The Promise

By Freda Lightfoot

House of Angels
Angels at War
The Promise

The Promise

FREDA LIGHTFOOT

First published in Great Britain in 2011 by
Allison & Busby Limited
13 Charlotte Mews
London W1T 4EJ
www.allisonandbusby.com

A CIP catalogue record for this book is available from
the British Library.

10 9 8 7 6 5 4 3 2 1

ISBN 978-0-7490-0829-1

Typeset in 11.25/16.5 pt Sabon by
Allison & Busby Ltd.

Paper used in this publication is from sustainably managed sources.
All of the wood used is procured from legal sources and is fully traceable.
The producing mill uses schemes such as ISO 14001
to monitor environmental impact.

Printed and bound by
CPI Group (UK) Ltd, Croydon, CR0 4YY

The Promise

San Francisco, 1926

I write in some distress to inform you that I am again in financial difficulties. Not for the first time, I know, but I fear on this occasion I may not recover without your help. I mention no names but iniquitous charges are to be brought. Bankruptcy looms and my situation has become intolerable. I would not ask otherwise.

You may already feel that you have paid too high a price, but I disagree. Weren't you always so much luckier than I? Don't I deserve the same luck in life? I know you will understand why I chose this particular messenger to carry this letter. He will act as a salutary reminder about how much power I have.

I trust you will not hesitate to assist in my hour of need. If not for the close relationship we once enjoyed, then because if you do not, the consequences could be dire, not least for yourself. I'm sure your children would be most interested to hear the whole story.

I look forward to hearing from you, and to receiving a large banker's draft with all due speed. You owe me this, Georgia, in return for the promise I've kept all these years, a state of affairs you no doubt wish to continue.

1948

Chapter One

A shaft of sunlight slanted in through the open window of the flat, together with the usual city sounds: the constant hum of traffic, the klaxon of a police car going about its business, a child indulging in a noisy tantrum. It also brought dust, a stifling summer heat, and an intense feeling of claustrophobia to the young woman patiently pouring tea into fine china cups.

Chrissie Kemp set a small mahogany table close to the invalid's side, covered it with a lace doily, then carefully put two ginger biscuits on a plate and placed them upon it with the teacup so that her mother would only have to put out her hand to reach them. The older woman eyed the result of her daughter's efforts with disdain.

'No cake again? And do close the window, dear. It's creating a dreadful draught round my neck.'

Chrissie stifled a sigh as she reluctantly did as she

was told, feeling even more trapped by the stuffy room. Her mother was not a patient woman, but she seemed even more crotchety than usual today. 'I queued half the morning, hoping to find some dried fruit or ground almonds, even a few cherries, since you're tired of plain sponge, but there were none to be had. And we can't afford to waste too many eggs in cake-making, Mum. Sorry, but there it is.' She tried a smile, but received only a frowning response.

'It is absolutely appalling that the government dares to continue with this iniquitous rationing. What did we win the war for, I wonder?'

'Don't let your tea get cold,' Chrissie gently chided, not wishing to go over this old ground for the hundredth time.

'Oh, do stop fussing, girl. Where are my pills? I'm getting one of my heads. Don't sit there looking stubborn. I need one now.' From an array of small bottles on the tray, Chrissie dutifully tapped out the required dose into a small cup to set beside the biscuits. She watched with sadness in her eyes as Vanessa greedily swallowed them with a slurp of tea. Though what good they would do, she couldn't imagine. Chrissie was quite sure the doctor only prescribed them in order that he may continue to call and add another fee to his steadily growing bill.

Nor would the introduction of the new health service this month make the slightest difference. Vanessa Kemp had no truck with anything that was free. If something did not cost a considerable sum then it was worthless in her eyes, a philosophy that had cost her dear throughout her life, and was really rather ironic when you considered the pittance they now lived on.

There was only Chrissie's small wage coming in, as her mother had never quite acquired the knack of working for a living, apart from the occasional foray selling handkerchiefs or perfume in Harrods or Harvey Nichols. She'd grow bored after a few months and walk out in a huff, although the last time Chrissie suspected she was dismissed for sneaking one too many shots of gin behind the counter.

Now they were behind with the rent, and would be out on the street were it not for Chrissie constantly dipping into her precious savings, and sweet-talking the landlord into allowing them a little longer to catch up. Not that these efforts on her part prevented him from sending out a constant stream of eviction notices, which any day now he would be sure to act upon.

The doctor too would be lucky if he ever got paid, although Chrissie did wonder if perhaps he took payment in kind from his still-beautiful patient. With her chestnut-brown hair, hazel-green eyes, porcelain complexion and deep-red lips there was no denying that her mother had lost none of her sex appeal, despite being past the dreaded age of forty. The pair were certainly very cosy, and there was nothing Vanessa loved more than being the centre of attention, particularly where men were concerned.

Chrissie did her best to cope but hated the idea of squandering every penny she possessed on attempting to pay off a huge unmanageable debt. It was rather like putting a finger in a dyke to stop a flood. But she lived in hope that she could stir Vanessa out of her depression, stop her drinking, and bring back the woman she'd once been.

Chrissie dreamt of escape, of release from this straitjacket of a life she inhabited. She longed to have a life of her own, to start her own business, perhaps a small bookshop. If she were ever allowed the opportunity.

Feeling bored and slightly irritable at having spent a precious Saturday afternoon once again confined to the house doing domestic chores, Chrissie picked up a newspaper, a copy of the *Westmorland Gazette*, and flicked idly through the pages while sipping her tea.

Her mother had been born in Westmorland, and despite her absolute refusal to speak of her birthplace or her family, still insisted on having the paper posted to her in London. Being a local newspaper there wasn't any mention of the Olympic Games, due to take place shortly in August, or the recent dock strikes. As if the outside world did not exist, it was largely concerned with the price fat lambs made at auction, the weather, a report of a man charged with poaching, and advertisements for home helps and farmhands. But then an advert a page or two in caught Chrissie's eye. It read:

Why not pay a visit this summer to Rosegill Hall in the beautiful English Lake District, a charming old house with spectacular views of the Langdales. It even boasts its own boathouse and jetty on Lake Windermere. This historic property, set in its own woodland gardens, has been converted into delightful holiday cottages and bed & breakfast accommodation. The owner, Georgia Cowper, offers a warm welcome to guests.

There followed a telephone number and postal address for bookings. The thought flitted across Chrissie's mind that she couldn't remember when she'd last had a holiday. Before the war, probably, as a young girl, when they used to go down to Brighton for a week each summer.

'I suppose you'll be going out later?' Vanessa remarked in self-pitying tones, interrupting her thoughts.

'We might go to see Katharine Hepburn in *Song of Love*. It's showing at the Alhambra.'

'Does Peter like musicals? How very odd for a man.'

Chrissie gave a rueful grin. 'Probably not, but he's happy to let me choose. He's very obliging.'

Perhaps too obliging at times. Peter would indulge any choice she cared to make, in particular a date for their wedding, if only she would accept his proposal. He repeated his offer almost on a weekly basis, in case it had slipped her mind. The trouble was Chrissie wasn't even sure if she loved him. She was fond of him, but was that enough?

Admittedly there wasn't exactly a stream of suitors paying her calls, but then when did she ever find the opportunity to meet new men? And surely she wasn't entirely unattractive? She was slim with long legs and a reasonable figure, soft brown hair and eyes, if a rather pale complexion and unflattering nose. There were creases between her eyes, so Chrissie was making an extra effort not to frown too much. Her mouth was perhaps a touch wide and didn't smile anywhere near enough.

Marriage, even to dull, boring Peter, might be infinitely preferable to spending her life waiting upon a hypochondriac mother. Had she not experienced both true love and marriage, however briefly, it might have been easier to come to terms with second best. But at only twenty-one it seemed rather young to admit defeat and marry simply to escape her mother's tyranny.

'Holy matrimony, dear girl, is not all it's cracked up to be,' Vanessa warned, as if reading her thoughts. 'You would be foolish to risk it a second time. Not that anyone would look twice at a mouse like you.'

Chrissie said nothing. She had learnt long since not to engage in pointless arguments with Vanessa. And since her parents' marriage had not turned out to be quite as happy as her mother had hoped, Vanessa's opinion was somewhat jaundiced, to say the least. But then Aaran Kemp had walked out on his wife when Chrissie had been but a small child, leaving his non-grieving wife with a legacy of debt, one there seemed little hope of ever paying off.

The moment tea was over Chrissie quickly cleared away the cups and plates, hoping for a short walk in the park, then an hour's quiet read in her room with the windows flung wide. After a week stuck in an office, filing and typing, and her weekends devoted to domestic duties, she snatched any spare moment that offered privacy, fresh air and freedom. But just as she was hanging up the tea towel to dry, the doorbell rang and Peter arrived, predictably early.

* * *

The evening at the cinema followed the usual pattern of all the other evenings they spent together. Peter would steer her down the aisle to their seats with his hand protectively glued to her elbow, almost as if he thought her incapable of walking unaided. He always insisted on paying for the tickets, and would buy her an ice cream in the interval without even asking if she wanted one. Then there would be the usual fumble under cover of darkness with him surreptitiously pressing her knee, or sneaking a hand around her shoulder which somehow lodged itself on her breast. Chrissie would be so preoccupied keeping track of his wandering hands that she would frequently lose the plot on what was happening on screen.

Afterwards he would walk her home and steal a brief goodnight kiss. That was all she did allow him, even after twelve months of walking out.

'Would you like a stroll in the park?' he offered. 'It's a clear moonlit night.'

The prospect of more tussles beneath the trees or on a park bench was more than Chrissie could contemplate this evening. 'I'm rather tired, sorry. Saturday is always a busy day for me, with the washing to get done and various other chores.'

His eyes gleamed. 'It would be so much easier for you if we were married.'

Chrissie wondered how that could be possible since she'd then also have a husband to care for, as well as a mother. 'Let's not talk about that tonight, shall we? You know I feel it's far too soon for us to be talking of marriage. I'm not ready for all of that yet.'

'I don't see why,' he said, in that small peevish voice he adopted, rather like a small boy denied a toffee apple. 'You wouldn't have to work at all if we were married.'

'Why wouldn't I?'

'You'd have no need to work, since I can perfectly well afford to keep a wife.' Rather as he might say he could afford to keep a dog.

Chrissie turned away and slotted her key in the lock, thankful to see the flat was in darkness, which meant Vanessa had gone to bed, so there would be no grilling about what she'd got up to. Her mother loathed the idea of Chrissie ever marrying again, no doubt for selfish reasons. Not that she had any inclination of doing so. One day it might be nice to find a good man, a kindred spirit, but not yet.

All Chrissie really wanted was to be free of duty and responsibility, to find some contentment and a purpose to her life. To make her own choices.

Peter was still talking. 'I'll call on Tuesday, shall I? Seven o'clock as usual. I thought we might try the new Italian restaurant that's opened on the high street, or we could go down the West End, if you prefer. Whatever you wish.' He was as predictable in his habits as night following day, turning up at her door regular as clockwork every Tuesday, Thursday and Saturday. Chrissie had never quite worked out why these particular days and no other.

There were times when she had to stifle the desire to tell him what she'd really like was for him to go away and never call again. But that would have been unkind. Peter could be good company, and, apart from the odd grope in the cinema, never anything but a perfect gentleman. She hated the idea of being sucked into a routine, and every now and then a small spark of rebellion would light within and Chrissie would make a feeble bid for freedom. She'd complained once that she'd no wish to be taken for granted, and Peter had showered her with flowers, chocolates and gifts for weeks, till she'd insisted he stop.

Now she said, 'Let me check my diary. I rather think Rosie, my friend from work, asked me to go out with her.'

Disappointment seemed to drain the life from his thin angular face, and Chrissie was instantly filled with pity and guilt, a feeling that seemed to mark the nature of their relationship.

'You should put *me* first, not Rosie; you're my fiancée, after all.'

'No, Peter, I'm not,' she told him, with exemplary patience. 'We aren't engaged, remember? How many times must I remind you that I have no wish to marry again, not now, maybe not ever.'

'Don't be silly. Every pretty girl wants to be a wife and mother. You'll change your mind, and I can wait till you're ready.'

As always, Chrissie gave up. Where was the point in arguing with him? 'I'll give you a ring from the office on Tuesday, or pop in the bank to see you,' she cheerfully informed him as she let herself into the flat, determined to stick to her guns for once. Didn't she too often allow other people to make decisions for her? Ever the good girl trying to please. It really had to stop.

* * *

It was barely ten o'clock but the flat felt empty and eerily quiet as Chrissie plumped up cushions, and folded away newspapers and magazines her mother had left lying about, tidying them away into the understairs cupboard before going to bed. One glance in the cocktail cabinet told her Vanessa had retired early with a half bottle of gin.

Chrissie had taken to removing bottles from the cocktail cabinet, or pouring the contents away. A pointless exercise, as the next day another would have appeared in its place. It was amazing how fit and capable this ailing woman could suddenly become when needing to replenish her supplies. Chrissie had tried many times to gently point out to her mother how she was ruining her life with drink, and popping pills she didn't need, and by shutting herself indoors for every hour of the day. But Vanessa would only weep and say that Chrissie didn't understand.

'You don't appreciate how hard my life has been – an endless trail of bitter disappointment.'

Chrissie had agreed that life was indeed full of disappointments, that she too had suffered, losing the one man she could ever love back in 1945, just as the war ended. 'How cruel was that?' she had asked her mother.

'Ah, but you were only eighteen, far too young to know what love truly is,' Vanessa had scorned.

Now, as she drew back the curtains on to the night sky, collected used cups and glasses, she noticed that her mother had been looking through old photo albums, as she so loved to do. She lived in the past, constantly recalling some golden era when she'd been happy, but then would launch into a diatribe about how badly her family had treated her. How they had cast her off because she'd married a man her mother didn't approve of. Chrissie had vague memories of holidays in the Lakes when she was small; other than that she knew little, if anything, about Vanessa's family. She'd once asked why there wasn't a single picture of Vanessa's own mother in the albums, and had got a sharp response.

'Why would I want a picture of that dreadful, unfeeling woman? She never did anything but lie to me.'

She absolutely refused to talk about it, speaking only of some fond romantic image she carried of the early years of her marriage, before Aaran Kemp, the love of Vanessa's life, had so callously deserted her. The albums largely comprised pictures of a father Chrissie could barely remember. Had he loved her? Chrissie held a precious memory of being cuddled on his knee, of him tossing her in the air. Or was that because she'd seen fathers do these things in films?

If he had loved her, why had he walked away and left her, never to be seen again?

He'd visited them once, she seemed to recall, about the time he was called up at the start of the war. She must have been eleven or twelve at the time. He'd felt like a stranger to her after all those years of silence, and Chrissie knew she hadn't exactly been very friendly towards him. Young as she was, she hadn't been prepared to forgive him for deserting them. Now, knowing he'd been killed at Dunkirk, she felt guilty, as that was the last time she'd seen her father.

Chrissie slid the albums back into the sideboard drawer, not even bothering to look at them. She'd given up showing any interest in their yellowed contents years ago, when she'd failed to get any answers to her youthful questions. It was as she was closing the drawer that she realised a folded sheet of paper had come loose and was sticking out from the pages.

About to tuck it back into place so that it didn't get torn, her curiosity suddenly got the better of her and she opened it.

It was nothing more exciting than her mother's marriage certificate.

Chrissie shook her head in sad resignation. How dreadful that the loss of this man, a runaway husband, had so blighted both their lives. What a tragic waste. Yet Vanessa must still be passionately in love with him as she'd never remarried, despite her many amours. She complained about the debts she'd been left with, but never once had Chrissie heard her mother utter a single word against Aaran. She was undoubtedly a bitter woman but her venom seemed to be directed entirely against her own parents, as if they were the ones at fault. Perhaps she hated them for being proved right in their assessment of a straying husband. But despite his betrayal, Vanessa had remained steadfast in her loyalty to him. How blind is love?

Chrissie's eyes filled with tears as she thought of her own love for Tom, a passion she did not expect to ever experience again.

But this was the first time Chrissie had set eyes on

evidence of her parents' marriage and she smoothed the certificate out, staring at the names: Aaran Richard Kemp. Again she desperately tried to recall her father's face. Occupation – businessman, and an address in Chelsea. No doubt the art gallery he owned, of which Chrissie had no recollection. That was back in the halcyon days of her mother's youth. No occupation was listed for her mother, who was given the usual description of 'spinster', and the same address in Chelsea. Good heavens, were they living together? How deliciously sinful. Chrissie glanced then at her mother's full name: Vanessa Margaret Cowper.

Cowper?

But wasn't her maiden name Shaw? Chrissie was almost certain that was what she'd been told. Frowning in puzzlement she began to look for something to prove her theory. She searched everywhere, including the little bureau, but nowhere could she find evidence of any birth certificate. And then Chrissie found the rental agreement for the flat. And there it was: Mrs Vanessa Kemp, née Shaw. How extraordinary!

Folding the marriage certificate and carefully replacing it within the leaves of the album, Chrissie closed the drawer and went to bed. Although not to sleep.

For some reason she found it oddly disturbing to discover that her mother wasn't whom she claimed to be. And if her maiden name was Cowper and not Shaw, as she'd always believed it to be, then who did that make Chrissie herself? Yet there was something vaguely familiar about the name Cowper. Where had she heard the name recently?

It was sometime in the early hours of the morning that she remembered, and sat bolt upright in shock. Of course, it was in the advertisement for Rosegill Hall in her mother's copy of the *Westmorland Gazette*.

What had it said? Ah yes, *The owner, Georgia Cowper, offers a warm welcome to guests.*

Vanessa had been born in the Lakes, where this Hall was apparently situated. So if she carried the same name as this woman, one she had apparently denied and kept hidden for half a lifetime along with all details of her family, were they in some way related? Was this reminder of her hometown the reason she was in a particularly sour mood today? And what was this woman to Chrissie?

Chapter Two

Her mother wept when Chrissie confronted her with what she'd discovered. 'All right, it's true. My maiden name wasn't Shaw. I changed it because I never wanted Ma to find me.'

Georgina Cowper had apparently objected so strongly to the man her own daughter had chosen to marry, she'd cut her off completely only a few years into the marriage, banishing her for ever from her life.

'Whatever did my father do to deserve such treatment? A lifetime of silence for not agreeing with her own daughter's choice of husband was surely somewhat excessive?'

'Nothing. Aaran did nothing at all. The woman is heartless.'

'But why has this family feud, this estrangement, lasted so long? What gives your mother, my *grandmother*, the right to consider herself the oracle when it comes to choosing a spouse? There must be more to it than simple disapproval. And did we never visit? I'm sure I have a vague memory of holidays in the Lakes.'

'Nonsense, you'd be far too young to remember such things.'

'Then tell me the whole story. I want to know all about this grandmother I can't quite remember.'

Vanessa firmed her lips and stubbornly shook her head. 'There's nothing to tell. I believe she was born in America, but I'm not certain. Isn't that sad? My own mother and I know virtually nothing about her. If there's one thing Georgina, or Georgia, as she likes to be called, hates, it's someone who attempts to pry into her private affairs. And she has to be the one in charge, you can't tell her anything. The woman is quite impossible.'

Rather like you, Chrissie thought, hiding a private smile.

But she knew at once what she must do. Perhaps it was an unrealistic dream but Chrissie resolved to bring about a reconciliation between these two women, or at least attempt to start the healing process. She leant forward, suddenly excited. 'We could visit her now. Why don't we both go to the Lakes and see this place? When did we last have a holiday? We could go and stay at this Rosegill Hall and start building some bridges. Wouldn't that do us both good? Cheer us up no end.'

Vanessa was appalled at the very idea. 'After so many long years of silence, any sort of reconciliation would be impossible. I refuse to set foot in that place ever again.'

The cause was lost before Chrissie had even begun, and when she responded by saying she would go alone, her mother was horrified and begged her not to even try.

'You don't appreciate how difficult that woman can be, how arrogant. She showed not the slightest compassion when Aaran and I fell in love, practically threw me out of the house, and I've had no proper relationship with her since. I forbid you to have anything to do with her.'

'Mum, I have to try. You're a widow, a woman alone, still with huge debts to pay off, no income and about to be evicted from your home. We have to do *something*!'

'Leave me some remnants of pride,' her mother snapped. 'That woman has never lifted a finger to help me throughout my entire marriage, and I'm certainly not going to ask for it now!'

'No, *I* am. She's your *mother*! She has a right to know how things stand with you. We can't let pride get in the way of practicalities, or a possible rapprochement.'

The older woman's cheeks were stained red with anger. 'Listen to me, Chrissie, this is one particular Pandora's box I do not want opening. Ever! *Is that clear?*'

They quarrelled for hours, Vanessa stubbornly refusing to accept Chrissie's idea as a possible solution to their difficulties. Probably because she hated to admit to the fact that Georgia had been right all along, that she never should have married Aaran Kemp.

In the end, weary of the argument, Chrissie let the subject drop. But not the plan. Without any further discussion on the matter, since she was a grown woman, after all, and surely capable of making her own decisions, she resolved to go ahead with it on her own. A holiday would do her good, and give her the time and space she needed to think properly about her own future, and whether Peter was the man to share it.

There would be no problem in getting time off from work as she hadn't taken a fraction of the leave due to her. Chrissie went straight downstairs to ask Mrs Lawson, their neighbour, if she would cook and clean for her mother while she was away.

'Course I will, chuck. Do you good to have a bit of a holiday. You've been looking a mite peaky lately. Go and get some sunshine and fresh air. I'll see to madam.'

'Bless you. I'll bring you back a stick of rock . . . oh no, Kendal mint cake, I suppose, from the Lakes. I really do appreciate this, and I'll pay you, of course.' They both knew she couldn't afford to, but Mrs Lawson simply smiled.

'Ooh, don't you worry about that none. What are neighbours for if not to lend a hand when folk are a bit down?'

'No, I insist. I have a bit put by, I'll see you don't lose out.'

Concerned that the summer holidays were almost upon them, Chrissie decided a booking by post would take too long and rang Rosegill Hall from the public call box at the end of the street. The housekeeper informed her that they were fully booked, but the loft over the boathouse was nearing completion, if she was prepared to take the risk that it would be ready in time. Chrissie was, and just ten days later, leaving a note for Vanessa on her dressing table, she quietly left.

The adventure had begun.

The train was late leaving Euston, constantly stopping and starting, once spending two hours sitting in a siding near Crewe in temperatures well into the seventies. And since it was July it was also packed to the doors with families going on holiday, screaming children, mothers fretting, soot and smoke and noise everywhere. The entire journey was a complete nightmare. Chrissie didn't even feel able to eat the sandwiches she'd so carefully prepared, robbing her mother of precious eggs, mixing them with even more scarce butter, crusts neatly cut off as Vanessa insisted upon. Yet the sight of those curled triangles filled her with a strange nausea, and she gave them to an old soldier who looked half starved.

The juddering and rocking of the train made her bones ache and she leant her head against the dirty window, tears blurring her vision. When he asked if she was all right, Chrissie blamed it on the smoke and pulled on the window strap to shut out the soot-encrusted air, but still the tears trickled over her hot cheeks.

This should have been a joyous moment, the start of an exciting journey of discovery, an adventure. Perhaps it was being on a train again, with its inevitable connection to painful goodbyes, but all Chrissie could think of was Tom, and the pain of losing the man she'd truly loved. It felt as raw as if it were only yesterday and not over three years ago.

She'd stood on the platform at Paddington one bright sunny morning in May 1945, kissing him and thinking he would be demobbed in a matter of months, and they could then start to put the horrors of war behind them. Tom had been granted compassionate leave and a special licence so they could be married. They'd known each other less than a year but had felt instinctively it was love at first sight, and believed they would be together for ever. The wedding had taken place at the registry office with only her disapproving mother and a couple of witnesses present. Their honeymoon had comprised one night in a cheap hotel close to the station, but it had been utter bliss. Not for a moment did Chrissie regret that night. Her last sight of Tom was his cheery grin, arm waving, as the train curved around the bend as it left the station.

Days later, Chrissie had heard that one of the V2s had hit his billet. All her dreams and hopes had ended in that moment.

Could Peter ever replace him? Could any man? Ten years older than herself, she'd met Peter Radcliffe while attending an evening class, either the one on pottery or pressed flowers, she couldn't quite remember. Peter was doing one on politics, or something equally dry. He'd pestered her for months before she'd finally agreed to go out with him on a date. Perhaps she'd given in out of pity, or desperation over the claustrophobic life she led. Seeking any excuse to get out of the house it had seemed like a good idea at the time.

Now he was making it very clear he was anxious to

regularise their relationship with marriage, and Chrissie was stubbornly refusing to agree. He'd been upset, angry even, when she'd told him she was going away for a whole month. Not only that, but she was leaving without giving him the answer he so longed to hear.

'It's too soon. I'm not ready,' she'd told him for the hundredth time. 'Although please don't take that as any cause for hope. I really can't see myself marrying again, not ever.'

'Don't be ridiculous, of course you must marry. You're far too young to spend your entire life alone. But this sudden decision to go off on holiday is so very selfish, not at all like you, Chrissie. What am I supposed to do while you're gone, twiddle my thumbs? And what about your poor mother? Deserting her in this way, leaving her in the care of a total stranger, is callous in the extreme.'

'Mrs Lawson is a kind neighbour who is glad to be useful because she's rather lonely herself, and I'm not being in the least callous. I wanted Mum to come too, but she refused.'

'I'm not surprised. The journey alone will be horrendous, and no doubt cold and wet in those northern climes.' As if they were going to the Arctic.

Chrissie had said no more. She certainly had no wish to mention the real reason for the trip. For one thing it was none of his business, but also she did feel a certain guilt over having kept Peter dangling for so long, and promised faithfully to consider his offer and give him a final answer just as soon as she possibly could. She knew that he too had suffered in the war, like many others coming back a changed man, although, unlike Tom, he had at least survived. Did he even love her? Or did he simply see her as good wife material, a useful helpmeet and prop to help him put the agonies of war behind him?

The train thundered through a tunnel and, pushing these thoughts from her mind, Chrissie decided there would be time enough later to make such decisions. First she needed a proper rest, and to bring about a family reunion.

After a while they left the hustle and bustle behind, and the countryside grew greener, the pale hint of mountains in the distance. Chrissie felt again that stir of excitement she'd long ago experienced when coming to the Lakes as a child for the summer, before the war changed everything.

Mother would close up the house in Chelsea, presumably leaving her father to cope alone throughout August. The move always demanded a great deal of fuss and bother, one minute Vanessa saying they needed very little in the way of luggage as everything was already there for them, and the next declaring she really couldn't go without her new silk frock, or that delicious pair of shoes.

She could afford to be extravagant in those days.

Nanny, of course, had been much more practical, studying railway timetables and supervising the packing of a hamper large enough for them to survive for a month, let alone the few hours it would take them to reach Windermere. And with the promise of four weeks of idyllic fun on the lake, Chrissie would excitedly collect together favourite books and teddies, plimsolls and shorts, wellington boots and waterproofs, for it often rained, even in August.

Chrissie couldn't help wondering what else she might remember, once she reached her grandmother's house.

She lost count of the number of changes as they headed north. Now it was quite late in the evening, almost dark, and raining, as the train drew into Lakeside station. Calling Peter was not high on her list of priorities. He could wait until she was in the right frame of mind for what would undoubtedly be a severe grilling, but Chrissie decided she couldn't avoid her mother, or the issue of her hasty departure, a moment longer, and made use of the public telephone on the railway platform while she waited for the bus.

Vanessa's tone was icy as Chrissie brightly offered reassurance of an easy journey. Pure fiction to stop her mother from worrying. 'When did we stop coming to the Lakes?' she went on to ask. 'It's not quite true, is it, that Grandmother cut you off completely after your marriage? I was right, I *do* remember coming here as a child, travelling in the train, messing about in boats, enjoying picnics by the lake. How old would I have been? Four? Five?'

'That must be your vivid imagination, darling. It can't have been more than two or three occasions. You certainly shouldn't be there now. I thought we'd agreed—'

'So why did the visits stop?' Chrissie interrupted, not wishing the argument to start up again.

'I really can't remember. Chrissie, it was very naughty of you to sneak off like that.'

'I didn't *sneak*. I'd made it perfectly clear what I intended to do, you just didn't agree, that's all.'

'I *forbade* you to go.'

Chrissie almost laughed, but managed not to as that would have been cruel. 'I doubt you can do that anymore, Mum. I'm a big girl now. Twenty-one, remember? Nearly twenty-two.' Free and single, and intending to stay that way. Stubbornly she returned to her original question. 'Was it because of the war that the visits ended?'

'What? No, it was long before then,' Vanessa snapped. 'Look, I don't remember. I expect Ma was being even more difficult than usual. Not that she ever made things easy for me, which is why . . .'

Chrissie gave a little chuckle. 'I don't expect she'll make things easy for me either, judging by how you describe her.'

'What name did you use?'

'I beg your pardon?'

'When you booked in, what name did you use? Did you use your maiden name?'

'Of course not. I used my married one, as always.'

'And not your first name, Susan?'

'No, what is this? Why do you ask?'

'I want you to promise me that you'll remain incognito. Get to know your grandmother a little, if you must, but *don't* ask too many questions and *don't* tell her who you are. She hasn't set eyes on you since you were five years old, so there's no reason why she would recognise you. And she has no idea you started using your second name. Do that for me, at least.'

'Mum, that's ridiculous. It's underhand, a lie.'

'Not a lie exactly. I know what a lie is, I've heard enough of them in my time.' There was a humph of disgust down the line, and her mother launched into the familiar lament that her entire life had been blighted by lies and deceit, and now from her own daughter of all people. Chrissie was saved from answering this charge by the blast of a horn. 'Sorry, the bus is here, I have to go. I'll ring later in the week, once I've settled in.'

'Promise you won't let on who you are,' Vanessa insisted.

'All right, cross my heart, not a word.'

It was a promise Chrissie would soon come to regret.

The moment Vanessa put down the phone, she picked it up again and dialled a number. 'Would you believe she went anyway?'

'Damnation, you said you could stop her. Have you no control over the girl?'

'About as much as you have.'

'We must do something.'

'Any ideas?'

'You're going to have to tell her.'

Vanessa jerked as if stung. 'Absolutely not. That's not a solution I could ever contemplate.'

There was a small silence, as they each reflected on the difficulties of their situation. The person on the other end of the line let out a heavy sigh. 'What alternative do we have?'

'There must be something you can do. You *owe* it to me.'

'She won't listen to me. Anyway, she knows nothing about you and me, about *us*.'

'So what am I supposed to do? I'm at the end of my tether here.'

'We're going to have to think about this problem a bit more. We can at least agree that Chrissie must be protected.'

'Yes, we can at least agree on that.'

'And what if she gets to the bottom of this mystery and discovers the truth?'

'Dear God, I do hope not.'

She'd half hoped to experience a blaze of recognition when she reached the hall, instead Chrissie felt a keen sense of disappointment, as she had no recollection of ever having seen it before. Nothing looked familiar, not the wide sash windows, nor the white-painted storm porch, but she could hear the slap of water against an unseen shore, a sound that kindled a warm sense of anticipation within. Perhaps a five year old would be more interested in the lake than the house, and it was too dark to see properly. She hoped something might nudge her memory in the full light of day.

Despite her eagerness to meet her grandmother and a curiosity to know what sort of person she might be, Chrissie felt oddly nervous as she arrived at the Hall. But there was no sign of her then, or the following morning when the housekeeper showed Chrissie round. The stalwart Mrs Gorran seemed to be very much the person in charge where keys, collecting ration books, and issuing rules and regulations were concerned.

'The Hall was used as a hospital for the wounded during the war, and you wouldn't believe the mess they left it in,' she tartly informed Chrissie, pointedly currying murmurs of sympathy and approval. 'We're only just getting it shipshape and in working order again.'

There followed a bewildering list of instructions, starting with breakfast being served at 8.30 on the dot; when the water was most likely to be hot enough for a bath due to the idiosyncrasies of the boiler; how to operate the ballcock in the lavatory if it refused to flush; where the fuse box was, should it become necessary to change a fuse; and where the candles were stored in case of a power cut. The rule which amused Chrissie the most was the one about 'no gentlemen callers'. It sounded rather like something out of a Victorian novel.

The seventeenth-century house, so far as Chrissie could see, had a faded grandeur about it, but was homely and clearly well loved, smelling of furniture polish and the lingering aroma of bacon and eggs. It boasted five double bedrooms for guests, all of them fully occupied since it was July.

'Mrs Cowper doesn't take families, as she does not consider the Hall suitable for children,' Mrs Gorran informed her. 'Too many steps, both in the house and the garden.' Chrissie wondered if it would be more accurate to say that Mrs Cowper didn't like children, particularly her own.

Behind the house were two tiny cottages which were self-catering, plus the loft above the boathouse which boasted a small but adequate bedroom and private bathroom, which suited Chrissie perfectly. She liked the idea of being slightly detached from the house, in her own private domain as it were, and felt a contented sort of anticipation about the weeks ahead. Perhaps she would find the fresh start she so craved as well as the solution to a family puzzle. Unless her alleged witch of a grandmother banished her too, simply for being the child of the devil who had married her mother.

Chapter Three

She was walking just above the waterline, the light summer breeze moulding her pale lemon frock to a slim figure and long slender legs. On her head was a straw hat which she kept clutching with one hand to stop it blowing away. She looked, Ben thought, like a piece of sunshine fallen from the sky. He watched, riveted, as she picked her way along the shingled shoreline that skirted the lake, sometimes lifting her skirt a little to jump over rocks, pausing to watch a tufted duck make its way through the reeds, or to pick yellow loosestrife and pale-lilac water lobelia before walking on.

Bowness-on-Windermere was one of those small Lakeland towns that clung to the rim of a lake that stretched for ten miles from Newby Bridge to Ambleside, its huddle of stone cottages seeming to lean against each other as if for support against the fickle winds that rattled up this valley. Here and there, amongst the lush woodlands, were scattered large Edwardian villas, often housing those who had made their fortunes in the industrial towns of the North and retired to Lakeland to enjoy the fruits of their labours.

The lake itself was always a hive of activity, bristling with masts, a couple of public steamers filled with holidaymakers, and a ferry that chugged back and forth taking cars and walkers from one shore to the other, providing a short cut to Far Sawrey, Esthwaite Water and Hawkshead. It was the kind of town where everyone knew everyone else's business. Ben could happily waste an hour watching young men struggling to row a hire boat as they showed off to their sweetheart, or listen unashamedly to family squabbles as sails were unfurled and small boats made ready to put out on to the water. There was always something interesting to watch. Now he'd found the most fascinating of all.

The screwdriver hung slack in his hand, the door hinge he was supposedly fixing quite forgotten.

'Pretty, isn't she?'

He glanced up, shamefaced, as his mother handed him a mug of tea. She was wearing her usual floral print smock, two sizes too big for her diminutive figure, her impish face beaming with mischief.

'I was only looking.' For a man who had enjoyed nothing but misfortune with the women in his life he was mad to even do that, but the girl was utterly irresistible. She was climbing the far steps up to the steamer pier now, looking so fresh and appealing he couldn't prevent a small sigh escaping. 'I don't suppose you know who she is?'

'She's the new tenant. Moved in yesterday afternoon, quite late. Taken the loft over the boathouse for a month.'

'A month?' Ben felt ridiculously pleased by this bit of news, then filled with guilt at the stir of anticipation he experienced deep in his gut. Don't even think about it, he sternly warned himself. Wasn't he already bruised and battered following his recent divorce?

His mother set down a large slice of her finest fruit cake on the wall beside him. 'Aye, a whole month. Longer than visitors normally stay.' There was a short silence while she considered this, then returning her attention to her son casually enquired, 'How long will Karen be away visiting that mother of hers?'

'I'd prefer you not to speak of Sally in that tone. She may no longer be my wife, but she's still the mother of my child.'

Hetty Gorran was no fool and knew her son inside out, better than he knew himself at times. Far too easy-going for his own good, which was how he came to get himself married in the first place. Thank heaven he'd finally seen the light. That flighty little madam was never any good for her boy. Hadn't she said as much to him at the time? Not that he ever listened to a mother's wisdom. Stubborn to a fault he was, and would stick to his point of view if only to prove he had the right to it, not unlike her employer who owned these holiday cottages.

'So you've had another falling out, eh?' she slyly remarked as she sipped her tea.

'Does everyone in this town know my private business?'

'If you will conduct it at top volume on a telephone in a public place . . . Anyroad, we Lakelanders like to pride ourselves on caring about our family and friends.'

'Lot of old gossips, more like.' Ben sighed, remembering how it should have been a quick call over train times for Karen's visit, but had found himself embroiled in a row over his ex-wife's demands that she have sole custody of their child, supported by half the profits from his joinery business. No wonder he'd lost his temper. He'd no intention of losing Karen, nor being left near-bankrupt. Not wishing to relate any of this to his interfering mother, he diligently reapplied his attention to the door hinge.

Hetty Gorran, however, was not one to let things go, once she'd set her mind to something. 'Wanting another chance, is she?'

'Something of the sort.'

'Is this her idea, or Karen's?'

Ben took a gulp of tea, then picked up the screwdriver again. 'What do you think?'

Hetty allowed her gaze to drift back to the girl in yellow. 'The lass will be gone some weeks, then?'

'For most of July, but you can never be too certain with our Sally.'

'Long enough, lad.'

Following the direction of her gaze, he quickly responded. 'Don't start your matchmaking, Mother. You're getting as bad as Mrs Cowper, thinking you can organise a person's life for them.'

Hetty Gorran adopted a wounded air of innocence. 'What, me? Never! But since that good lady has driven half her family away, maybe I'd best take care.'

'Aye, maybe you had.' Ben was smiling now, but as his mother hurried back to her kitchen his gaze searched again for that small portion of sunshine.

The sun was slipping low over the mountains, turning the lake to a molten gold as Chrissie let herself into the loft. She knocked the dust from her sandals, tossed her straw hat on to the sofa and moved instantly to the window to look out again upon the shoreline. Chrissie had been in Windermere for less than twenty-four hours and already knew that she wished to stay for ever. She was in love – with the town, with the woods that clustered the shores of the lake, the circle of brooding mountains, the air that was as pure and sweet as wine, with the whole magic that was Lakeland. How tempting it would be to create a new life for herself here. Was this the place she could follow her dream and open a bookshop, build a new future for herself? Did she even possess the confidence to try?

This journey was mainly about discovering her roots, about finding answers to the mysterious family quarrel that had blighted her mother's life. If she succeeded, then perhaps Vanessa too could finally put the past behind her and come home. It could be a new beginning for them both.

Chrissie began to set out her 'treasures' on the window sill: a pine cone, pebbles and pieces of slate of every hue and colour that had shimmered like jewels beneath the water. She arranged the buttercups and pink campion she'd picked into a jug and filled it with water. Later she would press them, perhaps stick them on to cards. Maybe she could sell them in this bookshop she might one day own. She smiled at this fanciful notion, not really believing it could ever happen as her mother would never agree to come back here. And Chrissie couldn't leave her alone in London. It was all a fanciful dream, nothing more.

Was it also a dream that she'd visited the Lakes before, years ago when she was small? Walking along the shore she'd had a sudden image of herself as a small child before the war paddling in the shallows, skirt tucked up her knicker legs, the air filled with sunshine and laughter. Is that why she loved the place so instinctively? Where had all that innocence, that happiness, gone? When and why had those long-ago Lakeland holidays stopped? Who was the shadowy figure she imagined walking with her by the lake, protectively holding her hand? Was that her grandmother? Chrissie's recollection, if that's what it was, of this supposedly crabby old woman was decidedly hazy, clouded by her mother's bitter descriptions.

But what would she be like in the flesh? Not for a moment did Chrissie expect it to be easy to bring about this reunion. Would Georgina Cowper live up to the horror stories she'd heard about her? Why had mother and daughter not spoken, not even seen each other, for most of Chrissie's own lifetime? Vanessa's father had apparently died in 1924 as a result of being gassed in the First World War. Maybe things would have been different had he lived. As a young girl Chrissie had envied her friends their fathers and grandparents, their normal family life. How badly she had longed for one of her own. But would she even like the woman when finally she got to meet her, let alone feel the love and respect she should?

Chrissie rested her chin on her hand and mused on the mysteries of life.

'That girl, the new guest in the loft, where did she come from?'

Mrs Gorran frowned as, later that morning, she set a plate of sandwiches on the table before her employer. 'London, I think.'

'What I mean is, how did she find us? How did she make contact, by letter or telephone?'

'She rang up a week or two back, said she was desperate to get away for a break and liked the sound of our advert. That was the one you put in the *Westmorland Gazette*, wasn't it, Sam?'

'Could've been,' her husband mumbled through a mouthful of ham.

'What treasures you both are,' Georgia remarked with feeling. 'I really don't know how I would go on without you. But that girl looks so familiar. Has she ever been here before?'

'Not that I know of.' Mrs Gorran took a large bite out of a cheese-and-pickle sandwich. The three of them always took lunch together in the kitchen these days, Mrs Cowper not being the stand-offish sort. But then they'd known each other a long time, Hetty having been housekeeper at Rosegill Hall for almost forty years, ever since the twins were born in 1912. She'd been fourteen then, and this her first job as under-nursemaid. Sam too had been just a lad, a humble apprentice gardener learning his craft. Now he was the only one, also doubling as handyman-cum-chauffeur.

Apart from a cleaner coming in twice a week, three times in the summer when they were busy, that was the extent of the staff these days. Hetty could remember when there used to be a cook, butler, several housemaids, parlour maids, skivvies and a whole regiment of gardeners back in those glorious days before the Great War, let alone this last one. All gone now.

'When do you reckon Mrs Cowper herself came here?' Hetty asked Sam as she washed up the few cups and plates after lunch while he sat on at the table, sharpening his shears. 'She talks so rarely about the old days, and never gives those sort of details. Was it sometime around 1910?'

'Mebbe earlier, I reckon.'

'When exactly?'

'I dunno, do I?'

'How did they meet, those two? Did you ever hear?'

Sam shook his head. 'Mr Cowper never did say, kept things very close to his chest, he did.'

Hetty sighed. 'They didn't spoil a pair in that respect. I heard it was in America. Do you reckon that might be true?'

Sam looked up, his old face creased into deep frowns, as he contemplated this notion. 'Old Mr Cowper did go a-venturing to sea, I do believe, when he was young. I mind once telling him how, as a boy, I used to catch eels, not that I ever fancied eating them. Then later we lads promoted ourselves to char, pike and perch, and they were real tasty. Said he loved fishing too, that he used to do a bit himself off Fisherman's Wharf when he lived in San Francisco.'

'There you are, then.' Hetty wrung out the dishcloth and draped it over the tap to dry. 'Mrs Cowper must be American, don't you reckon, with a name like Georgia? Although she doesn't sound it, does she? Course, she's lived here a long time, so the accent will have softened. Was that where they met, I wonder, in America?'

'You ask too many questions, girl. That's their business, not ours.'

'I dare say you're right,' she admitted, reaching for a towel to wipe her hands. 'And how many times have I told you not to clean your tools in my kitchen? The knife-sharpener chap will be here next week, wait for him.'

'I need it sharp today, woman. As sharp as your tongue,' Sam said with a grin, then popping a kiss on his wife's cheek, sauntered off, leaving her flushed and smiling.

At a little after five the following afternoon Chrissie was enjoying a quiet cup of tea seated on her little balcony, contentedly watching a few sailors venture out on to the water. A slight mist hung over the lake, shafts of sunlight giving it a golden hue. How lovely it was here, positively idyllic. She couldn't remember feeling this happy for an age, save for the nudge of guilt at the back of her head over abandoning both her mother and Peter. Chrissie did wonder what sort of reception she would get when she finally returned home, a worry she tried to ignore. She'd rung Mrs Lawson who said Vanessa was fine, if a little grumpy. Since that was par for the course these days, Chrissie resolved to put the problem from her mind, for now. There were more pressing matters to be dealt with, like meeting her grandmother, for instance.

Finishing her tea, she decided to explore the beautiful gardens and woodland that rose in terraces above the old house. Climbing a short rise of limestone steps she came upon a wide lawned area and suddenly there she was, deadheading the roses.

Despite having no memory of her, Chrissie knew instinctively that this was she. There was something about the tall stately figure that reminded her so much of Vanessa. Save for the clothes. Chrissie had never seen her own mother look anything other than beautiful and stylish, always decked out in the very latest fashion, even when she was playing the invalid. But there was none of her mother's elegance here.

This woman wore a tweed skirt that had seen better days, a droopy navy-blue sweater with holes in the elbows, topped by a green quilted waistcoat, its pockets stuffed with a pair of secateurs and ball of baling twine. She could see little of her face or hair beneath a large, ramshackle straw hat, but could hear her humming softly to herself. A Vera Lynn number perhaps, or something from Gilbert and Sullivan? More likely *Carmen*.

Chrissie instantly suffered from an attack of nerves. What should she say? Hello, I'm your long-lost granddaughter, the one you've never even been interested in seeing. No, that wouldn't do. Far too abrupt and confrontational. Perhaps her mother had been right to insist she not reveal her true identity, as she'd no wish to give the old dear a heart attack.

Taking a breath, Chrissie stepped briskly forward. 'What a wonderful view of the lake you have from here,' she said, sticking out a hand. 'Good morning, I'm so pleased to meet you. You must be Mrs Cowper?'

The eyes that turned upon her were steel grey and took her measure slowly through narrowed slitted lids. No effort was made to take the proffered hand and at length Chrissie dropped it, a flush of embarrassment touching her cheeks. Perhaps she'd got it all wrong and this was just the gardener, after all. She cleared her throat. 'I'm your new guest, Chrissie Emerson. Sorry if I'm being a bit presumptuous and pushy. Tend to act first and think later. Ever a fault of mine.'

There came a sudden bark of laughter. 'Me too. Far too impulsive and bossy for my own good, or so Hetty keeps telling me. Unfortunately, the old peepers aren't quite what they used to be, and I seem to have mislaid my spectacles so didn't at once recognise you. I remember you now, in the loft over the boathouse.' And wiping both hands on the back of the disreputable skirt, she grasped one of Chrissie's and wrung it hard. The grip was firm and strong, very much that of a young woman and not at all what you would expect from someone in her sixties.

'I hope everything's tip-top?'

'Perfect, thank you.'

'Good, good. If there's ever a problem I'm sure Hetty, that's Mrs Gorran, will sort it out for you.' She was busily patting pockets, poking the front of her jersey, peering about her in a bemused sort of way.

'Are these what you're looking for?' Reaching up, Chrissie unhooked a pair of spectacles from the ribbon of the tattered straw hat.

'So *that's* where I put them. Goodness, how dreadful. Please don't tell Hetty. I have no wish to appear more senile than I actually am.'

Chrissie laughed. 'I don't believe you're senile at all.'

'My dear, I am older than the century itself.'

'And a Lakelander born and bred, no doubt,' Chrissie teased, taking the chance some nugget might fall her way at this very first meeting.

'Oh, I do so wish I was. How marvellous that would be, to have been born in this lovely county.'

Chrissie smiled. 'I'm trying to identify your accent. It's unusual. Where do you come from, then, if not Westmorland?' She attempted to make the question sound casual, but somehow it fell rather flat.

Georgia Cowper half turned away, bending to retrieve her trowel before moving on to the next bush where she began to dig up a few weeds from around the stock. 'Do smell these roses, aren't they divine? I love the old-fashioned sort best, don't you?'

The failure to get a response to her impertinence was not entirely unexpected but Chrissie felt disappointed all the same. Mum was right, then, it was not going to be easy to draw any information out of her. Leaning close, she drank in the sweet heady scent of the bloom. 'Wonderful! Who maintains this amazing garden for you? Just look at all these rhododendrons and azaleas. You must need a whole tribe of gardeners to keep it looking so perfect.'

The older woman put back her head and laughed out loud. Her face was as brown as a nut, but with scarcely a wrinkle, Chrissie noticed. A face full of wisdom and strength, and a rare loveliness. She caught a glimpse of once-black hair, silvered with grey. 'Well, there's Sam, Hetty's husband, who does a marvellous job. He also drives the old Rover, should I feel the need for an outing, but he's getting on a bit. Not quite so doddery as me, but well on the way. This is not a house of young folk, which is why we enjoy our guests.' Dropping the secateurs into a trug standing nearby, she said, 'The garden is my pride and joy. Let me show you.'

It was indeed enchanting, Chrissie genuinely admiring every plant and shrub as she was taken from rose to kitchen garden along winding paths, through secret glades and the shrubbery, finishing in the walled garden inspecting the tomatoes in the huge Edwardian greenhouses.

As she paused by these, she asked, 'What about your own family, presumably they visit too?' Chrissie regretted the question almost the moment she'd uttered it. Far too soon. And clumsy.

Her grandmother gave what might pass for a smile. 'Those who wish to come when it suits them. Isn't that always the way with families?'

Chrissie was startled. Whatever answer she'd expected, it wasn't this. She instantly wanted to ask who these family members were exactly that visited. She'd always assumed her mother to be an only child as no aunts or uncles had ever come on a visit. But then they'd lived a strangely nomadic life, constantly moving, no doubt to escape debtors. Should she own up now to who she really was, and risk upsetting her mother?

But Georgia was speaking again, in firm no-nonsense tones. 'I didn't see you at breakfast this morning. I dare say that like all young women of your age you forget to eat properly. No, don't bother to deny it,' she went on, giving a soft chuckle. 'Mrs Gorran always produces excellent meals, and she'll never forgive you if you don't eat them. You shall sit with me at dinner tonight and while I make sure you eat properly you shall tell me all about yourself, as I'm quite the nosiest old woman in town.' Taking a firm grasp of her elbow, she began to lead Chrissie along the path. 'Are you married, dear?'

Chrissie would have answered but words failed her, as they so often did, even after all this time.

Georgia jerked to a halt to gaze at her in some concern. 'I'm sorry, that was clumsy of me. Was it the war?'

Chrissie bleakly nodded.

'Then we will say no more on the subject, although you must have been very young.' The older woman squeezed her hand in a warm grip. 'Am I allowed to say that you will almost certainly learn to love again, given time?'

'Thank you, I don't intend the loss to make me bitter,' Chrissie said, thinking of Vanessa.

'Very wise.' Georgia cast her a sideways glance. 'There's no one on the horizon at present, then?'

'There is someone, yes. A very nice man who is keen to marry me, but I'm not sure he's—'

'The right one? Then take the advice of an old woman and do not say yes until you are absolutely certain. Marriage is for life, remember.'

'I fully intend to take my time before making any decisions. That's partly the reason I came here, to give myself space to think. I'm afraid my mother never quite approved of my rushing into marriage at just eighteen. I'm glad I did, though, in the circumstances. At least Tom and I had one night together as man and wife.'

Later that evening, seated in the dining room at her grandmother's table, Mrs Gorran serving piping-hot Scotch broth and home-baked bread rolls, followed by a delicious steak-and-kidney pie, Chrissie was entranced as Georgina fussed gently over her. 'Tuck in and eat up every scrap, you look as if you need it,' she ordered, before continuing with their earlier conversation.

'Mothers don't always know what is best for their daughters, though they may fear for their happiness and sometimes be overprotective. I didn't get it right, and my own mother certainly didn't. But then it was a different age back then, with more rigid standards and moral codes than you youngsters of today would tolerate. My parents were very authoritarian, and I the dutiful daughter, the result of a lifetime of rigorous training. I did rebel in the end, however. Very much so.'

Chrissie felt surprisingly comfortable in her company, almost as if she had known her for years. 'Where were you brought up, Mrs Cowper?' She asked the question softly, not wishing to alarm the old lady by seeming too curious, but the answer came without hesitation.

'San Francisco, or "Frisco", as we called it. Oh, and didn't I just love that town: the undulating hills, the tramcars, the excitement of the wharves and waterfront, the elegance of it all, and the chatter in a dozen different languages, even back then.' The faded grey eyes grew misty with memory.

'You must miss it?'

She laughed. 'I certainly miss the Californian climate, but I love the Lakes too, despite the rain.'

'Tell me about your mother. Why was she so strict? Did she approve of your marriage with Mr Cowper?'

'Of Ellis? Goodness, no! She was outraged at the very idea. He was a foreigner, for one thing. She also dismissed him as unhealthy, because being British he was naturally pale. In those days we lived in fear of disease, of consumption and the like. Even worse, he was not at all of the right class and upbringing. You can laugh now, looking at all of this, but my mother didn't set any store by some ruin of a house in the backwaters of England, even if it had been in his family for generations. She saw him as a chancer, not the honest sailor that he actually was.'

'A sailor? Oh, how romantic.'

Her grandmother's eyes were radiating happiness now, her mind clearly picturing the handsome young man she'd fallen in love with all those years ago. 'I suppose it was rather romantic, at least at first. Before . . .'

Chrissie waited, holding her breath for whatever might

come next. 'Where did you meet him?' she prompted after an achingly long pause, anxious for her to go on.

'Ah, thereby hangs a tale.'

'I love romantic stories. Please don't stop now. Tell me how you met.'

Georgia folded her hands in her lap, the meal forgotten as her memory slid back to that distant time. 'It was a lovely warm day in June. A Saturday, which was always special as my sister Prudence and I would don our best fixings and promenade into town with Mama and Papa to see a matinee. Except this particular Saturday was to turn out rather more special, and decidedly more exciting, than usual.'

1904

Chapter Four

San Francisco

'Let me rub some cocoa butter on your cheeks,' Prudence offered. 'It'll make them soft. Not that you really need beautifying, but you know how Mama fusses if we don't take proper care of our skin. There, now I'll wipe it off with the Magnolia Balm.' She took up a pad of swansdown and began to pat my face till it was smooth and dry. 'Lovely, all fixed up pretty as a picture, and your skin as fine as porcelain.'

'Are you sure this is a good idea?' I asked, trying to decide if I liked this new paler version of myself. I was more used to a healthy glow on my cheeks. 'Don't you think I look a bit sickly? Mama so distrusts the pale washed-out look.'

'You don't look in the least washed out.' Prudence critically studied my face in the oval dressing mirror. 'Your lashes are so long and dark, Georgia. I envy you. Don't you, Maura?' she asked, turning to our maid who was lolling by the window, gazing out on to the street below in case she should see any handsome gentlemen go by in their carriages.

Startled out of her daydreaming, the Irish girl hastily agreed. What a silly question. I was well aware the maid envied me, and my pretty, little, spoilt sister. Why would she not, since she had nothing in the whole world, and we had everything our hearts desired? Poor Maura was plain and stick-thin, a result of the hard life she had suffered back in Ireland as a child, and on Ellis Island when she first came to America. I glanced through the window and saw she was watching a footman in livery hand a lady into a barouche. The whip snapped and the horses sprang forward. Thrilling! I expect she was dreaming that one day she would like to travel in a carriage just like that.

'Mine are so short and brown,' Prudence was complaining. 'As boring as my hair.'

Maura offered a bland smile. 'Why don't you black them, then?'

Prudence was all attention. 'Can you do that? How?'

'With a hot hairpin. Would you like me to fetch one? Though I doubt your mama would approve. Mrs Briscoe might think it too daring, miss.'

'Oh stuff, what if she does, I don't care. Hurry, Maura, do run and fetch one. We don't have all day.'

Now Maura would have to run down three flights of stairs to the poky little room in the basement where she slept, in order to find a hairpin. But then she did 'borrow' the odd scarf, pair of gloves, or ear bobs, whenever she'd a mind, so it seemed only fair she help us in return. Not that we ever let on that we noticed. Why would we, with so many clothes to choose from?

Besides, she had no wish to lose this job, bless her, and was becoming a valued friend to us both.

Prudence started brushing my hair, which hung halfway down my back. 'It's like a glossy cloud, such a lovely dark colour. And your lips are naturally red, I'm so envious. I do have other attributes, I suppose,' she said, turning to preen herself in the long mirror and admire her own shapely figure set off by a lovely pale-pink satin gown. 'I'd just love to give my hair a touch of henna. Do you think Mama would notice? I could say it had turned red all by itself overnight, couldn't I?'

I laughed at her nonsense. 'I doubt she'd believe you, Prue.'

'I shall at least put some rouge on my lips . . . There, much better.'

As Prudence tugged down the neckline of her gown to further reveal the enticing swell of her young breasts, I watched with amusement mingled with open admiration. Ever more daring than myself, I envied Prudence her spark of rebellion. Even now she was decking herself out in cheap jewellery which our mother wouldn't approve of either. But then Mama's jewellery was special, an inheritance from her own mother who was said to be European royalty, and therefore extremely valuable. It was kept safely locked away. Whenever I was asked to run and fetch a necklace or brooch from the closet, I always went in fear and trembling in case I should lose the key or bring the wrong piece by mistake.

Now I tweaked my own blue satin gown, checking I hadn't trodden on the hem and torn it, as I so often did. Or spilt fruit juice down the front, as I did at a recent soirée we attended. I've never seen Mother quite so angry, marching me off home and accusing me of being a ragbag and bringing shame and disgrace upon the entire family. For a *spill of fruit juice*? Heaven knows how she would react if I ever did something really bad.

At least the blue of my gown warmed the cool grey of my eyes a little. How I wished they were blue, almost as much as Prue ached to be a brunette. Why are we never satisfied with what we have? I was taller than my younger sister, whose figure was neat and trim, making me feel gangling and gawky, and far more plain than her sweet prettiness.

'If we don't hurry, the matinee will be over before we ever get there. Where is that girl?' Prudence complained. 'I declare she grows more mulish by the day.'

I giggled. 'You sound just like Mama.'

'Goodness, do I? Heaven forfend,' and we both fell into fits of laughter.

Maura burst in, not a moment too soon, gasping for breath and hot hairpin in hand. The next half hour was spent in frantic preparation as Prue's eyelashes were blacked, hair was pinned up, shoes and purses found before, at last, accompanied by our exhausted sulky maid, we presented ourselves for inspection.

Unsurprisingly we did not pass muster. One glance at

her younger daughter and Mama almost had the vapours. 'Is that rouge on your lips, Prudence? Remove it at once. And you are showing a vast amount of flesh. Pray run upstairs and change that dress this minute.'

Prue's face fell. 'Oh, Mama, that would take an age and we'd miss the matinee. Anyway, I think I look rather handsome.'

'You look like a shameless hussy. What your dear father will say, I cannot imagine. Maura, fetch me one of my lace handkerchiefs. Quickly! The largest you can find.'

Maura ran up and down two flights of stairs this time, and the handkerchief was tucked firmly into the bosom of the gown, quite spoiling the effect but certainly sparing Prue's modesty, or at least our mother's blushes.

There then followed the usual lecture about where we may and may not go after the matinee. 'You can take a short stroll but speak to no one with whom you are not already acquainted, is that clear?' she sternly warned.

'Yes, Mama,' we dutifully agreed, bobbing a curtsey, although I could tell that Prudence hadn't the least intention of keeping such a silly rule.

'How on earth would we ever meet anyone new and exciting if we never spoke to people?' she would say, and there was a certain logic to this argument. Unfortunately, I hadn't quite acquired my younger sister's knack for disobedience.

Father finally emerged from the library, carefully locking the door behind him, and that of the best parlour, to make sure the servants didn't rob us blind while we were out. In his silk top hat, frock coat and white silk cravat, he cut a fine figure as he walked straight-backed, head held high with his usual air of authority. Mama quickly gathered up her purse and wrap and the entire family set forth in our finest, to catch the tramcar for the short ride into town.

We walked arm in arm out of the theatre on to Bush Street, talking nineteen to the dozen as we recalled amusing little incidents from the plays we'd just seen. The matinee had been wonderful. The crimson curtains had swished back to gasps of excitement and enthusiastic applause from the audience, then we'd settled in our seats to enjoy an extract from *As You Like It*, and a short farce called *Her Sinful Secret* about a young society miss who pretends to be a maid and gets caught up in an *affaire*. Really quite shocking in its way, but very funny. All five of us had laughed till we cried.

The only disappointment was that few young gentlemen ever attended, Papa being rare in that he enjoyed theatre, as largely the auditorium was filled with women and children, all nibbling peanuts and chattering loudly. Fortunately, the performance rarely lasted beyond an hour, as the actors were anxious for a rest before the start of the longer evening performance, so there was still time for us to socialise elsewhere.

Papa had taken Mama off for tea and cakes, and we girls were now free to enjoy a short stroll up the street before returning home. Oh, and how we loved to browse in the smart shops and peer in curiosity as saloon doors swung open to reveal a brawl within, or some other sign of depravity. It was all very thrilling.

But first we had to negotiate the crowd of 'mashers' who milled about the entrance to the theatre. These considered themselves to be very much the fashionable men about town, but their object was to seek any opportunity to waylay some silly young girl and proposition her. As Mama had been at pains to impress upon us, it was quite wrong to speak to anyone unless you had previously been introduced. But the 'mashers' had their own way of getting around this rule.

I braced myself as one approached Prudence. 'How do you do, miss . . . er . . . um . . . oh dear, I am so dreadful with names. I believe we met at the Spinney's Social last fall, how lovely to see you again.'

Prudence, to her credit, sniffed with disdain. 'I very much doubt it, sir. I recall no such event.' But then spoilt the effect by falling into a fit of giggles which she quickly stifled with her handkerchief.

'Prudence, have a care,' I chided, but then as I tried to steer my sister through the pressing crowd, urging Maura not to fall behind, I found our way blocked by a rather large young man. Stout and broad-shouldered, he stood four-square before us.

'Ah, three beautiful girls, surely sisters. Indeed, did I not have the pleasure of meeting you all at Mrs Delaney's ball?'

I rolled my eyes in disgust at the same old line, and it was Maura's turn to fall into giggles at being taken for one of the Briscoe sisters. I decided to be kind and laughed good-naturedly. 'Nice try, but I fear you are mistaken, sir. Pray excuse us.'

Prudence tossed her brown curls and gave him an enchanting sidelong glance. 'I do declare we seem to be the talk of the town today. I wonder why that can be?' she said, hitching up her satin skirts as she pretended to twirl away from him so that he caught a tantalising glimpse of trim ankles.

I stifled a sigh. My young sister had an uncanny knack for choosing entirely the wrong moment to flirt, and at sixteen was as luscious and ripe as a fresh peach. As Prudence fluttered a hand to her breast, for one dreadful moment I feared she might be about to rip off the offending handkerchief, and quickly captured her hand with my own, just in case. Giving it a little squeeze I hissed fiercely in Prue's ear. '*Behave!* What are you thinking of?'

My silly sister had certainly caught his attention, for the arrogant fellow refused to budge, maintaining his stance blocking our path, so that in order to continue our walk we would need to physically push him to one side. Quite impossible.

We exchanged anxious glances while Maura cowered behind. Only a year or two older than myself at twenty, she was no match for this obnoxious bully.

'Why don't I walk you fine ladies home? We can stop off for a little drink along the way. My carriage awaits.' He reached out, as if to take my hand, but I flinched away, pulling Prue closer so that he couldn't grab her instead.

'I would prefer it, sir, if you stepped aside and allowed us to pass. We are in no need of an escort. We have our maid, and we will be meeting up with our parents again shortly.' This last was a lie, as we'd arranged to take the tramcar home and not wait for Papa and Mama, but he wasn't to know that.

Far from standing aside, he took a further step towards us, so close that I could smell the whisky on his breath. 'If three gels of such inestimable beauty are unescorted, and in such a flippant mood,' he added, giving Prudence a broad wink, 'they clearly wish to invite attention.'

'How dare you! We are doing no such thing. Pray get out of our way this instant.' I brandished my parasol at him, wishing it was raining, then I would have had my umbrella which was far larger. I had no other weapon at my disposal, and the crowd behind us had thinned by this time, with not even the door commissioner visible at the theatre entrance. I could see Maura desperately looking about for assistance, but there didn't seem to be any available. 'Come, Prue, Maura, we'll go this way instead,' and turning smartly on my heels I began to walk briskly in the opposite direction.

It was Maura's scream which brought me up short.

'Oh, the saints preserve us, he's grabbed Miss Prudence and is shoving her into that brougham!'

I whirled about in horror just in time to see the door slam shut, my beloved sister having been bundled inside. Before I had time to move a muscle, or even cry out, the horse set off at a brisk trot and the vehicle departed, soon vanishing into the crowd.

I wasted no time on debating what should be done but set off in hot pursuit, running as fast as my legs could carry me. I kept bumping into people, screaming at them to get out of the way, went sprawling at one point when I tripped over a kerb, and Maura hauled me unceremoniously to my feet.

'Are you hurt, miss?'

'No, I'm fine. What colour was it?'

'What?'

'The *brougham*. What colour?'

'Yellow, no, green and black.'

And we were off again, the pair of us darting in and out of bewildered pedestrians, checking every vehicle that bore even a vague resemblance to the one that had carried off darling Prudence. A tramcar drew up alongside but I didn't even pause long enough to climb aboard, quite certain I could run faster than a car straining uphill on its cable.

We crossed Pine Street and California, heading north on Kearny. No time now to enjoy the shops or pause to peep through open doors. Fortunately the streets were near-deserted as most people were still enjoying a matinee at one or other of the many theatres. So with our eyes fixed on a carriage some distance ahead which we hoped was the right one, we ran as if our lives depended on it, which Prudence's surely did. Eventually, we were forced to stop as we were both gasping for breath and needing to nurse the stitch in our aching sides. We were almost in despair.

'Damnation, there are times when I wish Frisco wasn't such a hilly town. Where can it be? Have we lost it?'

Maura was peeping down back alleys, growing

increasingly agitated. 'If we don't find her soon she might be taken to the Barbary Coast and sold off as a white slave.'

'Thank you for those few words of comfort, Maura.' We both jumped as a muffled explosion sounded in the distance. 'Was that fireworks? Are we near Chinatown?'

The Irish girl started to shake. 'It could be gunshots. We're almost at the wharves. Oh my, someone could shoot her!'

I cast Maura an anguished look. 'That's what Papa will do to us if we don't find Prudence. Come on,' and I set off at a trot again, soon breaking into a run, but sometimes obliged to walk a little to ease the growing stitch in my side. I felt hot and exhausted, had lost my hat and parasol some time back, and was having to bully the little maid to keep up with my much longer legs.

We were now approaching the dense area of warehouses, dives, beer halls and saloons that comprised the seamier side of San Francisco, all permeated by the rank odour of mud and filth and human excrement mingled with fish and salt breezes. The afternoon light was already starting to fade as damp mists were rolling in from the bay. I knew this was no place for two young girls to be alone, without escort. But nor was this the moment to be worrying about such niceties.

Maura, who again had been peering down side streets, suddenly cried out, 'There it is, at the bottom of this back alley. I recognise that awful pea-green colour.'

She was right. The vehicle was drawn up outside a beer hall. Somewhere inside that building must be my precious sister. I confess I did not pause to consider any possible danger to myself, or to Maura, my one thought being to rescue Prudence from her captors. I again set off at a run, but as I neared the vehicle a figure suddenly stepped out in front of me, and, quite unable to stop, I ran full tilt into him and landed flat on my back with the man on top of me.

Despite the fall having quite knocked the wind out of me, desperation allowed me to find my voice. 'Get off, you oaf,' I screamed at him, in most unladylike tones.

The fellow had the gall to roar with laughter.

I looked up into the bluest eyes I'd ever seen, set in a grinning face that boasted a delightful smattering of freckles. I could swear that I felt my heart literally turn over, which shocked me even more. What was I thinking of? I really had far more important matters on my mind right now than a young man's good looks. Opening my mouth to yell at him again, since he'd paid not the slightest heed the first time, to my utter dismay he stopped the cry by capturing my mouth with his own.

I couldn't believe this was happening. Here I was, lying in the filth and mud of a back alley where we'd followed the brougham that had kidnapped my lovely sister. There were all manner of stones and rubbish wedged hard beneath my back, and the pain of the long run was almost splitting my sides. Yet this stupid young man was actually *kissing* me!

I grabbed hold of his hair with both fists and yanked his head up. 'Are you deaf? *I told you to get off me!*'

He laughed as I unceremoniously pushed him off and scrambled to my feet, shaking out my skirts in fury.

'Bit picky, aren't you, for a whore? It was only a kiss, for goodness' sake.'

I was so furious at being thus described I swung my arm wide and slapped him hard across the face, then burst into tears.

Stunned by this unexpected attack and alarmed by its resulting reaction, he swiftly apologised. 'Hey, I'm sorry. Look, I didn't mean to offend.' He sketched a hurried bow. 'Pray allow me to introduce myself: Ellis Cowper, if you please, currently employed as deckhand and general dogsbody on the good ship SS *Kronus*.' He held out a hand which I coldly ignored. 'When I saw you running down the alley pell-mell, I meant to catch you, and swing you up into a kiss, just for a joke, you understand, only we both toppled over. I do apologise if I've made unwarranted assumptions about you.'

Unwarranted assumptions? How did a common sailor come by such grand words? Although his accent, I noticed, was British. I was about to give him the sharp edge of my tongue when Maura tugged at my arm.

'Look, isn't that him, the masher who blocked our way? He came out to get something from the brougham just now, then disappeared inside again.'

'Right. Whatever happens, Maura, stick close to my side. I don't want to lose you too.'

My young assailant was now attempting to brush down my skirts, still humbly apologising for his crass behaviour. I stopped him with one raised hand and my most imperious tone. Mama would have been proud. 'Pray unhand me, sir, I have no time for this. My sister has been abducted and is even now suffering God knows what fate in that beer hall below. Get out of my way this instant so that I may go and rescue her.'

The young man froze. 'Abducted?'

'Why do you think I was running? For the sake of my health?' Brushing past him, I strode to the door of the saloon, and again without pausing to consider the wisdom of such an action, marched straight inside, chin high and, I hoped, a very determined light in my storm-grey eyes.

1948

Chapter Five

The Lakes

It was the following morning and Chrissie had breakfasted alone, astonished that she'd eaten every morsel of Mrs Gorran's excellent porridge, toast and scrambled eggs, despite the substantial meal she'd enjoyed the night before. Perhaps it was all the walking in the fresh air that was giving her such a healthy appetite.

Oh, but she'd so enjoyed her grandmother's company last evening, had loved listening to her story of how she'd met Ellis, and begged for more. 'You can't stop there. What happened to poor Prudence?'

'Perhaps another time. Right now an old woman needs her rest.'

Chrissie could hardly wait. Now she asked Mrs Gorran if she may use the telephone in the hall, and rang Peter. The moment he answered she regretted her decision, as he was not in a good mood, castigating her at some length over the trouble she was causing, both to himself and her poor mother, by this foolish show of rebellion.

'I called upon Vanessa yesterday and I have to say she does not look well. You should be ashamed of yourself for abandoning your mother in this way.'

Chrissie tried to explain how badly she'd needed some time to herself but he was neither interested nor sympathetic. He asked few questions about where she was staying, seeming more concerned with his own situation. Chrissie listened with as much patience as she could muster; she had always tried to be understanding, knowing Peter was finding it hard to settle into civilian life, that he was discontented over being offered his old job back at the bank as a lowly clerk. He was even now harping on about this old theme.

'I should have been made a manager by now.'

'I'm sure you will be, in time.'

'I've been back almost *two years*, and still with no sign of promotion. Of course, if I had a wife—'

'You had a difficult war, Peter,' Chrissie quickly put in. 'You must allow yourself time to properly recover.' She privately doubted he ever would, that perhaps he'd always been dissatisfied with life. Chrissie also strongly disliked the idea of being used as a means for his promotion.

'And you had an easy one,' he sulked, snatching at her sympathy and milking it for all it was worth, as he always did.

'Hardly – bombs fell all over London. We would stand for hours in endless queues, spend night after night in air raid shelters and never know whether it would be our last.

The Blitz was the worst. We always feared the next bomb could easily have our name on it.'

'But we had it worse at sea. And you wouldn't believe what I went through in Africa and Italy, even if India was something of a sinecure. The heat, the fear, the knowledge we might be killed or fall into enemy hands at any moment.'

It was almost as if it were some sort of competition that he must win.

'It must have been dreadful for you, I know,' she said, doing her best to soothe him and dispel his black mood. 'But you must put all of that behind you now, remember? It's all over, in the past, and you can start to enjoy life again.'

Except that Peter somehow took pleasure in being miserable and complaining. Chrissie hadn't recognised that trait in him until he'd asked her to marry him, and appeared to relish her constant refusals. It was as if he believed he deserved her rejection because he was unworthy of her, and yet she constituted a challenge to him, a prize he was at pains to win in order to prove himself.

Rapidly running out of patience with his moans and groans, as so often in their conversations, Chrissie was relieved when Mrs Gorran walked into the hall ostentatiously carrying a feather duster, as if to indicate there was work to be done.

She quickly said her goodbyes and dropped the receiver into its cradle. 'Sorry I was so long. How much do I owe you for a call to London?'

'Ooh, I dunno. I'll need to ask Mrs Wren at the post

office. Don't worry about that now. I'll put it on your bill.'

Chrissie decided it would perhaps be wise to use a public call box in future, and reverse the charges. Not only might it be cheaper, but safer too, in case she accidentally mentioned any names that might be overheard by the ever-present Mrs Gorran. 'I'd rather pay for any extras as I go along, if you don't mind.' And pulling her purse from her bag, Chrissie began to count out pennies and sixpences, trying to guess what a call to London would cost. 'Will two shillings cover the call, do you think?' Better to err on the generous side rather than cause offence. Trunk calls were always expensive. And she was certainly in no hurry to call Peter again.

'Most kind. I'll see to put it in Mrs Cowper's telephone box.'

Chrissie was about to slip out for her walk when Mrs Gorran's next words stopped her in her tracks. 'I've arranged for you to have a boat trip this morning.'

She looked at the housekeeper, eyes wide with surprise. 'Boat trip?'

'My lad, Ben, he has this boat, see. Thought you'd enjoy a trip out on the lake, so's you can get a proper view of everything.'

Chrissie had intended to explore the straggle of shops that led up the hill from the waterfront. Then perhaps head out of town to the woodlands and meadows beyond. A good walk in the crisp Lakeland air would allow her to clear her head and gather her thoughts. A trip in a boat with a strange man was the last thing she had in mind. She didn't even know if she was a good sailor. But how could she refuse without appearing rude?

'How lovely,' she said, striving for a show of enthusiasm.

Moments later Chrissie found herself being led at a cracking pace down to a short jetty, the housekeeper talking nineteen to the dozen. 'Visitors flock to this little town for the beauty of its setting,' Mrs Gorran was saying. 'Others like to mess about in boats, climb a mountain, or simply enjoy a cream tea. Proper treat that is after all these years of austerity.'

Further along the shore Chrissie could indeed see holidaymakers revelling in the July sunshine: children trying to catch fish off the end of the pier, mums and dads fussing over little ones. Almost three years since the end of the war and optimism was high, helped in no small way by the King and Queen celebrating their silver wedding in April, and the announcement of a royal birth due at the end of the year.

A trip in one of the famous steam launches might be quite pleasant and offer an opportunity to do a bit of judicious probing. Perhaps her mother was right and keeping her name a secret would be no bad thing, might even give her a bit of leeway if she asked a few pertinent questions.

'Here we are. This is our Ben. He'll see you right, won't you, lad?'

Chrissie was so shocked by the sight of the boat – little more than a wooden dinghy with oars, for goodness' sake – she paid little attention to the young man who stepped out on to the jetty ready to hand her in. She was aware only that he was a head taller than herself, with fair hair and the kind of tan you'd expect from someone who spent their time working outdoors. But then she noticed how impatiently he slipped the painter loose from its ring, heard the irritation in his response.

'I'm sure Miss Emerson can manage without you organising her life, Mother.'

'I dare say, but a little helping hand never did no harm.'

Chrissie was suddenly aware of vibes of irritation. This young man had no more wish to take her out on a boat trip than she had to go on one. He'd probably got much more interesting plans lined up. With his girlfriend, no doubt.

She could feel his eyes upon her, assessing her, judging her.

They were a most interesting blue with laughter lines radiating from the corners. But there was a kindness in them, the face really quite good-looking. She found herself foolishly wishing she'd worn a pretty dress instead of this old cotton skirt and blouse; painted her nails, worn a touch of lipstick. How ridiculous! In any case, she really didn't need any more problems with men – wasn't her love life tangled enough?

So what was she even doing here, about to accept the hand he offered and step into a rickety boat with a perfect stranger, even if he did look like Gregory Peck? She let out a little squeal as it again slapped against the jetty, rocking dangerously from side to side.

'It's all right, she won't go over.'

'Yes, but *I* might!'

Waves slapped at the fragile vessel as the big public steamer went by, rocking and banging it against the wooden jetty. The little dinghy looked extremely precarious.

She took a step back. 'Um, let's do this some other day, shall we? There's really no rush.'

'Suit yourself,' he muttered, as if he really couldn't care less. Ben couldn't believe this was happening to him. Here was the girl in lemon yellow he'd longed to get to know from the moment he'd set eyes on her and compared her to a ray of sunshine. Now he was making a complete pig's ear of actually meeting her, just because his interfering mother had arranged it. Why was his life so beset with bossy interfering women? 'Perhaps you aren't used to being out on the water.'

It was Hetty who answered, in her usual forthright fashion. 'Course she isn't used to being on the water, coming from London. But she'll be fine, won't you, love?' She addressed this last question to Chrissie.

'Yes. Yes, of course, I'll be fine. Thanks.' Now what on earth had possessed her to sound so confident? Pride?

Chrissie groaned as the boat rocked precariously in the water, grabbing the sides as she sat down with a bump on the wooden seat in the bow. She'd much rather not be here at all. Her mind was still back in the dining room listening to the stirring tale her grandmother had so recently related. She could have listened to her all night.

'Now, you young people have yourself a lovely sail.' The housekeeper's bossy tones broke into her thoughts.

And, pleased at having finally accomplished her mission, she set off at a lick back up the jetty and left them to it.

'I'm sorry about this,' Ben muttered, by way of apology. 'She has a tendency to be a bit bossy, my mother. Nothing she likes better than to organise people.' He was wishing desperately that he'd never been put in this embarrassing position. It was perfectly clear this young woman had no wish to spend her morning in a boat with him, and no doubt thought him a sad case for having to rely on his mother for introductions to pretty girls.

Chrissie was embarrassed too, since these were her thoughts exactly. 'That's OK, I'm getting the hang of it now – I think.'

His bark of laughter was almost patronising. 'You don't look as if you are, not by the way you're clinging to the sides. You can relax – I haven't drowned many people, not recently anyway.'

'Sorry.' Now they were both apologising. Oh dear, this was dreadful. The worst of it was that in any other circumstances, if Mrs Gorran hadn't dropped this on them both, if Chrissie didn't still have Peter hanging on for her answer, and if she hadn't sworn on keeping to her single state if she ever did break free of her mother's chains, then she might well have fancied Ben Gorran. He was really rather good-looking, she decided, as she surreptitiously studied him from beneath her lashes. Nor was he obliged to resort to the oars, as there was an outboard motor which sprang to life at the tug of a cord, which was a huge relief.

Chrissie consciously unclenched her grip from the

edge of the boat and was almost surprised she didn't immediately topple overboard. Taking a breath, she told herself she would be fine. Ben began to point out various landmarks: the promenade, the Victorian splendour of the Belsfield Hotel, rows of tall Edwardian villas used mainly as boarding houses these days, every one of them bursting at the seams as accommodation was still in short supply.

'Did Mum mention that this lake was used for building and testing Sunderland flying boats during the war?' he asked her.

'Really?' Chrissie tried to sound interested.

'Not that anyone's supposed to know about that as it was top secret. Only those of us who live on the lake can say for sure. We used to see them coming in, testing them at one of the narrowest parts. If the pilot got it wrong, that would have been it. There was no room for error as he'd never have got up the other side and over the mountains.'

Ben went on with his tale but Chrissie couldn't take in half of what he was telling her, nor had she any wish to listen. He was speaking far too fast, babbling like some demented overcheerful tour guide. Except that this tiny boat was much less substantial than the steamers in which Vanessa enjoyed evening soirées on the Thames. Stifling a groan and attempting to concentrate on what he was saying, she rather thought it was going to be a long morning.

For a while, perhaps to give her confidence, Ben kept close to the shore where the woodlands were lush and green, overhanging branches skimmed the water, and moorhens paddled about in the shallows. Chrissie suddenly cried out, 'Oh, look, what was that big bird with the long neck that flew by, so close to the water?'

'A cormorant. And that's a Canada goose. Do you like birds?'

'I've never had time to find out. Oh, but they are so beautiful.' This trip was turning out to be really most pleasant. Ben had thankfully stopped striving to entertain her, and Chrissie was beginning to relax and enjoy herself.

As they approached Belle Isle in the middle of the lake, they looked back at the town, Ben pointing out how the gardens stretched right down to the shoreline.

'They are very elegant,' Chrissie agreed. 'Not much sign of flowers, though. Everyone is still busily growing vegetables. Got into the habit, I suppose.'

'I'll say, and keeping chickens. I don't know how folk would have managed during the war without their poultry and the fishing. Guddling for trout wasn't just a sport, it became a lifesaver. Generally brown trout in these waters. When I was a lad we'd sometimes go to Morecambe for the shrimping. I don't suppose you did much of that in London either.'

'We always had plenty of jellied eels,' she said, and they both laughed, easing the tension a little.

'See that big wooden shed just by the marina here? Boatbuilding used to be big in these waters, once upon a time, making those wonderful steam launches for the rich.' The marina still bristled with the masts of a dozen or so small yachts, but Ben chugged right past, to a quieter part of the lake. He told her more about the boats and this time she listened, about how the well-to-do would have their own crested crockery, and take their servants with them to serve a splendid picnic to their guests in Wray Bay or on one of the smaller islands. 'The gentlemen would be in their blazers and straw boaters, the ladies wearing their finest gowns with those preposterous hats, no doubt.' He grinned. She liked the sound of his voice – deep, and with a certain resonance to it.

'Do you build boats yourself?'

He nodded. 'When I can spare the time from my carpentry business. Only small ones though, so far.'

'Like this?' Despite her earlier reaction to the little dinghy, she was impressed.

Chrissie was fascinated too by his confidence in handling the tiller, steering the small boat through eddies and currents, and away from sandbanks. Or more particularly by the power of his hands and arms, and the way the breeze plastered the open-necked shirt he wore against his broad chest and muscled shoulders. He was wearing shorts, and his legs too were pretty impressive. She averted her gaze, embarrassed by her own interest.

Ben beached the boat beneath an overhanging willow. When he switched off the engine the silence rolled in upon them. There wasn't a sound save for that of a mallard as it quietly plopped into the water. Quite magical.

He handed her out and Chrissie was thankful to feel solid ground beneath her feet again, giving a little sigh of relief which brought forth a smile.

'I haven't drowned you yet, have I?'

'I'm hoping you won't.' She found herself returning his smile, noting how blue his eyes were, how she liked the way his hair had been bleached by the sun, and fell untidily over a broad brow. She felt a small glow start up inside, a sensation she hadn't experienced in a long time.

They picked their way over rocks and through bracken and furze. A bramble caught on her skirt and Ben helped her to untangle it. The touch of his fingers as they accidentally brushed against hers brought a sudden warmth to her cheeks with the awareness of how alone they were here, on the far side of the lake, the tension between them now of a very different hue.

Ben found a mossy patch for them to sit on, dry and cushioned. 'I like to sit here sometimes, in the quiet of an evening. I'll light a fire with driftwood and run out a line, catch some perch for my supper.'

The idea entranced her. 'And is this where you bring your girlfriends?' Now what on earth had possessed her to ask such a thing? Chrissie could have bitten off her tongue.

There was a short pause as Ben thought about his coming divorce, and Karen. He really didn't want to spoil the moment by going in to all of that unpleasant stuff right now. Nor did he want this girl's sympathy. Hadn't he been embarrassed enough by his mother's interfering and bossy organising? The last thing he wanted was for her to think he was seeking a replacement mother for his daughter. Yet neither did he wish to appear to lie or cover up his situation.

'Actually, I've just come through the nasty process of disposing of my wife. Through the divorce courts, I hasten to add, not in any more macabre way. Though there were times . . .'

She didn't laugh at his bad joke. 'I'm sorry.'

'Don't be, it was the best decision I'd made in years. How about you?'

Chrissie wrapped her arms about her knees, rested her chin on them with a small sigh, and told him briefly about Tom. 'It was probably the shortest marriage on record.'

'I don't know what to say.'

'There's no need for you to say anything. In fact, I prefer people to say nothing at all, rather than the wrong thing.' She tried a smile, avoiding his gaze so as not to see the pity in his eyes.

'I know what you mean. Divorce seems to disturb and shock people in some strange way too. Even my oldest friends have withdrawn slightly, as if it were a disease they might catch.'

She laughed. 'You're trying to get out of a bad marriage, while I'm trying to avoid being drawn into one.'

Ben was instantly alert. 'Really? There is someone, then, back home?'

'Not really . . . well, in a way. The thing is, I don't want to marry just because Peter thinks I'd be an asset to him as a wife, or because I need—' She stopped, unwilling to mention her demanding mother, not wishing to appear pathetic.

'You'd be an asset to any man, but I know what you

mean. You want to be loved for yourself, not because he fancies having a wife to look after him, or to chat up his boss.'

'Exactly!' Chrissie turned to look at him then and saw only warmth, and something she couldn't quite put a name to. Interest? Speculation? Those deep-blue eyes suddenly seemed as mystical and unfathomable as the waters of the lake. 'Thank you for understanding,' was all she could manage by way of response.

'You're welcome.'

There had been times recently when Chrissie had wondered if the grieving for Tom would ever pass. Sometimes she felt utterly bereft, a failure, less of a woman somehow, with no love in her life. Yet however frustrated and lonely she might feel, she was determined not to be pushed into something she wasn't ready for. What if Peter turned out to be a bolter, like her father?

'My mother tells me that men are all easy seduction, charming and romantic at first, full of kisses and sweet compliments. Then once the ring is on your finger, they lose interest and betray you without a second thought.'

'Not all men. And some women are like that too.'

Chrissie glanced at him, recognised the pain in his eyes. 'So that's how it was, eh? Then you were wise to call an end to the humiliation. You deserve better.'

His eyes kindled with warmth and humour. 'Are you offering?'

She gave a little chuckle. 'Cheeky! I've almost made up my mind not to risk marriage ever again. I'd found my soulmate in Tom. I think it very unlikely I could be so fortunate a second time, and have no wish to ruin my life by making a bad mistake.'

'Good for you, except that would be a sad loss to mankind. A beautiful girl such as yourself could surely take her pick of husbands.'

'Flatterer.' She was laughing at his teasing now, even as she furiously shook her head. But they were talking easily, like old friends. She could never talk to Peter this way. 'I mean to be my own person, or at least try.' Chrissie told herself she certainly wouldn't allow herself to be beguiled by soft words and flirting, however delicious. Nevertheless her insides seemed to melt just looking at this man.

'Is that why you're here? The Lakes tend to be an escape route for many.'

She looked down at her hands, clamped firmly between her knees. 'I felt the need for some time to think, to review my life and decide where I go from here. What a cliché. Everyone says that, I suppose.'

'It's still a good idea, to take your time over deciding, I mean.' He gazed out over the rippling waters of the lake. 'And this is as good a place as any in which to do it.'

'That's what I thought. This quiet solitude, the panoply of mountains, seem to offer peace, a sanctuary. So, how long have you lived in Windermere?' She brightened her tone, suddenly desperate to change the subject.

'All my life. My mother has worked for Mrs Cowper since she was a girl.'

'They do seem very close.' Chrissie paused, anxious to move away from her own personal troubles but worrying how to frame her next question without seeming too inquisitive. 'Does Mrs Cowper have much family of her own?' Surely a perfectly reasonable question to ask.

Ben plucked a blade of grass and began to idly chew on it. 'Her husband died some years ago, but her son comes from time to time, usually to issue lectures and tell her what she should be doing. Moving out, if he had his way, or at least retire to one of her cottages.'

So there was a son. Her uncle! Chrissie took a moment to absorb this detail.

'Ryall didn't approve of his mother's decision to turn the family home into B&B and holiday lets. I think his wife has a fancy to be mistress of Rosegill Hall.'

'I see.' She was struggling to disguise the growing excitement she felt at these unexpected titbits. 'And are there more . . . I mean . . . does Mrs Cowper have any grandchildren?'

He picked up a stone and skimmed it across the still water, counting the bounces. 'Five, not bad.' Then laughed. 'No, not five children, Ryall has two. A boy and girl, I think. Then there are the twins.'

'Oh, so he has four?'

Ben shook his head, laughing all the more. 'Sorry, no, I'm explaining this very badly. I mean Jenna and Corin, Mrs Cowper's twin daughters. They live in the Midlands, I think, and only come at Christmas and holidays. They were here in July, as usual, with their respective husbands and children. I rather like the twins. No-nonsense types, and very jolly. They are the only ones who can put their brother in his place.'

Chrissie was stunned into silence. So this was the

'family' Georgia had obliquely referred to, who came and went as they pleased. Not only did Chrissie have an uncle she hadn't been aware of, but two aunts and goodness knows how many cousins. Now, why had her mother never thought to mention them? Surely her siblings could have kept in touch, even if Vanessa had been told never to darken her mother's doors again. Or did they cast her off too? The fact that Vanessa had never even told her own daughter that these family members existed was distinctly odd, and clearly deliberate on her part. Was this one of the reasons Mum hadn't wanted her to come? There was clearly more to this estrangement than she'd at first realised.

Everyone had a right to a secret, except when it affected other people. But Chrissie was beginning to wonder which of these two women, Georgia or Vanessa, was the one really responsible for this family rift.

'Are you all right?' Ben was leaning close, looking concerned. 'You've gone all pale.'

'I'm fine.' She could smell the fresh mountain air on him, the sharpness of green grass, feel the warmth of his closeness. In that moment Chrissie experienced an overwhelming desire to rest her head on his shoulder and weep. No, not weep. Lean into his strength and kiss him perhaps, reaffirm that she was a person who mattered and not one to be either bullied into marriage by an overcontrolling boyfriend, or ignored by a selfish mother.

'It's very hot, fancy a swim?'

'I'd love one, sadly I didn't bring my costume.'

He grinned at her. 'I wouldn't mind.'

Chrissie laughed. 'I'm sure you wouldn't, but I would.'

'Next time, then? We could bring a picnic.'

So, he wanted there to be another boat trip, did he? One he'd arranged himself without his mother's assistance. Still, she wasn't against the idea. She rather liked Ben Gorran. Chrissie thought a girl could lose herself in those gorgeous blue eyes of his. 'Just name the day and I'll be ready.'

Chapter Six

San Francisco

Addressing the barman, who looked in dire need of a shave and a clean waistcoat, I spoke in a voice loud enough to carry to the furthest corner of this grubby little bar, and to whoever may be listening beyond. 'I believe my sister may have been brought in here and I'd be obliged, sir, if you would point me in the right direction where I might find her.'

He stared at me as if I were an alien who had fallen out of the sky. I'm quite sure the only women who ever entered his saloon were of the type whose morals were questionable to say the least. I might have appeared flustered, my hair awry and my skirt muddied, but I was undoubtedly recognisable as class. It radiated from my presence, was all too apparent in my crisp pronunciation, and must have shone out of my face like a ray of sunlight in hell, which was what this place was, near as made no difference.

'I wouldn't know nothing 'bout that,' he mumbled. 'Can't help you, ma'am.'

'Oh, I think you can, if you put your mind to it.'

I half turned in surprise at the sound of the voice at my elbow, startled to find my would-be assailant had come up quietly behind me. My young defender was casually dressed in brown jacket and trousers, a neat green silk cravat at his throat, and as he swept off his hat I noticed that his hair was a pale gold, almost as fair as mine was dark. Utterly entrancing.

Ignoring me completely, his attention was entirely focused upon the barman. 'I'd do everything I could to help this lady, if I were you, unless you want your precious saloon torn apart and wrecked. I could easily arrange that, should I find it necessary, by calling on my mates from the SS *Kronus*, who are just outside. They're handy chaps, and not too respectful of other folks' property, or particularly sober right now. So, do you reckon I've jogged your mind about what might have befallen this lady's sister?'

I rallied sufficiently from my surprise at the young man's unexpected support to pitch in with my own two dimes' worth. 'And if you refuse to cooperate I shall inform my father, Mr Isaac Briscoe. As you may be aware, he is an important and influential employer in these parts, owning several of these warehouses. You might find a good many people suddenly out of work, businesses closed or buildings razed to the ground.' It felt like an empty threat, as I hadn't the first idea which warehouses Papa owned, but I had to say something, and this was all that came to mind off the top of my head.

The barman hurriedly disappeared into a back room, from where we heard the mumblings of a furious argument ensue. I was instantly concerned.

'Where has he gone? If he runs off with her . . .' I turned to my companion. 'Could you really call on your friends? I didn't see anyone outside.'

'That's because they weren't there. I lied.' He gave a flicker of a smile by way of apology. 'It seemed worth the risk. I had to say something.'

My heart sank. 'Then we're on our own?'

'Afraid so.'

Knowing me too well, Maura began to whimper. 'Oh, please don't you go in there, miss. Please!'

I muttered some oath under my breath which would have caused Mama apoplexy. Not that I had a single plan in my head how I was to effect a rescue, but I was determined to devise one somehow. Only the terrible fury I was experiencing held back my fear, and in desperation I began a rapid search of the area behind the bar, seeking inspiration.

'What are you looking for?' asked my stalwart companion, coming to join me.

'Don't worry, I've found it,' I told him, and stormed into the room in pursuit of the barman.

The room was shrouded in gloom, so deep in shadow I at first found it well-nigh impossible to see what was happening. But it was the stink of the place which hit me the most, making me reel. It reeked of something overwhelmingly pungent and yet intensely sweet.

'It's opium,' my companion whispered in my ear. 'That's Shanghai smoke or I'm a Dutchman.'

'I'd rather gathered that,' I caustically responded. Once my vision had adjusted to the dim light, I could see two men slumped in chairs, their eyes unfocused, fixed grins on their faces, their whole demeanour tantamount to the effect of the pall of smoke that hung about them. One was the stout man who had blocked our passage and taken Prudence; the other was small and thin, probably the driver of the brougham. The barman was remonstrating with them in furious whispers, talking and waving his arms about in great agitation, perhaps explaining whose daughter it was they'd abducted, and what would happen to his premises if they didn't cooperate.

I fervently hoped they would, as I really had no wish to carry through this crazy plan of mine, if that's what you could call it, to bring about my sister's rescue. And there darling Prue sat, eyes wide with fright, wrists tied to the arms of a chair, a filthy gag rammed into her pretty mouth. I couldn't believe this was happening to us. Taking a breath I stepped quickly forward before I quite lost my courage.

'If you imagine you can get away with this, you couldn't be more wrong. I refuse to be intimidated by threats, so don't waste your time trying. Release my sister at once, or I promise you'll regret it.'

The silence following this reckless statement was profound as four pairs of eyes swivelled in my direction.

I was aware of Ellis Cowper watching me in open admiration. I hoped that my young sister's abductors were likewise impressed, despite themselves. This sort of thing happened regularly, of course. Pretty girls or young boys would be snatched off the street and sold to some ship or other as slave labour. For a girl the prospect was particularly disastrous. Even being here, in this hellhole, could ruin her reputation for life. I flicked my gaze about the room, sizing up possible escape routes, wondering whether these ruffians would be likely to own a gun. I'd heard that most preferred a knife or blunt implement in order to threaten their victims, as dead human merchandise were of no value to them.

My companion took a step forward to place himself firmly at my side, casting me a wry sideways glance, as if to say 'I'm with you in this'. I was immensely grateful for his support, but, not wishing to reveal my fear, I shielded my eyes with those thickly fringed lashes that Prudence admired so much.

'Well?' I asked the two kidnappers, in the tone of voice a schoolmarm might use to a recalcitrant child. 'Are you going to let her go or must we summon reinforcements?'

It was at this moment that the valiant Ellis Cowper suddenly noticed what I was holding in my hand, and I sensed his recoil. It was, of course, a gun, which was what I'd been looking for behind the bar. I guessed there'd be a weapon of some sort hidden there. I'm not sure what kind it was as I'm unfamiliar with weapons. Possibly the sort of pistol that would have been used in the American Civil War. A Colt, or a Smith & Wesson perhaps? I had no idea. No more than I knew how to fire it, but I didn't worry about that. All that mattered was that these ruffians recognised that I meant business. I pointed it straight at the two men, keeping my aim remarkably steady, considering how I was shaking inside like an aspen in a gale-force wind.

'Hey, steady she goes. Let's not be too hasty here.'

My sidekick reached out a hand as if to take the weapon from me and I swung it towards him instead, a wildness in my eyes and in my heart that gave him pause. Now he was the one staring down the barrel of a gun, and though he was evidently no coward, I saw how his blood ran cold. He certainly had no intention of tackling a gal with a gun, not one in such a state.

'OK, OK.' He backed off, hands held high. I prayed the thugs holding my sister would show similar wisdom.

Unfortunately, perhaps seeing an opportunity while I was thus distracted, the big man was rash enough to lurch drunkenly towards me.

'Hold it, let's all stay quite calm, shall we?' my companion cried, and quick as a flash jerked forward to bar the fellow's way. I'm not sure whether this was brave or foolhardy, but he obviously felt it incumbent upon himself to prevent any bloodshed. I saw how he braced himself in case the big man should hit him, but it was me who lashed out. Ellis Cowper had reckoned without my fury. Shoving my protector out of the way, I spun about, the gun wavering crazily for a second until I managed to steady one shaking hand with the grip of the other, and fixed my livid gaze upon the fat man along its sights.

'One more step and I shall take out your kneecap. The choice is yours. Now, untie my sister or give up all hope of walking out of here.' I deliberately kept my voice calm, as if I were offering him milk or sugar with his tea, while aiming the pistol firmly at his legs.

The fat man obviously believed the threat, or else he was too drugged to counter it, for he at once staggered back and began to fiddle clumsily with the knots holding Prue's wrists. Once she was free he grabbed her by the arm and flung her to the floor. 'Take the girl, see if I care. There's plenty more where she came from.'

Prudence scrambled to her feet and fell into my arms in a flood of tears. 'Darling Georgia, I knew you'd come for me, I just knew it. Don't you always save me when I get into a pickle?'

I gave her a quick hug while keeping my eyes very firmly upon the group of men before me. 'Don't move a muscle, any of you, and don't think to follow us. We have friends waiting outside, remember, who'll make sure you stay put.' The lie sounded so convincing no attempt was made to stop us as I quietly led my weeping sister from the room.

Once outside on the sidewalk, having thoroughly checked that no harm had befallen Prue, I thanked my partner in the rescue. Somewhere in the distance I could hear clanging bells and whistles, the clop of hooves and shouts of warehouse men going about their normal business, a comforting reminder that we were not in fact alone, and all was again right with my world. 'I am most grateful for your assistance, Mr Cowper, even if our earlier meeting was somewhat unfortunate.' I put out a hand to introduce myself. 'My name is Georgina Briscoe, and this is my sister, Prudence, and our maid, Maura Kerrigan.'

Prudence fluttered her lashes while Maura dipped a curtsey as Ellis acknowledged the introductions with a slight head bow. Taking the proffered hand, and holding it warmly between both his own, he kissed it. 'I am truly thankful our intervention had such a good outcome. I hope you are not too shaken up by what happened.'

I hastily retrieved my hand, which suddenly seemed to have grown terribly hot. 'I'm fine. I would never have forgiven myself if something had happened to my beloved sister.'

'May I say that I thought you exhibited exemplary courage in there. I was most impressed.'

Prudence rushed to agree. 'Oh, indeed, Georgia can be very fierce when she wishes. She is quite the bravest person I know, even if she is supposed to be the quiet one of the family.'

'I can bear witness to your sister's valour and dashing nature, Miss Prudence. But perhaps it would be wise if she were to hand me the gun now.'

I laughed, giving a careless shrug. 'Oh, I tossed it back behind the counter as we ran through the bar. I don't even know if it was loaded.'

'I rather suspect it was, judging by the men's reaction.'

'I was certain sure we were all going to be shot dead,' sniffed our frightened maid, dissolving into fresh tears.

'I agree with you, Maura. For a moment in there things looked exceedingly dicey.' He handed her a large white handkerchief, which Maura used to mop up her tears and blow her nose upon before handing it back to him. He declined, telling her she could keep it. Then turning to me, he continued, 'Had the big man known for certain that the gun wasn't loaded, he could easily have wrested it from your hand, Miss Briscoe. How did you even know there would be a gun behind the bar?'

'I assumed there would be, in case a drunken brawl should ever get out of hand. Seemed logical.'

Ellis acknowledged my quick thinking with an appreciative nod, then smilingly told Prudence, 'As for your sister's ability at running, she may wish to consider taking up the sport and entering the marathon in the next Olympics.'

We all fell to giggling then and Ellis crooked his arm. 'Now, shall we proceed and get the dickens out of here while the going is good? I beg you to allow me to escort you all safely home, if only for the sake of my peace of mind. I want no more brutes attempting to accost and abduct either one of you. I shudder to think what might have happened to such a charming young girl as yourself, Miss Prudence, by falling into the hands of those criminals. You should, of course, report the incident to the police.'

I frowned, saying nothing as I privately considered the implications of this suggestion.

Maura bent close to whisper urgently in my ear. '*Your mama would not approve of this gentleman seeing you home. You don't know him neither.*'

Ignoring her, I accepted the proffered arm. Normally I would have listened to such sound advice, not only because I liked and trusted Maura, but also because I tended to veer towards caution myself in most things. However, there were times when it felt safe to take a risk, and this young man had surely proved he was trustworthy. 'Thank you, we would be most grateful.'

Maura clicked her tongue disapprovingly. 'What your dear mama will say when she hears the full story, I shudder to think.'

I whirled about and gave the silly girl a little shake. 'Mama must *never* hear of this. Do you understand, Maura? Never! It must be our secret, for all time. Do you hear, Prudence? No weeping and wailing. Mama and Papa must never discover that not only did we dare to disobey her number one rule by speaking to a stranger, but the fellow took advantage by abducting poor Prudence. We would all be locked up for ever. You too, Maura. Kept within doors and never allowed to venture out alone ever again.'

There was a startled gasp from each of them as they acknowledged the truth of this, Ellis Cowper listening in respectful silence.

'It must be our secret, then,' Prudence softly agreed, beginning to shiver as reaction set in following her ordeal.

Ellis, noticing her distress, was at once all concern. 'Come, let us get you home with all speed.' And offering Prudence his other arm, we set off, Maura trailing miserably behind predicting a sorry future for us all.

Chapter Seven

I could tell at once by the frozen smile on our mother's face that we were not going to be in for an easy ride. We'd taken a tramcar for part of the way, then Ellis had walked us the last two blocks without a single complaint about the steep hills. I'd watched him closely throughout the journey, completely enchanted by his looks, his good manners, and by his English accent as we chatted about this and that – anything but the trauma we'd all recently endured. By the time we reached our tall house on Geary Boulevard, I felt as if I'd known him for months and not just an hour or so. Naturally wishing to show proper gratitude, I offered him refreshment.

'That really isn't necessary,' he demurred. 'I have no wish to be a bother.'

'Oh do come in,' Prue cried, batting her carefully

blackened eyelashes for all she was worth. 'It really is no bother at all.'

'Some iced tea, perhaps?' I added, by way of enticement, feeling a sudden reluctance to see this young man simply walk away, out of my life, never to be seen or heard of again, even as I told myself that was only because we were now comrades-in-arms following the Great Rescue.

'Well, it is rather hot still. A cold drink before I make my way back to quarters would not go amiss.'

So it was that when Mama and Papa returned home fifteen minutes later, it was to find their two daughters entertaining a perfect stranger in the front parlour with lemonade and coffee cake.

'Do please introduce me to your "new friend", Georgia.' The smile Mama offered this stranger, who had dared to invade her private sanctuary uninvited, grew ever more chilling as I embarked upon some makeshift tale of how we'd been pestered by the 'mashers' and Mr Cowper had rescued us, an approximation of the truth. Prudence fussed around offering our parents cake and lemonade, which they refused.

'Mr Cowper saved us from a seriously embarrassing encounter.'

'I was delighted to help, as the gentleman was in his cups, ma'am,' Ellis politely informed her, adding veracity to the yarn. 'It seemed proper to see the ladies safely home, and I am most pleased to make your acquaintance.'

'I doubt you have done that, not quite yet.' Mama was making it perfectly plain that it took more than a passing introduction to be classed as an acquaintance, let alone a friend.

Papa gruffly cleared his throat and all eyes turned in his direction, breaths held while we awaited his opinion on the situation. 'Haven't seen you around – are you new to Frisco, young man?'

Ellis Cowper smiled, looking far more relaxed than seemed possible in the circumstances. 'I come and go, making regular crossings between Liverpool, Australia and the Americas.'

Mama sat up very straight in her chair. 'You can afford to travel frequently, and in luxury?'

Now he was laughing. 'I'm afraid not. I'm currently with the SS *Kronus*. She's a square-rigger, and when I say I am with the ship, I mean I'm employed as a deckhand. Once she's taken on her consignment of Californian wheat we'll sail again for Liverpool, and I with her.'

'*Deckhand?*' The low boom of Papa's voice seemed to echo in the silence following this surprising remark.

'That's right. Sometimes I work as a steward on board passenger ships, but—'

'A *steward*?' interrupted my mother, in sepulchral tones.

'Indeed!' He acknowledged her interruption with a smile. 'And a fascinating job it is too. It demands untiring energy and patience, good sea legs, of course, and some simple first-aid skills to care for those less accustomed to life aboard ship. The pay is quite good but the hours long, as the job entails a high level of cleanliness in the passengers' cabins, even to cleaning their boots, as well as making sure they get the best service at table. I don't mind as I love meeting new people, don't you? But, as I say, at present I'm on the cargo service, handling wheat, and wool from Australia, jute and rice from India.'

'And are you responsible for loading these *cargoes*?' Papa asked in freezing tones. I listened in increasing horror to my parent's reaction to these quiet answers, which I confess I found absolutely fascinating.

'I am one of that number, yes.'

The young man's smile was pleasant, his aspect open and friendly. Not so my father's. I observed with dismay how his dark eyebrows seemed to bristle, the creases between them deepening ominously. Feeling rather nervous, I attempted to lighten the atmosphere. 'My father is in import and export too, are you not, Papa?'

'I *own* a company which deals in such matters of business, yes,' he said, clearly emphasising the difference in their status.

My father, Isaac Briscoe, was a stern Victorian with a strict code of morals as rigid as his spine, an authoritarian quite certain of his position in business and society. He was proud and ambitious, and certainly valued hard work and enterprise, but although willing to assist members of his own family in their endeavours to make a better life for themselves, perhaps because this reflected well upon himself, his standards were high – if these grateful souls should fall short in their efforts, or he should develop doubts about his investment, Papa would not hesitate to withdraw his assistance.

As for those who made no effort to better themselves, they were, in my father's unswerving opinion, beneath contempt. I saw quite clearly that he regarded this young man as one of that category.

Mama was frantically fanning herself with her lace handkerchief as if the shock that such a low-bred creature should enter her portals, without her permission, had brought her close to collapse.

Being in the right class was, to Cecilia Briscoe, a social necessity. The correct pecking order seemed preordained, the prestige of birth far outweighing any attempt at social climbing or success in business achieved since, however worthy that might be. Mama sprang from an impeccable lineage with a countess for a grandmother. The family had fallen on political hard times, and now names had been anglicised, the past safely buried, and she and Papa were American, true to the flag and all this wonderful country stood for. Neither parent ever referred to their emigration to the US, having wholeheartedly reinvented themselves in the New World.

And they most certainly had no wish to allow either of their daughters to associate with a nobody.

'What of your family, do they approve of your . . . your form of employment?' Mama asked, with the slightest curl to her upper lip.

Ellis smiled at the question. 'My mother frets constantly, as all mothers do, quite certain I shall end up at the bottom of the ocean, drowned. Father is far more philosophical and pragmatic, and willing to tolerate my passion for adventure.'

Again that moment of silent disapproval.

'You mentioned Liverpool,' Isaac reminded him. 'Is that where you hail from?'

Ellis shook his head. 'I live in what is known as the

English Lake District, situated in the North West of England. It is a very beautiful mountainous district, with numerous lakes and tarns, charming towns, and friendly people. My home is Rosegill Hall, situated on the shores of Lake Windermere.'

'Rosegill Hall?' Mama again perked up. I could see her thinking that this young man was perhaps filling in a few years adventuring before taking up a rich inheritance. 'Is your father a lord, then, or perhaps an earl?'

Ellis burst out laughing, not noticing how this reaction made her flinch. 'Not at all, just ordinary country folk.'

Papa thoughtfully tugged on his moustache. His shrewd brown eyes behind the gold-rimmed spectacles did not miss the anxiety that shadowed his elder daughter's face. Perhaps in a rare moment of kindness his next question seemed to be seeking some way to compensate. 'Your parents no doubt hold an important status in the town as members of the landed gentry. Isn't that what you call them in England?'

'They are very well thought of, yes, although I wouldn't go so far as to call us "gentry". The "Hall" isn't nearly so grand as it sounds. Once a large farm, it has been in our family for a century or more, but is sadly in a ruinous condition.'

'Ruinous?' Mama's gasp of dismay was dreadful to hear.

'I'm afraid so. My father does what he can to maintain the place, but much of our land has been sold off over the years. He still owns some property in the town, and holds shares in a couple of slate quarries, but the income is no longer there to sustain it properly.'

I knew, without glancing at my mother's shocked face, that any hope of sustaining this new friendship had just died before my eyes. It made me feel unaccountably sick.

If only I was able to tell them how very brave Ellis had been in supporting my rescue of Prue. I thought of him by his first name already, for surely after such an adventure we were bound together by a friendship forged through adversity. I recalled how he'd courageously stood before me, unarmed, to protect me when the fat man had made his move. However befuddled by the opium, the ruffian had still been acutely dangerous, more so possibly. But on no account dare I even mention what had occurred in that gloomy room to my parents, let alone that I'd voluntarily entered a seedy saloon in order to save my kidnapped sister. The shock would be too much for Mama, and our future freedom seriously curtailed. Prudence, I noted with some sympathy, had sat silent throughout this discussion. For all her bravado, she was no doubt terrified that a single wrong word could ruin her reputation for ever.

Mother was on her feet, moving with all her considerable dignity to the bell pull, which she tugged sharply, twice. 'We are most grateful for your assistance in this delicate matter of rescuing my foolish daughters from the mashers, Mr Cowper. Maura will show you out.'

Seconds later, to his very great surprise, Ellis Cowper found himself on the wrong side of the Briscoe family's front door.

* * *

'So there you are, my dear, that is the tale of how I met my dearest beloved. I'm not sure if it deserves the epithet *romantic,* but it was certainly memorable, exciting, and even rather frightening.'

'Oh, but what of Ellis, did you see him again? You must have done. When? How?'

'A dutiful daughter I may have been but I was in no way stupid, dear. Even then, on that first afternoon, I knew that I felt something for this young man and had no wish to lose sight of him. I also suspected, in my youthful arrogance, that he felt the same attraction towards me. I hoped he would linger outside for a while, and I was proved right in this. At the first opportunity I sent Maura out to look for him and give him a little note. She found him hiding around the corner, not having stirred more than twenty feet from my door.'

Her eyes were once more alight with pride and love, and Chrissie's heart went out to her. 'I think it *wonderfully* romantic, as well as exciting.'

The old lady frowned. 'If it was, then it gradually deteriorated into a horror story, which I really don't care to relate, or recall.' Her grandmother was on her feet, her expression now cool and determined. 'I'm glad to see you've taken my advice and are now relishing Hetty's excellent repasts. Now, I must attend to my neglected paperwork, which is just as well, as I've talked far too much.' Making it very plain she would say no more.

The morning spent with Ben had unsettled Chrissie somewhat. The following day, needing time to think and evaluate what she had learnt about her grandmother, she took a long walk out into the countryside. Escaping the town with its ice cream stalls, noisy trippers and crowded streets, she went through a kissing gate and walked up out on to the rocky summit of Brant Fell. It was a steep climb, taking the better part of an hour, but worth the effort. At the top Chrissie sat on a tussock of grass to catch her breath, enchanted by the magnificent view over Lake Windermere to the Coniston fells and Fairfield.

So much to think about, not least Ben's effect upon her, which had been startling, just when she'd resolved to give up men for good. How fickle she was. She really must not allow herself to be influenced by a winning smile. She really had no intention of falling in love, not ever again.

But the discovery that she actually had rather a large family was even more disturbing. Yet they were all strangers to her, and in that moment Chrissie experienced an odd sense of loneliness. She'd never been given the chance to get to know them, her own family. They hadn't been a part of her life, or she theirs.

Even more sad than losing a family she never knew existed, her one night with Tom had not produced the child she'd hoped for, and Chrissie realised that by denying herself marriage, she would also lose the opportunity to create a family of her own. It felt like a double blow. No children of her own, that most precious gift, nor a ready-made family to visit and be a part of. She couldn't help but regret the many delightful summers she might have spent here in the Lakes had it not been for this silly squabble.

But she couldn't find it in her heart to blame her mother for keeping quiet. If her own brother and sisters wouldn't even speak to her, then she must have believed it was for the best not to even mention them to her daughter. How could Chrissie judge whether that was right, since she didn't know the full story?

Vanessa had pretty well said as much yesterday afternoon when Chrissie had telephoned on her return from the boat trip, to challenge her with what she'd discovered.

'My brother and sisters didn't support me at the time, so why should I bother to keep in touch? They had ample opportunity to contact *me*, but never did.'

'Did they know where you lived?'

'They could have made it their business to find out.'

'How? We never stayed in one place longer than a few months.'

'We didn't leave Chelsea until 1932, and not even my sisters wrote to me after that, not once.'

Chrissie admitted that must have been hard. 'Why did you stop coming to the Lakes, Mum – was there another quarrel?'

'I've already told you, I don't remember.'

Chrissie didn't believe her. 'You could at least have told me they existed, if nothing else.'

'So that you could go poking and prying into places you shouldn't?' A familiar tone of aggrieved anger was mounting in her voice. 'That woman ruined our lives. Anyway, it was all a long time ago. Your father certainly wouldn't want you resurrecting the past and asking a lot of damn-fool questions. I want you out of there, Chrissie. *Now!*'

'Why wouldn't he? Dad was just as affected by their attitude as you were. How did you meet him anyway? You've never told me.'

There was a small sigh. 'He just arrived at the Hall one day, to see Georgia, I think.'

'When was this?'

'The summer of 1926.' Again a slight in-drawing of breath, as if it pained her to speak of him.

'You mean he just turned up, out of the blue?'

'I suppose so. Oh, Chrissie, does it matter?' The irritation was growing again.

'I'm sorry if it hurts you to remember that time, Mum, but I need to know, to understand. I don't want to shut him out completely. He was my father, after all. Why did he come?'

'I really have no idea. It never occurred to me to ask. He arrived in Windermere, perhaps to do some walking, I don't know. I was young and fell for him right away. It was love at first sight. We married the following year when I turned twenty-one in April.'

'And I was born in the May. Oh, Mum.' Chrissie's heart went out to her, knowing Aaran must have been the love of her life. She'd never remarried but stayed true to his memory, despite their alleged difficulties, which sadly they'd never resolved, and he'd been killed early in the war. 'But why did your mother not approve? Why would she accuse him of being unworthy of you? What was so objectionable about him? What did he *do* that so offended the family? Don't I have the right to clear my own father's name as an honourable man? OK, I know things didn't work out for you, but he wasn't two-timing you then, was he?'

Vanessa almost laughed. 'No, of course he wasn't. Oh, how can you possibly understand? You weren't *there*. And you're a *child*.'

'No, Mum, I'm not a child any longer. I really have no wish to hurt or upset you, but I would like some answers, some cooperation on your part to heal this breach. Don't you think that would be a good thing? OK, Georgia might be bossy and nosy, and interfering, but whatever she did to you all those years ago, your mother is old now. What if she were to die and you'd never made up? You'd be devastated, heartbroken. I know I would be if that happened to you and me.'

At that point Vanessa had put down the phone, leaving only the dialling tone purring in her ears.

Now Chrissie sighed with exasperation, chewing on her lower lip as she watched one of the steamers on the distant lake, packed with day trippers, make its way back to the pier. Was this obstinacy born out of a sense of guilt? Vanessa was certainly very good at avoiding unpleasantness. She liked *nice* things, *nice* clothes, *nice* people. Everything neat as a new pin, and she was a great hoarder, never threw anything away, just as if every little thing she possessed was precious to her. So why not her own family? It was a puzzle. And despite her problems now, she'd always been a loving mother to her, very caring and attentive, almost too fussy and possessive in a way, constantly reaffirming her love and needing reassurance it was returned.

It was as if a light had switched on in Chrissie's head. Maybe that was it! It wasn't her family's disapproval that had hurt her, it was their lack of affection. Vanessa hadn't kept in touch with them because she believed they no longer loved her, and she couldn't bear their rejection. If that was the case, then it was even more sad, yet knowing her mother as she did, Chrissie thought it made perfect sense.

But did that give her the right to prevent her own daughter from being allowed the opportunity to at least meet these family members, and make her own choices about whether she wanted them to be a part of her life? In truth, Vanessa could no more justify imposing her own views and standards than Georgia could. Surely each generation had to step back and allow the next to make its own mistakes?

Chrissie shook her head in despair. What a can of worms she'd opened.

And what had brought Aaran Kemp to Rosegill Hall in the first place? Had he come to the town on holiday and spotted her beautiful mother walking by the lake? Perhaps he'd followed her home, or asked where she lived. What other reason could there be for his suddenly turning up at the door quite out of the blue?

How Chrissie wished her father were still alive today, not simply to answer these puzzling questions, but because she had loved him so much. She'd adored him. The worst of it was, as a child she'd thought that he adored her mother every bit as much as Vanessa loved him. What little memory she had of those early years were happy ones, of much kissing and cuddling, hardly able to keep their hands off each other, in fact. And then everything had changed. Rows and sulks suddenly became common, father sleeping in the spare room, and long heavy silences that had gone on for days. What could have caused things to go so terribly wrong between them?

But she wasn't going to find any answers today, that was certain, and Chrissie was feeling decidedly hungry. Dusting grass from her skirt, she got up and began to retrace her steps down the stony path through the cool shade of the woods. Since it obviously caused her mother so much distress, perhaps she should let things lie and ask no more questions, at least for the present. She should simply enjoy her holiday, plan her own future, and try to think of a different approach.

Chapter Eight

Chrissie met Ben every day after that. He would take her out on the lake, stopping off at various quiet bays where he'd help her to collect flowers and leaves, wild grasses, seeds, old acorn shells and whatever they could find, always careful never to take a rare plant. 'Even the most common buttercups and wild geraniums can make a stunning design for greetings cards.'

'You must be very talented. I never saw myself as an artist's assistant, but I can see the appeal. It's like treasure hunting, isn't it?'

'I love it because you never know what you might find, particularly in this quiet backwater where few people come to disturb it.'

'And you were the finest treasure ever to be washed up on Lake Windermere's shores.'

'You won't get around me with flattery,' she teased,

attempting to sound fierce. 'I'm immune to masculine charm.'

He looked at her with a knowing smile in his eyes and Chrissie was forced to turn away, in case he should see how his words did indeed affect her.

Lying on the grass, their eyes closed, not speaking, not touching, just soaking up the sun, Chrissie was acutely aware of his nearness. It took all of her self-control not to roll over and rest her head in the crook of his shoulder. How warm that would be, how solid and comforting. Exciting even. She imagined him drawing her close, lowering his lips to hers . . . She quickly blocked the thought from her mind. 'Isn't there something more important you should be doing? Like working?' she asked, abruptly sitting up, determined to get a hold of herself.

'It's August, I'm entitled to a holiday too, even if it is in my own backyard.'

'Quite right.'

'Why, don't you like having me around?'

'No fishing for compliments allowed,' she said, and he laughed.

Ben never made any attempt to kiss her, which was something of a disappointment to Chrissie, despite her very firm resolution to avoid all emotional entanglements. One little kiss wouldn't have created a problem, would it? But then she'd look at him and think that perhaps it was wiser not to risk it. One kiss could lead to another, and another, and then where would they be? Even if she didn't have Peter waiting hopefully in the wings, she would be leaving Windermere soon, wouldn't she? Unless . . .

In the late afternoon when the sun had warmed the lake a little, they might swim in the glass-calm waters, picnic on delicious pasties made by Mrs Gorran. In the evenings they'd search out small fish restaurants in town, sip wine and talk about Chrissie's dream of owning her own small business.

'Will you do it, do you think?' he asked her one evening, as they sat frying sausages on a driftwood fire in the soft warmth of a summer's evening.

Chrissie sighed. 'I'm not sure I can,' she admitted. 'It's such a risk, and a huge commitment. Am I even capable of running a business on my own? Of dealing with things like suppliers and profit and loss accounts?'

He scoffed at that. 'Of course you're capable. You're an intelligent, wonderful woman, why would you not be capable? *I* believe you can do it.'

She looked at him, astounded. 'Do you?'

'Absolutely.'

Chrissie couldn't remember anyone having believed in her before, certainly not her mother who was far too self-obsessed, as was Peter in a different way. She half smiled to herself, thinking how these two were so alike in many ways: selfish, demanding, and yet vulnerable. She turned the smile into one for Ben alone. 'But you don't even know me terribly well.'

He gently touched her cheek with one finger, sending a tiny thrill flowing through her veins. 'I know you enough to appreciate how you weigh everything up carefully before you act, that you can feel vulnerable and a bit lost at times, as many of us did following the war. I certainly felt that way when I first came out of the navy, floundering like a stranded fish. But I've found my métier here with my carpentry, and . . . well . . . I have other compensations in my life too. Friends. Family. I'm grateful for that even if things haven't quite worked out as I'd hoped. It's important for you to keep faith too, Chrissie, and to be true to yourself. I have every faith in you.'

'Do you?' She was gazing up at him entranced.

'I do.' He leant closer, so close she could feel the warm draught of his breath on her cheek. 'Be brave. Nothing ventured and all that. But you'd best watch what you're doing right now or you'll burn that sausage.'

She started, almost dropping it into the flames, and they both laughed.

But she couldn't help wondering why he hadn't kissed her.

Almost three weeks had slipped by in this delightful fashion, and Chrissie had already asked the redoubtable Mrs Gorran if she might extend her holiday by another week. Even so, time was fast running out. She couldn't stay indefinitely . . . or could she?

Ben was right. It was time to have faith in herself, to summon up the courage to make some firm decisions about her life. She should banish this lack of confidence that was holding her back – or was it guilt over Peter? She hadn't meant to string him along, or give him the wrong idea, but she really should settle that matter once and for all. She'd sent him a few postcards, even a brief chatty letter, but hadn't rung him in weeks. It was long past time she resolved that problem, at least.

The very next day, taking her courage in both hands, Chrissie telephoned him. His choice of greeting was not encouraging. 'Ah, at last. I thought you'd forgotten all about me.' He sounded rather like a small child whining about having been abandoned. 'I'm tired of leaving messages with your mother that you choose to ignore.'

'Hello, Peter, I'm fine, thank you, I hope you are well too.'

'How can I be *well* when my fiancée is gallivanting off God knows where with God knows who? When are you going to stop this nonsense and come home?'

Chrissie took a slow breath, determined to remain calm. It didn't seem to matter how many times she made it clear that she wasn't his fiancée and never would be, the information failed to penetrate his obstinate brain. 'I'm sorry I didn't call sooner, but I felt I needed some time alone, to think and relax.'

'No doubt too busy enjoying yourself to even care about me!'

Ignoring that snide remark she brightly enquired, 'Have you spoken to Mum recently?'

'Vanessa? No . . . well . . . yes, but only briefly. Why?' He sounded decidedly touchy on the subject, no doubt because the two of them sat pulling her character to shreds like a pair of gossiping fishwives. Chrissie doubted either of them would have imagined she had it in her to rebel and stay away for so long.

'I just wondered how she was.'

'She's sick, that's how she is, needing the care of her daughter.'

'She is not sick, except in her reliance on the bottle, and on sleeping pills and goodness knows what else from the doctor, which do her no good at all.' Even as she protested, a rush of guilt flooded Chrissie's cheeks to a bright pink. Peter always did have the knack of finding her more sensitive spots. 'I've called her a couple of times, but I confess the weeks seem to have rushed by in a flash.'

'You should come home *now*, at once! Your mother needs you. *I* need you. What have I done to deserve such callous disregard? You're my fiancée, for God's sake.'

Chrissie closed her eyes for a moment in despair. 'Peter, I would much prefer to tell you this face-to-face, but the truth of the matter is that I am not, and never will be, your fiancée. I cannot marry you because I do not love you.'

There was a small silence while he digested this, followed by a heavy sigh. 'Now dearest, you know that isn't true. We've been together as a couple for over a year and are perfectly happy. We have both suffered the travails of war, so we're not silly young things needing all that romantic nonsense. You wouldn't even allow me to buy you flowers and chocolates, if you remember, as you said it wasn't necessary. But you know that I love you, Chrissie dear, and promise to look after you. I really don't see the problem.'

'You aren't listening to me, Peter.' When did he ever? 'I can't ever be your wife. At first I was still grieving over Tom, and glad of your company, a friend to talk to who understood. I like to think we helped each other recover from the terrible effects of war, but I can't take this "friendship" any further. It wouldn't work. We just wouldn't suit each other. We want different things out of life. It's time for you to forget about me, Peter, and move on.'

'Damnation, woman, don't you dare tell me to *move on*!'

The explosion of anger startled Chrissie, causing her to jerk the telephone receiver away from her ear. She'd grown used to Peter's black moods over the last fifteen months or so, his tendency to fall into a depression. She sympathised deeply, as he'd seen many of his comrades killed during the war, including his best friend. Chrissie had done her best to calm and placate him, even suggested he seek advice from doctors or old comrades, but had failed to persuade him to talk to anyone else about his grief. Nevertheless, this was the first time she'd heard his normally quiet voice raised in anger against her. It seemed to indicate a new low in his state of mind, perhaps a growing resentment against her refusal to do as he asked.

And standing in the town's small post office, in full view of customers queuing for stamps and postal orders, Chrissie wondered if they'd heard his shout as faces swivelled in her direction in open curiosity. Turning her back on them, she spoke quietly and calmly into the mouthpiece.

'Peter, if you're going to yell at me, then I shall ring off now. I'll be home soon, but first I have some important decisions to make about what I intend to do with my life. I've rung you first, out of courtesy, as I feel guilty over having kept you hanging on for so long. I'm sorry, but it's all over between us.'

'Absolute stuff and nonsense! You're only saying that because you're annoyed I refused to go with you on this wild goose chase to the back of beyond.'

'No, I'm not,' she patiently informed him. 'I didn't actually invite you, if you recall. I invited Mum. And it isn't the back of beyond. I rather like the Lakes, it's a beautiful place to live.'

'Heavens, you aren't thinking of staying, are you?' There was panic in his voice now, along with irritation, rather as a headmaster might speak to a recalcitrant child.

'I haven't quite made up my mind about anything yet, so please don't mention this to Mum. If I do decide to stay on, I want to tell her myself when I come home next week.' Chrissie was beginning to regret having confided this particular snippet of information with him.

'I wouldn't dream of doing any such thing. The responsibility for breaking your mother's heart is entirely yours. Have you found yourself a lover? Is that what this is all about, some silly holiday romance?'

'No, of course it isn't,' Chrissie snapped, but her denial didn't sound convincing even to her own ears.

'I shall expect you home by next week, and trust you will have come to your senses by then.'

Gritting her teeth, and not wishing to examine too closely the possible truth of his accusation, Chrissie very gently and firmly repeated her point. 'I assure you I have not taken a lover. And whether or not I had come to the Lakes, it would still be over between us. That is a fact, I'm afraid.'

He wasn't listening, just blithely continued as if she hadn't spoken. 'I won't have my fiancée cheapening herself in such a common way. I expect you to act with more decorum, not like some loose trollop.'

At which point Chrissie dropped the receiver softly into its cradle, the sound of his disapproving tones still echoing in her head. She leant her forehead for a moment on the glass panel in despair, then walked out of the post office, chin high, blind to the curious stares all about her.

Finding that her legs were shaking, Chrissie had to sit on a bench on the promenade until her anger had dissipated somewhat. What damage the war had done to that man, making him entirely oblivious to anyone's needs but his own. She appreciated that he'd suffered, that it had been long and difficult, with him only getting demobbed late in 1946 after a spell in India, but he seemed deaf to her words, oblivious to her needs. At first she'd found in him a sensitivity and a kindness not present in her mother, at a time when she'd most needed it. But lately he'd grown increasingly self-obsessed. Smooth, sympathetic, and always agreeable, yet stubbornly determined to have his own way. Chrissie could take no more. He was suffocating her, and in a very subtle way attempting to control her.

She refused to wallow in guilt over calling an end to a relationship that had turned into a nightmare.

Chrissie remembered then his remarks about the constant calls and messages he'd left with her mother. Had he bullied some information out of Vanessa? If so, she didn't much care for the sound of that. But then it occurred to her that even her mother wouldn't risk giving Peter her location. If she didn't want her own daughter investigating her past, she surely wouldn't encourage any possible future son-in-law to go poking his nose into her private business.

Peter knew nothing of the family feud – no more than Chrissie had, until recently.

She felt deeply offended, though, by that last cutting remark. 'Loose trollop' indeed. No doubt he was simply trying to frighten her into submission, hoping she would go crawling back to him. Well, it wasn't going to work. Far more important that she start to look forward, not back, make plans for her own future as Ben had suggested, and decide what she was going to do with the rest of her life.

Later, following lunch at her favourite café on Crag Brow, Chrissie was strolling in and out of shops, agonising over what she should do, when quite by chance she discovered one that was empty. It was situated up a small side street just opposite the church, its location excellent for passing trade. Today, being August, the town was buzzing, so many holidaymakers crowding the strip of pavement that they spilt right across the narrow cobbled streets. Out of season might be a different story. Could a small shop like this earn enough during the busy months to see her through the quiet ones?

Despite the risks involved, the prospect of staying on in Bowness-on-Windermere and making a clean break from all the painful memories of the war and London was most tempting. She felt a fluttery feeling inside just thinking about it, like a butterfly sensing escape.

Was it possible to persuade her mother to come too? Chrissie didn't feel she could abandon her entirely. Or could she perhaps find some other companion for Vanessa? Even if that were possible, a move to the Lakes would not release her from the responsibility of helping her mother financially. Chrissie knew she would need to take that cost into account when working out the figures.

She went to sit on the promenade for a while, to think. There were also practical issues to consider. Where would she live? She couldn't afford to stay long at Rosegill Hall. Even if she confessed to who she really was, Chrissie had no wish to encroach upon her grandmother's goodwill by expecting to be accommodated rent-free. That wouldn't be right.

She gave a mental shrug. OK, so there were a few problems still to be ironed out, but she was perfectly capable of resolving them, wasn't she? Ben certainly thought so. She turned her mind deliberately away from Ben, not wishing to acknowledge that he had any influence over her decision to move north. It was simply that she needed to stand on her own two feet. She was twenty-one, for goodness' sake!

Chrissie found herself back at the shop, gazing through the dusty window, striving to judge the size of the sales area. It was only small, but then she couldn't afford large premises. She would need to find out what rent was payable, what the rates were, heating, lighting and other costs involved. She'd have to take all of that into account before coming to a decision. Plus whatever she would need to contribute to keep her mother afloat. There was always risk with any new business, but wasn't it at least worth a try? She'd some savings put by, and could advertise in the local paper for people wishing to dispose of their old books, which would provide her with an initial stock. Maybe she could sell a few gifts and cards for the tourists as well, walking guides and maps, and the pressed-flower cards and bookmarks she made, which cost next to nothing.

The core of excitement inside her grew the more Chrissie thought about it. It would be her dream come true. There was a For Sale notice stuck on the inside of the window, and taking pen and paper from her bag she noted the address of the agent. Maybe she'd pop in and have a word sometime.

Chrissie glanced at her watch; nearly four o'clock. Goodness, she'd wasted an entire afternoon just walking, thinking and idling, watching the boats on the lake and generally doing nothing at all. Oh, but it was lovely to be able to do as she pleased for once, without fear of criticism, a lecture from Peter, or the responsibility of rushing home to make tea for her mother. She felt rather like a naughty child playing truant from school. And since she was gasping for a cup of tea, she might as well go the whole hog and treat herself to a cream tea. Could you get such a thing, she wondered, with rationing still in place?

But first, since the agent's office was only a little way up the hill on Lake Road, maybe she'd just pop in and collect full particulars. Armed with all the details, she'd be much better able to make the right decision.

Chapter Nine

The letting agent saw no reason why Chrissie couldn't take on the tenancy of the shop for a two-year lease as a trial period. 'It comes with a two-bedroom flat above. It's small, unfurnished and been unoccupied for some years, so it will need a good clean, and no doubt a lick of paint, but the property has bags of character.' He handed over a key there and then. 'Go and look it over, see what you think.'

Chrissie did just that, and thought it perfect. The shop was indeed small, a tiny kitchen and toilet at the back, no stockroom, but big enough for her purpose. And although it was as dirty and uncared for as the agent had warned, the flat above had great potential. It was spread over three different levels: living area, two bedrooms, plus the loft in the roof which would be useful for storage. There were beamed ceilings, and each floor sloped, sometimes to port, sometimes to starboard, and the three flights of stairs seemed to tilt in every direction at once.

Chrissie loved it on sight. With a thorough spring clean, curtains at the windows, and her bits and pieces brought from London, she'd be snug as the proverbial bug in a rug.

She studied the little shop's particulars, did some quick calculations and felt reasonably confident she could afford it, if this was what she wanted. All she had to do was decide, then summon up sufficient confidence to call in the agent's office and agree terms. What was so hard about that?

When she returned the key she told him she was seriously interested but needed a little time to think it over and deal with some issues at home first. He agreed to keep her informed should there be any other offers, and feeling happier than she'd felt in months, Chrissie positively bounced as she made her way back to Rosegill Hall.

She couldn't help wondering what her grandmother's reaction would be to her taking a shop in town. But then Georgia Cowper was unaware of who she really was. Chrissie was already regretting not having told her before now. When she did reveal her true identity, she was going to have some explaining to do.

Nevertheless, the truth must be told, no matter how much her mother might protest, and sooner rather than later. If she was to stay on here, how could she go on living a lie?

Summer lethargy and indecision seeped into every relaxed muscle. Chrissie felt filled with lassitude. These last years grieving for Tom, and dealing with her difficult mother, had put such a strain on her that it was a relief and a delight to have nothing at all to do, no pressure of any sort. She felt so relaxed and content she was reluctant to spoil the mood by worrying about anything unpleasant. Consequently she'd put Peter's bad reaction to her rejection of him right out of her mind. Nor was she quite ready to make a decision about the shop. Not just yet. It had even been some time since she'd done anything about this supposed mission to bring about a reconciliation between her mother and grandmother. Right at this moment such an enormous undertaking suddenly seemed quite beyond her.

But Ben wasn't for letting her off so easily. 'Well, have you made up your mind yet about staying?' he asked, as the end of her stay was in sight. They were sitting on a rock, their shorts and shirts rather grubby from a long walk over Claife Heights, and their feet looking like dead white fish, as they'd removed boots and sweaty socks to dangle them in the deliciously cold water.

'You're fishing again, and I'm still thinking.'

Ben grinned, having learnt there was no hurrying her. He rather admired this caution in her which seemed to indicate a certain lack of confidence. It made her seem rather vulnerable and sweet, although he hoped her indecision had nothing to do with this chap, Peter, who hovered somewhere in the background.

'There'll be a fishing competition of the more normal variety at our own little water festival the last Saturday in August,' he casually informed her, deciding it was politic to change the subject. 'Guddling for trout for the kids, speedboat and raft races, sailing competitions, and the usual prizes for the best fancy dress and decorated floats in the procession. Any ideas for a costume? I assume you'll be taking part.'

'Hmm?' She was only half listening, her mind racing as Chrissie reminded herself that this Saturday she was supposed to check out of Rosegill Hall, and she still hadn't made up her mind about anything. Time was fast running out.

'You could be a mermaid.'

Chrissie laughed. 'I think I'd need access to my feet.'

'Lady Godiva, then?'

She scooped up a handful of water and splashed him, soaking his hair and the front of his shirt. 'You're getting far too cheeky, Ben Gorran.'

'Ouch! You minx,' and he splashed her back.

This naturally provoked a water fight which ended with them both falling into the lake, splashing each other madly until Chrissie managed to swim away on smooth strong strokes.

For a moment she thought she'd escaped him, but then suddenly he came up beneath her and pulled her down under the water. Chrissie could see him grinning as he tried to grab hold of her, but managing to extricate herself she came up gasping for air. Barely had she caught her breath than he pulled her under a second time. His arms went around her and this time he held her tight in his arms. She could feel the heat of him even through the biting cold of the water. With his face just inches from her own she felt certain he was about to kiss her, knowing that she wanted him to kiss her, very badly, saw how his gaze focused directly on her mouth and that he wasn't smiling now. Her lungs were nearly bursting, her feet freezing, yet she couldn't find it in herself to swim away. It felt rather as if they were in a secret world, one throbbing with some indescribable emotion. But then he seemed to think better of it, and pulling her with him, struck out for the surface.

They came up together, splashing madly and gasping for breath as he helped her back to the shore where Chrissie flopped on to the rocks, exhausted.

What had just happened down there? Why had he hesitated? Had he considered kissing her, then changed his mind? Had he feared rejection, or decided he didn't want to get involved?

Chrissie stared ruefully down at the pool of water gathering about her as she sat huddled on the rocks, shivering in her dripping shirt and shorts. Keeping her voice deliberately bright, as not for a moment would she allow him to see her disappointment, she said, 'Now see what you've done, you idiot. I'm soaked through!'

Giving what might pass for an apology, Ben tossed her a towel.

'I really don't think that's going to help much.'

'Strip off those wet clothes and rub yourself down properly, then.'

'Oh, I do like your optimism. No one could deny that you aren't a trier. Or maybe just trying,' she teased, striving to shake off her misery.

Down there in the water she'd loved being held so close in his arms. Had he simply been teasing her? Was it all just a silly joke? Maybe she'd misinterpreted his intentions because Peter was so much more serious. And having carefully kept Peter at arm's length Chrissie knew that her experience of men was limited, other than her beloved Tom. Nor had she given Ben the slightest hint of encouragement, keeping him very much at a safe distance. Had he taken that attitude as rejection?

But what was she so afraid of, exactly? Commitment? More likely the pain of loss if she allowed herself to fall in love again and it didn't work out. Had he read fear in her face, was that why he'd turned away? Or maybe it was all in her imagination and Ben hadn't felt any urge to kiss her at all.

She glanced up, watching as he shook himself like a young puppy after a bath, combing his fingers through wet hair, and silently cursed herself for feeling this aching need. What were his intentions? That irrepressible grin was firmly back in place and nothing in his cheerful expression gave the slightest indication of his true feelings. He certainly didn't look overwhelmed by passion, or yearning with desire.

Ben was having great difficulty in keeping his hands off her. She looked so beautiful with the light of the setting sun turning her soft brown hair to a glowing gold, and the way her wet shirt clung to her breasts showed off her curvaceous figure to perfection. He longed to pull her down on to the rough shingle and make love to her there and then.

Oblivious to this need, and determined not to show her own momentary weakness, Chrissie made a great show of hugging herself in the towel, although there was no necessity to exaggerate her shivering as she was indeed cold. 'It's a miracle we didn't drown,' she teased. 'Stay in the lake a moment too long and it could easily have been our last. You play reckless games, Ben Gorran.'

The cold didn't seem to have affected him one bit and he laughed, arching one brow in wry amusement. 'You don't fancy another swim, then?'

She got quickly to her feet and started to back away. 'No, I do not. One wetting is quite enough, thanks all the same. I think we should go. Now! I feel the urgent need for a hot bath. And if I die of pneumonia before we get there, it will all be your fault.'

His expression turned rueful. Ben knew he'd messed up, but for the life of him couldn't think how. One minute they'd been having fun, flirting and laughing, the next he was getting the cold brush-off. He certainly hadn't failed to notice the 'don't touch' message he thought he'd seen in her eyes down there in the murky depths of the lake, and had quickly changed his mind about stealing a kiss. Difficult as it might be, it seemed safer to play it cool. Ben was determined to listen to that wise voice of caution in his head because he really didn't want to risk losing her. He picked up his jacket and wrapped it about her shoulders. 'We'd best make tracks, then. When you're dry and warm again, how about I treat you to a fish supper?'

'Just for a change, you mean?' She strived to match his careless tone, to recapture their earlier happy mood.

'You can buy the beer.'

'OK, you're on.' She breathed an inward sigh of relief that at least they were still friends.

'And you'll come to the festival?'

'Wouldn't miss it for the world. I'll come as Sarah Gamp from *Martin Chuzzlewit*, just in case there's another wetting.'

'Then I'll be Fagin. We'll make the most handsome couple of the day.' They both laughed at this picture of themselves, but his choice of words, and the fact he referred to them as a couple, for some reason set her pulses racing yet again.

Chrissie had got into the habit of helping Georgia for an hour or two each morning in the garden. She'd been deeply moved by the story of how the two lovers had met, and was anxious to hear what happened next, how Georgia had overcome her parents' disapproval. Her grandmother had rather hinted that their journey was fraught with difficulties, but said that even had they known at the time quite how traumatic it would be, they still would not have been able to resist seeing each other again. Somehow, Chrissie must find a way to persuade her to tell the rest of her story, although what any of this might have to do with the family feud she really had no idea.

As she helped prune and cut back overgrown shrubs, Chrissie worried over that vital piece of information she was keeping from her. How would she explain her neglect in not revealing who she really was? And what if her grandmother was so angry with her for the lie, she threw her out of the house, as she'd done with Vanessa? Why would she treat a granddaughter better than her own daughter?

This morning, while they battled with weeds, Chrissie was trying to find some way to approach the subject obliquely while agonising over doing so against Vanessa's wishes. Georgia interrupted her thoughts.

'I do admire your determination, your courage in going on,' the old woman commented, barely pausing in her labours as she dumped barrow-loads of weeds on to a garden bonfire. 'It's not easy going on with life when you've lost the man you love. I do hope your time here has helped you to find the way forward. Now that you've come through that first fog of grief and can start to think clearly again. Living in the past and relying on others isn't really an answer. Too much sympathy can be very debilitating.'

'Oh, I do agree, it all becomes almost self-indulgent if you're not careful. People would either shower me with pity – oh, poor dear Chrissie – or else relate their own loss, of which there has been no shortage during the war. But grieving is something you need to do alone, in your own way. There's nothing anyone can do to help.'

'Indeed not.'

'In any case, I don't find it easy to share my feelings with anyone. For weeks, months, I was unable to sleep or eat, or even think clearly,' Chrissie admitted. 'I went through the motions of living while inside I was dead too. I never want to feel that way ever again.' To her horror Chrissie found tears filling her eyes as she remembered the pain of hearing that Tom, the man she'd imagined she would love for ever and grow old with, was dead. Losing him had broken her heart.

'None of us do, dear.' Her grandmother had taken off her old straw hat and was making a great play of wafting the smoke from the bonfire away, as if that were to blame for her tears. 'People can be very kind and well meaning, but they do expect you to get better after a given period of time, as if pain ever ends.'

'Oh, that is so true,' Chrissie said, sniffing at her tears. 'And I found making decisions incredibly hard. Still do, after three years, yet I feel it's time I did.'

Georgia offered her a large white hanky to wipe her eyes as she led Chrissie to a garden bench. 'I'm sure you will succeed very well. Deciding to make a big change in your life is always difficult, but if something feels right in your heart, in your soul, then you have to go with it. You have to be true to yourself.'

Chrissie looked up at her in surprise, about to say that was what Ben had said, but her grandmother's gaze had turned inward. She sat in silence for some long moments – which Chrissie didn't feel she should break – cloaked in memories as old people tended to do. Then she seemed to shake herself out of the reverie and looked about her, as if to remind herself where she was.

She smiled. 'I like sitting here, where I can watch what's happening on the lake. And it is so peaceful. Listen!'

It was still early in the morning and oddly quiet, many visitors having already returned home to start the new term. All Chrissie could hear was the soft lap of water on the shingled shore, the wind in the trees, and somewhere high above, the lone cry of a curlew. A pair of swans sailed serenely by, a partnership that would last for life; then out of nowhere, as if she had no control over her own words, Chrissie found herself saying, 'To make matters worse, I've just refused an offer of marriage from a very dear friend who was there for me when I was at my lowest.'

'Ah, which has opened up old wounds. Did he not take it well?'

Chrissie made a little sound in her throat. 'I'm afraid not. If he doesn't like what he's hearing, Peter stubbornly refuses to listen. He seems completely oblivious to whatever I say.'

'I see.' Georgia sat back, folding her hands in her lap. 'Perhaps that's his pride at work. Some men react badly to rejection, even when they don't necessarily love you as much as they claim. Sometimes aggressively so.'

Chrissie glanced at her grandmother, a frown puckering her forehead. 'I hadn't thought of that. You may well be right.' But the comment seemed oddly personal, as if the old lady was referring to something – or someone – else entirely.

After another long pause Georgia continued, 'I'm sure you've done the right thing by refusing his offer. You only get one chance at life, and if you don't feel the marriage would work, then you had no choice but to refuse him.

Not everyone has that choice, more's the pity, and there's nothing worse than being married to a man you don't love.'

'You sound as if you speak with feeling, Mrs Cowper, yet you married the love of your life.'

The old woman smiled sadly at her. 'Indeed, Ellis was my first and only love, but, as I mentioned before, my parents did not approve of our friendship and had quite different plans for me, particularly Mama.'

'You did see him again, though, didn't you, after that first disastrous meeting with your parents? You said that you sent your maid, Maura, to look for him and he was still outside your house, waiting.'

That familiar warmth came back into the faded grey eyes. 'Oh yes, Ellis swore he would have waited till hell froze over.' She chuckled softly to herself. 'And I did secretly rebel and managed to manufacture an opportunity to see him again. After that, we saw each other regularly, although always in secret and nowhere near as often as we would have liked. It was very difficult, but Mama and Papa knew nothing. I never even told Prue, as she couldn't keep a secret to save her life. Only Maura knew, and acted as courier between us.'

'How romantic.'

The light in her eyes dimmed a little, her expression turning rather sad. 'Yes, for a time it was truly romantic, but also dangerous and rather cowardly of me. Ellis was for confronting my parents to tell them we were in love, but I was too afraid they might stop me seeing him altogether. I've thought many times since, that if perhaps

I'd been braver, or more outspoken and rebellious from the start, instead of so secretive, things might have turned out differently. But I was so young, and trained to be a dutiful daughter. I still believed in happy endings, that love would prevail in the end.'

'And did it?'

'That's a very good question, dear. A very good question indeed.'

Chapter Ten

San Francisco

That summer I told Mama my first lie. 'I've been asked to help out at the Seamen's Institute. Maura and Prudence have both volunteered to come too. You wouldn't have any objections, would you, Mama?' They hadn't asked me at all; I'd called in and offered my services, which were readily accepted. And my sister had only agreed to come with me after considerable persuasion, but then I knew Mama would never allow me to go alone. Even so, she was no fool.

'This hasn't something to do with that dreadful English sailor, has it?'

I put on my most innocent expression. 'Of course not – why, I'd forgotten all about him.' My second lie. 'Didn't you bring us up to be useful and care for those less fortunate than ourselves?' My mother was a governor of many local high schools, as well as involved with charity work at the church. She was looking decidedly uncomfortable.

'Well, I dare say there could be no harm in your helping, perhaps once a week. I insist that John drives you in the brougham, and he will wait outside for you on Steuart Street until you are done, in order to conduct you safely home. And I want you all back home on the dot of nine. You will not wander about unescorted, since I remember only too well the trouble last time I allowed you to come home alone, and that was in broad daylight. Nor must you fraternise with any of those young men,' she sternly warned, fixing me with her gimlet gaze.

'As if I would do such a thing!' My third lie, but not, I'm afraid, my last. On my first evening at the Institute I learnt two surprising things about sailors; one was that they loved to sing. We could hear their voices booming out in a full-throated body of sound even as we stepped down from the carriage. It brought with it the rush and smell of the sea. I could imagine them singing against the wind as they sailed into the bay. The second, and perhaps more important thing that I noticed, was that they were not the scum of the earth most people claimed them to be. As I stood at the door, Maura and Prudence beside me, feeling oddly shy and awkward, what I saw was a hall filled not with ruffians who had come here to drink, but men who were neat and tidy, scrubbed clean and smartly attired in their best uniforms. They looked as respectable as any gathering of Frisco's crème de la crème.

One group of young sailors were engaged in a three-legged race, clearly enjoying themselves while a laughing audience cheered them on. Some were playing cards or dominoes at tables set out for that purpose, and to my very great surprise one or two seemed to be actually knitting, although I doubt it was the kind of lacy stole Mama made. At the end of the hall was a stage upon which stood what must have been over fifty men, all singing a sea shanty that threatened to lift the roof. I was enchanted.

'Oh, my goodness,' murmured Prue, equally entranced, though perhaps for a different reason. 'So many men!'

A round-faced, smiling young woman in an apron bustled over. 'Ah, Miss Briscoe, and your sister, is it? Oh, and you've brought along a friend too. Excellent. So delighted to meet you all, and deeply grateful for your offer. We're rather pressed and desperate for a helping hand. Molly and I are just preparing supper – would you and your friend mind serving the tea? I've set up the urn in the corner, out of the way.'

Maura turned pink-cheeked at being so addressed and started to interrupt. 'I'm Miss Georgina's maid, ma'am, not—' but I quickly hushed her.

'What does it matter who you are? We're in this together, Maura,' I whispered. 'More importantly, have you any idea how to operate that urn?' The plump young woman had already bustled away with almost as much haste as she had received us, so I was feeling very slightly stunned.

Maura's round plain face broke into a grin. 'We have one in the kitchen just like it, miss.'

'Splendid. Then lead the way.'

During the next hour we hardly had time to breathe as we poured tea, helped spread peanut butter on thick slices of bread, and served hot red pepper soup. The seamen were impeccably polite and welcomed the good food with a hearty appetite. There were many young boys who hadn't yet grown a beard and hardly seemed old enough to have left their mothers' arms. Old veterans with powerful physiques and battered weathered skin as tough as old leather, yet with the manners of gentlemen as they helped themselves to food. And all the while I was seeking one face in particular.

I'd almost given up hope of finding him when Maura whispered in my ear. 'There he is, miss, coming down from the stage. He must have been one of the singers.'

My heart gave a painful lurch, and as my eager gaze searched the crowd of men pouring off the stage, politely forming an orderly line for their own supper, there he was, and my eager gaze greedily devoured him. He looked different in uniform, and even as I daringly admired the length of his legs and the power of those shoulders I was worrying about how soon he might be leaving. Any day he could sail away on one of the many steamers, big sailing ships, mailboats or smaller craft that crowded the bay.

The wharves extended for some miles, taking in Mission Bay, Fisherman's Wharf, numerous piers, the Ferry Building and the new Embarcadero still under construction. Some ships were laid up in the foul-smelling mudflats at Oakland Creek. Others chose to anchor at one of the more favoured and sheltered spots some miles from the congested bay area. But if Ellis was at the Institute tonight, his ship couldn't be too far away, could it? I wondered why it mattered. For reasons of basic humanity, I told myself. There was far less likelihood of typhoid fever in the Bay of Sausalito, for instance, but I knew in my heart there was much more to it than that. I *needed* to see him again, to speak to him, to feel again that rush of excitement as he kissed me.

Prudence came up close and pinched my arm. 'I guessed as much. This was your real reason for turning all charitable. You wanted to meet the brave and handsome Ellis Cowper again.'

'You won't tell Mama?' I gave her my most beseeching look. 'I beg you, Prue. How else could I get to see him?'

She gave me one of her pitying looks. 'He is charming but it will only end in tears.' For all Prue was younger than me by two years, she liked to give the impression she was far more sophisticated and worldly-wise than I. Maybe she was.

But I smiled and gave her a quick hug, knowing I'd won her round. 'I do hope not.'

I ladled out soup as fast as I could, desperately hoping to reach the end of the line before we were obliged to leave in order to meet Mama's curfew. Then suddenly he was holding out his empty bowl and I was filling it with a strangely shaky hand.

'I thought it was you, but couldn't quite believe it. It is you, isn't it? Or are you a magical mirage I've dreamt up?'

I looked up into those entrancing blue eyes. 'Would you like a peanut butter sandwich?' I asked, as no more sensible reply sprang to mind.

'I'd much rather have you instead.'

I must still have been pouring soup as his dish was almost brimming over. I quickly stopped, my cheeks burning as hot as the red peppers that made it, and handed him a sandwich. 'I didn't realise you could sing. It sounded wonderful.' I should have guessed that he could, since the resonance in his voice had been one of the first things I'd noticed about him.

With some reluctance he edged towards Maura, who was manhandling the tea urn with professional efficiency. 'I must see you, if only for five minutes,' he whispered. 'Alone.'

I was already smiling at the next man in line. 'When I've finished this I'll come over to you, but I can't stay long,' I managed, just before he moved out of earshot.

Eventually the two hundred or so seamen were all served and we ladies were then kept busy collecting up dirty dishes. Maura had her arms elbow-deep in soapsuds in the tiny kitchen at the back of the hall, washing up with the kind of happy grin on her face she never exhibited when tackling this same task in the kitchen back home. Prudence was carrying loaded trays, along with the other women, chatting and flirting with the sailors with the kind of aplomb Mama would consider cheap.

With both of them safely occupied, I glanced quickly about the room. Ellis was standing by the back door and he jerked his head, giving me a look which said everything. Desperate not to waste this precious opportunity, I slipped away and quietly followed him outside.

* * *

There was a cool nip in the air and a mist rolling in off the bay, but I noticed neither. I felt an overwhelming urge to walk straight into his arms. Only my innate caution and shyness held me back. 'Good evening, Mr Cowper,' I said, in my most ladylike tones.

'Good evening, Miss Briscoe, I trust you are well and have experienced no further difficulties since our last meeting.'

He was smiling at me in that disarming way he had and I found myself smiling back. 'Not in the least. As you see, Prue has made a full recovery. I couldn't exactly claim she is a reformed character, but I fear our adventures have been somewhat curtailed since that day.'

'A cause for regret, I should think.'

'Indeed.'

The words might have been those exchanged between perfect strangers but the manner in which he was looking at me, the way he was edging ever closer, told quite a different story. I could scent the sea on him, and the freshness of the soap he'd used, despite the less pleasant odours drifting in with the fog, and was overcome with a strange breathlessness.

'Will you be in port long—?'

'Do you ever have time to yourself—?'

We'd both started speaking at once, and laughed with embarrassment. My own query had come of its own volition, expressing the one thought uppermost in my mind, but I didn't repeat it, rather answered his. 'Sometimes I walk in the Golden Gate Park, with Maura, or my sister.'

'And does this walk take place at any special time?'

'I find Wednesdays at two o'clock quite pleasant, as Mama is at her bridge club, Papa about his business and Prudence often visits with her friends, so on that particular afternoon there is only Maura. She and I enjoy a quiet stroll together.'

'How fortuitous. I believe Wednesday would be most convenient for me too. I may perhaps see you there one day.'

I couldn't answer, feeling the blood rise in my cheeks at my own daring. 'I really must go. Mama insists we be home by nine and it is gone eight-thirty already. I dare not be late.'

'No, that would be most unwise.'

As I turned to go he grasped my wrist very gently. 'I won't be leaving before we've had time to . . . to talk properly, maybe get to know each other a little. The SS *Kronus* has sailed, but I can find another berth any time. When I'm ready.'

I looked deep into his eyes and felt my heart soar. 'Good,' I said. 'I'm glad.' Then I fled, grabbed Maura, chivvied Prue away from her gossiping, and we ran to the brougham. We walked in the front door just as the hall clock chimed the hour.

At that first illicit meeting, Maura keeping a tactful distance, I felt a shudder of expectation ripple through me even as he hurried towards me on his long-legged stride. I knew it was wrong, and certainly Mama would consider my behaviour both wicked and wanton, yet I cared nothing for convention, or even my reputation, in that moment. I wanted nothing more than to see this young man again and bask in the glorious knowledge that he was as captivated by me as I was with him.

'I thought you might not come,' he said, snatching up my hands and giving my fingers a small squeeze before dropping them quickly, as if he feared he'd overstepped the mark.

'I'm sorry I was late, only we were held up helping Mama find her favourite brooch. She is most particular about which jewellery she wears, and that it is kept safe, but then has a tendency to carelessly leave it lying about, I'm afraid.'

'It doesn't matter, I'm just glad that you're here.'

We walked in the Botanical Gardens, admiring the collection of rare plants from all around the world as Ellis talked about the different ships he'd worked on, the people he'd met, the places he'd visited. He told how he loved the banyan trees in Hawaii, the hot gushing geysers in New Zealand, Rotten Row in England where the fashionable ride their horses, the Ponte Vecchio bridge in Florence. He also spoke about the mountains and lakes of his home, how at this time of year the leaves would all turn gold, yellow ochre and crimson, the red deer would shyly forage in the deep forests, and curlew and eagle soar high above the mountains. Clearly well travelled, I asked him what it was that had led him to leave home if the English Lake District was as beautiful as he described.

He gave that irrepressible grin that I loved to distraction already. 'I have itchy feet, I suppose. I'm an adventurer of the old style, born into the wrong age. I would love to have sailed the world with Drake, been with the *Santa Maria* when Columbus first discovered this beautiful land, perhaps met Pocahontas and traded with the Indians.' He laughed. 'Or I might have sailed with John Cabot when he went seeking the North-West Passage. I don't know what it is but I never stay anywhere too long. Maybe I quickly grow bored, but I just have to see what's around the next bend, or over the next hill.'

I was smiling at his boyish enthusiasm, savouring the warmth of his shoulder brushing casually against mine as we walked, yet his words troubled me. 'Don't you ever feel the need to settle, to return to your own home port of Liverpool, then restore that ruin of a house you mentioned?'

A frown puckered his brow. 'It's true that one day I should – probably must – do exactly that. Until that day dawns, and I trust it will be long in coming as I have no wish for my father to die, then I intend to enjoy my freedom to explore this beautiful world.'

There was a short pause while I considered this remark. Was he warning me, I wondered, that this friendship, this budding romance, if that's what it was, would be transient? That after a time he would move on and forget all about me. Isn't that what sailors did all the time? Disappointment settled in my stomach like a lump of cold porridge.

'But enough about me,' he said brightly. 'What about you?'

I turned to look at him, drowning in the warmth of his

gaze even as the common sense voice at the back of my head was urging me to walk away now, before it was too late. 'Oh, I lead a very dull life by comparison, one filled with duty, and no freedom at all.'

'It is different for young ladies, I can see that,' he sympathised. 'But you seem to manage very well to make good use of your time. Your work at the Seamen's Institute, for instance. How long have you been working there? I confess I've never noticed you before.'

I couldn't help but giggle. 'I've never been before. That was my first time.'

'Ah, and what made you decide to come, might I ask?'

I raised my chin a fraction, knowing he was teasing me and understood full well why I was there. 'I'd heard they were short-handed and thought I could help,' I primly remarked.

He cleared his throat, as if choking on a laugh. 'And I should have better manners than to ask. But you will come again, I hope?'

'Oh yes!' The eagerness in my tone quite put an end to my false hauteur, and brought the usual betraying flush to my cheeks. Then he was holding my hands in his, and this time making no attempt to let go.

'I'm delighted to hear it. I do hope we will see much more of each other in the future, Georgia. I may call you that, mayn't I? We are friends now?'

'Of course,' I whispered. Words seemed to desert us both and a silence washed over us, the sounds of the city fading to nothing as I traced the glorious line of his aquiline nose with its delightful smattering of freckles, the square strength of his jawline. His face seemed to have drawn nearer somehow, only inches from mine, so close I could see my own reflection in the depth of those blue eyes. It wouldn't do to allow him to kiss me again, not here in a public place. Not at all, in fact. Mama would not approve. But then my mother wasn't anywhere near and the blood was pounding in my heart, roaring through my veins, making my fingers and toes tingle. The very touch of his hand, skin against skin, was filling me with a desire I had never before experienced. He drew closer still, his warm breath caressing my face.

'It's time to go, miss.'

Maura's voice shattered the moment and we both sprang apart.

'You will come again next week,' he called as I raced away.

'I'll be here,' I shouted back, quite forgetting he would soon sail out of my life and go adventuring again.

'You can't stop there,' Chrissie cried, as Georgia rose stiffly from the garden bench, picked up a garden rake and began to scrape up more leaves. 'I want to know how things progressed between you. Did he leave or did you see him again?'

She smiled. 'I think that's enough talk for one day. Old people should never bore the young with their memories. Run along now and enjoy yourself. Don't you have a costume to make for the water festival on Saturday?'

Chrissie picked up a long brush to help sweep the

leaves. 'I intend to leave all of that stuff to the locals, but I'll certainly attend. Will you?'

Her grandmother shook her head. 'I shall watch from the sanctity of my eyrie.'

'Then perhaps you'll tell me more another day?'

She didn't glance up from her task, just kept on collecting leaves into a big pile. 'I'm surprised you're so interested. People aren't usually wanting to hear tales from a crabby old woman. Certainly my family doesn't, which is a relief in a way, I freely admit. Some things that happen in life are best not spoken of, best not even remembered.'

Chrissie's heart went out to her. If only she could tell her that here was one family member who would listen all day to her stories. But she couldn't say that, not yet. On impulse Chrissie hugged the old woman, kissed her papery soft cheek. 'I hope you'll change your mind, but I'll leave you in peace, for now.'

Chapter Eleven

The Lakes

Saturday came and Chrissie took some trouble with her appearance, choosing a new cotton skirt in her favourite blue, and a white, silk, peasant blouse. She carefully shampooed and curled her soft brown hair, and added a discreet touch of coral lipstick and mascara, simply for her own self-esteem, she told herself unconvincingly. Taking such trouble made her feel young and attractive again, something that had been sadly missing in recent months. But she had no wish to examine too closely the reason behind the effort she made.

The Water Festival went ahead with great gusto. There were model yacht races, apple bobbing and bursting water-filled balloons for the very young. Every kind of madcap race you could imagine including speedboats, home-made rafts and rowing skiffs, and fishing and diving competitions for the more adventurous. And for those oldies who preferred to keep their feet on terra firma, they could play quoits or throw balls at coconut shies.

In one race the lads had to run through Bowness, up the hill, collect a bucket of water from behind the picture house, carry it back to the lake then row it across to Belle Isle, spilling as little as possible. Ben managed to win that one, much to Chrissie's delight, and she rushed to offer him a kiss as a reward, in addition to the red rosette that was pinned to his vest.

'Never again,' he laughed, almost scarlet in the face from the exertion. 'That hill is a killer even without carrying a bucket of water, let alone having to row half across the lake at the end. Look at me, I'm soaked to the skin and the bucket is near-empty.'

'Wimp,' she teased. 'Stop complaining – you won, didn't you?'

'And your kiss was the best part of the prize. Any chance of an encore?'

Laughing, she was backing away from his pursuit of her when a rival group of lads from the neighbouring town of Ambleside suddenly rushed at him, and, picking Ben up shoulder high, flung him into the water. There followed the kind of ferocious water fight that made Chrissie thankful she was safely on dry land. She stood on the jetty with the rest of the crowd laughing uproariously at their high jinks.

When Ben finally emerged, fortunately unharmed and still grinning from ear to ear, he begged her to wait for him. 'You won't run away while I go and get dry, will you?'

'I'll be here,' she promised, pretending to heave a

resigned sigh but feeling inside that familiar nudge of excitement. With wet shorts and vest clinging to his muscular body, he was a sight to see, so intensely masculine she could feel her cheeks growing pink just looking at him. When Ben returned, looking fresh and even more startlingly handsome in grey slacks, navy jacket and a blue shirt open at the neck, Chrissie caught her breath at the sight of him. His fair hair was slicked back, and there was something about the way he was smiling down at her that made her go all warm and fizzy inside. He bought her an ice cream cone which she licked with great enjoyment, as if she were a child again. The emotions running through her were, however, very far from childish.

The highlight of the occasion was the firework display, which took place as soon as dusk fell, and after that came music and dancing by the marina for those still with the energy to take part.

'May I?' Ben was holding out a hand for a dance, but Chrissie shyly demurred.

'I don't think I can remember how.'

'That's OK because I have two left feet, so we can stagger round together.'

She laughed. Ben made a joke of everything, and she liked that in him.

It turned out to be a fun polka which they danced to 'I Don't Want Her –You Can Have Her – She's Too Fat For Me', which reduced them both to helpless laughter. But then the music changed to something far more seductive, a Doris Day number: 'It's Magic'. The pace slowed till they were barely moving, and Chrissie was all too aware now of Ben's arms about her, holding her so close she felt stirred by the press of her breasts against his hard body. Her eyes drifted closed as she swayed to the lilt of the music, and somehow his chin was resting against her forehead, his hand holding hers against his chest and it was all deliciously romantic. She'd forgotten how wonderful it felt to be in a man's arms, even if it was only in a dance.

'So this is what you get up to when I'm not around?'

'Karen!'

The music was still playing but they were no longer dancing. Ben had jerked away and the romance of the moment had quite vanished. He seemed to be staring in open-mouthed dismay at someone over her right shoulder. Chrissie half turned to meet the furious gaze of a young girl. Dressed in red shorts and white top she couldn't be a day over nine or ten, although standing there, hands on hips, she gave a good imitation of a middle-aged harridan.

She was glaring at Chrissie as if she hated her. 'Like pinching other people's fellas, do you?'

'Karen, don't start, please,' Ben began, but Chrissie interrupted.

'I beg your pardon?' She was dumbfounded by such rudeness, even as she experienced a prickle of discomfort between her shoulder blades. Was there something – or more accurately some*one* – Ben hadn't thought to mention? She recalled talk of a pending divorce, but not a word about him having a daughter. She waited for an explanation, an introduction even. He did neither. His arm tightened protectively around her waist as he addressed his next words to the girl, and they weren't in any way loving ones.

'What the hell are you doing here? You're supposed to be with your mother.'

A shrug and a pout, in that grumpy way young girls have. 'I got bored, so I came home.'

'Bored? What do you mean you got *bored*? And *how* did you get home? Does Mum even know you're here? Don't tell me you ran away without telling her?'

'I'm not stupid, Dad. Not like you,' she added, casting another furious glare in Chrissie's direction. 'She put me on the train, OK? Grandad picked me up. I'm perfectly capable of travelling on my own. Looks like I arrived just in time.'

Chrissie quickly disengaged herself, thinking this might be wise judging by the thunderous expression on the girl's face. 'Look, I'll make myself scarce. I can see you two have things to talk about which don't concern me.'

'And just you leave my dad alone, right?' snapped this very angry child, poking Chrissie in the chest with one stabbing finger, so hard that Chrissie staggered back a pace or two.

'Excuse me, I've done nothing. I don't even know why you would object to my dancing with Ben . . . er, your father. I understood he was a free agent.'

'Well, that's where you're wrong, see.' The girl punctuated her next words with further stabs at Chrissie's chest, each one more vigorous than the last, forcing her to back off, much to the amusement of the other dancers who'd paused to watch the fun. 'This is my dad, so that means he belongs to *my mum*! And don't think there's going to be a divorce, because there isn't. Mam's packing so she can come back home. She'll be here any day. Got that? They're getting back together, so you can buzz off and find a chap of your own.'

Chrissie heard Ben's groan, saw him dart forward as if to stop her, but it was too late. The girl suddenly slammed the flat of both hands into Chrissie's chest and shoved her backwards into the lake. Chrissie hit the water with an explosion of shock that knocked all the breath from her lungs. In an instant, freezing cold water closed over her head and she found herself floundering once again in the murky depths of Lake Windermere, only this dipping was much less fun than the first. She flapped her arms, kicked her legs, quite certain that at any moment some weeds, or anchor chain, would wrap themselves around a foot and drag her down, or her lungs would explode and she'd drown anyway. Then hands were grasping her wrists and she was being pulled to the surface. Chrissie emerged gasping into the moonlight.

Several people had rushed to her rescue, including Ben, and she was dragged unceremoniously from the water, beached like a stranded fish. Karen stood close by, laughing and giggling with her friends as if this was the funniest sight they'd ever seen. Which in a way it probably was. Chrissie's beautiful new blue skirt and silk blouse were now a dripping wreck, her carefully curled hair plastered to her scalp. Yet another outfit ruined. This was developing into a habit.

Ben's face was a picture of horror. 'God, I'm sorry,

Chrissie. I should have told you about Karen.'

'Yes, I think perhaps you should. Still, no need to bother now, eh? I think I understand perfectly why you didn't.' And she strode briskly away, chin high, gathering whatever dignity she had left at her command.

Ben came chasing after her. 'Are you OK?' His handsome face was creased with concern. 'Let me see you home.'

'I can manage, thanks.' She kept on walking.

'Oh, your lovely blouse, and it looked so beautiful.'

He pulled a string of water weed from her hair but she shook him off. Water streamed down her neck, but as every part of her was soaking wet it hardly seemed to matter. 'You know how much I relish a ducking, particularly on a chilly evening in a freezing lake.' Her tone was sharp enough to cut flint, her mind resolutely fixed upon the possibility of a hot bath, assuming the boiler at Rosegill Hall was working. Ben caught at her arm and jerked her to a halt.

'I want you to know that what Karen said isn't true. The poor lass has been a bit upset by her mum and me splitting up, but Sal is history, I swear it. It *is* true that she's coming back home, but not permanently. At least I don't think so.'

'You don't seem too sure.'

'It's hard to say with Sal, but I won't allow that to happen.'

'Do you have any way of stopping her?'

He had the grace to look a bit sheepish. 'No, I don't suppose I do. It probably won't happen, anyway. I expect she's finding that life on her own is not quite so much fun as she'd imagined it would be, or else her latest fella is creating difficulties. But the divorce went through OK. We have the decree nisi and everything. I'd hate you to think I was cheating on you.'

Despite herself, Chrissie was both surprised and elated by this explanation, expressed with every sign of sincerity and compassion. But what exactly was he saying? That he was serious about her, or just no longer in love with his ex-wife? That he couldn't bear to let her go? That he was prepared to make his own daughter's life a misery by continuing to see a woman she strongly disapproved of? Not a promising prospect. Or did he just want a bit on the side, to help get his own back on his wife's infidelity?

Wary of getting involved, she backed away. 'The state of your marriage is of no concern to me,' she told him, rather frostily. 'It's really none of my business. Although it might have been tactful of you to mention, in passing, that you had a daughter.'

'I admit I should have told you about Karen, only she is something of a trial at present and—'

'You didn't want to put me off?'

'No, that's not it – well, partly I suppose. Mainly, it was because I didn't want to look like a desperate male seeking a replacement mother for her.' He gave a philosophical little smile.

Chrissie was suddenly angry. 'Yet that's exactly how it seems. Did you hope to get me hooked on your charms, then when I'd fallen hopelessly in love with you and could resist you no longer, you'd casually mention her existence?

A sort of, "Oh, by the way, this is my daughter who just happens to be in need of a new mother."'

'Are you?'

'What?'

'Hopelessly in love with me?'

'Don't flatter yourself. You are a *cheat*, and a *liar*.'

A stain of crimson spread up his neck. 'Is that what you think?'

'Don't all men think only of their own needs? Utterly selfish creatures, that's what they are. Men! I've had enough.' She strode away, so infuriated when he easily kept pace with her that she continued to rail at him. 'Stupid men want to get married, even when there's a war on and they might get killed. They pester you for years and take it for granted you'll marry them, even when you tell them over and over again that no, you never want to marry again, thank you very much. Ever!'

'I think you're confusing me with other men in your life.'

'I am not!' she cried, skidding to a halt, quite beside herself with cold and anguish, and bitter disappointment. Not because Ben had a daughter, who was probably a perfectly nice girl, if a bit churned up by the storm of events in her life. But because he'd kept quiet about the child, rather as if she were a shameful secret. And because in all these weeks together he'd given every impression that he cared for her, *and yet still hadn't so much as kissed her*. 'Your actions were not those of an honourable man. Presumably you simply wanted to lure me into your bed. Well, hard cheese, it didn't work.' The lack of logic in

Chrissie's argument failed to register. She was too cold, too wet, too far gone in her rage.

'Do men ever think of anyone but themselves?' She yelled the question at him then answered it herself. 'No, they do not! Do they ever listen to a word you say to them? No!' Chrissie wagged a furious finger in his face. 'If your feelings for me were genuine, you should have spared me, *and* your daughter, the humiliation of meeting like that. It wasn't fair on either of us.'

'OK, so I got it wrong. I'm sorry. I accept I should have told you, all right?'

'No, it is not *all right*. Feelings are involved. You can't go messing about with people's emotions like that.'

'Have I?' he calmly enquired.

'Have you *what*?' She was almost spitting with fury at his obstinate refusal to see any sort of a problem.

'Messed about with your emotions?'

'Damn you, Ben Gorran!' And spinning on her heels she started to march away, except that as she was still dripping wet she slipped in the mud, would have fallen had not Ben caught her. Tears standing proud in her eyes, she slapped him away. 'Get off me! Leave me alone.' She was crying, although she hadn't realised it until now. 'I don't ever want you to touch me. Actually, I don't give a toss about you.'

'Actually, I think you do.' Then he pulled her into his arms and this time he did kiss her, very thoroughly. It was a savage kiss, hard and brutal, but Chrissie made no protest, rather gave a little moan deep in her throat. She leant into him, couldn't seem to help herself, all her resolutions melting away at the sensations racketing through her body as his mouth moved possessively over hers. Demanding and insistent, he coaxed her lips open and, to her shame, she allowed his tongue to tease and dance with hers. Chrissie couldn't ever remember feeling like this, as if this was the place she wanted to be more than anywhere else in the world, the place she belonged, in Ben's arms.

And then she remembered how she'd vowed never to let herself feel anything for a man ever again. How she had vowed not to fall in love, not to risk the pain of losing that love. Bursting into tears she thrust him from her and ran to the loft without looking back.

He was sitting outside the next morning when Chrissie finally emerged, rather late and bleary-eyed, for breakfast. The night before she'd taken a hot bath and been ashamed to find herself crying into the soapsuds like some foolish young schoolgirl. What had she expected? What had she hoped for? That Ben Gorran might suddenly become the new love of her life? What dangerous folly that would be. Look at how weak she'd been over Peter, letting things muddle along because she couldn't bear to be alone when she was still grieving for Tom. And consider how she allowed her own mother to control her life, running her errands, waiting on her hand, foot and finger, even telling lies for her. Hadn't she firmly resolved to make a fresh start, to be strong, and fight for her freedom and independence, to think for herself in future and stop being the good little girl who wanted to please everyone? Now look at the state of her, all because she'd been stupid enough to forget her own rules. Well, it would not happen again. She would build a shield of iron around her heart which no good-looking male could breach.

'What are you doing here?' she asked, stomach churning despite her resolve.

'I've waited by your door all night to beg your forgiveness,' he murmured.

'Don't be ridiculous.'

'Maybe I am ridiculous, but it's the truth. I'm sorry I messed up.' And taking her hand he kissed it. Encouraged when she didn't protest, he kissed her mouth, very softly, then the pulse of her throat.

Only then did it occur to her how dishevelled he looked, how his rough, whiskery chin had scraped against hers. Chrissie pushed him gently away to study him more closely. He was still wearing the same clothes, save for the navy jacket which he'd discarded and now hung over the gate. The smart blue shirt was badly creased and grubby, sleeves rolled up, his hair tousled, as if he'd spent the intervening hours constantly combing it through with agitated fingers. Perhaps he had. Her senses skittered, for the rumpled look rather suited him, making him look sexier than ever.

'I don't believe you would do such a thing,' she protested, eyes fluttering closed on a faint murmur as he continued to trail kisses round to her ear.

He held her away from him, his gaze warm as it met hers. 'I am so sorry for my daughter's behaviour. She's just turned nine, going on thirty-nine. Feels she has to watch over me, and is very bossy. I've told her to apologise to you herself. Please don't say it's over between us before we've even begun. I beg you to please give me another chance.'

There was a desperate appeal in his voice, in his eyes, which Chrissie found dangerously alluring. She could find no words to answer him, her mind in a whirl, a torrent of emotion searing through her just by the way his hand was smoothing her arm.

'You must know how I feel about you, Chrissie. From the moment I first saw you walking along the shore in that yellow dress, it felt like a little piece of sunshine had fallen into my life. I've done my best to be patient, knowing how vulnerable you are, afraid I might frighten you off if I spoke too soon. I'm just hoping that I haven't completely blown it. Could we start again, do you reckon?'

He was looking at her with such pleading in his eyes that she felt something shift inside, as if her heart had flipped over. Her lips twitched, the corners lifting slightly into the shadow of a smile.

So he'd put off telling her about his daughter because the girl was being difficult. And like all men he would hate emotional confrontations. No doubt that was the reason he was having problems with the child in the first place.

But what was he asking of her? What did he want? Could she trust him? Should she forgive him for not being open and honest with her? And had he truly given up on his marriage, or was there some truth in what Karen said?

She felt herself trembling at the top of a slippery slope

which could swoop her into a wonderful, new exciting life, or lead her down into a morass of problems she'd much rather not be involved with. Chrissie closed her mind to the sweetness that had flowed through her a moment ago at his touch, and, keeping her tone deliberately cool, almost indifferent, she calmly informed him that she intended to return to London. 'I shall be leaving first thing in the morning.' She saw how his face fell, his disappointment all too plain to see, and she relented a little. 'Don't worry, I'll be back. I mean to take that little shop.'

'You do?' His joy was transparent, rather like a small boy on Christmas morning.

Chrissie couldn't help but laugh. 'I've signed the contract and everything. As for you and me, I'll think about it. Let's take things slowly, shall we, one step at a time? I'll be away for about a week collecting my stuff. Then we'll see.'

'I'll be waiting, just as long as it takes.'

Despite herself, Chrissie rather hoped that he would.

Maybe the episode with Karen, or else the kiss, had acted as a sort of catalyst, but Chrissie rather thought that she'd at last made up her mind. She wasted no time in returning to the agent to set the necessary arrangements in motion. He was delighted by her decision. She agreed to bring in a cheque for the deposit before she left for London and he promised to have the lease ready for signing on her return the following week. She still needed to go home to London to pack her belongings, and no doubt there'd be some explaining to do, arrangements to make for her mother. Vanessa would not be pleased by the news, and would no doubt hit the roof in one of her tantrums.

But no matter how difficult a challenge she faced, Chrissie was determined that she wouldn't allow herself to be persuaded out of this decision. Her mind was made up. It was time to put herself first.

If she'd anticipated surprise when she announced she was staying for good, she had seriously underestimated Georgia. 'Ah, yet another to fall victim to Lakeland's charm?'

'Well, it is rather irresistible. I feel the move would be good for me since I'm in need of a fresh start.'

'That's what people always say when they come here, then once under the town's spell they never move again.' Georgia gave her gentle smile. 'Consider carefully before you decide. It could be a lifelong change.'

Chrissie couldn't help but laugh. 'I'm willing to risk it. I've decided to take a little shop, initially on a two-year lease, which I hope will give me sufficient time to see if I can make a go of it. But I was wondering,' she hurried on, 'if I could extend my stay in the loft for a little longer, maybe another month. I shall be moving into the flat above the shop but it needs some work doing to it first, a good scrub down and a lick of paint mainly. I also need to pop back down to London to collect some of my things.'

'And to tell your family of your decision, I imagine. How will they react, do you think?'

The question sounded so odd coming from her own

grandmother that it unnerved Chrissie a little and she took a moment to recover. Should she blurt out who she really was here and now? Would that make things worse for Vanessa, or better? Perhaps she should at least have the courtesy to tell her of this decision first. 'I'm sure my mother will point out the likely problems, as all parents do. But I believe this one is right for me.'

'I'm sure it is, and it's really nobody's business but your own what you choose to do with your life.' Georgia settled on her favourite seat in the garden. 'So tell me about this shop. What will you sell in it?'

Chrissie went to sit beside her. 'Second-hand books mostly, plus maps, and a few cards and gifts.'

'How wonderful. We could do with a bookshop in town. I love reading. We have a huge library here at Rosegill Hall. In fact, I'm quite certain there are several books you could have to help get you started.'

'Oh, that would be wonderful, thank you. I was also thinking of putting an advert in the paper.'

'Good idea, but take care how you word it. You don't want damaged books on your shelves that have been kept in a damp old cellar for years. Do insist they are clean and in good condition.'

'Oh, don't worry. I mean to make a success of this business.'

'I have no doubt you will succeed, my dear.'

They talked as they worked contentedly side by side, harvesting potatoes, leeks and onions, sowing winter lettuces and transplanting cabbages, while Chrissie spilt out her ideas. She grew increasingly enthusiastic and confident as her grandmother listened so patiently, only interrupting to offer suggestions, or approve a particular plan. She didn't issue the kind of lectures Chrissie had grown accustomed to from Peter. Nor did Georgia make any demands upon her as Vanessa constantly did. They talked as equals, and the old lady listened with interest to what Chrissie had to say, respecting her answers.

'It all sounds such fun, and of course you are welcome to stay on here as long as you like, till you've got the flat entirely to your liking. There's absolutely no rush. Hetty and I will be glad to help in any way we can. I'm rather handy with a paintbrush myself.'

'Bless you, you're very kind, I do appreciate your support.' Was this the moment to reveal her true name? But how to break the news gently? 'I seem to be able to talk to you so easily, easier than with my own mother. Why is that, I wonder?'

'Ah, the mother-daughter relationship is not an easy one. It is fraught with underlying jealousies – the mother fearful of her child's growing independence and awakening beauty, the daughter testing out her new powers.' She gave a sad little smile. 'And on top of all that comes the guilt. Whatever a mother does, she feels she should do better, because she's the mom, right? And in her turn, every daughter loves and wants to please her mother, needs her approbation, although the price of achieving that is sometimes too high and goes against her own needs or desires.'

Very softly, Chrissie asked, 'Did you pay too high a

price for the decisions you made? What happened with you and Ellis? Did your mother discover your secret? What plans did she have for you?'

'Oh, marriage with a suitable young man, of course, and she set about the matter with her customary zeal. The consequences were very nearly catastrophic.'

Chapter Twelve

San Francisco

Suitors were allowed to call on Thursday and Sunday afternoons. Prudence would flash her eyes and flutter her lashes, then reject them all. But still they came back for more, entranced by my sister's wit and beauty. She would offer dazzling smiles at their compliments while Mama regaled them with tales of how her darling daughters had personally baked the scones and cakes with our own fair hands. An absolute fiction, particularly in Prue's case, as she wouldn't have the faintest idea how to begin. I too was a walking disaster in the culinary arts and Cook had actually banned me from the kitchen, my having burnt one too many meat rolls for her patience. But the fiction must be upheld that we were proficient in the feminine arts of baking muffins, embroidery, crochet, tatting and other fancy work. That way, Mama was confident we would attract a suitable husband.

I was gifted in none of these skills, nor in the art of seduction, certainly not with young men I found dull and unattractive.

One wet Sunday afternoon that autumn I was enduring yet another 'At Home'. Today our guests were Leonard Stibley, a dandy who was fussy and fastidious; Willie Wyman, profligate and selfish; and Samuel Morgan, about whom the least said the better. And it took every ounce of my strained patience and feeble charm to fend off Marcus Coleson's advances.

He was plump with bright-red hair and had already grown a moustache, at barely nineteen, which lay like a dead rat above a full upper lip. He had fat fingers that were constantly fidgeting, smoothing his superfine jacket, adjusting his silk cravat or primping said moustache. The thought of those hands ever touching me made me feel quite ill.

But he was the eldest son of a wine exporter of considerable means, therefore a candidate of note in Mama's eyes. Even now she was conversing with him far more than I, telling him how I had embroidered the napkin he was using.

Smirking disdainfully at the article in question, he used it to dab at those moist, full lips of his, and inclined a slight head bow. 'I am deeply impressed. However, Miss Georgina's greatest charm is her beauty, her glossy black hair, red lips and delightful smile.'

Since I was not considered to be the beauty of the family, and hadn't smiled once at him all afternoon, this was all fanciful nonsense on his part.

Mama simpered, sending me a furious glare in a silent plea to converse with him properly.

'Prudence is the pretty one,' I firmly responded. 'And Mama, you know I cannot embroider for toffee. That is actually one of Prue's napkins. My effort was a grubby mess that you quite rightly threw in the trash.' I smiled at Marcus. 'My skills lie in quite another direction. I have a fancy to be a nurse, Mr Coleson. Now what do you think of that?'

'Do you mean to tend the sick?' He looked quite shocked, as if I'd said I wished to enter a bawdy house.

'I do, I can think of no better calling than to help those less fortunate than ourselves. What say you?'

'I . . . er . . . um . . . really couldn't say.' He glanced about in desperation as if he might catch some dread disease simply by talking about it. The podgy fingers suddenly grew quite agitated as they eased a neckcloth that seemed to have become oddly tight.

To be fair, everyone lived in fear of sickness, and families would leave the city in summer to avoid any risk of contagion. To have a wife who deliberately laid herself open to such risk would be quite beyond the pale. Which was why I raised the subject.

Mama was fanning herself furiously with her lace kerchief. 'What she means, dear Marcus, is that my *darling* daughter may well find herself obliged to take up some unseemly profession if she is unsuccessful in making a suitable marriage.' As she most certainly will be if she does not make more effort, her flint-like gaze silently informed me. I dropped my own, realising

I'd gone too far in my teasing. I would indeed enjoy having a job that involved caring for others, even as I recognised Mama would never allow it. But there were limits to my acts of rebellion, and mine were already beginning to wither on the vine. I did not have my sister's skill with banter, nor her desire to flirt with a noted bore.

He left soon after that, as did the other young men, without any requests to call again, much to Prue's amusement and Mama's despair.

After they had gone there followed the inevitable analysis. Mama would order Maura to clear away then bring us a fresh pot of tea while we picked over the afternoon's offerings and issued our judgement, rather like a talent competition or horse fair. Really most degrading.

'So what did you think of Wyman? Pleasant enough, I thought, but not quite up to the mark.' It was Mama's favourite phrase.

Prudence would make some cutting remark, as she was doing now. 'Samuel Morgan's crowning glory is undoubtedly his nose, but I couldn't abide the constant honking.'

This reduced even Mama to choking giggles.

My mother then turned her gimlet eyes upon me. 'Georgina, why can you not just once show a little interest in your suitors. Is it asking too much that you at least be polite and entertaining? Marcus Coleson is a charming young man, and of considerable means. Any young gel he takes as a wife will live in a fine house in the

Napa Valley, in the lap of luxury, and consider herself blessed.'

'I have no great wish to live in luxury, and I really do not care for him, Mama.'

She let out a heavy sigh. 'You cannot go on finding fault with these fine young men or you will live and die a spinster, my girl.'

'I don't care if I do,' I stubbornly responded. 'Better that than marrying such as Coleson. He would simply bore me to death. Anyway, I don't like his hands.'

'What on earth is wrong with his hands?'

'His fingers are most dreadfully podgy.'

I could see her struggling to disagree, and finding it quite impossible she settled for her usual bland remark. 'He is a fine, upstanding young man, of solid worth.'

'Certainly solid,' giggled my irrepressible sister.

'Prudence!' Mama reprimanded in her sternest tones. 'I shall invite him again on Thursday, allow him one more opportunity to shine.'

'Please don't, Mama,' I begged. 'I assure you I could never like him. Nor do I care for his red hair.' Horrified by this suggestion, I was desperate to find something, anything, to put a stop to her matchmaking.

'Don't be ridiculous. What does the colour of his hair signify?'

She was quite right, of course. It did not signify at all when choosing a husband. It was just that I preferred a certain pale gold, and a face with a wry grin and a smattering of freckles. But I couldn't tell her that. Or could I?

* * *

For some weeks I suffered these At Homes in silence. Hopeful young men would come and attempt to dazzle us with their wit and charm, then quietly steal away disappointed or disillusioned. Prudence continued to flirt outrageously while I would sit like a wooden dummy, saying nothing, feeling stiff and awkward, wishing I were anywhere but in Mama's front parlour. I ached to be out in the fresh air, walking with Ellis in the Japanese Gardens, my hand warmly held in his, or sitting beneath the eucalyptus trees talking about nothing in particular. Following that first tentative meeting we'd met regularly, usually in the park. I constantly chewed over in my mind how I might persuade Mama to invite this certain young sailor, with whom I'd quickly fallen head over heels in love, to tea, but never quite plucked up the courage.

Dearest Ellis, who had been my partner in a most thrilling adventure. Life seemed dull when he wasn't around. We met also at the Institute, and I enjoyed my work there. I found great satisfaction in seeing how much pleasure we brought these men, who were so far from home, with the home-made suppers we provided, and the games and entertainment we organised for them.

One of their favourite activities was a tug of war. The men absolutely loved the challenge and were hugely competitive. The British would vie with the American ships to win, the French against the Germans or Russians, the floor slippery with their efforts despite the sawdust that was constantly thrown down. The winner was always the best out of three, and some of the men, the

Scandinavians, for instance, were powerfully built and formidable opponents.

One particular evening Ellis was in the team pulling against these Norse giants and I was filled with pride to see Ellis take his place . . . By no means the broadest but certainly one of the tallest in the British team, and with some power in those shoulders.

The captain gave the signal to start, and after much tugging and heaving, grunting and gasping, the British pulled the Scandinavians over the line, then repeated their success a second time. I was so thrilled that as Ellis turned towards me, a grin of pure triumph on his laughing face, I threw myself into his arms and kissed him.

The entire room erupted. The assembled seamen roared and cheered, stamped their feet, and I would not wish to repeat the ribald comments I received. I quickly broke away, crimson-cheeked with embarrassment. Prue was laughing along with the rest, seeing no real harm in my impulsive gesture. Surprisingly, it was Maura who was the most disapproving, and she lectured me all the way home.

'What if someone should tell your mother?'

'Mama doesn't know anyone who attends the Institute.'

'That Molly person might tell her, or – what's her name? – the woman who organises the suppers? She must be somebody's daughter, some woman who in turn might attend one of Mrs Briscoe's bridge parties or sewing bees.'

'Oh, for goodness' sake, Maura, you really are worrying unduly. I think it highly unlikely.'

'Stranger things have happened. You should be more careful. It was a foolish thing to do, miss, to kiss him like that in front of everybody. You might even consider calling an end to this madness.'

I looked at her askance. 'It was just a spur-of-the moment kiss. What is so wrong with that?'

'It was rather public, old thing,' Prudence whispered.

'And clear to everyone that it was not your first,' Maura added, her face unusually stern.

I was surprised by her sharpness, and said so. 'I think you exaggerate. In any case, I get the distinct impression that you are rather sweet on John, and really have no objection to these little escapades.'

My maid's blushes told their own tale, and I laughed. 'I know I can rely upon you to keep my secret. You won't breathe a word either, will you Prue? I know I can trust you both with my life.'

Prudence hastened to assure me that was most certainly the case. 'You can, of course, rely upon my absolute loyalty. Oh, but Maura's right, you must take more care, dearest. But she won't tell either, will you, Maura? We can depend upon your discretion, can we not?' And she turned to our ever-loyal maid.

After a short pause, Maura answered. 'Indeed, haven't you always been able to trust me?' Her tone was dry, the words rather lacking in the required conviction, something which didn't occur to me until later. Far too late. I did, however, appreciate their concern, and realised Maura had made a valid point. I vowed to be more circumspect in future. But not for the world would I give him up.

I stubbornly continued to meet Ellis every Wednesday without fail, and there were many more stolen kisses. Only to yield my mouth to his sent my senses skittering with fresh desire, filling me with an exquisite pain. I would curl my fingers in his tousled hair, and he would press my soft body against the hardness of his own, murmuring my name over and over. He never asked for more than kisses; even so, I was aware how I sinned, and was quite unable to resist him. Touching, tasting, my mouth bruised and swollen from his kisses, I would have to sneak quickly upstairs to the bathroom on my return. Had Mama ever set eyes on me before I had freshened up, she would have guessed at once, just by the glazed expression of love in my eyes.

I continued to meet Ellis and defy my parents, sometimes without even Maura at my side, slipping out for a prearranged tryst at the corner of the block. The risks we ran in order to be together were both reckless and dangerous. But I did not hesitate to run them, nor pause to worry over what punishment Mama might inflict were she ever to discover my deceit, knowing it would be severe and long lasting. It made no difference; I would take any chances to be with him. I could have lived for ever in his arms, loving him as I did with all my heart and soul.

Sometimes Ellis would take me down to the waterfront

so we could watch the ships come and go in the bay. I didn't care where we went, so long as he was by my side, although he was adamant that he would never take me to the more dangerous wharves, among the shabby bars, or into the seedy underbelly of Frisco.

'That is no place for a lady.'

'Huh, and I'm no fainting violet,' I briskly informed him, cuddling close with his arm tight about my waist. 'I can look after myself,' and he burst out laughing.

'I've seen the evidence of that with my own eyes. Even so, if I am ever to be received by your family that must never happen again.'

His words sobered me, for it was true. Meeting in secret like this was all very well – delightful, exciting, thrilling – but what of the future?

I lived in fear that any day he would tell me that he was leaving. I was thrilled that Ellis had let the SS *Kronus* leave without him. I flattered myself that he couldn't bear for us to part, but I knew he must take another berth soon. At some point he would need to go back to sea as he had his living to earn. Besides which, hadn't he made it plain that he never stayed anywhere very long, that he was an adventurer who suffered from itchy feet and must move on? I just prayed it wouldn't be soon.

Perhaps driven by this fear as much as by the risks we ran, one afternoon I at last plucked up the courage to put forward my request. 'Mama, may I invite a friend of mine for our next At Home?'

She looked up from her sewing to glare sharply at me.

'A *friend*?' As if it were impossible to imagine that I should have one. But then I had little opportunity to make the acquaintance of young gentlemen who were unknown to her. 'And who might that be?' Then she set down her embroidery with an irritated click of her tongue as she read the truth in my face. 'Not that dreadful sailor, the one who allegedly rescued you from the masher? I knew it was a mistake to allow you to help out at the Seamen's Institute.'

I took a quick breath. Having got this far I wasn't for giving up easily. 'Mama, the Institute is a perfectly respectable place, and Ellis Cowper didn't *allegedly* rescue me. Without doubt or question he saved both Prudence and myself from a highly embarrassing and possibly dangerous situation.' If only I dared tell her exactly how dangerous, how Ellis had faced threats to his own life to save us, but Prue's reputation was at stake, which I could not risk for the world. 'I assure you he is a perfect gentleman. Please allow him the opportunity to at least call and prove his worth.'

Mama drew herself up ramrod straight in her chair. 'I think not, Georgina. He's a common sailor who flits from port to port with no settled abode, no status, no fortune other than a ruin of a house in some godforsaken spot, nothing to recommend him at all. And he is a foreigner to boot, about whom we know nothing. A most dreadful young man.'

'But you may find that you like him, if you would only allow him to call.'

'I said no,' and placing her pince-nez upon the end of her nose, which she really didn't need as she was as sharp-eyed as an eagle, she consulted her list. 'Next week we have the Levy boys coming, and Drew Kemp. I have great hopes of the latter, a charming man, and most comfortably placed. I believe you will find him an interesting prospect. And there will be no more helping out at the Seamen's Institute if this is how you repay my generosity.'

'Oh, but Mama.'

'Not another word. I will hear no more of this English sailor, Georgina, is that quite clear?'

The subject, it seemed, was closed.

'Why will Mama not allow us to choose our own suitors?' I bitterly complained to Prue, stripping off my gown in a lather of hurt feelings without waiting for Maura's assistance as we prepared for bed that night. I was almost in tears and my sister hugged me close, alarmed and upset by my distress.

'You know full well that suitors need to be properly vetted first, before they are allowed anywhere near us. All the matrons sit around gossiping over their sewing bees and bridge parties, busily devising a list of suitable young men. If one isn't on the list, there's no hope for him.'

'But *why* is it like that? Why can we not invite friends of our own?'

She frowned at me, then sadly smiled. 'You fell for that young sailor in a big way, didn't you, Georgia dear?'

I found myself flushing. 'I did nothing of the sort, I'm simply speaking in general terms. He is an example, that is all, of how our freedom is curtailed.'

Prudence looked at me with that knowing smile of hers. I could tell she was in no way deceived. 'You aren't still seeing him, are you? Enjoying secret trysts in the park? Exchanging kisses in the sweet meadow grass or beneath the redwood trees?'

My cheeks burnt scarlet as I hotly denied it. 'Of course not, don't be silly!' But I had to quickly turn away, pretending to fuss over the clasp of my necklace, thankful now of Maura's help, as well as the sympathy in her eyes. I'd long since won her soft Irish heart round with evidence of our love. Or believed I had.

'Well then,' Prue said, already shrugging the problem away. 'You should do as I do. Encourage them all, then choose the richest and most handsome.'

'Oh, Prue, don't be so heartless.'

'A gel has to look after herself in this world.'

I sat on my dressing stool while Maura wrapped my hair in rags, pointlessly hoping for curls. 'But what about love? Don't you want to fall in love with the man you marry?'

'Mama says love will follow as we get to know the young man in question. I'm sure it can be easily conjured up between two agreeable people. Money, however, is a different matter entirely. You either have it or you don't, and I have no intention of living in poverty. Marrying a poor sailor, even one as handsome and beguiling as the steadfast Mr Cowper, would not suit me at all.'

It would suit me very well, I thought, but to my headstrong sister I simply smiled. 'I don't believe you are half so money-grubbing as you pretend, Prue dearest. I, for one, have every intention of marrying for love. I shall insist upon it.'

She gave me what I can only describe as an old-fashioned look. 'Well, good luck with persuading Mama and Papa to agree.'

Chapter Thirteen

Drew Kemp was not at all plump. Nor did he have red hair, or seem in the least boring. He was tall, olive-skinned, with dark-brown hair and strange, deep, chestnut eyes that never quite looked at you directly. He was also extremely handsome, albeit with a somewhat cynical curl to a thin upper lip. According to Mama he'd recently inherited, on his father's death, not only a considerable business of real estate which he had plans to expand, but also a sizeable fortune to go with it.

Therefore he represented an excellent suitor for either one of her daughters.

Prue was happily flirting with Richard Denson, an amiable enough young fellow, willing and ambitious, the sort who would be an asset in any business. Papa would certainly approve of him. And as the son of a textile exporter, quite comfortably placed – an asset which ranked high in Mama's list of requirements.

I couldn't help smiling at my capricious sister as she batted her eyelashes, gazed at him adoringly and trilled with laughter at his feeble jokes. He was clearly most anxious to please and enchanted by empty-headed little Prudence, which was just as well, for once she'd set her cap at him the poor boy wouldn't stand a chance, and that was before she called in Mama as backup.

She'd already riffled through my wardrobe and borrowed my most flattering gown in pale mauve, which showed off her porcelain skin to perfection. And very charming she looked in it too.

Sighing with some small degree of envy at my sister's uncomplicated outlook on life, I looked about for further diversion. Unfortunately the Levy boys, who were always entertaining, seemed content to tinkle silly tunes on the pianoforte, so that left me with the indolent and haughty Drew Kemp. I thought him rather full of himself, oozing with artificial charm and self-confidence, so decided to ignore him and settle for listening to a stilted rendition of 'In the Shade of the Old Apple Tree'.

My mind turned, as always, to the image of another young man, mentally tracing the line of his lips with mine. How I ached to be with him now, this very minute.

The last time we'd met was at the Institute on Thursday, when the Seamen's choir had given a concert before the worthy citizens of San Francisco in aid of their homeless sailors charity. Prue and I, with Maura's help, of course, were serving the refreshments during the interval. We barely had more than a moment to exchange a few desperate words secreted in the wings behind a curtain, long enough for Ellis to gently warn me that he was rapidly running out of funds.

'I'm going to have to go to sea soon, Georgia. I've been laid up for some weeks now, but it can't go on indefinitely.'

I could feel a physical pain clench my heart even as I assured him that I fully understood, choking back a rush of tears as I'd no wish for him to think me selfish or needy.

He cradled my face between the palms of his hands. 'You will wait for me, won't you? You are my girl?'

That was the first time I'd ever heard him use those words and my heart swelled with pride and love. 'Oh, yes, Ellis, my darling. For ever and always.'

He had to go on stage then for the second part of the show, and afterwards there were so many people crowding around to congratulate the singers that I couldn't get near. Then there was John, our driver, impatiently urging us out the door, so I never got the chance to speak to him again. I hoped and prayed he wouldn't be leaving quite yet. It seemed long enough to wait till next Wednesday when we would meet for our regular walk in the park.

Stifling my regret and fears I attempted now to focus on Drew Kemp. Glancing at him, I thought his face somewhat angular, with long harsh lines drawn between nose and mouth. I guessed he was older than myself by some six or seven years, maybe more.

Mama had set out a dish of fruit beside Cook's blueberry muffins, perhaps despairing of winning approval for our non-existent baking skills, and with not a single topic of sensible conversation in my head I offered him the dish. He selected a strawberry, nibbling it slowly till the juice ran down his jutting chin, his dark piercing eyes fixed upon mine in a most disturbing manner. 'I hear you are considering taking up nursing as a career,' he suddenly said, quite taking me by surprise. His voice was oddly light and with a slight rasp in his throat.

I lifted my chin. 'You've been talking to Marcus Coleson, I take it?'

'The poor fellow seemed stunned by such an unusual ambition; alarmed by it, in point of fact. He rather assumed such tasks were performed by ancient harridans, not a nubile young miss who'd rather caught his eye. What a waste that would be,' he drawled.

'You think women should not be educated, or have any ambition other than marriage?'

The grating sound of his chuckle was strangely irritating, and not a little patronising. Reaching for another strawberry he bit into it with strong white teeth, sucking up the juice in an expression of blissful ecstasy while his eyes mocked me. 'I would never dare,' he said, once the fruit had been consumed with relish. 'Women, I've always found, are highly talented and can achieve whatever they set their minds to. Assuming they have a mind, that is.'

I was outraged by this remark, but, all too aware of Mama's anxious glances in my direction, rigorously maintained a show of politeness. 'You think us lacking in intelligence?' I asked, a smile firmly fixed to my stiff lips.

'I would not dream to issue such a damning indictment

on American womanhood. Lacking in judgement, perhaps, but that is bound to be the case if they do not have the benefit of a man to advise them.'

I gasped, feeling my cheeks start to burn. It would have been asking too much of my feminine pride to allow this remark to pass unchallenged. I took a breath, still desperately attempting to keep my voice calm. 'I would like to remind you that San Francisco possesses some of the finest schools in the state, if not the entire country. I have several times visited our local education establishments with Mama, and found the children there not only busily scratching on their slates, but bright and neat, well mannered and eager to learn. The scholars receive the best education from talented teachers, covering such subjects as arithmetic and geometry, geography, the history of our nation, grammar, and even philosophy. Are you saying that this excellent curriculum should only be made available to boys?'

He considered my comments with a lazy grin, the curl to his lip together with an icy coolness in those dark eyes destroying any evidence of amusement. 'They are the ones who will need to earn a living by the sweat of their brow.'

'And why cannot women do the same?'

He laughed, a harsh bitter sound that I did not care for in the least. 'Because there are more important things for women to do.'

'Such as?'

'Why, pleasing their husband, what else? And providing him with a son.'

'Like a brood mare, you mean.'

His laughter this time was a throaty chuckle, although the eyes remained cold and hard. 'Your choice of words, not mine, but yes, the epithet fits well. Any wife of mine would most definitely be required to present me with a parcel of children – at least two, if not all of them, male. She will also devote herself entirely to my pleasure and comfort, and wait upon my every whim. Isn't that the lot of women? Isn't that their proper purpose in life?'

I felt the heat of my anger bubble through my veins, the urge to leap to my feet and stalk away almost unbearable. I did not like this man, not one little bit. His arrogance was deeply unpleasant. Even Marcus Coleson now seemed like a harmless puppy by comparison. But I certainly wasn't going to allow him to best me. 'Then I should think you'll have a hard time finding such a woman.'

'On the contrary, I offer the kind of inducements no sensible Mama could bear to ignore. I shall have the pick of the crop. It is simply a matter of which one I decide to choose.' And hovering his long fingers over the fruit bowl, thoughtfully commented, 'Now which shall it be, a peach or a nice soft plum?'

That's when I got up and walked away, in high dudgeon.

Sadly, I was alone in my dislike of Drew Kemp. Mama was seriously smitten. Even silly Prue could see no fault in him as we picked over the day's crop of candidates with our usual scrutiny while enjoying a glass of iced tea.

'But most men hold that view about women, Georgia, and they all want sons to follow them in their business. What do you expect?'

'Did his hands meet with your approval?' Mama asked, with a rare show of wry humour.

'Yes, I will admit he has very fine hands; pale, with long tapering fingers.'

'And his hair did not displease you?'

'No, Mama, only his manner, which I found cold and unfriendly.'

She made a dismissive sound in her throat. 'We don't want you growing too friendly at this stage. Time enough for warmth later. He is exceedingly well placed, dear, and with an engaging wit. I shall speak to Papa about him, and invite him next Thursday, as well.'

'But Mama . . .'

Too late, she sailed from the room in a flurry of taffeta with a light in her eye that I found deeply worrying.

The following Wednesday found me at the park, as usual, but this time Ellis was not there waiting for me when Maura and I arrived. The pair of us sat on a park bench for a while, twiddling with our gloves and parasols. Maura always made a valiant attempt, I noticed, to look smart and tidy, not wearing her maid's uniform since I did not wish to draw attention to my status when we were out together. I preferred us to be seen as two friends, rather than mistress and maid. I admired the efforts she made to better herself and often gave her cast-offs of my own to wear, which I know she took great pleasure in. She would even try to emulate my style, matching the colour of her gown to mine. I once caught her in my room secretly trying on one of my ball gowns, but crept away again unseen, having no wish to embarrass her.

After about half an hour we grew tired of sitting and walked a little, not too far in case Ellis should suddenly appear. But as the minutes ticked by I grew increasingly anxious. 'Where can he be?'

'Did he mention he might be leaving?' Maura asked, and my reluctance to answer her question told its own story.

'He did say funds were running low. But surely he can't have found a new berth already?'

'And he wouldn't leave without saying goodbye,' she agreed.

It dawned on me then that perhaps those few hurried words in the concert interval had been his way of doing exactly that. Ellis had indeed gone to sea, and I had no idea how long for or when he would return.

The very next day I was called to Papa's study whereupon he informed me that I had been fortunate enough to receive an offer from Mr Andrew Kemp, and that he had accepted on my behalf. I made one almighty fuss. 'I hardly know the man, and I do not like him!' I screamed. 'I shall certainly never agree to marry Drew Kemp.'

Father simply ordered me to my room to collect myself, where Mama later found me pacing the floor in a fury of tears.

'Have you lost your senses, child, to refuse such an excellent proposal? I am at a loss to understand why you do not appreciate your good fortune.'

'How dare Papa accept a proposal on my behalf? Why was I not consulted?'

'Consulted?' My mother looked aghast at the very idea. 'Why would he feel the need to consult you, madam, I wonder? Instead of complaining, you'd do better to appreciate the pains your dear father is taking in looking after your well-being and future security.' She was wearing her frozen do-not-argue-with-me expression, which for once I was ignoring.

'So *I* have no say in the matter?'

She clicked her tongue in annoyance. 'How can a young gel be allowed to make such an important decision without the proper guidance? Quite out of the question.'

'Why?'

'Because it is simply not done. It is a father's duty to consider and plan a daughter's happiness, and hers to obey.'

'To marry where my heart is not engaged is surely a recipe for disaster, not happiness. I will not endure it.' I was angrily fighting back fresh tears, desperately struggling to hold on to my self-control while I challenged the accepted logic of a fashionably arranged marriage which, to my mind, was anything but logical. 'I will not marry a man I do not love!'

Turning away from her, I stood, arms folded, stubbornly glaring out across to the bay, wishing with all my heart that a certain sailor had not chosen this week as the time to leave, willing his ship to turn around and return home, bringing him to my rescue yet again.

My mother jerked me round to face her, wagging a

stern finger in my face. 'You will do as your father says and be grateful.'

'Never!' Inside I was shaking, a burning sensation in my chest, as I couldn't ever remember defying her with such stubborn determination. She too was stunned by this unexpected rebellion and instantly opted for a more reasonable approach.

'Georgina, dearest, please stop looking at the negatives and start to think more positively,' she wheedled. 'Marriage will bring many benefits. With Kemp as your husband you will be granted the income to dress in the latest fashions and take a full part in society here in Frisco, not far from your family. There will be a home of your own, servants, children. Marriage will provide the freedom you crave.'

'What freedom? Instead of being accountable to my father, I will simply be transferred to the dictate of a husband, a man I do not even like.'

Mama heaved a sigh. 'I really cannot see what it is that troubles you so. Drew Kemp is a charming man, handsome, debonair, rich. What can you possibly have against him? And love will come, in time. Do you see your sister making a fuss? Dear Prudence has more sense. In fact, I can see another wedding on the horizon before the year is out if Denson comes up to snuff. She, at least, appreciates that she'll require a pleasant home and a regular income coming in to feed the children she will one day have. All of which requires considerable care when choosing who will supply these essentials. While you, dear girl, go around with your head in the clouds as if life were a romance novel. Well, I do assure you that it is very far from the case. *Love*, however delicious and exciting it may sound, will soon fly out the window when poverty comes in through the door.'

'Please don't spout old wives' tales at me, Mama. Those silly sayings are far too simplistic.' And I walked away from her to angrily plump up the pillows on my bed, before flinging myself upon it.

'That is because they are true,' she snapped, standing before me with arms akimbo like some avenging angel. 'Flirting with a passing stranger who rescues you from an embarrassing situation is not a suitable foundation upon which to build a friendship, let alone a secure future.'

I sat up, clenching my hands together as if in prayer in an effort to make her understand. 'But Ellis Cowper is everything that Drew Kemp is not.'

'How would you know that?'

'I know because I have the intelligence to form my own judgements,' I cried, and saw at once that my pride had betrayed me. The shock on her face was palpable.

'Georgina, are you telling me that you have met this sailor again?' She put her hands to her cheeks in horror. 'Oh, my goodness, you fraternised with him at the Seamen's Institute, didn't you? Quite against my specific instructions to the contrary.'

'Mama—'

'Dear heaven, if so then you are ruined. You stupid girl, what were you thinking of?' Her knees suddenly gave way and she slumped down on to the edge of my bed. For a moment I feared my mother might actually faint, something she'd never been prone to in her entire life.

'I am not *ruined*, Mama. I've done nothing wrong.' But as I did battle with the wisdom of proclaiming the depth of my love for Ellis, and whether I dare confess he had actually kissed me, more than once, she quickly rallied and was on her feet in a second.

'And where was Maura when all of this was going on?'

'Nothing was *going on*. We talked quite a bit, that's all.'

'Alone, and unchaperoned?'

I rolled my eyes heavenwards. 'Well, yes, for a few moments we may have been alone, if Maura was serving tea or washing up in the kitchen. What of it?'

'What of it? *What of it?*' Marching over to the bell pull she gave it a hefty tug. 'We'll see what that young miss has to say in her own defence. The girl will have to go, of course, and without a character. She was charged with looking after you, and I will not tolerate a disobedient servant. As was John. He shall be dismissed too.'

I was horrified, and instantly leapt to my feet. 'But you can't blame Maura, or John. It wasn't their fault, it was mine. I will not apologise for liking Ellis . . . er, Mr Cowper. He's interesting to talk to, has travelled the world and enjoyed all manner of adventures.'

'I dare say he has,' she dryly remarked. 'And can you swear, hand on heart, that you never did anything but talk?'

I was saved from answering by a tap on the door, but before I had time to call for her to enter, my mother flung it wide. 'So there you are, madam, skulking as usual, I see,' she stormed, somewhat unkindly.

Maura was visibly startled, her mistress being the last person she'd expected to see in my room, and one glance at my devastated expression told her she was not there for any happy reason. 'You c-called, ma'am.'

'I did, Maura. I wish to allow you one last opportunity to defend yourself, although what you could possibly say in your own defence I cannot for the life of me imagine. I wish to know why I should not turn you out on the streets this minute.'

All the colour drained from poor Maura's face. 'On the streets, ma'am? W-why would you do such a thing?'

'Why would I not?'

'I-I'm wondering what it is you think I've done, ma'am. 'Cos I swear I've not done not'ing, to be sure.'

Her Irishness always came to the fore when she was in distress. She'd come to America as a young girl, endured a difficult time on Ellis Island while trying to find employment in New York, before coming west to Frisco. Now she was facing the possibility of life on the empty streets again. My heart filled with pity for her, and no small degree of guilt. Mother, however, was intransigent. 'I believe you have failed in your duty to my daughter.'

'Ma'am? Miss?' Maura looked at me, a frown puckering her round anxious face, obviously hoping for some indication of what this was all about.

Hating to see the fear in her eyes I quickly stepped forward. 'Mama, I've already told you that Maura is not to blame. *I* chose to volunteer my assistance at the Seamen's Institute, and bullied Maura, and Prue, to come with me. I did it, yes, because I wished to see Mr Cowper again. He's a fine young man whose company I enjoy. But it was not Maura's doing. On the contrary, she urged me to call an end to our friendship.'

'Oh, I did so, ma'am,' Maura hastily agreed.

'Obviously not forcibly enough.'

'I did me best, and I never left them alone, not for a minute . . . well, never longer'n a minute or two at most, not even when we were in the park.'

'The *park*?'

'Oh, Lordy,' Maura said, clapping her hand to her mouth. 'Now I've blown it.'

I was utterly mortified by this revelation. The little maid's eyes were sparkling at me above the flat of her hand and for an instant I had the chilling sensation that her blunder had been intentional, that she took pleasure in my discomfort. Surely not. Why would she do such a thing? I dismissed it as fancy almost at once. Maura was not only my maid, but my most loyal friend. She may suffer a little jealousy from time to time, but I knew she would never do anything to hurt me.

Mama was glaring at me, aghast. 'Is this true, Georgina? Did you meet this young man, this unknown *foreign* sailor, alone and unchaperoned in the park?'

I took a moment to catch my breath before answering, but there seemed little point in denying it. 'Yes, I did.'

'Heaven help us, then you are indeed ruined!'

'No, Mama, I swear I—'

'Answer my question, did you ever do more than talk?'

'Mama, I . . .' Should I tell the truth? Should I say that I had every right to kiss him as I love him, and he loves me? Would she stop me seeing him again if I did, or could I persuade my unsympathetic parents to give Ellis one more chance? I may well be able to win my father round, in the end, but Mama was another matter altogether.

'Well?'

I glanced across at Maura who was biting hard on her lower lip, her small hazel eyes darting from one to the other of us in total panic. If I chose to say nothing, my secret was surely safe with her. Perhaps that would be the wisest course, at least until Ellis returned from his latest voyage. 'No, of course not. I just liked to listen to tales of his adventures.'

I might have gone on to describe some of them, to prove my point, but Mama was pacing the floor, wringing her hands and no longer listening to me. 'Your hesitation says it all. I can no longer believe in your innocence.' She halted before me, her gaze glacial. 'You do realise, Georgina, this changes everything. You have confirmed my worst fears. There will be no further visits to the Seamen's Institute, which is clearly a place of utter depravity, no more of these love trysts in the park, nor any more tantrums of this nature. It is long past time you faced reality. In future you will, at all times, behave like a lady.'

'You want me to graciously accept my fate, is that it? To put my head on the block with a smile on my face?'

'Please do not overdramatise, it does not become you.

You are usually so patient, Georgia, so quiet and sensible. I blame this man, your *lover*!' Her tone was bitter. 'He has evidently brought out the worst in you and ruined you in the process.'

With the patience she so admired in me I repeated my point like a mantra. 'He is not my *lover*. I am *not* ruined. I have done *nothing wrong*.'

'You have done *everything* wrong!'

A terrible fear was growing inside of me, and I understood, in that moment, what it meant when someone said that a face could go purple with rage. My mother had always been strict, but I had never seen her quite this angry before.

Now she spun on her heel and strode to the door, where she paused to issue her parting words. 'I shall give you time to reflect upon the misery and near-catastrophe your ill-judged rebellion has brought upon us. If you have any sense of loyalty or pride left for your father and me, if not for yourself, then you will think very carefully on this excellent proposal. It is not too late to salvage your reputation, not yet. But do not hesitate too long or you will indeed be lost, a woman no man would touch, not even a penniless sailor. Fortunately, Drew Kemp is ready to call the banns and wishes the marriage to take place within the month, six weeks at most. Your father and I saw no reason why that shouldn't happen. Now it seems speed is even more imperative. We'll visit the dressmaker to discuss your gown first thing in the morning, just as soon as you have recovered your equilibrium. As for you, Maura Kerrigan, thank your lucky stars there is a way out of this mess, which has saved your bacon too.'

Maura bobbed a hasty curtsey. 'Thank you, ma'am.'

With that Mama left the room, ushering the subdued maid before her. And to my utter dismay I heard the key turn in the lock. Not that there was anywhere, or anyone, to run to, even were I free to do so. I took off my slipper and threw it at the door.

Chapter Fourteen

London

'I expected you home long before this. What have you been doing all this time? You must have been gone for *seven weeks*!'

'Six, actually, and I've been getting to know my grandmother,' Chrissie told her mother with a wry smile. 'Which has been most enlightening.'

They were sitting in the lounge of Vanessa's London apartment and even through the windows, always kept firmly closed against the dust and rain, Chrissie could hear the familiar hum of the city: buses and cars swishing by, the steady chatter and clatter of feet and tongues, a church bell and the distant whine of a siren. Sounds she had once taken for granted and now couldn't help comparing with the peace and solitude of the Lakes.

'Don't be pedantic, it doesn't suit you,' Vanessa snapped.

'I found Georgia to be really rather a remarkable

woman, obviously well liked and much respected in the town.' She wanted to say 'and with a remarkable story to tell' but didn't quite have the courage. Perhaps she could approach the subject later, when Vanessa was in a better frame of mind. At least there was no sign of a bottle anywhere around. Maybe she was off the booze, at last. Not wishing to risk upsetting her mother if that were the case, Chrissie decided she would stick to more practical matters.

'According to Mrs Gorran, her housekeeper, the pair of them were thoroughly involved in WVS work during the war, and have spent the years since restoring the family home. A splendid job they've made of it too. Rosegill Hall has a charm and beauty all its own, yet manages to remain homely and welcoming, as does the hostess.'

Vanessa gave a scornful sniff. 'Now you sound like a travel brochure. A house is an inanimate thing. My mother is far less caring of people, particularly members of her own family.'

Chrissie frowned, remembering what Ben had said about Georgia's son and daughter-in-law. And although her grandmother had in the end attended the Festival along with everyone else in the town, there hadn't been a single member of her family present. Certainly not the son, whom Chrissie had been hoping to meet before she left.

'There does seem to be an issue with *your brother*. You know, the one you forgot to mention,' Chrissie pointedly remarked, 'in that he wants Grandmother to retire and move out of the Hall, but she refuses absolutely to do so.'

'He always was a greedy little tyke; on the other hand, he may have a point. Ma is getting rather old to be running such a large house.'

'Actually, she's extremely fit and active, so why should she move? And the twins, *your sisters*, visit her regularly apparently. I'm sorry, Mum, but I can no longer see her as the wicked witch of the woods, even if she has cast you in the role of the black sheep of the family. Oh dear, now I'm mixing my metaphors, but you know what I mean.'

'This is no joke, Chrissie.' Vanessa's tone was sharp with anger, and jumping up she began to pace about the room in a strangely agitated fashion.

'I do appreciate that,' Chrissie conceded, already regretting her flippancy. The last thing she wanted was to drive Vanessa back to the gin bottle. 'I'm sorry, I'm just trying to understand what's going on between the pair of you; why you've kept your entire family a secret from me all these years, even to the extent of lying about your maiden name.'

'I had my reasons.'

'What possible reason could you have? None of this makes any sense. The fact of the matter is, Grandmother has been most friendly towards me, and, before you ask, no, I didn't reveal my true identity, although I was tempted to do so on more than one occasion. I chose not to because of my promise to you. One from which you will have to release me, as I can't go on living a lie.'

'I don't see why your "true identity", as you call it, should be a problem. You are unlikely to see her again, certainly if I have anything to do with it.'

'Ah, but you don't have anything to do with it,' Chrissie quietly pointed out. Then, taking a breath, she continued, 'Look, there's something you need to know.'

Vanessa's eyes sharpened with a new anxiety, and almost as if her knees could no longer support her she sank again into a chair. 'What? What do I need to know?'

'I've decided to move to Windermere, if not necessarily permanently, at least for the foreseeable future.'

All colour drained from her mother's face before flooding back to a dull crimson. '*I will not allow it!*'

Chrissie very gently took her hand. 'Mum, do I have to remind you again that I'm a big girl now. I need a fresh start, somewhere far away from my grief and memories of the war, as well as Peter and the way he's trying to take control of my life in his quiet, unobtrusive way.'

'He loves you, and wants only the best for you.'

'I'm not so sure.'

'I'd be the last person to advocate marriage, but Peter has been a good friend to you and at least deserves your appreciation and friendship in return.'

'I do value his being there when I most needed a friend, but it's time to move on. The fact is, I've taken on a shop, only a small one, but where I intend to sell second-hand books and cards. It will be fun and give me the independence I crave.'

Face tight with anger, Vanessa said, 'You could do that in London. Enjoy this so-called freedom and independence you crave, here, where you belong.'

'I'm sorry, but I've made up my mind. I've also spoken to Mrs Lawson from the flat below. She's happy to step in and help with the cleaning, meals and suchlike. And I will, of course, continue to help out with your living costs. Once the business gets going, anyway,' Chrissie added, still hoping her mother might rouse herself and take control of her own life again.

'And what about poor Peter?'

'I do wish you wouldn't refer to him in that way. I've told him countless times it's over between us, that we were never anything more than good friends. Unfortunately, he doesn't listen. I believe it will be better for us both if I go. His persistence is turning into something very like harassment. I do hope you didn't tell him where I was staying.'

'Of course not. I may have mentioned you'd gone north, for a holiday, but I didn't say where. I have no more wish than you for him to go poking his nose into our private affairs.'

'If for different reasons,' Chrissie shrewdly remarked. At which point her mother took out a half-bottle of gin from the cocktail cabinet and went off to bed.

Vanessa did not appear for breakfast, which was no surprise considering the vast amount of alcohol she'd drunk the night before. Chrissie made a start on her packing, sorting through some old books she might be able to sell. When Vanessa finally did appear, she absolutely refused to talk about the proposed move.

Later that afternoon, as Chrissie was carrying a pile of books to the hall, where she was stacking stuff ready to be transported to her new home, she heard her mother speaking to someone on the phone. Presumably a woman friend, but there was something in Vanessa's tone of voice which clearly indicated distress. Chrissie paused, and, nervous of bounding unannounced into the middle of a private conversation, stepped back to hide behind the dining room door.

'What am I to do? I'm at my wits' end, she simply will not listen.' There was a pause, presumably as the person on the other end of the line offered sympathetic advice. 'No, I've tried that, I've tried everything, but she is quite obdurate.'

Another long pause, in which Chrissie began to wish she'd either made her presence clear from the start, or quickly retreated to her own room. Or else vanish through a crack in the floor. Now she was terrified of moving a muscle in case one of the books should tumble off the stack in her arms and reveal her as an eavesdropper.

Her mother was talking again, her normally well-modulated tones tight and high-pitched. 'The terrible thing is that it's partly my fault. I insisted she went incognito, and now, having kept her identity secret for so long, Ma will have fifty fits if she reveals it now.'

A lengthier pause this time, one in which Chrissie miserably imagined the caller on the other end filling Vanessa's ready ear with other possible dour consequences when she revealed this wicked deception.

'Oh, she's already made it very clear that her decision to move has nothing whatsoever to do with me. None of my business, evidently. I really don't know what else I can say to dissuade her. She has no idea what she is meddling in, or what the consequences might be. I don't know how I shall cope if she goes through with this.'

And to Chrissie's complete and utter horror, her cool sophisticated mother fell to weeping. She heard her say, 'I have to see you. It's been too long. You must come, I need you.'

Instantly swamped with guilt, Chrissie longed to dash in and beg forgiveness for her thoughtlessness, for pushing the beautiful but always vulnerable Vanessa into something which obviously caused her immense distress. Instead, she slunk back to her own room, and softly closed the door behind her. Giving in to emotional blackmail had always got her into even deeper water in the past.

After a largely sleepless night worrying over the phone call she'd overheard, and filled with guilt over abandoning her mother, Chrissie decided it was time to put forward her suggestion. She'd been careful up to now not to rush her, but waving her toast about in a flush of enthusiasm, as if the notion had just occurred to her, she cried, 'Hey, I've got a brilliant idea. Why don't you come back to the Lakes with me and stay for a while in the flat? You could help make it presentable. It could be fun splashing paint on, sewing curtains and cushions, buying bits and bobs for it.'

'Chrissie, it's very sweet of you to invite me to do your sewing for you, but your little ploy won't work.'

'Damn, didn't think you'd see through it quite so quickly. You know how hopeless I am with a needle and thread. Anyway, why wouldn't it work? It would at least give you the opportunity to see Georgia again. The pair of you could start to heal the breach, talk to each other like civilised human beings.'

Vanessa was shaking her head in steadfast denial. 'What a very cosy view of the world you do have. She would absolutely refuse to see me.'

'How do you know? Time may have mellowed her. She might be experiencing regret for mistakes long past.'

Her mother gave a bitter little laugh. 'I very much doubt it. While it's always been clear to everyone that she is the one responsible for this split in the family, she blames me entirely, insists I stormed off in a huff or some fit of adolescent rebellion, even though I was almost twenty-one at the time. It's a moot point who is the victim here. My mother is a difficult woman, obstinate and unyielding, stern in her views, and with a strong sense of duty to family.'

'And what is so wrong with that? It doesn't mean you can't forgive and forget, put the past behind you and make a fresh start, as I am doing. Going round in circles arguing about who was to blame, or who was the real victim, is pointless, isn't it?'

Vanessa began to noisily clear the table, rattling cups and saucers as she almost tossed them into the sink. 'Sometimes what happened in the past never does quite go away, and is best forgotten. You'll learn that as you get older.'

Hadn't Georgia said something very similar? But Chrissie was fast losing patience. 'Don't patronise me, Mum. I'm not a child. I know about pain and suffering, remember?'

'You know nothing!'

They washed up in a strained silence, then concentrated on the packing while tempers cooled. Chrissie was struggling to hide her irritation by trying to decide which were the most sensible items of clothing to take with her in her new life, and which she should discard. They couldn't even seem to agree on that. 'It's cold in the Lakes,' Vanessa tartly reminded her, 'you'll need all your warm woollies, waterproofs, boots and wellingtons, not those silly shoes.'

'You used to wear silly shoes, I seem to recall.'

'I was young then.'

'I'm young now. I might go to a dinner dance where silly shoes are essential.'

'How could you without a man?'

'I might find a man.' Might already have found one, the thought came, unbidden.

Her mother's expression was scathing. 'Far too soon for such nonsense.'

Chrissie thought of her watery drenching following the romantic smooch with Ben, and said no more. Perhaps mothers did sometimes know best.

The situation, Chrissie thought, was untenable. If she told her grandmother who she really was, then Vanessa would fall to pieces, was already doing so, bit by bit. Yet if she didn't own up to this deception, what would Georgia think of her once the truth came out, as it surely must in the end? Oh, what a muddle!

Her grandmother had hinted at some nostalgic regrets

over the past. Surely her mother must have some too. Chrissie decided to have one more attempt to winkle a little more out of her before she left.

On her last day, as Vanessa helped Chrissie to choose which pieces of furniture she might take with her for the flat over the shop, she stubbornly returned to her argument. 'So why are you so against visiting the Lakes, even if you have no wish to actually move there permanently? Why will you make no attempt to patch up this quarrel and make friends with your own mother, who is now, I suspect, quite a lonely old woman?'

Vanessa's lips momentarily tightened. 'You know very well, Chrissie. I've told you a hundred times. She practically threw me out just because I fell in love with your father.'

'Perhaps she thought you were too young, as you did with me, I seem to remember.'

'It wasn't the same. I was older than you for one thing, almost twenty-one, and there wasn't a war on.'

'The war was just ending when I married Tom. I thought we were safe.' There was a bitter sadness in her voice and Vanessa gave her a quick hug.

'I'm sorry, darling, but you know what I mean.'

Chrissie wasn't sure that she did, but inwardly resolved to keep the discussion light, choosing her next words with care. 'OK, fair enough, but I have the distinct impression there's much more to this matter than you're actually telling me. You've never explained, for instance, how you two lovebirds met. Was it at the house, or by the lake? You said something on the telephone about my father coming to see Georgia. Why was that, do you know?'

'I told you, it was no concern of mine. Anyway, I don't remember.'

Chrissie let out an exasperated sigh. 'I can always tell when you lie, Mum, or at least prevaricate. If it was love at first sight you must surely remember where the two of you met. Come on, where did you first clap eyes on this handsome man of your dreams?'

'Oh, Chrissie, what does it matter now?' Vanessa cried, folding a pair of woollen socks and tossing them into the suitcase.

'I'm just interested, that's all. I asked my grandmother the same question and she told me a most romantic and adventurous tale. It was absolutely fascinating, involving kidnap, opium dens, and yes, love at first sight, a love that was very much frowned upon by her parents. You have more in common than you might imagine.'

Vanessa's eyes darkened and she snorted disdainfully. 'She once told me all that romantic nonsense. I didn't believe a word of it.'

Chrissie was instantly alert. 'Hey, I thought you said you knew nothing about her, not even where she was born.'

A flush stained Vanessa's cheeks. 'I might have exaggerated somewhat. I know some basic details. But I think she makes these stories up simply to divert people so that she doesn't have to tell the truth, whatever that is.'

'It sounded real enough to me. Very detailed, in fact. I'm waiting, with bated breath, to hear the end of that particular story, of how she was rescued from an arranged marriage.'

Vanessa looked at her askance. 'Arranged marriage? Don't be ridiculous! You mustn't believe half what she tells you. It's all a fiction. Pure fantasy. Georgia has never been open and honest in her entire life, so why should she start now, with you?'

Chrissie wondered if perhaps her mother was experiencing some jealousy over the fact Georgia had confided so readily in her, a supposed stranger, yet refused to talk to her own daughter. If so, then she felt some sympathy for her. She decided to capitalise on the point. 'So if mothers and daughters are supposed to be open and honest with each other, and share their thoughts and experiences, tell me yours. I repeat, when and how did you meet the gorgeous Aaran?'

Vanessa gave a sad little grimace of resignation. 'I'll make us some coffee.'

They sat on the rug by the gas fire that Vanessa had lit against the chill of a damp autumn day, a casserole gently simmering in the oven, Chrissie saying nothing as she cradled the comforting warmth of the coffee mug in her hand, patiently waiting for her mother to speak. For some long moments Vanessa quietly sipped her coffee as she stared into the popping blue flames, then suddenly began to talk. 'We met at the house. It was the very first occasion I recall my mother ever fainting. I heard some commotion in the hall and came running downstairs to find Mrs Gorran and several maids all in a flap administering sal volatile and little slaps to her face. Ma was lying prostrate, quite out for the count.

'To my shame, I was more interested in the gorgeous

male hovering at the door. He was tall with dark curly hair, pale complexion and eyes that seemed to look right to the heart of me. Oh, and he was incredibly handsome. I was struck dumb, utterly captivated from that moment on.

'Ma quickly recovered, but it was clear that whatever news he'd brought must have been bad for her to faint like that. She's not normally the delicate type. Later, she took him to her study and I compounded my shameful behaviour by listening at the keyhole. Not that I could hear very much as mostly they kept their voices low-pitched.'

'"How dare you come here making outrageous demands and accusations?" Ma cried at one point, her voice raised to anger. "This letter sounds shockingly like blackmail to me."'

'Blackmail?' Chrissie interrupted. 'That's rather melodramatic, isn't it?'

'My mother is prone to melodrama. I only repeat what I heard.'

'What was this letter? What else did you hear?'

'Not much, as I say, their voices would drop to a hissing whisper, which was most frustrating.'

Chrissie sipped her coffee. 'Did you discover later what the argument was about? When you and Dad got together, I mean.'

'Money. Isn't it always?' Vanessa shrugged. 'Aaran had come to plead the cause of his poor distressed mother, who was living in penury, apparently. I assumed the two women were once friends in their youth. On that first visit I did hear Aaran say that his mother had asked him to remind Georgia of a promise they'd each made years before. Even then, before I knew him, my heart went out to this young man, for I guessed he would have little hope of success as my mother considered it embarrassing, almost shaming, to discuss money. Her answer to his impertinence confirmed my suspicion. I've never forgotten it.

'She said, "Promises sometimes seem perfectly simple and straightforward when people first make them, but while I have certainly done my utmost to keep mine, I do wonder if your mother will continue to honour me with the same consideration."'

Chrissie was intrigued. 'So what was this promise? Or rather two promises. It sounds as if they each made one. Did you ever find out?'

Vanessa shook her head. 'Not then, nor since. I heard Aaran ask in what way his mother had not kept her word, but of course Georgia refused to explain. And Ma always avoided difficult questions about her past. Obstinate old fool that she is. Some years later, when his mother fell ill, Aaran felt it was time to go back, to be by her side in her last days.'

'So you went to San Francisco and met her?'

Vanessa nodded. 'Oh yes, I met her all right, and she was charming. My mother-in-law welcomed me with open arms, wanted us to stay in Frisco, with her. She adored you and wanted the next child, a son naturally, to be born in the States.' Vanessa shrugged off her failure to conceive again with a philosophical smile.

'I don't remember any of that.'

'You were very young.'

'How long did you stay?'

'Not long, six months maybe, until she died.' A shadow crossed Vanessa's face at this point in the story. 'It was on her deathbed that she revealed the lies my mother had told. Her terrible secret.'

Riveted by this revelation, Chrissie quietly asked, 'What lies? What terrible secret?' Chrissie waited, itching to hear more, but nervous of pressing too hard. Vanessa seemed to have drifted off into some private world, back in San Francisco all those years ago.

At last she looked up, her eyes oddly blank. 'That was in 1932.'

'About the time we stopped visiting the Lakes, and you and Daddy started having those big rows?'

'About then, yes.'

Again a long silence and Chrissie tried a different tack. 'Did you challenge your mother with what you'd learnt?'

Vanessa gave a bitter little laugh. 'Oh, yes, I challenged her all right. Not that she welcomed my questions or was prepared to answer them in any satisfactory manner. She denied everything, of course, but then she'd be bound to. Why had I ever imagined it would be otherwise? Yet she offered no convincing explanation, and had already accused my husband of being some sort of con man, of only wanting to marry me for my money. Aaran refused to come with me on that occasion. She never saw him again after that visit to America. Once I'd learnt just how completely ruthless she truly was, I knew there was no hope for us ever to be friends.'

'And you never saw your mother again?'

'Never. The damage had been done. I could never forgive her, not after learning what she'd done.'

'And what had she done exactly?' Chrissie again asked the question she most needed answering as quietly and unobtrusively as possible, but somehow it did not surprise her when Vanessa set down her cup with a sharp click, and got to her feet. 'I'm sure that casserole must be ready by now. Let's eat.'

So the story was left frustratingly unfinished, and no amount of probing on Chrissie's part could squeeze any more information out of her.

As Chrissie prepared to leave the next morning, mother and daughter shared a warm hug, both anxious to part on good terms. Chrissie was quick to offer what reassurance she could. 'I won't say anything to Georgia yet, if that's what you prefer. I'll keep quiet about who I really am until you've had time to consider how we might set about healing this row. I do see that it might be more difficult than I at first anticipated, even if I don't fully understand why.'

As she saw relief light up her mother's eyes, Chrissie's heart clenched with pity. She'd hardly slept a wink, worrying about this whole can of worms she'd opened. 'I do love you, Mum, and the last thing I want is for this crusade to cause you any further anguish. There've been quite enough tears spilt already. I'll keep quiet, for now, if you agree to keep off the gin for good this time. Will you try?'

Vanessa gave her a rueful smile. 'I'll do my best.'

'Good girl, that's a deal, then.'

Then she climbed into the taxi that was to take her to the station. Chrissie only had with her a small suitcase, the rest of her belongings to be sent on later. But there was no promise of a forthcoming visit from Vanessa.

Chapter Fifteen

The Lakes

Despite her mother's obstinacy in insisting she didn't reveal the truth about who she really was, Chrissie felt she'd learnt a great deal of new information which was both exciting and intriguing. But these discussions also inspired a whole new raft of questions. It appeared Aaran had come to Rosegill Hall asking for money and Georgia had refused to help his mother, an old friend, despite having previously promised to do so. Had the other girl made a similar promise? If so, what had caused this distrust to spring up between them, and in what way was it connected with the family feud?

And what was this secret best left untold?

This entire campaign, if you could call it that, had been started in order to heal a family breach. But far from mending the fractured relationship, the mystery seemed to be deepening. One which could well be difficult to solve, and didn't she have enough to contend with right now?

Settling into the flat, Chrissie discovered, was going to take all her energy, and far more work than she'd appreciated. It really was in a dreadful state. Every room would need to have the wallpaper stripped, the walls coated in size and repapered. And since money was tight, it was a job she would largely have to do herself. Chrissie told herself she was a capable, practical person, and if she was careful with her savings it didn't matter if it took all winter. Which would also give her plenty of time to source and buy stock before the spring. Thankfully, the busy holiday season was almost over, and Georgia had agreed she could stay on at the loft as long as she wished.

Even so, Chrissie was feeling slightly overwhelmed by the whole enterprise, wondering what she'd let herself in for.

She was thrilled to be back in Windermere, of course, and there was surely no better place to be than the Lakes in September. Clear sunny days, children picking blackberries, the stags clashing their antlers in their challenge to attract available females. Best of all were the glowing colours of the woodlands: saffron, crimson and gold. Quite breathtaking.

And judging by the proliferation of notices in the post office and corner shop, there was much to look forward to: the excitement of the local Sheepdog Trials, a Flower Show, Best Puppy Competition, Cumberland wrestling, and the Women's Institute famous cake contest. So many events Chrissie thought it was as if everyone wished to prove that they'd finally put austerity and the travails of war behind them, even though they still had to queue, and rationing remained very much in place.

But there was a lot to plan, a great deal to worry about.

A few days after her return, as Chrissie was walking around Cockshott Point, filling her lungs with clean air as sweet and crisp as wine, she rounded a bend by an ancient ash tree and Ben came strolling along the path towards her.

And suddenly all was right with the world.

The two of them stood transfixed for a long moment, smiling shyly at each other. 'I can't believe you're actually here,' he said. 'I was quite convinced you'd never come back.'

'I did say that I would.'

'But you might easily have changed your mind, and the way I behaved – not telling you I had a daughter – well, it wouldn't have surprised me if you'd decided to stay in London after all.' Hands in pockets, Ben shuffled his feet, glaring furiously down at his own boots, as if they were the ones at fault.

Chrissie gave a soft chuckle. 'How is Karen?'

His head jerked up and Ben let out a small sigh of exasperation. 'As impossible as ever, and not in the least bit remorseful. That's kids for you.'

'And what about her mother? Has she moved back, as threatened?'

A flush crept up his neck. 'I assure you, Chrissie, Sal and I are history.'

'That's not what I asked.'

'All right, yes, she's back in Windermere, but not with me. We're no longer a couple, no matter how much Karen might like us to be. She's staying with a friend. We have the decree nisi. It's over.'

Chrissie wasn't entirely sure she could believe that. She wanted to, very badly, but if a couple had been together long enough to produce a nine-year-old daughter, could it ever be over between them? Karen obviously thought there was still hope, had perhaps persuaded her mother to return. A physical presence in the town was surely much more difficult for him to ignore. She decided to err on the side of caution and maintain a cool distance. 'Young daughters certainly know how to apply the thumbscrews on their father to get what they want.'

Had she? Chrissie remembered climbing up on to her daddy's knee, kissing his rough chin and pleading for an ice cream or some other treat. She'd thought she was the apple of his eye, his adored child. But that hadn't stopped him from walking away.

'Thumbscrews won't work in my case. Sal is only here on a short visit, and I fully intend to avoid her like the plague.'

Chrissie's tone remained steadfastly chilly. 'Easier said than done. It's a small town. Must be hard to miss folk trekking up and down Crag Brow. Or you might spot her feeding the ducks or walking by the lake.'

He gave her his winning grin. 'I don't go in much for duck feeding. Anyway, I've been too busy to get out and about much. Got a lot of work on at present.'

'I'm pleased to hear it, and I'm sure your mother will

keep me informed of what's going on.' Despite her best efforts, her mouth twitched.

'I dare say she will,' he dryly remarked. 'Mam has taken quite a shine to you, but then so has her son.'

A silence fell, as if some agreement had been reached, an acknowledgement of difficulties but a refusal to be cowed by them. They were by now sitting on a fallen beech tree, Ben looking quite relaxed, his hands hanging loose between spread knees. Studying him from beneath her lashes, Chrissie couldn't help noticing how a whorl of fuzzy hair grew along the backs of them. His arms were strong and muscled, the sleeves rolled up, a white line of an old scar just above one wrist. Nor could she fail to take in the breadth of his shoulders, or note how the width of his chest tapered to narrow hips, and strong thighs. He was, without doubt, a fine-looking man.

Deliberately she turned her attention to the view, to passengers alighting from the ferry, perhaps to enjoy the long walk through the woods over to Claife Heights or Esthwaite Water.

Following the direction of her gaze, Ben gave a vague wave of a hand. 'Near Sawrey, over there, is where Beatrix Potter lived, or Mrs Heelis as she was known locally, at Hill Top. She bequeathed the house to the National Trust after she died a few years back, plus various farms and a great deal of the land around here, so that everyone can continue to enjoy it in perpetuity.'

'How wonderful. I'm glad she did, as it is so beautiful,' Chrissie softly agreed. 'I could stay here for ever and never grow tired of looking at this view.'

He looked at her. 'I hope you will, stay here for ever, I mean. It would be good for you. Good for me too.'

Ben Gorran seemed to be a gentle man, caring and considerate, appreciative of her vulnerability in only just coming to terms with her grief, and clearly a caring father. But there was a strength in him too, both physically and in the promise of passion she'd tasted in that single stunning kiss. But then they'd both been upset by events that night, and it was certainly an exciting way to end a row. Now he appeared to be his normal, courteous, chivalrous self, perhaps waiting for her to give him permission to let loose that passion again. She wondered how it would feel if she did.

Very softly, she said, 'You must understand that I have no wish to start a relationship or romance, whatever you choose to call this thing that is growing between us – not with a man on the rebound.'

He turned to her then, all eager reassurance. 'That's not how it is at all. You must believe that. You must know how I feel about you, Chrissie.'

She looked at him, at the genuine sincerity in his eyes, and felt her insides melt with affection. He was a fine man, a good man. Why would she not trust him? Maybe she had these doubts because she was too used to Peter pestering her and attempting to take over her life. On a sudden impulse she decided to put the ex-wife from her mind and take Ben at his word. She would believe him when he said it was over between them. At least she could offer him friendship. No more than that. For now. Pushing back her hair, she rewarded his patience with a smile, warmer this time. 'Er, this workload you've got on at the moment, does that preclude you from taking on any more jobs?'

He was instantly alert. 'Why, do you want something doing?'

'I need some fitted cupboards in the kitchen area of the flat, and bookshelves putting up in the shop.'

'I'm sure I could manage that,' he said, a grin stretching from ear to ear. He glanced at his watch. 'I have to pick Karen up from school shortly, but I could come and measure up once I've done that, if you like.'

'OK, thanks. I'd appreciate that.'

They walked back together, chatting easily, Chrissie answering a few polite enquiries about London – the packing of her belongings which were to follow when she'd organised a room in which to store them. She was curious to know what he would think of the shop, and the flat above.

'I'll be ten minutes,' he promised her. 'I just have to drive up the hill and back.'

It took him thirty, but the delay didn't trouble Chrissie one bit. The extra time allowed her to freshen her lipstick and tidy her hair, put the kettle on for coffee, although there was nothing she could do to improve the look of the place.

'It's very small,' Chrissie warned, as she let him in, 'but then I intend to stock it only with words. Come to think of it, that's what I shall call it. "Words".'

He nodded. 'I like that.'

'Indeed.' Then over his shoulder her gaze locked with

Karen's. The girl had been left sitting in Ben's van parked at the door and was glaring right at her. 'Oh, do bring your daughter in. Maybe I've got some lemonade somewhere.'

'No, she's fine,' he said, pulling out a notebook and a stub of pencil. 'She's used to hanging around waiting for me when I'm working. She'll do her homework, or something. Now, what is it you want, exactly?'

Chrissie frowned slightly, but said no more, just left the door ajar so it didn't look as if she were closing it in the girl's face. She began to outline where she wanted shelves fitting, along each wall to just above eye level, leaving space for a table in the centre which she could use both as a counter and sales area for large books.

Ben at once pulled out a roll of tape and started to measure up. His reaction to the little shop was all she could have hoped for, warm with approval. 'I can see it has great potential, and an excellent position being so close to the main street. Bowness is very popular with tourists. I'm sure you can make it into a great little shop. What's the flat like?'

She gave a wry smile. 'Needs work.'

'I'm your man.' And as he clumped up the stairs behind her in his big boots, a part of her rather wished that he was.

Maintaining a cool distance she said, 'There's just the one room on this floor which I intend to use as a living room with kitchen area at the back, furthest from the windows overlooking the street.'

'Complete with beams and a sloping floor, I see.'

'I like a bit of character to a place,' she agreed, smiling.

'So do I. Not much into the smart modern look myself.' His gaze was teasing and all-encompassing, and Chrissie wondered if he was also referring to her check shirt and baggy blue coveralls which she'd had for years. Oh dear, she needed only a turban to reinforce the Rosie the Riveter look.

As Chrissie explained what she wanted he quickly sketched a plan of the cupboards he could build for her. She held the tape measure while Ben added measurements to the drawing, listened carefully to his advice and suggestions, agreeing with some but rejecting others, which didn't seem to trouble him. He was easy to talk to, seemed to quickly pick up on what she had in mind, and time sped by as they became engrossed in the task in hand.

'How are you with wardrobes?' she asked at length, when the kitchen plan was fully mapped out. 'I don't have anywhere to store my clothes and wondered if you could fit in a cupboard-cum-wardrobe in the bedroom. Can I show you?'

'Lead the way.'

The main bedroom on the second floor was empty save for a small Victorian iron fireplace, somewhat rusty but nothing a good scrub and coat of black enamel paint couldn't put right. Between this and the window was a gap. 'I wondered if you could put doors on this alcove to form a wardrobe? The floor slopes even more here – would that present difficulties?'

'Nope, I can take the slope into account as I make the toeboard.' Pulling out his notebook again Ben licked the pencil, but as he started to draw his usual quick plan, the lead broke and the pencil flew from his hand. For some reason they both dived for it in the same instant; Chrissie caught her toe in a large crack in the floorboards, and in trying to save her, Ben skidded on the slope which suddenly seemed as treacherous as a ski run. They both fell in a tangled heap of arms and legs, Ben sprawled on top of her, knocking all the breath from her body. They laughed, a mixture of embarrassment and amusement. But then, perhaps remembering an earlier encounter at equally close quarters, the laughter quickly faded, and when his mouth came down on to hers Chrissie made no protest whatsoever.

'I thought this would be what you two would be up to, and not carpentry at all. Just wait till I tell Mum. She's already got the dinner on, did you know that, Dad?'

Ben groaned as he quickly leapt to his feet. Chrissie just wanted the sloping floorboards to open up and swallow her.

'It's not how it sounds. Sal offered to cook me a meal tonight, that's all.'

'Something you failed to mention when we were talking earlier.'

'I thought you might jump to the wrong conclusion.'

'Now I wonder why I might do that?' Chrissie dryly commented.

They were standing at the front door, the girl was back in the van, still sulking, and Chrissie was keeping her eyes anywhere but on that bleak condemning gaze. Ben didn't seem to notice, far too anxious to prove his own innocence.

'You have to believe me, Chrissie. We'd agreed Karen should stay with me so as not to interrupt her education, but there have been a few problems. She got terrible marks in her end-of-term exams back in July, and Sal had an appointment to speak to her teacher today. We share a child, not a future. She has her life, I have mine.'

'Karen doesn't seem to agree with you.'

Ben sighed. 'I know, but getting that fact across to the poor kid without upsetting her still further is the hard part. Sal is as bothered by her reaction as I am. She only came back to please Karen, and to sort out this school problem. Unfortunately, having her mum back in town seems to have given the child fresh hope, the opposite of what we intended. I really didn't think she'd take our split this badly. I thought she'd be relieved that at least the rows had stopped.'

Chrissie said, 'Maybe she thinks that's a good sign, the fact you've stopped arguing.'

'Hell, I never thought of that.' He ran a distracted hand through tousled fair hair, and Chrissie glanced up at his face, her heart clenching at the woeful expression she saw written there.

'Look, why don't we take things more slowly, give Karen time to get used to the idea of me being around. Anyway, I need to concentrate on getting this place in order. I need those shelves.'

'And all *I* need to do is to stop thinking about you, stop dreaming about you, and somehow keep my hands in my pockets whenever I'm near you. Not as easy as it sounds.'

He looked so forlorn she actually laughed out loud. Eyes

glowing with sympathy and amusement in equal measure, she said, 'Did you get the necessary measurements for the wardrobe doors?'

He shook his head. 'Nope. In the circumstances maybe I'd best pop back for those tomorrow, while Karen's in school. I'll also drop off some wood and stuff, ready to start work in the next week or two, hopefully.'

Keenly aware of the desire that still hummed between them, Chrissie put a hand on his arm. 'Don't be too hard on the kid. We were rather a long time and she must have got terribly bored with waiting. You should have brought her in with you, as I suggested.'

'Now that *would* have been boring.'

'Stop it. She's a child, worried about her dad. She feels very much pig in the middle, poor girl, and still longing for a fairy-tale ending. I rather like the way she sticks up for her mum, *and* challenges you. Good on her, that's what I say. Just try to point out, if you can, that you and Sal were over long before I put in an appearance. I refuse to be classed as the wicked Other Woman.'

'I'll do that. Hey, why don't you join us for the meal? Give Karen the chance to really get to know you and see you as a part of my life.'

This was too much, too quickly, Chrissie thought, experiencing a sudden panic. She liked Ben a lot, but was she ready for yet more emotional turmoil? 'Some other time, OK? It might be a bit awkward with Sally around.'

'Sal wouldn't mind.'

'Maybe, but Karen obviously does. Let's leave it for a bit, shall we?'

'Just remember that I want you in my life, Chrissie, no matter what my grumpy daughter says.' And there was not a scrap of teasing in his voice now, only tenderness and need.

The door of the van opened and a sharp little voice called, 'Dad, are you coming, or what? I'm bored sick with sitting here.'

'OK, love,' he called, yet still he lingered. 'When can I see you again, tomorrow perhaps?'

'Maybe next week would be better, after what happened just now.'

His face lit up. 'Great, I'll speak with Karen about that meal, then we'll fix a date.'

'Go!'

When at last he climbed into the van and drove away, Chrissie locked the shop door and leant against it with a sigh. 'Do you have the first idea what you've let yourself in for, girl?' she asked herself, and when she got no answer, plodded back upstairs to continue with her decorating.

A few days later, Chrissie was invited into the conservatory at Rosegill Hall as Georgia had sorted out a few books for her. 'There are some old classics here: *Anna Karenina*, *War and Peace*, various Dickens and Austen novels, all of which I seem to have collected spare copies of over the years. And quite a few Agatha Christie and Dornford Yates books which I shall never read again.'

'Perfect.'

'There's a pile of old Pears' encyclopaedias and year books here too. Are they any good?'

'Everything is useful to get me started,' Chrissie agreed, enthusiastically leafing through the books her grandmother had set out on the wrought-iron table. 'This is very generous of you.'

'Nonsense, my bookshelves were in serious need of a good clear-out, and it's even more generous of you to help with the gardening.'

'I quite enjoy weeding, and you've been so kind in agreeing to let me stay on a bit longer. Oh, look, the *Just So Stories*, and the *Arabian Nights*, I love those old tales. Several books about the four Georges, and seventeenth-century theatre. I must read those. And *Walking in the Lake District* by Symonds. How wonderful.'

Georgina was smiling broadly as she watched Chrissie's enthusiasm mount. 'I probably have more books by local worthies, and numerous old maps. I'll look some out for you.'

'Have you thought of writing a book yourself? Your memories of San Francisco, for instance.' Chrissie enquired, keeping her tone deliberately casual.

'Goodness, I'm no writer, nor have I anything of interest to say.'

'Now that's where you're wrong, I love to hear your stories, and I'm sure others would too. Your family, for instance.' How Chrissie longed, in that moment, to confess that she was one of their number. But her visit home had not gained her the permission she needed to put this dreadful muddle right. 'You really should write them down. Perhaps I could help with that too. Then you'd have something to pass on to your family. We'd reached the part where your mother had discovered you'd been seeing Ellis secretly, and was determined to arrange a more suitable marriage for you. Did you manage to get out of it?'

Georgia sank into a chair, her hands still clutching a book, but her mind now elsewhere, already centred on some other, more distant, concerns. 'It was well-nigh impossible to defy my mother, once she'd set her sights on a course of action. And on this occasion Papa was not on my side either. No one was, not even dearest Prue.'

Chapter Sixteen

San Francisco

I couldn't believe how quickly my life had changed. One day I'd been happily falling in love with my handsome sailor, promising to stay true to him for ever, the next I was about to walk down the aisle with a man I loathed.

'I won't do it! Why would I, when I don't even like Drew Kemp, let alone love him?' Mama and I were sitting in the carriage heading for the dressmakers, the road ahead jammed with broughams and hacks, cable cars straining uphill.

'I want the best for you, child, what is so wrong in that? Drew Kemp is a man of property and affairs. It is perfectly plain to me that any future with him will pan out far better than with some two-bit sailor.'

'How do you know that, Mama? I'm well aware this is a town for those who have struck it rich, for men who love to flaunt their wealth. It's also one full of speculators, gamblers, hoodlums, cheats and money-sharks. It's not an aspect of Frisco life I like, as there are far more important things in life than the size of the cheque a man can write.'

'Oh, for goodness' sake, come down out of your ivory tower, girl. At least Kemp has some sand in him and doesn't waste his time and energy working in a menial capacity in the belly of a ship, for heaven's sake.'

There was no talking to her, I could see that. Mama would never understand how I felt because our values were entirely different.

Prudence reached over to squeeze my hand. 'You should start to look on your fiancé in a more positive light, dearest. Drew Kemp is charming, handsome, witty, and cuts quite a dashing figure in society. You will never be short of pretty gowns to wear or social functions to attend.'

I looked at her in pity. 'Is that how you view life, Prue, as one long party?'

She flushed, this carefree sister of mine with her pearly cheeks and porcelain-like shoulders who all the men drooled over, looking uncharacteristically cross. 'I know you think me shallow and silly, but I would consider myself most fortunate were I in your shoes. What is so wrong in wanting to step out with a man of ideas, one with boundless faith in himself, and the fortune to go with it?'

'What indeed?' Mama echoed. 'Quite contrary to this sailor of yours. What could *he* offer? Does he even love you?'

'Yes, I think he does.' A recklessness born of desperation

must have come over me to admit such a thing. Maura, sitting opposite, cast me a warning look which I chose to ignore.

'You *think* he loves you? You don't sound too sure.'

'Of course I'm sure. Is it so wrong to fall in love at first sight?'

'Has he declared his love in so many words? Did he offer for your hand in marriage? Did he promise to stop his adventuring around the world and make a proper home for you? Did he ever suggest, for one second, that he would do the decent thing and make a respectable woman of you? Has he considered putting your needs before his own?'

I couldn't answer her. How could I? Certain as I was of Ellis's love for me, he had done none of these things. I couldn't even prove that one day he might well have got around to proposing, because in a miserable hollow in the pit of my stomach I rather feared he was very content with his life the way it was. Hadn't he been at pains to point out how he loved to see what was round the next bend, over the next hill? He'd given no hint that he was ready to abandon his wandering lifestyle and settle down to all that love and marriage entails. I saw, in that moment, that perhaps Mama may have a point. Was Ellis's love simply a summer romance, as fleeting as a butterfly that would light on a flower to enjoy its fragrance and then fly away?

'Well?' she queried, jolting me out of my melancholic reverie. 'Has he?'

As the carriage lurched forward I turned my face away and stared out the window, recalling the scent of opium and fear, sweet meadow flowers in the park, and the taste of his kisses. 'We have known each other but a few short weeks, during which time you refused to even receive him, Mama, so what is a young man to do in such a situation?'

She offered no answer to this challenge. 'Where is he now, this romantic hero of yours?'

I shifted in my seat with discomfort, falling once more into a gloomy silence. It was Maura who answered. 'Please, ma'am, Mr Cowper has gone back to sea for a while as his funds are running low.'

I closed my eyes so that I would not see the light of triumph in my mother's eyes.

'Exactly,' she said. 'Now we will hear no more of this foreign wastrel, is that clear? This morning you will be measured for your bridal gown. Prudence will be maid of honour, and when the time comes you will accept your new husband with good grace and offer proper gratitude to your dear papa for arranging this fortuitous marriage.'

The wedding was a mere four weeks away, to take place on the last Saturday in September, as decreed by Drew Kemp. When I complained about the unseemly haste, Mama simply cited examples of other young girls in a similar ruinous situation as myself who had not been so fortunate in finding a suitor in time. What their fate had been was apparently too dreadful to relate, but she maintained a close eye on my waistline despite my protests that I remained as untouched and virtuous as she could wish. But why would she believe in my innocence? It was enough that I had met this common sailor in private, without a chaperone, and allowed him to take liberties with my person.

Time rushed inexorably by and no ship sailed over the horizon, not the right one anyway. No dashing sailor came to save me, nor any letter from him saying that he missed me and wanted me for his wife. But then Ellis would never dare to write to my home address, knowing my parents would intercept any such correspondence, and if he'd left a message for me at the Seamen's Institute I never received it as I was banned from helping there ever again.

When not going about the business of preparing for this dreaded celebration, my days were largely spent confined to the house, mostly in my room, sulking or railing against my fate. Sometimes I was obliged, nay forced, to sit in the parlour and talk to my fiancé, or rather sit and listen while he told me what a very fine man he was, and how grateful I should be that he had even deigned to look my way, since I did not possess my sister's beauty.

'You should have chosen Prudence then, instead of me. It's not too late to change your mind. I'm quite sure she would not be unwilling. She constantly praises your charm and good looks.'

He laughed at that, was at pains to point out that a wife needed to be far more than a pretty face. 'She must be dutiful and reliable if she is to be good for my business, and for my image. And it goes without saying that she should provide me with the son I need to carry on the company after me. As the eldest daughter you were a much better bet.'

Self-centred, cold and unemotional, this man saw our union in terms of a business contract, as a useful alliance with my father, his biggest competitor. He loved himself far too much to spare a thought for anyone else.

I learnt how he was never shown proper love and affection by his own parents, his father being far too busy making his fortune to pay any attention to his only son, and his mother a fly-by-night female with a string of lovers to keep her amused in her husband's absence. Perhaps, I thought, this was the source of his low opinion of the female sex. Kemp the man was now more than content to take his revenge by spending his late father's money as fast as he could. Although he intended to add to it, he assured me, through any opportunity that presented itself. He would continue to prosper, he insisted, by his own efforts, with help from no one.

'Am I supposed to admire that in you,' I asked, 'or pity you for not having enjoyed a happy childhood? I feel more likely to pity myself.'

His dark cold eyes stared at me unblinking. 'You should appreciate how very fortunate you are that your own parents gave you a loving home and took such excellent care of you.'

I realised this was probably the case, despite their arranging my marriage in a manner that did not meet with my approval. Even as I continued to protest against the plan, Mama would alternate between stern lectures and impulsive scented embraces, promising me that all would be well and I would be happy, while Papa would gruffly inform me that he'd wrung out all the necessary reassurances for my care from my future husband. His choice of words – 'wrung out' – troubled me slightly, which was perhaps why I felt the urge to clarify my position now.

'And will you treat me with equal consideration?' I challenged him.

The thin lips twisted into that too-familiar cynical smirk. 'I am of the view that a person gains in life the consideration they deserve, do you not think so?'

I looked at the way his cold eyes glinted with pleasure at my obvious misery, and struggled to believe this could be a show of concern on his part, rather than some sort of subtly disguised threat. But I was determined not to let him bully me. 'In which case you too should take care. A wife only loves a husband who is kind to her.'

He laughed at this, as if at my naivety in making such a remark. 'A wife will learn to love where she is told, and do what is good for her, if she has any sense.'

Maybe I lacked that sense, or was not quite so obedient as my parents would have wished. I was certainly lacking in the required gratitude to my father, and in one last desperate bid for freedom I confronted him in his study to tell him so. 'How can you do this to me, Papa, your own beloved daughter? You know full well that I do not love this man. Do not say that love will come, in time, for I don't believe it. How can you be so heartless as to force this marriage upon me?'

He turned from me with an irritated *tck* sound in his throat, avoiding the plea in my gaze to stare out the window. 'You are young yet, and understand little of the complexities of life. Marriage is a partnership, the same as any other, and this one will bring you many benefits and advantages.'

'And utter and complete misery. You must see that I loathe the man, Papa. I cannot bear to be near him.'

His glare was firmly fixed upon our neighbours going about their business: the portly Mr Crocker trotting off to eat porterhouse steak and French fries washed down with champagne at the Palace Hotel, as he did every lunchtime; young Ted Foggerty rising late after yet another poker party attended by a certain breed of unaccompanied ladies. Papa stood, hands clasped behind him, his back as rigid as his code of morals, looking over his spectacles with marked disapproval upon the entire world. Then he focused that condemning glare upon me. I had never seen my father look so angry. 'Your problem is that your silly head is stuffed with romantic nonsense. Stop being so damned stubborn, Georgia, and give the fellow a chance.'

Mindful of Prue's warnings to tread carefully and not lose my own temper, I softened my voice to one of gentle femininity. I had heard both Mama and Prue adopt this tone when wishing to wheedle something out of him, and thought it worth a try for all I felt more like screaming and shouting at the stubborn old fool.

Resting a hand upon his arm, I looked adoringly up into his face. 'Dearest Papa, it is not that I don't wish to please you, because you know how I love and respect you. I simply wish you to treat my opinion with equal respect. You know how very sensible I am, how dutiful a daughter. Nevertheless, Mama has greatly exaggerated my friendship with Mr Cowper. Whilst it is true that we have fallen in love, and equally true that he still has his fortune to make, we have done nothing . . . untoward . . . nothing you could reproach me for. And certainly nothing that demands my being hastily shunted off into matrimony with a man I do not even like.'

'Enough!' he commanded, in that tone of voice I most dreaded, my feminine wiles having failed me yet again. 'I will hear no more of this.'

'But Papa—'

'I said, enough.' He wagged a furious finger in my face. 'Listen to me carefully, Georgina.' The use of my full name was always a bad sign. 'I am prepared to accept your innocence, but it makes no difference. You *will* marry this man. I had no choice but to accept his offer on your behalf.' The sternness in father's face suddenly softened, his temper vanishing almost as swiftly as it had come, and he gently patted my cheek. 'Do not fret, my dear, I have made certain you will be well treated. But you are growing up now, and must face the harsh realities of life. The truth is that we are not quite so well placed as you, or your dear mother, might imagine. My business is not exactly thriving, not as it once was. Drew Kemp has proved to be a far more formidable competitor than his father before him, and while I am not yet in debt, if I do not agree to this alliance then the company could well go up the flume.'

I was shocked. This was the last thing I'd expected to hear and I let out a gasp of horror. 'That surely cannot be true, Papa. We are well off, always have been. The house, the servants, Mama's dress allowance and jewels, they—'

He gave a sad little smile, his gaze again shifting, this time to some far distant place in his head. 'Ah yes, your mother's jewels. And you will appreciate how important, how precious, those jewels are to her. They were a legacy from her own mother, a countess no less, in old Europe, which she brought with her when she married me and we came to America. I will tell you in all honesty, Georgia, that in recent weeks I have come close to selling them, or at least taking them to the pawnshop.'

'Oh, Papa, no, that would have broken Mama's heart.'

'Indeed! Mine too, for I could not have borne to see her thus. But then Kemp offered me a way out, so there we have it.'

I gazed up at him in open horror. 'Are you saying that if I do not marry him, Drew Kemp will deliberately set out to ruin your business? And that you'll then have to sell Mama's jewels to save it?'

The sadness in his eyes was heart-rending to see. 'You put it somewhat bluntly, but that is about the nub of it. Kemp's way of dealing with the competition is to take it over or destroy it. He fully intends to be as rich as Croesus, to own and control everything himself. And even then, despite the sacrifice, selling the jewels may not have been enough. The house would have gone next, the carriage, everything. Kemp is a powerful man, with a great deal of influence in this town. He is not a man to cross.'

'So I am to be sacrificed instead?'

Papa winced, and turned away as if unable to witness the pain he had caused me. 'If I could find any other way . . .'

My fate, it appeared, was sealed.

It was a beautiful sunny day in the fall, the ships in the bay looking like toys set out on a sheet of blue, a cloudless sky above. Egrets and sandpipers paddled and pecked at tidbits in the mud, swallows swooped and dived, and somewhere a meadowlark sang. But my heart felt grey and leaden as Papa led me down the aisle in the church I had attended regularly from being a small child. My sister followed behind, preening herself in her new rose-sprigged gown, although I knew she ached for the chance to be the bride, and not simply a maid of honour.

My bridegroom, still little more than a stranger to me, stood waiting at the altar rail. He certainly cut a fine figure in his grey broadcloth suit, glossy dark hair and handsome looks, but my heart sank to my satin slippers as my father passed my hand to his. His grip was cold and somehow remote, as if he were oblivious to my presence. He did not even trouble to turn and glance at me in that moment, let alone offer a smile of encouragement or word of reassurance. I might just as easily have been a parcel, or a stray horse put into his hand, rather than the woman he was about to marry.

How had it come to this, I thought? Why had Ellis not returned? Where was he? Did he think of me, or even remember who I was?

It was only as I repeated the prescribed words spoken by the pastor that the full import of what was happening dawned upon me. 'Till death us do part,' I obediently intoned. Vows meant to last for life. Promises that were irrevocable.

Like it or not, I had, in very truth, become Drew Kemp's wife. There followed the usual rejoicing and congratulations that you find at weddings, in my case from giggling cousins and approving aunts. My bouquet was tossed and caught by my silly sister who claimed to be green with envy, and spent the next several minutes flirting with my husband to prove her point. Even Maura hovered about him like some adoring nymph. Wine flowed, the finest food specially ordered by Mama was served, but I could eat or drink none of it. There was dancing and music, but all I could think of as my new husband whirled me on to the dance floor was that these were not the right arms, this was not the right moment for marriage. This was not the man I loved.

What had I done? What had my father done? I looked into Papa's eyes and saw his shame.

Should I have fought him more, put more effort into my rebellion, forced my proud mother to sell her precious inheritance, even move out of her fine mansion? I could not ask such a terrible thing of her. It was unthinkable. I would much rather sacrifice my own happiness than hers. And where could I have turned for help? Aunts, uncles, cousins, my entire family thought Kemp something of a catch. Prue, and even my own maid, were equally enchanted, so there would have been no assistance forthcoming from that quarter had I recklessly decided to run off with my sailor.

Besides, my beloved Ellis was far away at sea, enjoying life on some far distant shore.

The truth of it was that I was young, barely eighteen, trained to be dutiful and in no position to disobey my father or devastate my mother. All I could do was cling to the reassurances offered by dearest Prue, that at least I would remain close to my family, that I would enjoy wealth and position in society, and have some sort of freedom.

And if my heart longed for romance, still ached for a certain young sailor, then I could only hope the pain of losing him would pass in time.

How wrong I was, on every count.

The first hint of reality came within hours, on my wedding night. My parents and sister drove home in their carriage, tired and content, while I went with my new husband to his house on Nob Hill. Maura came with me. We were shown into a lavishly appointed bedroom, all frills and furbelows in yellow and powder blue, a room that seemed entirely inappropriate for a single male. Had he decked it out purposely to please his new bride? Or had it once been his mother's boudoir, I wondered, where she had entertained her many lovers? Whatever its origin I was thankful to at last stop this pretence of revelling in new-found matrimonial joy. I sank on to the dressing stool with a sigh. My relief, however, was short-lived. Maura had barely begun to unlace, unbutton and unpin me, when Kemp burst in without even knocking. My maid was instantly dismissed, and I was alone with my new husband.

* * *

'Take them off,' he ordered, the moment the door had closed on her retreating figure.

I stared at him dumbstruck for some long seconds, looking about me in cold panic. No maid to help, not even a screen to hide behind. I had never taken off so much as a slipper in front of a man before, not even my beloved Ellis. Surely he couldn't seriously expect me to disrobe before him? As he lounged in a chair opposite, hooking one leg over an arm, he made it very clear that was exactly what he demanded. Even so . . .

'I-I beg your pardon?' I stammered.

'Your gown and underthings, take them off.'

'B-but I shall need Maura, and a degree of privacy. Pray allow me some respect.' I wanted to tell him that I was shy, and a virgin, but did not know how. He clearly thought my blushes highly amusing.

'Privacy, my dear, is not the privilege of married ladies. As my wife you will dance to my tune. Now remove your clothes this instant. If you do not, then I shall do it for you.'

There was no doubt in my mind that this was no idle threat. With trembling fingers I fumbled with buttons, pulled off my gloves, my shoes and stockings one by one, took off the circlet of rosebuds from my hair, my jewels and rings, everything I could think of whilst remaining fully clothed. He sat smiling, his eyes fixed on me throughout this pantomime, like some lascivious creature from a netherworld. Eventually, there were no more accessories to remove, nothing further I could do to delay the inevitable. Lifting my chin high, I made one last plea. 'A gentleman would withdraw and return when a lady was properly attired in her night things.'

'Ah, but I am not a gentleman, not in the sense that you mean. And there is nothing more diverting than watching a lady undress.'

I gaped at him. 'What a wicked thing to say! I assure you my parents would never have given their consent to this marriage had they known I would be so ill-treated.'

He laughed at that, as well he might. 'Your parents sold you to the highest bidder. They bought you position and status in society, a rich husband who would add to their own rapidly diminishing fortune through a most profitable business arrangement. You were merely a part of that deal, a bargaining chip at the casino table.'

I gave a little cry of distress but still I hesitated, my arms clamped about me, shielding my bosom as tears slid silently down my cheeks. I was filled with a cold fear, and a terrible sense of loathing. Mama had done her duty, so far as a lady of her gentility was able, in explaining the duties of the bedchamber to me. I'd thought I was not entirely ignorant on the subject, and I had welcomed and enjoyed the many kisses Ellis had given me.

But this was different to anything I had imagined. This man was making it very clear that he cared nothing for my feelings. He spoke of me as if I were a possession, an object he had purchased and could treat as he pleased.

Losing patience, he stepped forward, pushed my hands aside and stripped the gown from me. He swiftly unlaced my corset, a task Maura had not been allowed to do, and ripped it from me. Slipping my camisole from my shoulders, within seconds the garment was on the floor, followed by my petticoats and drawers, then he stood back for a long moment to examine every bare inch of me. I burnt with humiliation. To stand thus, naked as the day I was born, before this man was abominable, but he wasn't done with me yet.

Stretching out a hand he squeezed one breast. 'Hm, not exactly voluptuous, are you? Pity. Still, pert enough, I suppose, if rather small.'

I was utterly mortified.

Was this how a husband usually looked at his wife, as if she were a piece of merchandise he must scrutinise in every detail? I half prayed that since he'd found a flaw in me, he might agree to return me as unwanted goods. 'Turn around, let me see the rest of you.' He smoothed a hand over my rump, and my hopes were instantly dashed. 'That's better. Soft and round as a ripe peach.'

My heart almost stopped with fear, and I closed my eyes so that he would not see how they sparkled with tears. Was this the joy of the wedding night my mother had haltingly hinted at? Was this what I had dreamt of as a young innocent girl? Aware of my blush spreading to every exposed part of me, I must have let some plea or whimper escape my tightly pursed lips, for he chuckled.

'No nightgown yet, my lovely. There's business to be done.' And shoving me down on to the rose-pink satin quilt, he eased himself free of his trousers, parted my soft thighs and thrust into me. The shock of it, and the pain, was overwhelming. I felt I would surely split in two, his grunting, sweating body obscene as it pounded against mine. He made no attempt to kiss or fondle me, did not trouble to prepare me in any way to receive him, or allow me a moment to catch my breath.

I doubt the act itself took more than a few minutes, although it felt like hours, a lifetime in fact. I might have screamed from the pain had I not been all too aware of servants listening at doors, of Maura hovering nearby, and the certain knowledge that there was no one to come and rescue me.

I belonged entirely to Drew Kemp now, and, as he'd made very clear, he could do with me as he willed. If I did not comply, he would destroy my entire family. With a wisdom beyond my years I did not fight him. I bit my lip till it bled and wept silent tears of anguish for what might have been.

But had I had access to that barman's gun I'd once flourished with such crazed bravado, I would not have hesitated to use it.

Chapter Seventeen

The Lakes

It was a Friday and Chrissie was sitting on an orange box sipping her morning coffee when the doorbell rang. Her heart leapt, as it always did at the sound, knowing it would be Ben. He'd measured for the wardrobe, dropped off the timber, and already started work on the bookshelves in the shop. She glanced at her watch. Eleven-fifteen. He was late this morning, he usually started work by eight. She'd been coming earlier herself for the last week or two, wanting to get the work finished.

Chrissie gazed down at herself in rueful dismay. Trouble was, he always saw her looking her worst. Old overalls, hair in a turban, paint on her face, and stinking of turps.

'The way to a man's heart indeed.' The bell rang again, for much longer this time. 'OK, OK, hold your horses, I'm coming.'

Quickly wiping the worst of the paint from her hands,

which left her smelling even more strongly of turpentine, Chrissie ran down the stairs, worrying slightly about the lunch she'd been invited to share with Ben and his family on Sunday. She'd put it off as long as she could but would certainly look smart for that, and remember to be on her best behaviour with Karen around. She flung open the shop door, ready to share the joke at being caught looking a mess yet again, but her smile instantly died.

'What the—?' She couldn't quite believe her eyes.

'Ah, good, I got the right address, then. May I come in?'

'Peter!' Just a few weeks ago she'd quietly celebrated her freedom, believing she'd at last got the message through that it was all over between them. Now here he was turning up in her life yet again like the proverbial bad penny.

'Chrissie, darling, I've missed you so.' He leant over to kiss her but she managed to turn her face at the last moment, so that the kiss landed on her cheek instead.

She instinctively found herself comparing Peter's dry hard mouth to Ben's more generous one. The memory of Ben's kiss, so soft and warm, brought a sudden ache to her heart. But then Ben was more generous and caring in every way, while Peter seemed increasingly repressed and withdrawn. Even his brown hair was plastered down with Brylcreem, not a strand allowed to escape, and his eyes had a deadness in them. His narrow face with its close-set eyes and pointed chin rarely smiled, and it saddened her to see him looking even more mournful than usual. But she was also astonished she'd felt any sort of affection for this man, who already felt like a stranger to her.

'What on earth are you doing here?'

He scowled, not looking pleased by her lack of welcome. Chrissie could tell at once that he was in one of his black moods, the kind she'd come to dread. He was a man of inconsistencies, one minute all agreeable, affable and obliging, nothing too much trouble, the next as if the devil himself was sitting on his shoulders.

She made no move to let him in. 'How did you know where I was? I mean, how did you get this address? I only took this place over a few weeks ago and—' Now he did smile, in that patronising way he had as if she were a small child and life was far too complicated for her to understand. 'If you'll let me in, instead of keeping me freezing on your doorstep, I'll be happy to explain.'

With reluctance Chrissie pushed open the door and allowed him to follow her up the stairs to the flat, bracing herself for the inevitable put-down. She was not disappointed. The look of disdain on his face as he walked into the living room spoke volumes. Even Chrissie privately acknowledged the place was not looking its best, being empty save for paint pots and brushes, rolls of wallpaper, a decorating table and the orange box upon which reposed a half-eaten sandwich on a cracked plate.

'Good Lord, what on earth possessed you to take this place on? I've seen dog kennels more habitable – and bigger, for that matter.'

Chrissie couldn't help but compare his reaction to that of Ben's. How approving and optimistic Ben had been, at once seeing the potential in the little shop and flat above, despite its diminutive size. Peter saw only its deficiencies, which said so much about their respective characters. She put on her brightest voice. 'Actually, I rather like the place. Once I've done it up, I shall be very cosy here.'

'More likely suffer from claustrophobia.'

'Are you going to tell me why you're here?'

'Are *you* going to offer your neglected fiancé some refreshments?'

She felt again that combination of despair and furious exasperation at Peter's great talent for blithely ignoring everything she said to him. He seemed to do exactly as he pleased, making arbitrary decisions without reference to her. Not even asking first if it would be convenient for him to call. Come to think of it, when had he ever warned her of any decision he made? This notion she'd had that he would do whatever she wished or asked of him had all been a clever ploy on his part in order to control her without actually seeming to. She shuddered at the thought. He declined to explain the purpose of his visit until he'd downed two mugs of tea and eaten most of the biscuits out of the tin. With her patience fast running out, Chrissie tried again. 'So, are you going to explain how you found me?'

'It was surprisingly easy. I paid a call upon Vanessa yesterday, and accidentally came upon the advertisement you used to book your holiday.'

'You went snooping through my mother's things?'

'Of course not. I found it lying about on a table somewhere, can't exactly remember. You know how Vanessa never tidies up after herself.'

Chrissie couldn't believe she'd been so careless as to leave that paper lying about. More likely he had indeed gone searching for evidence. It was certainly not beyond his devious nature to go nosing into cupboards and drawers, seeking clues.

Peter merely smiled. 'You'd rather foolishly drawn a ring around the one for Rosegill Hall, and, noticing that something was obviously troubling Vanessa following your recent visit, I asked her what was wrong. She refused to say, but admitted that you'd decided to relocate north and open a small shop. It wasn't difficult to put two and two together.' He grinned at her, rather like a Cheshire cat that had swallowed an entire pot of cream.

'OK, so you've found out where I'm living. I still don't understand why you're here. We agreed this is supposed to be a new beginning. For us both,' she pointedly added.

'No harm in my checking that my fiancée is well, is there?'

'For the hundredth time I am not, and never will be, your fiancée.'

Ignoring her interruption, Peter went on, 'I thought it only polite for me to pay you a visit, just to make sure you were settling in after all this unnecessary trauma. And your dear mother was distraught. I called at the Hall first. It was the old woman who directed me here.'

'Mrs Gorran?' Chrissie made a mental note to speak to the housekeeper on matters of privacy, although it would be a bit like closing the stable door after the horse had bolted.

'No, the other one. Mrs Cowper, is it? She gave me your new address readily enough when I introduced myself as your fiancé. Although I must say she seemed quite surprised when I happened to mention, in passing, that you two must be related. She is your grandmother, I presume?'

Chrissie felt as if every drop of blood was draining from her body. She went hot and cold all over, and actually started to shake. 'H-how did you—'

'Know? I really can't remember. Ah yes, it was something your mother said. Dear Vanessa asked if it mattered if she hadn't used her correct maiden name when opening an account. It obviously troubled her and I was able to advise her, as a bank clerk, that there is nothing illegal in calling yourself by any name you choose.'

'And she told you what it was, did she?' Chrissie wondered how many gins that had taken.

Peter shrugged. 'She did happen to mention it in passing and when I saw the advertisement I put two and two together. It seemed the logical conclusion for your reason to visit such a backwater. Why, does it matter?'

Chrissie was at a loss for words. Of course it mattered! It mattered so much she'd been obliged to deceive her grandmother. She'd so wanted to tell the old lady the truth herself, gently and carefully, not have it applied with a blunt instrument by a perfect stranger. But she couldn't say any of this to Peter, not without owning up to the fact that she'd lied to Georgia from the start.

'I believe you did this on purpose to make trouble. You must be aware by now that my mother has some unresolved issues with her family, and because I'd let you down you decided you'd come and stir things up a bit, to pay me back. That's the nub of it, isn't it? Some sort of cheap revenge for my leaving you?'

His expression of feigned innocence made her almost want to vomit.

'Chrissie, dear, it was nothing of the sort. I wanted only to give you every opportunity to come home, with me,' he mildly pointed out, in his most reasonable tone.

'I'm not coming home with you, ever! This is my home now, not London. And this really is none of your business, Peter. I don't understand why you thought it necessary to mention any possible family connection.'

'It seemed the right thing to do. I'm family too, after all. Well, almost, as I explained to her.'

Chrissie's patience finally snapped. 'No, Peter, you are not!' Fury was now replacing her distress, and she longed to lash out and smack that self-satisfied smirk off his face. Not that it would do any good. Arguing with Peter was like battling with blancmange. You were never able to make any impact as it just wobbled away from you.

He gazed at her, completely unmoved by her anger. 'I must admit the old dear wasn't too welcoming, or friendly for that matter.'

The hollow feeling in the pit of Chrissie's stomach yawned wider. 'W-what was her reaction?'

'She slammed the door in my face, then I heard a crash, rather as if the old bird had collapsed.'

'Oh, dear heaven, what have you done?' Chrissie

practically did likewise to this most unwelcome visitor, then grabbing her coat and bag she hurried to the telephone box at the end of the street and called her mother.

Vanessa had refused to come, on the grounds that Chrissie had got herself into this mess, therefore it was up to her to find a solution. There seemed no alternative but to see Georgia forthwith, and offer a most humble apology. Taking a breath to steady her nerves Chrissie grasped the heavy knocker, its gargoyle grin almost mocking her. The front door, built of strong solid oak with many curlicues and studs, was opened by Mrs Gorran, and Chrissie was made instantly aware, if only by the grim expression on her face, that she knew. The housekeeper's stance was rather as if she were guarding the gates of Paradise, across whose threshold no mere mortal would be allowed to cross.

Chrissie felt as if she were some loathsome creature that had crawled out from under a stone.

'G-good m-morning, I wondered if . . .' She cleared her throat, tried again. 'May I speak with Mrs Cowper, please?'

'The mistress is unwell and not accepting callers.' The housekeeper's tone was icily cold, brooking no argument.

'I-I'm sorry to hear that. Perhaps what I have to say might make her feel better.'

'I very much doubt it. I rather think you've already done sufficient damage to Mrs Cowper's health. Her heart is not strong and the doctor has prescribed rest.'

'Oh!' Worse and worse. Had the news of her deceit brought on a heart attack? Chrissie felt sick at the thought. 'Perhaps I may speak to her later then, when she is feeling more herself.'

'We'll see.' She began to close the door. Recklessly, Chrissie stuck her foot in the gap.

'It wasn't my idea not to tell. It was my mother's.' She sensed rather than heard the startled gasp in response to this plea, and there was a slight slackening of the woman's tight grip on the door.

'Your *mother*?'

Encouraged, Chrissie ploughed on. 'You do remember my mother? Of course you do.'

'It was a long time ago,' the older woman said, her tone softening slightly with nostalgia as she clearly recalled the child and young girl she'd once nursed and no doubt been fond of. 'Are you saying that Vanessa sent you?'

'I'm afraid not. It was entirely my idea to come here,' Chrissie admitted. 'I thought I could help to mend bridges between her and Georgia, heal whatever had driven them apart, only my mother was so distressed by the idea she made me promise not to say who I was. Even when Peter told me what he'd done, that he'd revealed who I really was, I rang Mum to tell her, but she point-blank refused to come anywhere near, insisting that would only make things worse.'

'I see.' The older woman seemed disappointed by this news, as if her own bright hopes for a reconciliation had also been dashed.

'I'm so very sorry, Mrs Gorran, about all of this.'

Impulsively, Chrissie reached out to clasp the other woman's hands in an effort to plead her case. 'Please believe me when I say that I meant no harm. At least allow me to apologise, to try to put things right.'

'The harm has already been done, I'm afraid. Old wounds have been reopened, and I doubt those can ever be healed.' The housekeeper drew up her spine, ramrod straight. 'The young master, Mr Ryall, arrived earlier. I believe he would like a word, if you're agreeable?'

A hollow sensation opened inside Chrissie. This must be the uncle she'd never met, hadn't even known existed, who hadn't spoken to his sister in sixteen years. The one who, according to Ben, constantly urged his mother to sell up or move out of Rosegill Hall and allow him to take it over. This didn't seem quite the moment for, and certainly not the way she would have wanted, their first meeting to take place.

'That would be lovely,' she said, putting as brave a face on as she could. And Mrs Gorran stepped back on the black and white tiled floor and allowed her to enter.

Chrissie was deeply aware of the slow thud of her heart as she was shown into the library. Her immediate impression was of a small cosy room, cluttered with books. These were stacked untidily on wall-to-wall shelves, on circular tables, on window sills, or left lying about on worn wing-backed chairs. She could imagine her grandmother sitting here of an evening, a glowing fire burning in the iron grate as she savoured the delights of her favourite authors.

Yet there was a definite chill in the air today.

She did not have a good feeling about this coming interview, and was hardly reassured when the man standing before the fireplace, with his hands clasped behind his back, turned to face her. The expression on his face was dour, the deep creases of a frown puckering his brow. Of slight build, he sported a small goatee beard, perhaps to compensate for a prematurely bald pate, circled by a rim of dark hair, although he couldn't be much over forty. He wore half-spectacles, over which he peered censoriously at her.

Smiling brightly, she stuck out a hand. 'Chrissie Emerson.'

Making no attempt to take it, he said, 'I rather think that can't be right. Perhaps you would care to try again, with your correct name this time.'

Chrissie stiffened, letting the hand drop. Though she knew she was in the wrong, she really didn't care for this man's superior tone. 'That *is* my correct name actually. I don't use my first one, which was Susan, and Emerson is my married name, although my husband was killed in the war. My maiden name was Kemp, as I believe you are aware.'

'We are now, Mrs Emerson, but until your fiancé chose to reveal the full facts to my mother, you had very cleverly avoided mentioning this essential detail. Now why was that, I wonder? Could it be that you were afraid of spoiling the nice little friendship you were building up with her? Very clever.'

Chrissie could feel the betraying burn of guilt warm

her cheeks. 'Peter is not my fiancé and he had no right to interfere in my private affairs. But I'm not sure what it is you're implying by that remark.'

'Aren't you? You don't think it's obvious that you've been attempting to make yourself indispensable? Helping her in the garden, breakfasting at her table, a privilege none of the other guests are awarded, and apparently encouraging her to talk about the past. My mother, Mrs Emerson, *never* talks about the past, with anyone, not even her own family.'

'Perhaps that's because you do not show sufficient interest in it, or in her.'

The scowl darkened, if that were possible, his next words rising in pitch almost to a shout. 'My mother is an old woman in uncertain health, and sadly an easy target for charlatans such as yourself who attempt to exploit her good nature.'

Still standing facing each other across the Persian rug, this most difficult conversation was being conducted as if the pair of them were about to commence a duel. The trouble was, Chrissie was now trembling so badly she felt her knees might give way. 'May I sit, please? I'm sure I can explain everything to your satisfaction and put your mind at rest on that point, and any others you may have.' When no such offer was forthcoming, her uncle's expression remaining as frozen as ever, Chrissie steadied her nerves as best she could and battled on. 'I have called today to offer my most sincere apologies, so if I may be allowed to see Georgia . . . er . . . Mrs Cowper.'

'I'm sure Mrs Gorran made it clear that my mother is

not receiving visitors. In fact, I doubt she'll wish to see you ever again.'

Chrissie was mortified. This was the last thing she wanted, to damage the delicate friendship which had been growing between them. 'I never meant any harm by the deception. Many times I longed to tell her who I really was. I only kept quiet to avoid causing distress to *my* mother, *your* sister,' she added pointedly. 'Although I was hoping to talk Mum round, if I was successful in achieving the reconciliation I'd hoped for.'

'Ah yes, of course, the reconciliation.' Sliding his hands in his trouser pockets he rocked back and forth on his heels. 'How very touching. And highly unlikely.'

'I don't see why. Difficulties between family members can surely be overcome if there is sufficient goodwill, and love, on both sides.'

'Do we *look* like a family bursting with goodwill and love? Naturally, the presence of considerable wealth makes the effort worthwhile, whatever the circumstances, wouldn't you say, Mrs Emerson?'

Cheeks now fired to a bright scarlet, Chrissie hotly protested her innocence. 'How dare you suggest such a thing! Money was never my motive.'

'Was it not? I wonder. If I know my sister, not to mention that useless fellow she married, their financial state will not be a healthy one. Do you deny that your parents are in a parlous state?'

She could not deny that, of course, but neither would Chrissie give this arrogant man the satisfaction of being proved right. All her mother's warnings now seemed to be coming true, alarm bells ringing loud and ominously in her head. 'As a matter of fact my father was killed during the war, at Dunkirk. My mother and I are far from well off, that is true, but we get by.' This didn't seem quite the moment to mention the long-standing debt Aaran had left them with, or her mother's fondness for the bottle.

Ryall let out a sharp disbelieving snort of laughter. 'I can't pretend to grieve for the loss of that man, although I'll admit Vanessa was besotted with the fellow. She always did have poor taste in men and quickly fell pregnant. With you, I presume. The silly chit allowed a few moments of carnal passion to ruin her entire life. But it was her choice, and to stay away all these years was another unwise decision. It devastated my mother. You have my absolute assurance, Mrs Emerson, that there is not the slightest hope of a reconciliation, nor of you inheriting a penny from my mother's estate when the time comes.'

All of Chrissie's nervousness had quite vanished during the course of this bitter homily, replaced by a very real sense of aggrieved anger. Nevertheless she kept those feelings firmly in check, if only out of loyalty and love for her mother. But she most certainly had no intention of standing silently by while being falsely accused of what amounted to fraud and extortion by this arrogant man. She took a step towards him, which instantly brought a flash of alarm into his blue-grey eyes.

'My mother may have made many mistakes in her life, but marrying my father was not one of them. They fell in love. What was so wrong in that?' Chrissie arched a brow at him as if challenging him to deny it, yet didn't wait for his answer. 'I'm sorry if Georgia was distressed by this family feud, but so was my mother. Where was your support when she needed it? Where was that of her other siblings? And if you think that ignoring your own sister – for what, sixteen years? – isn't cruel, then I pity you. You are clearly a man with no heart. My mother, unfortunately, is a woman with too much of one. But I tell you, *Uncle* Ryall, I'd rather have that flaw any day than be the frozen, selfish, unfeeling person you clearly are. You're welcome to Grandmother's fortune. Large or small, I wouldn't accept a penny of it, even if it were offered.'

A round of applause greeted this remark, although not from her uncle. 'Bravo! Well said, and clearly spoken from the heart.'

The woman's voice came from behind, and spinning on her heels, Chrissie came face to face with her grandmother.

Chrissie's heart soared with new hope. Might she be forgiven? Perhaps it wasn't too late after all. She took a quick step forward. 'May I have the chance to explain?'

'I rather think this isn't the time for a protracted discussion,' Ryall intervened. 'Thanks to you, my mother is unwell.'

'I'm perfectly willing to listen to what the girl has to say,' Georgia quietly objected, ensconcing herself comfortably in her favourite chair. 'Even if I won't necessarily believe a word of it.'

'Mother, I don't think . . .'

'You can leave us, Ryall. I'll deal with this.'

'But . . .'

'Leave us, please.'

There was no doubt that Georgina Cowper was a formidable woman, one not even her own son could entirely control, and giving Chrissie one last fierce glare he strode in fury from the room, slamming the door behind him. The sound reverberated in the silence for a long time before, drawing a shuddering breath, Chrissie found the courage to speak.

'I don't want to put all the blame on to Mum, but I'm afraid she was very much against my coming to see you, hence her insistence I remain incognito.'

'I can imagine.' The tone was sardonic, the steel grey eyes riveted upon Chrissie with a coolness that chilled.

'I-I'm most dreadfully sorry. And truly, deeply regret that you should find out in this way. Unfortunately, the longer I left it, the harder it was to own up to the deception. I do hope you can forgive me. It was a stupid thing to do, a foolish misjudgement.'

'Is that what you call it, a misjudgement? Not a deliberate lie then?'

Chrissie found her cheeks grow warm with embarrassment beneath the direct scrutiny. 'I always hoped it wouldn't be viewed as such, although the last time you shared your reminiscences with me, in the garden, I itched to confess, but felt I needed to speak to Mum first.'

'And did you succeed in persuading her?'

Chrissie shook her head, dropping her chin so as to

avoid the gimlet gaze. 'I can't think why I ever made such a promise.'

'Ah, promises are always easier to make than to keep.' Georgia let out a small sigh. 'I should have guessed who you were. You were certainly asking a great many questions. And I'm not usually so forthcoming in talking to strangers.'

Reading hope in this remark, Chrissie met her grandmother's eyes with frankness in her own. 'May I tell you the reason?'

'If you wish.' There was a weary resignation to the tone that was not particularly encouraging, nevertheless Chrissie valiantly explained, as best she could, about her honest desire to bring about a reconciliation between mother and daughter. She took far longer over the explanation than was strictly necessary, repeating herself somewhat as her grandmother sat silent, never interrupting, nor in any way making it easy for her. When Chrissie finally ran out of steam the silence in the room lasted for several long moments, as her grandmother seemed lost in some distant time, some place far from here.

Chrissie knelt before her, took the old woman's cold hands between her own. 'Whatever it was that went wrong between you, you are still my grandmother, and I – I care about you. I thought we were friends, you and I, but I'd like us to be more than that. Family is important, isn't it? Or perhaps you only think that when you don't have one.' There was a tight feeling in her chest, a blockage of tears bursting to be shed that was burning into the heart of her.

The faded grey eyes focused upon Chrissie more kindly now. 'Happy families, in my experience, are entirely dependant upon a woman marrying the right man in the first place.'

'And you didn't,' Chrissie softly finished for her.

'No, I didn't. And that's where all this trouble for poor Vanessa began.'

Chapter Eighteen

San Francisco

Following my initiation in the rites of the marriage bed, repeated with only marginally less trauma the following morning, Maura tenderly bathed me and dried up my tears, consoling me as a mother might, although she was but a few years older than myself. She changed the bloodied sheets, counselled and advised me on how to protect myself better next time, even what position to adopt so that it wouldn't hurt quite so badly. I listened carefully, taking in every word. I had little hope that any such futile efforts on my part would save me. This was a man, I realised, who took pleasure in the pain of others.

'How will I endure it?' I begged her.

'It will get easier, and I will always be here to help you.'

The physical pain did ease in time but my loathing for my husband increased. The few precious hours of freedom when he was out and about on business became increasingly important to me. Dressed in our best we would don our bonnets and stroll in the park, remembering the good times now lost, a time when I'd still possessed hope for the future, when I'd still believed in Santa Claus.

I was warming to my Irish maid more and more, not simply as a servant, but as a friend. One I greatly needed in the life I was living. We'd make a great fuss of getting ready, doing our 'fixings' as we called them, just as I had once done with Prue when we were girls together, which now seemed like a lifetime ago. I so welcomed Maura's friendship that I readily encouraged her to borrow any of my gowns that took her fancy. She was slightly taller than me, but otherwise they fitted her well. But then I lent them to dear Prudence too, whose social life was far more exciting than mine.

'I do like the blue, ma'am. Ooh, but then it's your favourite, seeing as how it sets off your grey eyes.'

'It really doesn't matter, Maura. You are welcome to wear it if you wish. I shall wear the yellow.'

And off we would go, while I would be instinctively keeping an eye out for the swaggering walk of a certain young sailor.

My afternoon calls twice a week to Geary Boulevard to see Mama and Prue, and even Papa, also became like a lifeline to me. But not once, not for a single moment, did I let slip any hint concerning the depth of my unhappiness. I feared the disaster that might befall them, were I to be so reckless.

And on Saturdays I still met with dearest Prudence for

our regular trips to the theatre. She was always full of chatter about her latest beau, although the outing did not hold quite the same appeal for me as it once had. All I could hope for now was that my dear sister be granted greater happiness than I. Certainly I did my best to help, lending her money as well as gowns, to buy her fripperies in order to attract the attention of the young man currently in favour.

'Didn't I lend you fifty dollars last week, which you've not yet repaid?' I might gently remind her, and she'd pout in that delightful way she had and talk of her allowance being late this month.

'Thirty would do, Georgia, or twenty, but I really must have a new outfit to meet his parents, and a darling new hat I saw, or I shall look an absolute frump.'

Where my silly younger sister was concerned, I was putty in her hands, just like her adoring admirers.

I, meanwhile, was the plaything of a heartless husband. On a whim he would order me upstairs. This could happen while I was quietly reading a book by the fire, sewing, or seated at table halfway through a meal. It mattered not what I was doing, or what time of day it was, and there was never any warning. Nor did he care if the servants witnessed my humiliation. He would remove the book or piece of needlework that occupied me, or order me to leave my food half eaten. Then he'd jerk his head, the curl of his upper lip almost a snarl of gleeful anticipation, his mocking eyes willing me to resist.

'Upstairs, wife, I have need of a different sort of sustenance.'

I always meekly obeyed, nervous of upsetting him and making things worse for myself. But then I became unwell, and was actually sick some mornings. I couldn't work out what was wrong with me, soon feeling faint and sickly for most of the day.

Maura said, 'You've fallen.'

'Fallen?' I tried to think what she meant, as I rarely left the house, save for our afternoon walks in the park. 'Did I stumble over a tree root or something? I can't recall having done so. And why would that make me sick, if I had?'

She put her hand to her mouth and started giggling. 'I mean you're expecting. You're going to have a baby, ma'am.'

I stared at her, eyes wide. 'Oh, my goodness, I never considered . . . never thought of a child.'

'That's what happens when you . . . well . . . when you do what Mr Kemp does to you all the time. You'll have to take things a bit easier now.'

I brightened as a thought struck me. 'Could I perhaps refuse him access to my bed for a while?'

An odd sort of calculating look came into her eyes. 'Aye,' she agreed. 'You might well do that, although I doubt he's a man to take kindly to abstinence.'

'Then he must learn,' I primly responded.

But in the weeks following I never quite managed to pluck up the courage to tell him of my condition, let alone issue any rules regarding it. Until the day I was seated at dinner, forking a piece of crab cake around my plate.

My appetite was small these days; even so, I was anxious

to eat something for the sake of the baby. I really hadn't quite worked out how I felt about becoming a mother, of holding Kemp's child in my arms, but instinct told me I must do right by it. It was important that I remain healthy, and not damage it in any way. So on this occasion when he ordered me upstairs, I refused, absolutely, to leave the table. 'I have not finished my meal. Your needs must wait until I am done.'

'I beg your pardon!' The way his face darkened was terrifying to see. 'I wait for no man, and certainly not a woman. Upstairs, wife, *now*!'

Blithely ignoring him, I cut a portion of the crab cake, speared the piece with my fork, and put it in my mouth.

Flicking out a hand, he swept the plate from the table. It fell with a crash to the floor, splintering into a dozen pieces. Not a servant in the room moved a muscle to clear up the mess, nor blinked an eyelid. This in itself should have warned me they had witnessed similar tantrums in the past, and I should have followed their patient example. Instead, I was incensed, and taking up my glass of water, flung it in his face.

'Don't you ever dare do that to me again,' I screamed at him.

Somewhere in the back of my mind I heard Maura's small gasp of horror, but only when I saw what my husband was holding in his hand did I appreciate the true reason for her dismay. He'd snatched up the poker from the fire irons, and, pulling me across his knee, he beat my backside till it was black and blue. Then dragging me upstairs he took his fill of me, as he'd first intended, only with far greater brutality. No one came to my rescue. Every maid had slipped silently and swiftly away to hide in the kitchen, just in case he should turn on them instead. Only Maura remained close by, hovering outside the door throughout my ordeal, then she held me sobbing in her arms when finally he stormed off, no doubt to get drunk in some hellhole.

Later that night I began to bleed heavily and it soon became obvious to us both that I had suffered a miscarriage.

It was never wise to defy him. I'd learnt that lesson the hard way.

I grieved for this child I could hardly visualise as a reality. How tragic that its precious life should end so prematurely, and I took some pleasure in telling my husband the catastrophic result of his temper. 'Your brutality cost the life of what might well have been your son.'

I saw by the flicker in his eyes that he was startled by the news, but as always he twisted things around to blame me. 'It's entirely your own fault. You should have told me you were pregnant, you stupid woman.'

'Would it have made a difference?'

Grabbing me by the throat he pulled me to him, flecks of his spittle spattering my face. 'I want to know *everything* you do, *everything* that happens in this house. Do you understand? You are my *wife*!'

'God save me.'

He hit me then, slapped me back and forth about the head until I cowered in a corner of the bedroom and begged for mercy. 'Perhaps you'll manage to hang on to my son next time,' he shouted, before striding away and leaving me sobbing on the floor.

I was grief-stricken, terrorised by what had happened. But however sympathetic Maura might be, she was still only a maid, with no influence or ability to help. Desperate to talk to someone about the tragedy that had befallen me, the very next afternoon that I visited Mama and Prudence, an opportunity presented itself when my mother remarked on how peaky I looked. 'You look in dire need of a square meal – are you eating properly, girl?'

I took a breath. 'My appetite has been down lately, that's true.'

She looked suddenly hopeful as she cut me a large slice of coffee cake. 'You aren't expecting, are you?'

This was the moment I'd so longed for: to tell my mother the truth at last. But for some reason I couldn't quite find the words to describe how my husband liked to rape and beat me on an almost daily basis. Or that as a consequence he'd caused me to miscarry. Mama had a severely restricted view of life, nurtured by my father, who never told her the truth about anything. Not least their financial situation. I chickened out, and said instead, 'I'm not finding it easy adjusting to my new life. My husband is very . . . demanding.'

Mama gave me one of her long looks. 'Marriage is all about give and take, about facing your responsibilities, not pining for what you can't have. Now eat every crumb of this delicious cake. It's your favourite.' And she took a large bite of her own, as if the matter were settled, before quickly changing the subject. 'Did you know that Prudence is now walking out with Bronson Wade? He's a fine young man, I have to say, and with excellent prospects.'

I turned to my sister, who was blushing furiously. 'Do you like him, Prue?'

'He seems pleasant enough,' she said, casting a half-glance at our mother.

'Because if you don't, do not allow yourself to be persuaded into marrying him. Not at any price.'

Mama spluttered crumbs everywhere as she clicked her tongue in annoyance. 'Do not say such a thing! Dear Prudence has more sense than you, and will gladly do what's good for her without complaint, will you not, child?'

'Well—' Prue began, but our mother was too busy lecturing me to allow her to finish whatever she'd been about to say.

'No wonder you aren't settling if you're still harbouring resentment about what might have been. But all of that romantic nonsense is in the past now, and you'd do well to leave it there. It is far better to marry a man whose stocks are booming than a two-bit homeless sailor with no future.'

'Ellis did have a home, and a future, as a matter of fact, in England, but you're right, it is all in the past now,' I said, unable to quell the sadness in my tone. 'But does a wife have no say at all in what . . . what happens between a man and a woman?' I could feel myself blushing even as I said these words. My mother and I had never been prone to open discussion on personal matters, and I could almost feel her discomfort, as this question was far too delicate.

'A wife's duty is to please her husband,' she snapped. 'And I hardly think this is the time or place to discuss matters of such intimacy with your young unmarried sister present.'

'Put your hands over your ears a moment, Prue dear, if you wish, but I have to ask this question, Mama. Should not a husband ask permission of a wife before he—'

'That is enough!' she cried, almost dropping her teacup in shock. 'What goes on in the bedroom is not for public discussion. This desire of yours to wallow in foolish nostalgia won't do you a lick of good. My advice is to pull yourself together, child, and grow up!'

So much for maternal sympathy and support.

My father's explanation for procuring this marriage for me had already alerted me to the fact that my new husband's air of charm was entirely superficial. Within months, if not weeks, of my marriage, the truth of that warning became all too apparent. He was not only a brute and a bully, but also a compulsive gambler, a cheat and a charlatan. Most evenings, after we had dined, he would go out, to the casino or one of the many gaming houses – for all I knew to the filthy dives and hash houses on the Barbary Coast. In addition, men would often come to the house and be closeted in his study for hours on end. If it were not for the parade of servants carrying whisky or food on a platter to the room at regular intervals, you might not even realise they were in the house at all.

'What do they talk of, I wonder?' I whispered to Maura as we hid on the landing one afternoon, watching them arrive.

'They say in the kitchen that he lost out at being mayor in the last election.' Maura was good at picking up tittle-tattle, and I loved her for that as gossip was one of the few ways to brighten my days. 'Kemp talks fairly openly before the servants, thinking them dumb, if not exactly deaf, but they understand enough to know that he's furious and is determined to do better next time. He means to win in 1905 and wants every businessman, every railway magnate, every brothel keeper and wharf rat to support his bid to be the next mayor of Frisco. He's formed some sort of alliance and his cohorts are offering protection to shops and businesses across the city, even to the boarding house keepers on the Barbary Coast, if they will persuade the seamen to vote for him. Otherwise . . .'

I frowned. 'Otherwise what?'

Maura's shrewd eyes met mine. 'They would no doubt live to regret it if they didn't do as he asked.'

I fell silent, understanding fully the kind of man I had married. 'Yes, I can see that they might.'

Later, after I'd done my duty by him, as per usual, I asked him about the purpose of these meetings. 'Is it true that you are using bribes to win votes at the next election?' I never baulked at challenging him, determined to hang on to my self-esteem and pride at least, even though he was generally only amused by my 'quarrelsome ways', as he termed them.

Even now he was smiling. 'The crimps and their ilk have become so powerful that they think they can control the police and the courts through bribes. They mean to buy exemption from interference in their nefarious activities.'

'And you intend to stop them?' I dutifully asked, even as I doubted my husband could be motivated by anything so noble as honour or care for the community.

'I very much doubt that is possible. In any case, if they are willing to hand over a portion of their substantial profits to ensure the authorities turn a blind eye to practices that would take place anyway, why should I not enjoy my share? Most councillors and city officials are involved.'

'The dishonest ones, you mean.' I flounced away from him, which was perhaps a mistake as he did seem to be obsessed with my bottom. I stifled a shudder as he smoothed a hand over my buttocks in that way I'd come to dread.

'What a child you are, wife.'

'But what you are doing isn't fair,' I argued, reaching for my nightgown. 'Some of these businesses, the people whose votes you are buying with your own bribes, are honest folk and not crimps at all.'

He took the gown from me, and, tossing it aside, straddled me. 'You really should not trouble your tiny female brain with matters which do not concern you.'

Pushing him away, I sat up, incensed by this put-down. 'But where are they supposed to find the money to pay you if not by exploiting their own tenants, the poor? And if sailors are overcharged for their lodgings, or robbed blind and turned out on to the street, how would they survive?'

Kemp was laughing now, highly amused by my concern. 'Why would I care? They can always go back to sea.'

I flounced out of bed and went in search of my nightgown, thinking of Ellis, wondering where he was living and what kind of life he had. If he still thought of me. Slipping the silk gown on, I remembered the time dearest Prudence was kidnapped and he'd helped rescue her, a perfect stranger, despite risk to himself. I turned on my husband, defiant. 'And if young girls or boys are pressed into servitude in brothels, or on board ship, what will you, as mayor, do to help them?'

'What can I do?' he drawled. 'As a man of the world I know these things happen.'

I was appalled by this casual dismissal of what was surely a major problem. Yet why would I have imagined any other reply? If he cared not a jot for his own wife's feelings, why would he consider the welfare of those he chose to defraud of their money? Drew Kemp may well be a man of power and influence, but he was interested only in using those advantages for his own ends.

I wanted to march off in high dudgeon, to run from him, from this house, to get as far away from him as humanly impossible. But he was already pulling me back into bed, stripping off my nightgown, and, as I well knew, there was really nowhere for me to run to.

* * *

While I might yearn for another man, I was in every respect the good and obedient wife, prudent in my spending and dutiful in my habits. My husband's dinner was always ready at the appointed hour. I supervised the provision of his clean laundry, or at least the servants tolerated my interference with commendable patience. For what did I, a young girl of eighteen from a sheltered background, know of such things as the operation of Chinese laundries, or the proper ordering of dry goods for the kitchen larder?

So far as my everyday social life was concerned, my sister had been right. I did indeed enjoy a certain degree of freedom. There were regular balls, social functions and dinner parties I must attend, and no limit to the number of gowns I might purchase to wear at them. The opera too was ever a favourite with Kemp, and I was expected to entertain my husband's guests, to act as hostess at his dinner parties, or to at least wait upon them with wafers, wine and ready smiles should he invite his friends round for a game of cards of an evening.

I did whatever he asked of me, without complaint, and then escaped into a world of my own: my favourite books and needlework, my little outings. Sometimes, I even wrote letters to my darling Ellis, although as I had no address to send them to, and was fearful of them being discovered by my husband, I would then have to burn them on the fire, tears rolling down my cheeks as the paper curled and scorched. If only I could see him one more time.

Then one day in the new year, as Maura and I walked

in the Golden Gate Park as we did on most afternoons, I rounded the pagoda in the Japanese Gardens, and there he was. It was as if he had been waiting for me, as if he had known that I would come. Ellis swept me up into his arms and kissed me just as if it had only been yesterday that he last saw me, and not in those soft days of summer nearly five months ago.

Chapter Nineteen

How difficult it was to tell Ellis that I was a married woman now, and see the devastation and dismay in his face. Briefly, I described how it had come about. He held my hands and it felt so wonderful, so warm and comforting, I couldn't bring myself to pull away. He looked tired, I thought, older, and I wondered what had brought those lines of fatigue to his dear face. I longed to hold him in my arms, but dared not, determined to keep a firm check on my emotions. I set Maura to keep watch while we sat together on the grassy sward.

'I understand now why I was locked up.'

I stared at him in horror. 'Locked up? Do you mean in jail?'

'In Broadway Jail. It's in the Tenderloin district, the worst part of town, and the most evil-smelling hellhole you could imagine. I knew that the order for my arrest had come from Kemp, but didn't understand in what way I could possibly have offended such a powerful man. Now I can see why, very clearly. He must have heard about our feelings for each other, and got me out of the way by having me thrown in the clink.'

'Oh, Ellis.' I wanted to say that my husband would never do such a thing, but how could I when I knew only too well that Drew Kemp was capable of anything? He certainly wouldn't baulk at disposing of a rival who was in his way.

Ellis dismissed my cry of dismay with a shrug. 'After several days of unexplained incarceration in a dank cell, I was manacled and shipped out on an eastward-bound clipper. I've spent the last several months desperately trying to escape the bilges and work my way west.'

'But who told him about us?'

'Maybe Prudence mentioned seeing me at the Seamen's Institute, without even realising he would put two and two together.'

'That makes sense, she's such a scatterbrain. Oh, Ellis, but we've lost all chance of happiness as a result.' I was crying now, tears rolling down my cheeks and he tenderly mopped them up with a big blue hanky. I cried partly out of despair and disappointment, but also because I'd been right all along. Ellis did still love me, had never stopped loving me, through all these long lonely months. 'If only I could have held on and waited for you. Sadly, I wasn't given the chance. I tried to resist but it was quite impossible. There were financial difficulties for my family. They too would have been destroyed.'

Ellis lovingly tucked a curl behind my ear as he kissed it. 'Don't fret, my love, I do understand that you didn't deliberately betray me. And the fact you are married doesn't make the slightest difference to my feelings. I still love you and always will. Perhaps our time hasn't come yet. I'm not going to give up, not ever.'

'No, Ellis, it's too late for us now. I can't ever see you again. It would be far too dangerous. I am striving to be a good wife to him, and at least I have Maura, thank heaven.' I could see my little Irish maid was growing fidgety at her post, stationed by the tiny bridge that led over the pond, as we'd talked for so long. I said nothing to Ellis of my wedding night, of the rape Kemp had subjected me to, or the beatings since. Where was the point in making his pain worse, or risking retaliation between the two men? Even now his blue eyes sparked, whether from anger or loss I didn't dare to consider.

'May I have one last kiss?' he asked, but I shook my head.

'No, my darling, one kiss would not be enough, and yet too many.' He lifted my hand to his lips and kissed that instead. 'Please don't,' I groaned, snatching it away. 'Please go now. Just walk away. I shall sit here on the grass until you are gone.'

'If that is what you wish, but I swear I will never give up waiting for you, Georgia. I promise I shall be here every Wednesday afternoon at two, just as I always was. And if I have to go to sea for a while, don't give up on me but keep on coming, then we'll always meet up again, one day, as soon as I'm back in port. You will remember that, my love, will you not?'

He was on his feet now and I was kissing his fingers, clasping his cold hands tightly between my own, wanting to hold on to him even as I urged him to leave. 'I will remember. But you must take care not to let my husband realise you're back in town. It would be much safer if you found yourself another berth immediately, sail to somewhere far away from here, where there is no likelihood of Kemp ever finding you and putting you back in jail.'

'I'm staying in Frisco for as long as I can afford to, but I promise to take care, for your safety rather than mine. We must keep the faith that one day we can be together.'

'Farewell, my love, and go safely.'

Then I buried my face in my hands and did not look up until I felt Maura's arms come about me in a big warm hug. Knowing then that he had gone, I turned my face into her neck and wept as if my heart would break.

Since moving to Nob Hill, Maura had become my very dear friend. It didn't matter that she was a little jealous of me. I'd always been aware of this trait in her. At Geary Boulevard I'd been amused when I discovered she was secretly trying on my gowns, or borrowing a scarf or hat. After my marriage I'd gladly lent her gowns to wear as she now seemed more of a companion than a maid, and therefore should be more suitably dressed. I knew she was desperate to better herself and was at first flattered when she began to imitate my style, my manner of speech and brisk way of walking, even picking up and repeating my pet hates and favourite topics of conversation.

One cold afternoon in early March I was looking for my fox fur tippet. Prue and I were going to the theatre to see *Boccaccio*, a popular Viennese operetta, but I couldn't find the fur in my wardrobe. Guessing that Maura might have borrowed it, since the weather had been particularly chilly lately and she'd developed this increasing appetite to emulate my style, I tugged on the bell pull to call her. When, after some moments, she still hadn't come running as she usually did, I surmised she must be out running errands for the housekeeper.

'No doubt it is in her room,' I said to myself as I started up the flight of stairs that led to the servants' quarters. Hurrying along the top landing I tapped only once on her door before pushing it open, quite certain she was out.

But she was not out. She was in bed, with my husband on top of her.

I stood transfixed, staring in shock at their writhing grunting bodies as he pounded into her. I could not believe what I was witnessing, and then it came to me that Maura was being violated. Kemp was doing to her what he had done to me. I was outraged, overcome by anger. 'What the hell are you doing to her?' I cried.

My horrified shout made both of them jump but Maura was the one to move first. Wriggling from beneath him, she dived for her dressing gown that hung over the bed rail. Kemp simply swivelled about and grinned up at me.

'It's not your turn today, wife. Unless you'd care to join in?'

Spinning on my heels, I ran, skittering down the stairs so fast I almost fell over my own feet. I did not stop until I gained the privacy of my bedroom and slammed shut the door. Leaning against it to catch my breath, it was only then that I properly recalled Maura's expression when I'd interrupted them. She was not screaming, nor even silently crying in agony, the look on her face had been one of complete ecstasy.

She came to me within minutes, contrite, and yet oddly triumphant. Bobbing a curtsey she cast a sideways glance up at me. 'I'm sorry, ma'am, that you should find out like this. I should've told you meself, only I thought mebbe you'd guessed since he wasn't troubling you as much as he used to.'

Her words made me stop and think, and it dawned on me in that moment that it was true. My husband had not ordered me upstairs, nor kept me awake half the night with his attentions quite so often of late. Nevertheless, I stared at Maura, stunned. 'Are you saying that you were a willing participant? But what of your fancy for John, our driver at Geary Boulevard?'

A sorrowful expression washed over her face at this. 'I rarely see him now, do I, save when we pay a call? I think he's forgotten me. Anyway, Mr Kemp is a hard man to refuse.'

'I confess you did not look as if you were protesting just now.'

She gave a little smirk, a secret smile in her hazel eyes. 'Mebbe I don't have your sensitivities, ma'am, but it doesn't bother me in the slightest – him wanting to have his way with me, I mean. Not that I had much say in the matter. Anyway, if it keeps him away from you . . .'

She let the sentence hang unfinished, as if implying she was doing me a favour by sleeping with my husband. Perhaps she was. I certainly didn't want him in my bed any more than was absolutely necessary.

I sat down, rather abruptly, on my dressing stool. My mind was in turmoil, not quite able to take in the full implications of what had occurred, or how it might change my relationship, both with Kemp and with my maid. 'This is a dangerous path you tread, Maura. He is not an easy man, or a considerate one. You are making yourself exceedingly vulnerable in letting him use you in this way.'

'I really don't mind,' she said, with an almost stubborn lift to her chin. 'That is, if you don't, ma'am. If you don't think it above my status, as it were.'

So there was the challenge. If I accepted the situation, my little Irish maid would consider her position to have risen to that of mistress to the master of the house. What difference would that make to her and me? I had no idea. Yet if I protested, I would lay myself open not only to the kind of attentions I did not relish from my husband, but also his censure. He was not a man who cared to have his behaviour curbed by a jealous wife. In any case, I was not jealous. Not in the slightest. It would not bother me in the least if my husband never visited my bed again, in fact I would welcome such an outcome.

'Ma'am?' Maura was still waiting for my answer, an appeal in her hooded eyes which seemed partly fearful and yet strangely knowing. She'd probably guessed my reaction already.

It came to me then how much I depended on her, how she could almost read my thoughts, how she understood my feelings, succoured and cared for me when I was down or depressed. I had made few friends thus far in this part of town, and the servants were too scared of their master to exchange anything more than a few essential 'thank yous' and 'yes ma'ams' with me. I couldn't bear to consider how lonely life would be in this house without her, even more confined than I was already, as Kemp would never allow me outdoors alone. I could hire another maid, of course, but she would be a stranger to me, and who's to say Kemp wouldn't bed her too?

'I think, Maura, we will say no more about this matter. We must each do what we must, I can see that. But I want you to know that while I greatly appreciate your concern for me, I can take care of myself. I am willing to do my duty as his wife, whether I like it or not, and you must never think to sacrifice your own happiness on my behalf. Is that understood?'

She was smiling now, although I still felt uneasy at her tranquil acceptance of the situation. 'Perfectly, ma'am.'

The subject was never mentioned between us again, nor did I risk venturing to the top landing, even though many more of my personal belongings unaccountably vanished from my wardrobe.

Very gradually, almost without my realising it, Maura took over the running of the household. She issued orders to the servants, insisting these came directly from the master, and it was to Maura they went now for instructions, not to me. Sometimes I thought they were laughing at me behind their hands, no doubt highly amused by this shift in power between my Irish maid and myself.

Maura no longer ate in the kitchen with the other staff, but in the dining room at the table with Kemp and myself. She would simper and laugh at my husband's bad jokes, feed him tidbits from her plate, and openly kiss him in front of me. She would always appear utterly fascinated by his conversation, their heads together as they talked and laughed, while I sat mute and ignored. Sometimes, I would walk into the drawing room and find her sitting in my chair, reading my book, or stitching at my needlework. And she borrowed not only my gowns, shoes, bags and trinkets without even troubling to ask my permission, but also the barouche, should she wish to go into town for supplies. Even asked for a little pocket money from time to time, in addition to her regular wages.

No longer did my obedient little maid come running whenever I tugged the bell pull. She was generally there with my hot water of a morning and evening when I needed it, to brush my hair and help me dress, but then she would vanish for hours at a time. And I did not dare to ask where she went, or how she spent those hours away from my side.

She behaved, in fact, exactly as she pleased, as if she were mistress of the house as well as my husband.

There were benefits, of course. Kemp came less often to my bed, although still far more frequently than I would have wished. He rarely stayed long, and never for an entire night. Once he'd done the necessary duty, he swiftly rose from my bed, donned his dressing gown, or dressed in his street clothes if it was daytime, and quickly departed.

'Why do you even bother to come?' I asked him on one occasion as he strode to the door, having spent less time servicing his wife than he would grooming his horse.

He paused, his hand on the door knob. 'I come for one purpose only, as you well know. Once you have provided me with a son, your task will be done, and you can go to hell in a handcart after that, for all I care.'

The result was that I began to feel oddly sidelined by all of this change, and lonelier than ever, which in turn made me long for Ellis more and more. But, fearful that I would be unable to resist him were we to meet again, I began to stay away from the park. Not that Maura was quite so available to come with me on my afternoon strolls as before, or accompany me on my visits to Prudence and Mama. She seemed to have developed a life of her own, one that was entirely private and beyond my control, while I felt increasingly trapped, almost living the life of a recluse.

One day she walked into my bedroom without even knocking. I looked up from the book I was reading, rather startled by her sudden entrance, and slightly irritated by it. Was I to be allowed no privacy? But I sensed at once that something was wrong as the self-satisfied look she normally wore these days had quite gone from her face.

'I thought you should know where your husband goes of an evening.'

‘I doubt it is any of my business, but I assume he is at the gaming houses or beer halls.’

‘’Tis a fact that he does visit those places. But isn’t he also visiting houses of ill repute and sleeping with whores,’ she bluntly informed me, falling into her Irish lingo as she always did when upset. ‘Did you know that?’

‘I did not.’ I stared at her, bemused, shocked by this news, although why I should be surprised by anything my husband did I cannot imagine. I felt sickened and disgusted by the thought that the man who still visited my bed, however infrequently, now consorted with women of the night, the lowest of the low. I shuddered at the thought. ‘What do you expect *me* to do about it?’ I asked.

‘Sure an’ I’m telling you that you should make him stop these shenanigans, at once.’

I gave a self-deprecating laugh. ‘You want *me* to tell Drew Kemp what he should and should not do? I thought *you* were the one with the influence these days, Maura, not me. So why don’t you tell him yourself?’

There were deep creases marring her brow, lines gouging her round face from nose to mouth, making it look plainer than ever, her eyes like hard pebbles in the bright light of my reading lamp. ‘Haven’t I told him already, but he won’t listen. He just laughed at me.’

‘So why do you think he’d treat me any different?’ I patiently enquired.

Her lips thinned with disapproval. ‘Because you’ve not yet provided him with the son he so desperately needs.’

‘Ah!’

She took an eager step closer. 'He'd be much more likely to listen to you because for all he knows you might be pregnant. And he wouldn't want to risk any future son of his catching some nasty disease, now would he?'

The prospect of sharing my bed again with such a man filled me with horror. I was unwilling to get involved in my husband's affairs. 'As it happens, I'm not pregnant, Maura, thank heaven. But it's rather late to be worrying about such things as diseases now, don't you think? How long has he been calling upon these women?'

She gave a little shrug, her face a picture of misery. 'I don't know. He wouldn't say.'

Her eyes, I noticed, were filling with tears. What was this? Surely she hadn't fallen in love with him? Could this be a lover's tiff? 'One thing is very certain, Maura, in future you can have my husband all to yourself. He will never grace my bed ever again. So he can kiss goodbye to any hope of a son.'

Telling my husband of this decision was, however, another matter entirely. As the following day was a Wednesday, I slipped out without either Kemp or Maura noticing, and took the cable car to Golden Gate Park where I flew into Ellis's arms. Just to be enfolded in his embrace was balm to my soul, making me feel human again, and loved. 'What am I to do?' I asked, once I had told him the news. His answer was unequivocal.

'You leave him. Now! At once! Don't even go back today.'

'I couldn't do that. The scandal! My parents would be mortified.'

'Forget about the scandal – it's your life, not theirs.'

My instinct was indeed to run home, to Mama and darling Prue, but how would that help? They would be sure to take Kemp's side, for one thing. And Geary Boulevard would be the first place my husband would look, then he'd bring me back, kicking and screaming if necessary. 'The problem is that my father's business is not in such good shape, thanks to Kemp, who has largely taken control. But there's no knowing what my husband might do if I went back home. He could destroy my parents completely.'

Ellis was frowning, his eyes sparkling with anger as he held me close, stroking my hair, kissing my forehead. 'But that isn't *your* problem, my darling, it's your *father's*. He sold you down the river, and for what? To save his profit and loss account? To evade bankruptcy?'

'He did it for the sake of my mother, whom he adores. Mama comes from an aristocratic background. She has always had money at her disposal and has little grasp of reality.'

'She certainly didn't approve of me.'

'I'm afraid not. Oh, Ellis, what a muddle.'

'There must be a solution. We have to find a way to beat Kemp at his own game. You need to find grounds to divorce him. What about this affair with the maid?'

The prospect of fighting my husband in the law courts made me feel sick to my stomach, though it may well come to that in the end. 'I'm sure half of Frisco businessmen have affairs with their wife's maids. I doubt any judge would grant one on those terms. Isn't a wife supposed to turn a blind eye?'

'Then we need more, something stronger. Has he ever struck you or hurt you in any way?'

I fell silent, for some reason ashamed of the beating Kemp had given me, as if I had been responsible in some way and allowed it to happen, which was nonsense. Nevertheless, if it served to free me from this man then it must be spoken of, and brought in as evidence against him. I briefly told Ellis how my husband had caused me to miscarry. Not unnaturally, he was livid. The rage brought a flush of crimson to creep up his throat and over his clenched jaw.

'Damn the man, I could kill him with my own bare hands.'

'Don't say such things, Ellis. We mustn't stoop to his level, and he is a powerful man in this town. We have to be clever, and patient. We must carefully think through our options.'

'Devise a proper plan, you mean. All right, we'll do that, my darling. But promise me you will at least move out of his bed.'

'How could I not?' My eyes were bright with love, and I made no protest this time when he kissed me.

Being the coward that I was, and anxious to avoid confrontation, I wrote Kemp a note explaining my reasons for moving out of his bedroom. Leaving it on his tallboy for him to find, I had Maura move all my belongings into a spare bedroom further along the landing. She guessed at once what was going on.

'You've seen Ellis again, haven't you?'

'Oh, please don't tell.' I grabbed hold of her in my anguish and gave her a little shake. 'Promise you won't say anything. Kemp would kill me if he ever found out.'

She looked at me out of those enigmatic hooded eyes. 'You know that I am ever loyal, that whatever I do it is with your well-being in mind.'

'I know that,' I agreed, but I had the uncomfortable feeling that I'd put myself even more under her power.

I sat in the strange bed that night with one ear cocked for the sound of my husband's step on the stair, quite certain Kemp would come and order my return, drag me back by the hair if necessary.

As I lay tossing and turning with anxiety, sleep quite beyond me, I heard voices below on the breezeway. Getting out of bed I went to peep out of the window. Unfortunately, I could see nothing because of the roof over it, so pulling on my dressing gown I crept down the stairs on bare feet. The front door was slightly ajar and I edged through it, slipping out on to the porch where I hid myself behind a potted palm.

Kemp was standing arguing with two men, one with powerful broad shoulders, looking very much as if he was about to shove a fist in my husband's face at any moment. The exchange seemed to be growing ever more heated, but his weasel-like companion, standing quietly by the steps leading into the garden, took no part in the altercation. There was something about them both that looked strangely familiar, but then I'd seen so many men come to this house in recent months that it barely signified. I was more fascinated by seeing my husband not have the upper hand for once. Grasping hold of Kemp by his collar, the big man almost lifted him off his feet and shook him, as a dog might a rat. His next words rang out loud enough for me to hear.

'I've paid you good money to see that I'm not hounded like this. You get them cops off my back, pronto, you hear? Or you'll discover I've ways of making you sorry that you couldn't even imagine in your worst nightmares. OK?'

Kemp almost stumbled as his assailant let him go, then brushed himself down in an attempt to regain lost dignity. 'OK, you need have no fears, the matter will be dealt with forthwith.'

'Good, and I'll have double the cash for the inconvenience caused. By tomorrow.'

'Drat you, that wasn't the terms of our agreement! I can't find that sort of money, not so quickly.'

'You will if you know what's good for you. I just changed the terms, OK? If you don't want any comebacks, you'll find the cash.'

Kemp gave a low growl of fury deep in his throat. 'And you'll keep your side of the bargain, if I do?'

The big man smirked. 'You can certainly hope so.' And turning, he loped away down the steps. He so resembled a gorilla that you might see at the zoo, I almost giggled. The smaller man was about to follow him, but then suddenly glanced across and looked me straight in the eye. Had

I made a noise, or rustled the palm leaves? I thought, in a sudden panic. I couldn't begin to guess, but in that heart-stopping moment I recognised instantly where I had seen the pair before. In the opium den. They had been the mashers who had waylaid us outside the theatre and kidnapped Prue.

As spry as ever, he caught me before I'd even reached the foot of the stairs. I would have cried out but his hand clapped over my mouth, stifling any sound. With consummate ease he half marched, half carried me out on to the porch, my feet pummelling his legs with all the energy I could muster. Watching all of this with an expression of wry amusement on his face, the big man merely jerked his head, issuing a silent order to his companion to take me out to the pea-green brougham waiting out front. Then to Kemp, he said, 'We'll take the little lady along with us for now, as insurance. Once you've got the dough, you know where to find us.'

Chapter Twenty

The Lakes

When Sunday came at last, Chrissie felt a nervous wreck, yet today she must somehow impress Ben's rapscallion of a daughter, because despite her better judgement she was falling in love with him.

Delighted as she'd been to receive an accolade of support from her grandmother, following that difficult interview, relations between them were still not exactly comfortable. It was encouraging that Georgia was at least still prepared to talk to her. But, perhaps wearied from relating her tale, she'd finally sent her away, warning Chrissie to take no further action with Vanessa until she'd had time to think further on the matter.

Chrissie had avoided the Hall ever since, not even taking breakfast there. And as no invitation to call was forthcoming, she was beginning to wonder if it was wise to stay on at the loft. Camping out over the shop may well be her best option.

So today she'd made an extra effort to look her best, choosing to wear a smart navy suit with a nipped-in waist, full skirt and pink blouse which seemed suitably conservative for the occasion. Surely dealing with a nine-year-old child would be nothing compared to that most difficult interview. Even so, Chrissie presented herself feeling very much like a lamb to the slaughter.

With the now-familiar grim expression on her face, Mrs Gorran led her into the housekeeper's parlour where Karen sat perched on the arm of the sofa rather like a malignant gnome, her small face alight with triumphant amusement. Chrissie inwardly groaned. Word obviously spread quickly. There was no sign of Ben, and even old Sam, Mrs Gorran's husband, was absent. A polite enquiry revealed they were out fishing, but would be back in time for lunch.

Gathering her courage Chrissie smiled in a friendly fashion, offered a few inane remarks about the weather, gaining nothing by way of response save for a frosty silence. She decided to grasp the nettle. 'I want you to know, Mrs Gorran, that I have spoken to my grandmother and my apology was accepted.'

'I wouldn't jump to conclusions too quickly, if I were you,' the housekeeper snapped, her tone showing no sign of any thaw. 'Mrs Cowper isn't prone to impulsive gestures. She might have listened to your apology, but that's not the same as accepting it, nor of finding it in her heart to forgive your lies.'

Chrissie felt suitably chastened. 'You're right, of

course. Forgiveness is often the hardest won. I shall have to hope for the best, shan't I?'

'You'll have to go back to where you came from,' piped up Karen in her shrill childish voice. 'Whatever hole that is where worms like you live. We don't want no liars here, do we, Nan?'

'Here, you mind your manners, miss,' chided her grandmother. 'You're that sharp you'll cut yourself one of these days. Now, I have vegetables to prepare, do you reckon you can entertain Mrs Emerson without giving her any more of your lip? We might not approve of her behaviour, but she's our guest, all right?' There was no response to this beyond a sulky shrug. 'Good. I'll fetch the sherry when I'm done, and a glass of sarsaparilla for you, miss, if you behave.' With that she marched off to the kitchen leaving Chrissie alone with Ben's rebellious daughter.

Determined to remain friendly and calm, and dreading yet another ordeal, she selected a seat and made herself comfortable.

Karen smirked, her small face a picture of malice. 'That's my nan's chair.'

Chrissie almost leapt to her feet, but then thought better of it. Playing musical chairs with this imp wasn't high on her list of priorities. Smiling, she settled back against the cushions. 'I shall be happy to give it up when she returns.'

'Why did you do it?'

'I beg your pardon?'

'Why did you tell those porkies? Mam tells me off

when I tell fibs, but then she's a good person, my mam. She doesn't go around stealing other folk's husbands for a start.'

Chrissie leant forward, her face soft with sympathy. 'Karen, I'm sorry about your parents' divorce, truly I am, but it happened long before I came here. I'm not responsible for that.'

Karen slid from the arm to flop across the sofa full length, propping her chin on one hand as she glared across at Chrissie, bottom lip trembling slightly as she stubbornly stuck it out. 'They were going to get back together till you showed up, I know they were. We was planning a new wedding, Mam and me, with orange blossom, organ music and everything, and me as the bridesmaid. Did you know that?'

'Er . . . no. Are you quite sure?'

'Course I am. Who else would Mam marry? Not that other bloke what hangs around all the time. Not when I don't like him. Granddad says he's her jigsaw.'

'Jigsaw?'

The eyes screwed up in thought for a moment. 'No . . . what was it . . . ? Her jiggle low.'

Chrissie nodded, struggling to keep a straight face. 'Ah, I see.'

'And I know me own dad, don't I? He still loves her – me mam. He said so. So they're bound to get back together, 'cept you juiced him.'

'I what? Oh, you mean I *se*duced him. Actually, you're wrong, Karen. Nobody has seduced anyone.' She wondered if this child even knew the meaning of the word. 'Your dad and I are just good friends. And I'd like to be friends with you too, if I may.'

The girl stuck two fingers down her throat and pretended to vomit. 'That's another lie. I know you juiced him 'cause I saw you kissing.'

'Oh, well, he is rather nice to kiss, your dad. But it wasn't quite how it looked.' By this time Chrissie was having a hard time not laughing. She was deeply relieved when she heard the front door bang and the sound of men's voices in the hall. Except that she was jangling with nerves again. If everyone else had heard the story of her deceit, Ben would certainly be aware of it. What would be his reaction? Would he too condemn her for a liar and a cheat, only interested in the old lady's money? He walked through the door, and coming straight over to her, drew her into his arms.

'Sweetheart, how are you? What a terrible thing to happen.' Ben seemed to accept, without question, that she was not the one responsible for the lies and subterfuge. He also made it clear that not for a moment did he believe she would have any ulterior motive in going along with what her mother had asked.

'You're just not that sort of person. I'm surprised anyone could even think that of you.'

'Uncle Ryall doesn't even know me, so why would he believe in my innocence?'

'You could equally well ask why he would believe you to be guilty. He's not an easy man at the best of times, but I can't see Mrs Cowper allowing him to influence her too much. She very much likes to make up her own mind about things.'

'Thank goodness. You too, I see.' Chrissie put her hands to Ben's face and kissed him. It was meant as a light kiss of friendship, as she was all too aware of a pair of gimlet eyes watching them closely, nevertheless it was filled with warmth, and promise. 'Thank you for that. I appreciate your loyalty, and those few words of comfort.' His faith in her was wonderfully reassuring, giving her hope that all might not be lost.

Lunch passed off surprisingly well, considering the circumstances. There was an unfortunate incident with a spill of gravy in her lap when Karen was passing her the sauce boat, which made Ben snap at his young daughter, ordering her to behave, rather as her grandmother had done earlier. But Chrissie dismissed it as unimportant. A scrub of cold water with a kitchen cloth got the worst of the sticky mess off.

'It's not a problem. The suit needed dry-cleaning in any case.'

Mrs Gorran cast the girl a sharp look and, after a surprised glance in Chrissie's direction, as if she'd expected a far worse reaction, Karen dutifully applied her attention to the excellent roast lamb.

After lunch had been cleared away Ben suggested that Karen sing for them. 'I'm sure Chrissie would love to hear you sing "Now is the Hour".'

'Indeed I would,' Chrissie agreed. 'I didn't realise you could sing, Karen. What a marvellous gift to have.'

'I take after my mum,' Karen said, pouting a little as she leant against her father's arm. 'She has a really lovely voice, doesn't she, Dad?'

'I think Sal would disagree with you there,' Ben laughed, clearly not prepared to play the game of 'Mum is best'. 'She would say you have far the better voice. Come on, I'll accompany you.'

Ben went to the piano and played a few opening chords. 'Ready?'

The girl sang beautifully, capturing each note with perfect pitch and reaching the high notes with ease. Everyone joined in with the final chorus and when the song ended Chrissie applauded with genuine appreciation and enthusiasm. 'That was lovely. Do you know anything else?'

Wrapping her arms about her father's neck, Karen sulkily shook her head.

'Course you do,' said her grandfather, happily sipping his glass of port. 'Sing that "Zip-a-dee-doo-dah" song, and "There's No Business Like Show Business". I like them jolly ones.'

Casting a dismissive glare in Chrissie's direction she kissed old Sam's weathered cheek. 'All right, Grandad, just for you.'

After a while, thanks to the encouragement from her grandparents, the genuine appreciation of her audience, and joy in her own singing, Karen opened up a little. She stopped sulking and began to giggle and laugh as a young girl should, allowing Chrissie to see how charming she was when not intent on doing battle and causing mayhem. She shone with happiness, and by the way father and daughter teased and played together, it was obvious they enjoyed an excellent relationship.

Chrissie felt privileged to be part of this delightful family scene with everyone relaxed and happy, and her own delicate situation seemed to have been forgotten, or at least set aside. Ben took pains to make her feel included, frequently asking her opinion on something, or just squeezing her hand and grinning at her. She wanted to tell Karen how very fortunate she was, both in her singing voice and her close family, but was nervous of reopening the issue of her parents' broken marriage, so kept quiet.

Eventually the piano was locked up again, Sam went off to see to his precious hens, and Karen for a bike ride. Ben too offered his apologies. 'I've a repair to finish in my workshop, for Mrs Johnson. I've been replacing a pane of stained glass in her cabinet. Do you mind? It won't take long but I just need to finish it off and polish the whole thing up. I promised I'd deliver it first thing in the morning.'

'Of course I don't mind,' Chrissie said. 'I should be going anyway. Lunch was lovely, Mrs Gorran. Thank you.'

Ben looked instantly disappointed. 'Oh, I thought we could take a walk later, when I'm done. Could I call for you?'

'Why don't you stay and keep me company for a bit?' his mother suggested, quite taking Chrissie by surprise. 'I've just to take Mrs Cowper her tea, then we could have a pot ourselves. I don't know about you but I'm ready for a brew, and mebbe a slice of fruit cake?'

Delighted by this sign of a thaw in the housekeeper's

attitude, Chrissie smilingly agreed. 'That sounds lovely.' It might also offer an opportunity to ask a few further questions.

'So, you're Vanessa's girl? Did she have any more children?' Mrs Gorran had taken a tray to the library for her employer and Mr Ryall, one loaded with cucumber sandwiches, slices of fruit cake and scones all carefully arranged on a cake stand beside a silver teapot, strainer, and china for two. Now she settled back in her chair ready for a gossip, and sipped thankfully at her own tea.

Chrissie shook her head. 'No, there's only me.'

'That's a shame. Vanessa always used to say she wanted a quiverful, two of each if she could choose. I'm sorry that didn't work out for her. But at least she's happy, eh?'

There was a small silence as Chrissie pondered on how best to answer this question. In the end she settled for honesty. 'Not exactly. Mum has never really got over losing Dad at Dunkirk, or his leaving her some years before, for that matter. He was very much the love of her life. No one else could ever hold a candle to him.'

Mrs Gorran nodded, smiling softly. 'I remember. Besotted they were, struck dumb by Cupid's arrow from the first moment they clapped eyes on each other.'

'Yet my grandmother did not approve of their marriage. According to my mother, she accused Aaran of being a charlatan and a chancer, who only wished to marry her for her money.'

The older woman frowned. 'I wouldn't know about that. I do seem to recall there was some history of a problem with the boy's mother, of which we weren't fully conversant.'

'Really? What sort of problem?'

'I couldn't say, but there was talk of Vanessa going to America. Mrs Cowper was terrified of losing her daughter, and her new grandchild.'

'America is a long way away, I suppose, particularly back then. Yet they did go in the end.'

'I believe so, yes, though I can't recall quite when it was. I do remember the big row afterwards. Vanessa storming out. Poor Mrs Cowper was devastated. She kept saying over and over, "I should have told her the whole story." Like a cracked record she was.'

'What was it, this whole story? Did you ever find out?'

Mrs Gorran sadly shook her head. 'She wrote screeds of letters to their shop in Chelsea, begging Vanessa to call, but they were all returned unopened, marked "gone away", so I suppose she never got the chance. It was very sad.'

'That must have been the time my parents sold the gallery, the time their marriage fell apart. I wish I knew why. I may be prejudiced but I thought my father was a lovely man. Why would Grandmother hate him so much?'

Mrs Gorran stopped heaping raspberry jam on to her scone, looking slightly surprised by this remark. 'She didn't hate him. Like I say, it was the boy's mother she distrusted, due to some old grudge between them, apparently.'

'But Mum says she never accepted Aaran, and that

money continued to be a source of dispute between them.'

'That may well be so, though as to the reasons, I couldn't say for sure. All I do know is that I once saw young Aaran here with my own eyes. He was alone on that occasion, without your mother, and the pair of them looked fairly friendly to me.'

'When was that?'

'Nay, it's too long ago to put a date on it. I'd just come out of a bedroom on to the landing, my arms full of dirty laundry, when I heard his voice below. He and your grandmother were talking in the hall. I couldn't hear what they were saying, exactly, as their voices were quite low, but they seemed very earnest, almost urgent. Later, when I heard the young couple had gone off to San Francisco, I assumed that must have been the subject of the discussion. But at the time I didn't think they were having a row. I did hear Mrs Cowper say, "I want her kept safe, the baby too, that's all I ask." Then she put her arms about him and they embraced, just a brief hug but friendly enough. After which he left and Mrs Cowper leant against the door and wept a little. I remember feeling rather sorry for her and hurrying down to make her a cup of coffee, black and sweet, just how she liked it, and a slice of her favourite coffee cake.'

'How odd. That doesn't sound at all the way you might expect a disapproving mother-in-law to behave.' Chrissie thoughtfully sipped her tea, which had gone a little cold, so she allowed Mrs Gorran to top it up for her. 'Did she ever speak of that conversation to you?'

'No, dear, not a word.' Mrs Gorran reached for a slice

of her excellent shortbread, offered one to Chrissie, which she reluctantly declined, being full to bursting with good food. 'She rarely speaks of private matters, or of that time, although she does sometimes mention the earthquake, and the fire.'

'Earthquake? Goodness, I didn't know about that. Was it serious?'

'Oh, I believe it was, yes, very serious. Happened in 1906. Mrs Cowper says it changed everything.'

'Oh, tell me more. What has she said about the earthquake?'

'I'm not sure it's my place. Happen Mrs Cowper should tell you herself.'

Back in the library Georgia settled in her favourite chair by the fire, eyes closed, thankful her son had at last left her in peace and gone off to telephone his adoring, ambitious wife. Dearest Clare was already threatening to catch the next train down to 'talk some sense into her', which made Georgia shudder at the prospect of further lengthy lectures. Yet, what did it matter? What did anything matter? Who could one trust these days? Certainly not your own family, and perhaps not even a young woman who pretended to be friendly and interested in you.

The girl had apologised for her deceit, which was something, even if her words and attitude had not impressed Ryall. And it made perfect sense that the idea for subterfuge would come from Vanessa, rather than from her. But she'd lost her lovely daughter long since, and had no wish to remember the pain of that parting.

She'd made such a mess of everything. Got it all wrong. Though even now she wasn't sure what would have been the right thing to do.

Now there was this new grandchild. Did she want to lose her too? What a pity that had gone badly wrong. And she'd seemed such a nice, open, friendly girl. Could she trust her, that was the question? What was she after? Was she really only trying to bring about a family reunion, or were her motives deeper and less honourable, as Ryall suggested?

'If only you were here to advise me, Ellis. I must consider what you might have said, or thought, of all of this.'

In seconds she was smiling, her mind slipping back to the past, to Frisco, her heart filled with love for her darling Ellis. And when the door quietly opened and Chrissie appeared, she reached out a hand to beckon her in.

Chapter Twenty-One

San Francisco

It wasn't the same room where they'd taken Prudence. This time, rather than a beer hall, it was situated at the end of a dark courtyard, behind a Chinese laundry. I could hear the chatter of foreign tongues, which I presumed to be speaking Mandarin, as my captors pushed me up a rickety staircase ahead of them. My heart was pounding and my brain racing, but coming up with no answers as to how I could escape this place. Not even Maura knew where I was, and I had little hope that my husband would care what these men did to me. Still only in my night attire, I was shaking with cold.

As we entered, I was again overwhelmed by a sickly-sweet, slightly nutty scent. I'd gone to bed early but it must have been almost midnight by this time and I could see, even in the dim light, that the room was full. The walls were lined with what looked like wide wooden shelves or bunks, and on each lay the prone figure of a man. Many, but by no means all, were Chinamen dressed in blue tunics, with long pigtails, and white stockings on their feet. Each bunk had a tray attached, upon which stood a small lamp, ivory box and long-stemmed pipe. As my abductor pushed me into a chair and started to bind my hands, exactly as he had done with Prue, the one nearest to me dug out a small piece of soft paste from a box and held it on the end of a wire to the flame until it solidified in some way. Then he stuffed it into the tiny stone bowl of his pipe and inhaled through the long bamboo stem, drawing the smoke deep into his lungs and blowing it out again down his nostrils.

I recoiled, horrified by what I had just witnessed, knowing how the drug would leave a trail of poison in its wake. This was far worse than what Prue had been subjected to. I looked about me, desperate for help, but none of the other occupants took the slightest notice of me. They were too occupied smoking their pipes, some insensible already.

'Havee smokee?' the man asked, happily beaming a lopsided grin as he offered me the pipe.

'No, thank you,' I gasped. My hands were clammy with cold sweat, and I was deeply afraid he might force me to take part in this fatal game. Fortunately, his eyes instantly glazed over, the pipe drooped in his hand and his head fell back as he sank into a doped stupor. I wondered if he was even breathing.

My weasel-like abductor, his bald head shaped rather like a bullet, had by this time got me firmly anchored to the chair, even tying my ankles together. Any hope of escape instantly died.

His larger friend said, 'Keep your mouth shut and be a good girl, if you know what's good for you. If you're lucky, your rich husband will cough up the necessary dough tomorrow.'

I almost said I very much doubted that would happen, but thought better of it. I could be signing my own death warrant if this pair ever got the idea that holding me would be a waste of their time. God knows what they would do to me if Kemp didn't appear on the morrow. I could only pray that even my heartless husband would find a modicum of decency and do what he could to get me released.

The pair left then, and the hours ticked slowly by in what turned out to be the longest night of my life. I was in bleak despair, every minute feeling like an hour, my fears and hopes see-sawing as the night wore on, till finally the pink of dawn crept around the edges of the partly shuttered windows.

My doped companions slowly began to wake, tottering away one by one like sleepwalkers. I called after them, 'Fetch help, please. Untie me. Help!' None replied, or even appeared to hear. Gradually the room emptied and I was left alone, silently weeping, in total despair. And then I heard the clatter of boots on the step and the door opened.

'Thought you might be hungry.' It was Weasel, as I'd mentally dubbed him, bringing me a bowl of steamed noodles, and tea, all set out neatly on a tray. I was deeply touched. He even untied my hands so that I could eat and drink in comfort.

'I'm most grateful,' I told him, and was, for his kindness if nothing else. Yet I didn't for a moment trust him, wondering why he bothered, and what his plans were for me.

He perched himself on the edge of the table as if ready to talk. 'I remember you now. You're that spunky gal with the gun who dared to outface Big Billy. Put the wind up him good and proper, you did. Gave me a good laugh afterwards when I realised the gun wasn't loaded. Took guts, that did. You 'minds me of my sister, Pol, she's a spunky lass too.'

I began to breathe more easily at the compliment, and tucked into the food, realising I was ravenous. 'A gal has to do what a gal has to do,' I joked, and he laughed.

'So now you're married to Drew Kemp, eh?'

'I am, more's the pity,' I muttered.

'Ah, he's not your idea of love's young dream, then?'

'Not at all.'

He wanted to know how it had all come about, and, since I was grateful for his company and his generosity, I told him, sparing no details.

'That sounds about right,' he said, nodding, as if he understood far more than I. 'Kemp is good at disposing of the competition, both personal and in business matters. Your friend had a lucky escape if he only got shipped out on a clipper. It could've been much worse. I'm sorry a nice young lady such as yourself has got caught up in this mess.'

Smiling, I sipped the hot green tea, which was most

welcome, and as we seemed to be mates by this time, dared to ask a question of my own. 'So what's your connection with my husband? Don't worry, I know all about his acceptance of bribes in order to buy votes and get himself elected as mayor at the next election.'

My new friend refilled my teacup from the little pot on the tray, then glanced nervously over his shoulder before telling his tale. It was as I had thought. My husband was heavily involved in fraudulent practices and corruption. If the crimps wanted to continue their business without interference it was in their interests to hand over large portions of their profits to Kemp.

'Kemp is heavily into protection rackets – charges a monthly retainer, cash only, no paperwork or receipts, in return for favours. If it's called a retainer for services rendered, the theory is it's not illegal. There's plenty like him in this town,' said my friend, who'd now revealed his name as Eddie. 'But Kemp is one of the big guys. He's hand in glove with some of the worst crimps in the opium trade, taking his cut of every shipment that comes in to the bay. He also grants liquor licences, in return for "retainers", for them "French" restaurants, so-called not for the food but for what goes on upstairs on the top floor. Everything has a price, and Kemp's the guy who fixes it.'

'I see.' I was, in fact, beginning to understand a great deal about my husband. Information which may well prove useful. Eddie talked for some time, naming names, filling me in on the secret side of my husband's life. But it was my own situation which most occupied my mind right now. I cast my new friend what I hoped was an appealing look, though I was so desperately afraid I had no need to manufacture tears – they were already welling in my eyes. 'Eddie, the honest truth is that I have no great faith my husband will come and rescue me, or pay this extra cash, whatever it is. What will happen to me? What am I to do?'

He grinned at me. 'That's why *I'm* here. I'm right sorry I dragged you into this. I admired you the first time we met. You'll be a real handsome woman one day, when you've done growing up. I ain't gonna let anything happen to you, gal, any more'n I would our Pol. I thought you could slip out while Billy is busy eating his breakfast.' He was untying my ankles now and hope bloomed in my breast.

'Won't he blame you if I just disappear? I would be sorry if he did.'

Weasel, or Eddie as I should call him now, shook his head in disbelief. 'D'you know, that's the nicest thing anyone ever said to me since my ma died. What a lovely gal you are, a real lady. But don't you worry about me none, I'll blame it on your companions of the night. I'll say they were so far gone they were quite capable of doing anything you asked of them. Now get you gone. Once you're out of here, remember, you're on your own.'

'Don't worry, I'll cope. I'm an independent sort of gal.'

He grinned at me, acknowledging this with a nod of his bullet-shaped head. 'Keep back,' he instructed as he opened the door a crack, then poked his head out to check if the coast was clear. 'OK, quiet as you can. Go!'

I didn't need telling twice. I popped a quick kiss on his cheek then flew down the steps on my tiptoes and fled.

Within a couple of hours I was back in my own bed, Maura by my side with a tray of hot chocolate, a plate of oat muffins, and a consoling smile on her face. 'As if Kemp would ever leave you in that place. I'm surprised you didn't have more faith in your husband.'

I looked up at her, wondering if I did indeed know this woman. She'd become like a stranger to me, and yet because she knew my secret, one whom I relied upon entirely. It was a most disturbing sensation. 'I wasn't about to hang around and wait to find out. I saw my chance and ran for it. Anyway, has my husband ever given me reason to trust him?' I asked, unable to keep the bitterness out of my voice. But it was pointless arguing with her, nor with Kemp when later he came to check on me.

'Serves you right for interfering in matters which do not concern you,' was his predictable response, with not a word of praise for effecting my own escape. 'What the hell were you doing wandering about the house in your night things anyway? You should learn to keep your prying nose out of my affairs. And what the hell is all this nonsense about you moving bedrooms? You'll move back into the marital bed, where you belong, this very day or rue the consequences.'

I ignored the threat. One thing I had learnt during the long night with the Chinamen, who had in no way molested me but taken their pleasure in private without interfering with anyone, was that I was much stronger than I'd realised. And I had learnt a great deal from my friend Eddie.

Now I faced my husband with new courage. 'I am fully aware of your involvement in – what do they call it? – graft. Corruption, I believe, is rife in Frisco politics right now, and you are one of the worst offenders, or so I'm reliably informed.'

'Who told you that? Absolute rubbish.' But I could see he was startled.

'Never mind who. Hardly matters, does it? I *know*, that's the point.'

Kemp's upper lip curled, as it so often did, matching his caustic thoughts. 'Who the hell do you think you are? You know nothing.'

I smiled. 'I know enough. I can name names, point fingers in the right places, make your life very difficult indeed. I can put a stop, in fact, to all your plans and dreams, should I choose to do so. You admitted to me yourself that you took bribes in order to win votes to have yourself elected as mayor, only you didn't quite get enough and lost. No doubt you hope this year will be different. And running for office must cost a packet these days, so a few favours here and there has a double benefit. Cash in hand, and election as mayor at some point.'

His rage was such now that his face had diffused to a deep purple. But my husband was no fool. Tight-lipped, he asked, 'So what is all this leading up to? What is it you want?'

'My freedom, of course. But I can see that a divorce

right now wouldn't help your political prospects one bit. I'm prepared to wait, at least for a little while. But it will be on *my* terms, which I now feel in a position to make. It's quite simple: leave me alone, or I'll spill the beans and tell everyone what you're up to.'

I stayed where I was while Kemp took a room on the floor above, conveniently closer to Maura. The new arrangement worked fine so far as I was concerned. And as I pointed out to my husband, there wouldn't be a breath of scandal as no one would be any the wiser. The reward for my patience and silence, he agreed, would be paid in full with a divorce, once he'd achieved his aim and become mayor of the city.

In truth, I had no intention of waiting that long, but I wasn't going to tell him that.

From that moment on I considered my marriage to be at an end. I could not live with a man who made use of prostitutes, who exploited those less fortunate than himself, and who cheated and took bribes in order to win yet more power. I had done my best to be a good wife to him, and he had rewarded my effort by abusing me. Not that the marriage had much hope from the start. It wasn't a wife Drew Kemp wanted, but a slave. The only solution was to somehow break free from the chains that bound me.

To do that I needed advice on how to procure a divorce, but my husband was so well known in the city, and so powerful, that I dare not seek out an attorney. I had to find some other way of escape. At least to begin with. I didn't trust him an inch, and held little hope of him keeping his word in our bargain.

Ellis and I began to meet regularly, albeit in secret.

Maura would let me out of a side door the moment Kemp was out of the house, or in a meeting, promising to keep him distracted should he re-emerge, so that he would not miss me. Then, leaving her to get on with her new role of mistress of my marital home, I would slip away to see my lover. I knew it was wrong, and it wasn't a comfortable situation to be in, rather one filled with danger. But I was young still, and deeply in love. I was also fully aware that the hold I had on Kemp would not last for ever, and could endanger others by my seeming acceptance of his corruptive practices.

Our long-term plan was to escape to Ellis's home in England, which was far enough away for even Kemp's reach to be blocked. But how to achieve that?

For now I was content simply to be in Ellis's arms. He would kiss me and I would feel the sweetness of his love run through me like fire. Summer was upon us and we would walk in the Japanese Gardens, over the little bridges, watching the carp playing in the ponds, or visit the beautiful Victorian conservatory in the Botanical Gardens. Later we'd find somewhere off the beaten track and hide in the bushes, with not a scrap of shame in our daring caresses. Tasting, touching, exploring our love for each other, which grew with each passing day. His tongue would dance with mine, his hands fondle the curve of my breast, and I gloried in his touch. How could I not when I loved him so? Wanting him as much as I did was both intoxicating and dangerous, yet not for a moment did I consider stopping seeing him. We took every opportunity to be together, savouring what we'd been denied for so long. He was a part of me, and I only felt whole when I was with him.

I took terrible risks to escape the house, with Maura's unfailing assistance. But once, I was so certain I was being followed that I walked for six blocks in the wrong direction and almost got lost in a rabbit warren of streets dangerously close to the wharf area. Fortunately a cable car came by and I jumped on board, travelling on it to the end of the line where it was swung round by the conductor, then headed back downtown. I reached our rendezvous safely, if an hour late.

Should my husband ever discover our secret I would lose whatever small hold I had over him. And he would then most certainly refuse to grant me a divorce.

'Perhaps we should stop seeing each other,' Ellis said, when I spoke of these fears. 'Should I go back to sea, then you would be safe? I'll have to go soon, I suppose, for financial reasons if nothing else.'

But I wouldn't hear of it, fearing I might lose him for ever. 'No, not yet, please don't leave me now,' I cried, desperate for his love. 'I need you here, with me. You are a part of me. I want you to love me.'

'I do love you, my darling. You know that I do.'

'I mean I want you to show me how much you love me. I want you inside me.' I started to kiss him then as I never had before, more urgent, more demanding, tugging at the buttons on his shirt. I felt so vulnerable, so afraid that I might never break free of Kemp. 'This might be all we get, Ellis, you and I. We should take what we can, love each other now. Think only of today.' I heard his small groan as my hands smoothed his bare skin. Then I was fumbling with my own buttons, and he was helping me, pulling, tugging, unlacing, so many silly clothes getting in the way. Nothing seemed to matter but the heat of our desire. When flesh finally touched flesh it was as if we had been set alight, and seconds later we found what we had been seeking for so long. We became one person, joined in spirit, in our hearts, and with our flesh. No one could part us now.

It was the most glorious summer of my life. We continued to meet in the park, as often as we could, but sometimes he took me to out-of-the-way hotels where we could be quite alone without fear of interruption. It was perfectly wicked, and dreadfully dangerous, but nothing could have stopped me from taking the risk. I owed nothing to Kemp now, not even my loyalty.

But finally summer passed, fall arrived with the smell of sweet chestnuts and the glory of falling leaves, and the knowledge that I was pregnant.

Chapter Twenty-Two

I had never felt so alone. Ellis was away at sea, had been for a week or two by the time I realised my predicament. I wasn't expecting him back any time soon, so had no alternative but to keep my pregnancy secret. I knew that the moment he returned we must make haste to escape. No matter how sketchy or dangerous our plans, however little money we had, we could afford to wait no longer. I couldn't believe how naive and foolish we'd been in dallying this long, how complacent. We might talk about practicalities, about saving every cent and dime we could, waiting until the moment was right when Kemp had been elected mayor, but really we were simply happily savouring the bliss of being together at last, enjoying our love without a thought for the consequences.

In any case, Kemp had lost. My husband hadn't been

alone in standing for mayor, there'd been several other candidates from various political parties, but no one could deny he hadn't campaigned hard. Kemp had been out and about every waking hour on the campaign trail, talking, advising, bribing, bullying, but to no avail. And I, as his wife, had hosted more dinner parties than I cared to recall. Despite all his protection rackets, his dubious 'retainers' and devious little tricks to pull in votes, he'd failed to win the number required. Instead, the tall charismatic Eugene Schmitz had been re-elected. No doubt because he was more a man of the people than my husband could ever be.

And Kemp was still visiting brothels, even though I assumed he still slept with my maid. My own relationship with Maura remained as complex as ever, and she took to complaining to me regularly about his habits. I refused to get involved.

'Why did you do it? I have never understood.'

'Because you didn't want him, and I did.'

'But *why* did you want him when you knew what sort of man he was?'

'I don't think I did,' she admitted, 'but I love him, so what can I do?' And on impulse, my heart softened by my own love for Ellis, I put my arms about her and hugged her. She wasn't a bad person, I told myself, only a very unwise and greedy one. A young woman rather full of her own importance.

Nothing about my husband's conduct had changed, and I made it a rule to keep well out of his way. I started to loosen my corset, drape shawls about my shoulders, hoping and praying that he wouldn't discover my secret. My heart raced with fear at the thought. Heaven knows what he would do to me if he ever found out I was carrying another man's child.

Fearful also of Maura discovering my condition, I dispensed with her services, not wishing her to see me naked or even in my underclothes.

'Let's stop this pretence of being maid and mistress, shall we?' I said to her one day.

She didn't flicker an eyelid, perhaps relieved by the suggestion. 'Very well. If you wish I'll ask one of the young maids to take my place. But I hope you and I can still be friends.'

'We will always be that, Maura.'

And strangely we were, despite the fact I had grown to hate and almost fear her. We would sit together of an evening, with our needlework or a book, chatting about inconsequential matters. We did not speak of my husband, or the oddness of our situation. To all outward appearances she was my friend and companion, nothing more, nothing less. In reality she took from me whatever she wanted, whether it be the loan of my gowns, my husband, even my position and status in my own home. And I dared not object.

But once Ellis returned and I was free, Maura could have Kemp all to herself, and welcome. I could hardly wait for that day to come as I ticked the days off my calendar with growing impatience. Then my love and I would never be separated again.

* * *

It was my mother who first grew curious. 'You've gone all peaky-looking again, girl. What have you been doing to yourself?'

'Nothing, Mama, I feel fine, thank you.'

'Well, you don't look it.' She cast me a sideways smile from beneath her lashes. 'You look to me like a young lady with a secret.'

My heart stopped. 'I-I can't think what you mean,' I babbled. How thankful I was that Maura had not accompanied me on this occasion, having taken to her bed with a cold.

'Hm,' Mama said, looking thoughtful.

Deeply grateful that she let the matter drop, I took my leave as hastily as I could. But I could sense her watching me closely every time I called after that, and she would ask Maura veiled questions about the state of my health.

'I wish I had half her energy,' Maura would reply. 'Considering the charity work, and the entertaining she is required to do, she's a veritable tornado, never still for a moment.'

'And what of you, Prudence dear?' I interrupted. 'I'm sure your social life is much more exciting than mine.'

I always did my best to direct the conversation away from myself and talk about my sister's latest beau, a favourite topic for speculation. She seemed to have a whole line of young men paying her court, which delighted me. And she continued to wheedle money out of me so that she could keep up appearances. Papa's business had largely been taken over by Kemp, and ready cash seemed in increasingly short supply. It was galling to realise that my sacrifice in going through with this marriage had not paid off financially. For that reason alone I never demurred at helping my spoilt sister, hoping that she, at least, might be allowed the privilege of choosing her own husband.

Christmas came and went, my condition becoming harder to disguise, and still with no sign of Ellis. I was distracted from this worry by Maura suddenly deciding to leave, claiming she couldn't stand to be near Kemp anymore. How could I argue with that, although I begged her not to go? 'How will I manage without you?'

'You weren't planning on staying yourself for much longer, were you? Or have I got that wrong?'

I said no more, but despite the awkwardness of our situation I was sorry to lose her. She'd been my only companion and the house seemed empty without her. Nor was I convinced her reason for going was genuine. For all I knew, my husband may well have set her up in a house of her own somewhere. I told myself it was no concern of mine. As soon as Ellis returned to port, I would be leaving too, just as Maura had suspected.

A week or two later my mother's curiosity burst forth more forcibly than ever. 'I have to say you're looking much better.'

'Thank you, Mama.'

'Come now, you can't fool your own mother. I know that certain look in the eye, that softening of the features, not to mention the bloom on your cheeks. Why, you're looking almost pretty, child. You're expecting, aren't you?'

I was devastated. This was the last thing I needed. I

tried to deny it, without exactly telling a lie. 'I can't think where you get these ideas from, Mama.'

She leant forward, sharp eyes narrowing as she closely scrutinised me through her pince-nez. 'Then why did you shudder when Prudence poured you that cup of coffee just now? There isn't anything worse for a pregnant lady than the smell of coffee. Unless it is oranges. I never could tolerate fruit of any kind in either one of my pregnancies.' Collecting her own coffee cup she leant back to quietly sip it, as if she'd solved a major enigma. 'So, when are you due?'

There seemed little point in arguing. The morning sickness had largely stopped but I still felt somewhat delicate. And that coffee was indeed making me feel decidedly ill, so much so that I was obliged to make my excuses and run for the bathroom. But Mama was still sitting waiting for me in the parlour, bright-eyed and bursting with the excitement of this new knowledge.

I returned to my seat with a resigned sigh. 'All right, it's true, I believe I may be pregnant, but please don't tell a soul. I haven't even told Kemp yet.'

Mama almost beamed her satisfaction at being proved right. 'It's a husband's privilege to be the first to hear, although I never can understand why they don't guess, when it's plain for all to see.'

'Not everyone sees with a mother's eye,' I said with a wry smile. 'And not all husbands pay such attention to their wives as Papa does with you.'

Setting her coffee cup down with a clatter, Prudence rushed to my side to grasp my hands in hers, a look of anxiety on her sweet face. 'Is something wrong, Georgia?'

'Not at all.' I had no wish to discuss the state of my marriage with my sister.

'I'm sure Drew will be delighted by the news. How fortunate you are to have such a charming handsome husband who adores you, and to be about to bear his child. I'm furiously jealous. I shall be eighteen soon, and still haven't found my soulmate yet,' she pouted.

I smiled at her. 'That's only because you are spoilt for choice. You have, to my knowledge, declined half a dozen proposals.' But I didn't disabuse my sister of this romantic view she held of my life, merely begged her to hold her chattering tongue, as it was early days yet.

'Prudence will end up an old maid, for sure, if she doesn't stop being so picky,' Mama sternly warned. 'And if you've any sense you'll tell your husband right now, girl, before the entire society of San Francisco is buzzing with it.'

'I will tell him when *I* am good and ready,' I said.

As luck would have it, Mama, Papa and Prue were coming for dinner to Nob Hill the following Saturday, and barely had Kemp put a glass of sweet sherry into my mother's hand than she gave him a knowing wink. 'I dare say Georgia has told you the news?'

'News, what news?'

I silently groaned. 'Not now, Mama, please. You promised. Can we talk about this some other time?'

'Talk about what?' Kemp asked.

'Why,' she said, eyes glinting. 'The fact that your wife is carrying your son, that's all.'

Silly Prudence gave an overly dramatic squeal of delight and, running to hug and kiss me, told me how clever I was and how she would just adore being an aunt, giving every impression that this was all a great surprise to her. Papa gruffly offered his congratulations, saying something about it being about time. But the silence from my husband was profound. If I was even breathing I was unaware of it.

At last Kemp drawled, 'Well, well, who would have believed it?'

'Oh dear,' said my mother, pretending to fluster. 'Have I spoilt the surprise?'

'It's certainly that,' my husband admitted. 'Although I did think there was something different about her, but couldn't quite work out what it was.'

Probably because he rarely saw me from one week to the next. I'd made very sure to keep out of his way, even to having my meals sent up to my room.

Mama was giggling like a schoolgirl, batting her eyelashes up at him in a most ridiculous manner. 'Of course, we don't yet know that it *will* be a son. It might be a daughter. How would you feel about that, Drew?'

He stared at her for a long moment, then smiled his wintry smile. 'I'd say there's always another time, except that I'd much prefer not to wait any longer.' He came to stand behind me, planted a cold kiss on my cheek as he patted my shoulders. 'But this is good news. We'd rather given up hope, hadn't we, dear?'

And as I looked up into his eyes, I felt the icy draught of his knowing gaze shiver down my spine.

* * *

He came to my room later, after our guests had gone, walking in without so much as a by your leave. But I made a mental note to have a lock fitted. Hands in pockets, Kemp stood contemplating me with the kind of smile on his handsome face that I'd come to dread.

'Only you and I are aware that this child has nothing to do with me. So whose is it?'

Somehow I kept a smile fixed to my face, hoping he wouldn't notice my fear. 'I-I don't really think that is any of your business in the circumstances, do you? We are separated, if you recall.'

He glanced about him with a feigned air of innocence. 'From what I can see we are not only still living in the same house, but both now occupying the same room.'

'No, we are not. *I* am occupying this room. *You* are visiting, albeit without my permission. I kept my word and stood by you until the elections, now I think it's time we put our separation on a more official footing. I want that divorce you promised me.'

He leant across the bed towards me, one clenched fist resting on the quilt at either side, trapping me within. 'There will be another election in two year's time, and another after that. I mean to be mayor one day, so my moral standing in the community must be unimpeachable.'

I actually laughed out loud at that. 'You've failed miserably in that respect already,' I scoffed. 'I can think of no one less moral than you.'

He continued speaking with barely a pause, as if I hadn't dared to interrupt him. 'You will remain my wife until I no longer need one, is that clear? Which could well be some years.'

It seemed that my opinion, my needs, my *life*, didn't count for anything. I fidgeted crossly in my confined space, sitting very straight so that I did not touch him. 'No, actually, it isn't clear at all. You're sleeping with my maid, no doubt set her up in a house somewhere, and with *whores*, not to mention the corruption you're involved with. How moral is that? I could spill the beans at any time.'

He stepped away from the bed, put back his head and laughed out loud. His obvious amusement at this remark lasted for so long that I began to prickle with unease.

'You're wrong about Maura, I've no idea where the silly chit is. But the fact of the matter is, dear wife, that whatever hold you once had over me has now quite lost its bite. The power has shifted back into my hands, as I knew it must if I was patient. Should I choose to do so, *I* could be the one to divorce *you* now. Charged with adultery, it would be *your* reputation that was ruined. Not only that, but were I to refuse to accept this child as my own, once it is born, I could turn you out of *my* house and refuse to allow you to even see it.'

I let out a strangled gasp of horror. 'You would never do such a thing.'

His gaze on mine was flint hard. 'Would I not? Did you pick up another homeless sailor, is that it? Since you've developed such a passion for them you could move in with him, whoever he is, at the Seamen's Institute, or in one of the dives on the wharves, or live on the streets for all I care. And if, by any chance, it happens to be the same sailor, one Ellis Cowper, then I could have him transported. I seem to recall I did that once before. How very enterprising of him to return. This time I could send him further, to the bottom of the ocean, for instance.'

I was shaking so much by this time that my teeth were chattering. It hadn't simply been foolish of us to delay our departure, it had been profoundly dangerous. 'Even you wouldn't go so far as to commit *murder*!' No sooner was the word out of my mouth than I wanted to pull it back, as if by using it I'd given the threat credibility.

By way of reply he gripped my face in one hand, with such power in his fingers that I thought my jaw might actually crack. 'I can do exactly as I please. Haven't you learnt that yet? And *you*, dear wife, will do as I tell you. Tomorrow you will move back into the marital bedroom. If this child is to be accepted as mine, then we must be seen to be living as a happily married couple. Rather late in the day, I accept, but necessary. We shall call it a happy rapprochement.' And having settled the matter to his own satisfaction, he sauntered to the door.

By the time he reached it, I'd collected what was left of my wits for one last show of defiance. 'I will not return to your bed. Ever!'

He snorted with laughter. 'Oh, yes, you will. If you want to keep this child, and your lover, safe, there'll be no more talk of divorce, nor of spilling any beans. Otherwise, it could be blood and tears that are spilt, and I do assure you, my dear, they will not be mine.'

* * *

Determined not to be bullied by his threats, the very next day I secretly packed an overnight bag. The moment Kemp went off to one of his business meetings I slipped out through the breezeway and down a side street where I called a hackney cab. It was far preferable, I decided, to live in a dive on the Barbary Coast, or even at the Seamen's Institute, than share a bed again with the monster I had been forced to marry.

The driver insisted I pay him extra when he learnt my destination was an alley just off Battery Street, where I knew Ellis was staying at a lodging house. When we arrived I understood why. The place was as far removed from Nob Hill as you could imagine.

There seemed to be people and vehicles swarming everywhere: handcarts and wagons, peddlers selling anything from buttons and shoelaces to soda pop and peanuts; Chinamen in their cone-shaped hats, pigtails bouncing, hurrying about their business with their hands tucked up their wide sleeves. Two women were brawling in the street, swearing and cursing and rolling in the mud as they tore each other's hair out. Someone was singing 'Wearing of the Green' accompanied by an old man on a banjo. And over all were the sounds of drunken laughter and ribald curses, the shrill peep of a police whistle.

'Do you want me to wait?' my driver enquired, looking anxiously about him as we pulled up beside a rickety old frame building with a painted sign announcing this to be 'Pete's Place'. A lamp swung above the door bearing the message: Lodgings 25, 50 and 75 cents per night.

'No, thank you,' I recklessly informed him. 'This is the place.'

Across the street a woman lounged in a doorway, flaunting her brazen charms in a faded yellow and blue gown that had never seen a bar of soap, plump breasts spilling out above the plunging neckline. She called to my driver. 'Why don't you come in for a drink, dearie?'

He didn't answer, didn't even glance in her direction. Handing me my bag, he asked in a hoarse whisper, 'Do you know what this place is?'

'It's a lodging house where sailors live.'

'And that bar opposite is a deadfall, the lowest of the low when it comes to beer and dance cellars. You pay 50 cents for a dance, half to the establishment, half to the girl, and maybe a drink to go with it. Any greenhorn stupid enough to accept her offer could find himself with a broken head and empty pockets come morning. He may well find himself married to the kind of gal he could never take home to Mama. And too often the sawdust on the floor is stained red with blood. You'd do better, miss, to let me take you home right this minute.'

I could see his concern was valid, and, suddenly remembering that Ellis might not even be back in port yet, was almost of a mind to accept. Then the door of the lodging house burst open and Ellis himself appeared, his face ashen with concern. 'Georgia, what on earth are you doing here?'

I flung myself into his arms, leaning against his broad chest in relief. 'Oh, I can't tell you how pleased I am to see you. Can we go inside, then I'll tell you everything?' And gathering up my small amount of luggage, he paid off the driver and led me into what might easily be a reincarnation of hell.

It turned out to be a tiny hall used as a small office or reception area. An old man, looking very like a pirate with a patch over one eye, sat behind a desk, his purpose clearly being to take payment in advance. 'And who might we have here?' he asked, giving Ellis a knowing wink.

'This is my wife, Squint-Eye, come on a visit,' Ellis lied, and I did not protest. How else could we share a room? It was obvious that sleeping quarters on the Barbary Coast would not be anything like the standard I was used to, and taking my driver's words to heart I had no wish to share with strangers in this dangerous place.

Pete, or Squint-Eye as he was more oddly named, accepted the few cents Ellis gave him with a grunt of satisfaction, then jiggling the coins in his hand, cast me a cunning look out of the corner of his one eye. 'You'll not be wanting to take yer *wife* into the bunk room, will you, son? Stinks of male sweat and cheap whisky in there, as you well know. You could have a room of yer own for double.'

With a sigh, Ellis handed over another 25 cents, and I was at once filled with guilt that I should already be costing him money. 'Oh, I can pay for myself,' I started to say, but Ellis silenced me with a fierce squeeze of my hand, laughing as he turned back to the curious Squint-Eye.

'A bit of a harridan, my wife; thinks she should call the tune even though she doesn't have a dime to her name.'

The old man laughed. 'That's women for yer, allus after yer hard cash. Right, this way,' and picking up his lamp, he led us along a dark passage which emerged into a large central area, around which were a number of little rooms. 'You can rent these by the month,' he was telling Ellis. 'Let me know tomorrow how long you'll be wanting it for. They're furnished and everything; wash yer own dirty sheets and blankets, and find yer own food a' course.'

The room might be considered furnished in so far as it boasted a chair as well as a rope-strung wooden bed with a straw mattress, a couple of pillows, and a not-very-clean pile of folded sheets and blankets. I looked about me, struggling to hide my dismay, almost wishing I had accepted my driver's offer, after all. This was far worse than I'd expected, or hoped for. Hell indeed.

'Some of the beer-slingers live here,' our guide was explaining. 'With their fella or husband, whoever it is who robs them blind of their earnings, and makes their lives even more of a misery than it already is.'

'What's a beer-slinger?' I whispered to Ellis.

'A girl who works in a dive serving beer, and other services too in some cases.'

Handing me a couple of tallow candles, the old man kindly patted my hand. 'There's a grocery store on the corner, little miss, that sells everything you'll need, but these'll get you started.' Then he shuffled off and Ellis quickly closed the door behind him. Turning the key in the lock, he wasted no time in asking what had gone wrong.

I sat on the edge of the bed and told him everything.

Chapter Twenty-Three

The Lakes

'How dare you! How dare you interfere in family matters in this way? You have absolutely no right to even be here trying to take control of my life.' Chrissie was taking out her disappointment and frustration by shouting at Peter.

She couldn't understand why the old lady was proving to be so obstinate. Hadn't she apologised, most humbly? Hadn't they talked? She was aware that Ryall's wife, Clare, had arrived but no invitation had been forthcoming for Chrissie to meet her – a pleasure to be looked forward to, she thought wryly. Chrissie rather thought it might be these two who were blocking her visits.

This morning she'd risen deliberately early, then hung around the gardens for a while hoping to find Georgia, as she had so often in the past. Chrissie was quite certain that if only she could catch her grandmother on her own, this whole unfortunate matter could be cleared up. But there was no sign of her.

Eventually she gave up and hurried to the sanctuary of her tiny shop, to her paint pots and rolls of wallpaper. She took the path along by the lake, cheered by the sight of the mallards paddling serenely by, moorhens with their little red beaks pecking happily in the mud. And beyond the lake, in the distance, was the breathtaking vista of distant blue mountains. The beauty of the scene made her appreciate the reason she loved this place. Why should she give it all up just because of stupid Peter?

As usual, her words were rolling off him like the proverbial water off a duck's back. They were standing in the empty shop, their raised voices echoing soulfully. Chrissie strove to recover her composure, and absolutely refused to invite him upstairs.

He started wandering around the shop, examining the half-finished shelves, smoothing a hand over the unvarnished wood and checking the fittings as if he were an expert in such matters. 'I have every right to be here. What we had together isn't something you can just shuffle off because it got a bit difficult. I was ready to make a vow to love you till death us do part.'

Chrissie closed her eyes in despair. 'I didn't ask you to do that.'

'Oh, I know you have a thing about not marrying again,' Peter scoffed. 'But what is so wrong in being a good wife to a man? Isn't that the role of women, the way of the world?'

'Look, there's really no point in going over all this. I'm

sorry things didn't work out for us, but there it is. We aren't the only couple to have been badly affected by the war. You were – are – a good man, Peter, and I'm still very fond of you, but that doesn't give you the right to follow me here and interfere in my life in the way you have. Grandmother is old and fragile, and with a bad heart. Shocks such as you gave her could have a devastating effect upon her health.'

The familiar peeved expression came into his face, as if the entire world were against him. '*I'm* not to blame for this situation. *You* were the one who lied and deceived her, making out you were an innocent stranger when the truth is very different. Dangerously so, in fact.'

Chrissie's eyes narrowed. 'What do you mean, "dangerously so"? What are you talking about?'

He raised both hands in a defensive gesture, and clamped his lips tight shut, making the point that he was obeying instructions not to get involved in family business.

'What else did my mother say when you called on her the other day?'

By way of reply he arched one brow in that irritating way he had when he knew something she didn't, or felt he was in the right and she in the wrong.

'Oh, for goodness' sake, I'm tired of listening to your innuendo and veiled threats. I think you should go. Now!' She pulled open the door to find Ben hovering on the doorstep, loaded down with his toolbox and lengths of wood. 'Oh, hello, I didn't hear the doorbell.'

He grinned at her. 'I was struggling to find a spare finger to press it.' Then as Peter stepped into view, taking a stance beside Chrissie as if he had every right to be there, Ben's face changed. 'Ah, sorry. Didn't realise you had a visitor.'

'He's just leaving. No doubt you'll be heading home tomorrow, Peter. Do call in to say goodbye before you leave.'

'I was hoping we might have some time together. I could take you out for a meal. There must be somewhere halfway decent to eat around here, and we really do need to talk.'

He attempted to slip an arm about Chrissie's waist but she hastily disengaged herself. 'I've already told you, Peter, you and I have nothing more to say to each other.' Then turning quickly to Ben, 'Let me help you with that. It looks a heavy load.'

'I can manage, thanks. I'm not too early, am I?'

'No, of course not.'

Ben set the load down on the shop floor, and, by the way he was watching his rival, she rather feared one wrong move on Peter's part and Ben would welcome the excuse to lay him out cold right next to those planks of wood. He'd not been pleased to learn that it had been Peter who'd upset Mrs Cowper by spilling these particular beans.

With an artificial smile pinned to her face, Chrissie started to ask after Karen, but was interrupted by Peter's sarcastic laugh.

'Don't try to pull the wool over my eyes by asking if it's too early. I'm quite sure you've only just left her bed in order to fetch that wood. I did know she'd taken a lover.'

He looked at her rather sadly. 'Chrissie, I'm no fool, so don't treat me as one.'

The silence following this remark was profound, and despite her innocence Chrissie was embarrassed to discover that a tide of hot colour was flooding her cheeks. But before she had the chance to find her voice, Ben bounced forward in a fury.

'Don't you speak to Chrissie like that or you'll find your chin making a close acquaintance with my fist.'

Terrified he might actually carry out the threat, Chrissie rushed to grab Ben's arm and pull him away as she hastily addressed Peter. 'Actually, you couldn't be more wrong. Ben is simply a good friend and nothing more.'

She could feel Ben's gaze burning into her, querying this hot denial.

Peter too was evidently unconvinced. 'You're becoming quite the accomplished liar, Chrissie. It must run in the family. Your mother is the real expert, of course.'

'Will you please keep your nose out of our family affairs.'

A cruelty came into his expression then, one that startled her by its coldness, and he almost snarled, '"Affairs" being the operative word. I'm beginning to think that I've had a lucky escape. Marrying you, let alone starting a family, would have been a complete disaster.' He glanced across at Ben. 'I should warn you, young man, that all is not quite as open and honest as it may seem in this family. Did you know, for instance, that Chrissie's parents were brother and sister? So if you've no wish to become entangled with the consequences of an incestuous relationship, I'd recommend you leave right now.' Chrissie was too shocked to respond. It was Ben who forcibly ejected Peter from the premises, then warned her not to believe a word. 'It's pure jealousy. Take no notice.'

'I've no intention of doing so.' But her heart was pounding in her breast, fear cascading through her even as she denied it. 'The trouble is I have this passion for digging out my roots, a humble desire for everyone in this family of ours to get on. Have I gone too far, that's the question?'

This time when Chrissie rang Vanessa, her response was barely audible. 'Oh my God, I hoped and prayed that was a question you'd never ask.'

Chrissie began to shake so much that her knees gave way and she sank to the cold concrete floor of the call box. She felt as if she'd been drenched with ice and yet there was a burning sensation in every limb, her heart thundering in her ears. She could hear tiny sobs coming down the phone, sounds not of outrage or indignation, but fear and horror. The last thing she wanted to hear, given the circumstances.

Had she indeed opened Pandora's box?

Her mother arrived by train late the following day, and Chrissie could hardly bear to witness the anguish on that still lovely face.

'Don't worry, Mum, I don't believe a word.' Outrage was loud in her voice as she held her close for a long moment, deliberately shutting out the memory of Vanessa's first reaction, as well as the image of Ben's face looking completely poleaxed. 'This is all some sort of petty revenge on Peter's part because I've refused to marry him. I shall never forgive him for this, never.'

When no response came, Chrissie busied herself finding a taxi, stowing her mother's luggage on board, then stared bleakly out of the window, not taking in the beauty of the autumn colours, or the way the lake gleamed almost blue in the sunshine. They drove into Bowness, passed the steamer pier, turned into Rayrigg Road and parked by a large Victorian detached property, now used as a private hotel.

Having paid off the taxi and unpacked her mother's small brown suitcase, her mind still blessedly blank, Chrissie gave what might pass for a smile. 'I've barely eaten a thing since yesterday, so why don't we go and eat? I don't think I can face a long discussion on an empty stomach.'

'That would be lovely, darling,' Vanessa agreed, as if everything were perfectly normal and this was some sort of unexpected holiday. For Chrissie, it felt as if nothing would ever be normal again. They ate supper, freshly caught trout, at a small café on Ash Street, although neither woman had much appetite. Chrissie's misery and guilt were keen, making her feel quite ill. She understood, or at least sympathised, with why her mother had insisted she shouldn't identify herself. Oh, but she did so wish that she'd gone with her first instincts and told Georgia who she really was from the start. And if only Peter hadn't taken it into his head to come looking for her.

Chrissie sipped her wine, struggling to sort out the

confusion in her mind while this huge unacknowledged problem loomed between them. Unable to bear the silence any longer, she said, 'Can you explain how this crazy notion that you and Dad were – you know – related came about?'

A flush crept over Vanessa's pale cheeks.

'It's all a nonsense, right? You and Peter were drinking together, weren't you? You promised me you'd give up the booze, the gin and the champagne cocktails, but you didn't.'

'I'm sorry.'

'You know how crazy you get after a glass or two. Were you pleading for sympathy, trying to find some way to force me to come home, and he got completely the wrong end of the stick? Or did he go snooping through your things?' Chrissie had blocked from her mind that telling remark: *Oh, God, I hoped and prayed that was a question you'd never ask!* 'Come on, Mum, what did you say that put such a daft idea into his head?'

'Chrissie, please don't lecture me, and don't be cross with silly Peter. I certainly don't remember saying anything of that sort, but he may well have riffled through my private letters while I was under the influence – in which case . . .'

A cold feeling began to creep over her. 'And what would he find, if he did?'

'I think you should listen to my part of the story first – all of it – before you judge me.'

Chrissie took a steadying sip of wine, then set it down with a click. 'All right. I remember that Aaran came to the house, and that Georgia fainted and you fell in love at first sight. Then something about a letter, a request for money from his mother? Some sort of promise. I've heard snippets from Mrs Gorran, which tantalise more than explain, so yes, I would be interested in the rest of your story. I'm listening.'

Vanessa cleared her throat. 'We were like a pair of lovesick ducks.' Her face softened into a smile. 'Do ducks get lovesick, I wonder? Anyway, we couldn't keep our hands off each other, or bear to be apart for a moment. My mother was perfectly aware of what was going on, and it didn't seem to bother her, not at first anyway. We were deeply in love, and soon I suspected I was pregnant, with you. I didn't dare say a word to anyone, not even to Aaran, let alone my mother. Then, quite out of the blue, on a romantic sail one moonlit night on the lake, he proposed.'

Vanessa's eyes were shining, the radiance in them that of a young girl in love, not the disillusioned middle-aged woman she'd become. Chrissie couldn't help but warm to her. It was a long time since she'd seen her mother look this happy.

'What did you say?'

'I accepted in a flash, as he'd known I would.' She gave a soft laugh. 'I admitted to him then that I'd fallen pregnant. Oh, I was so nervous, scared that I'd lose him, but he was thrilled, kissed me and said we'd just have to bring the date forward a bit. Mother had to be told, of course.'

'That must have been difficult,' Chrissie said, thinking

they must now be coming to the part where they fell out, for the most common reason of all: an unexpected pregnancy.

'Surprisingly Ma wasn't in the least bit disapproving.' A thoughtful frown creased Vanessa's brow. 'She was all smiley and weepy, delighted at the prospect of becoming a grandma.'

'So what changed?'

Pausing while Chrissie refilled their glasses, she took a long slug of wine before going on with her tale. 'Aaran was concerned for his own mother, naturally, as there was to be no offer of financial assistance forthcoming from Georgia. He suggested he should return to San Francisco and help her sort things out. Then he pointed out that I should go with him, as his wife. And that did it. Ma absolutely blew up. She was furious. She lashed out at him like a whip, accusing him of underhand behaviour, of trying to steal her precious daughter. Oh, and a great deal of hysterical nonsense of that nature. She got quite upset and angry at the prospect of our child being born in America. She wouldn't hear of it. Once we'd made that decision she turned against Aaran completely, wouldn't lift a finger to help us. Even ordered me to stop seeing him, but it was far too late by then. I loved him too much to give him up.'

'Perhaps she feared you might never come back, that she'd lose you for good.'

Vanessa frowned. 'I didn't consider that possibility at the time, although I suppose you might have a point. America doesn't seem quite so far away today perhaps, not now ships have a much greater speed, although it's still halfway across the world, isn't it?' She made a little scoffing sound in her throat. 'Anyway, that wasn't the reason. Her behaviour was outrageous, so cruel and heartless, accusing Aaran of only being interested in my money. She just turned against him.'

A shadow crossed her face at this point in her story, and the happiness faded, almost as if the memory were too painful. Chrissie reached out to squeeze her mother's hand. 'So what happened next? Did you go to America?'

'Oh, we stuck to our guns for a while, absolutely refused to change our plans. Ma was bitter and angry, claiming it was all some sort of plot, saying Aaran had manipulated the whole thing, planned it as revenge because she'd refused to bail out his mother from yet another financial crisis. She made the most outlandish claims. Utterly ridiculous; as if you can legislate to fall in love, and make someone love you.' Vanessa shook her head in despair. 'In the end we stopped arguing with her and just ran away. We married the moment I turned twenty-one and no longer needed her permission. You were born a month later, as you know. So no, we didn't go to America, not then.'

'How did that work out? Was she pleased that you were staying?'

'Yes, I think she was in a way. Ma seemed to calm down a bit, made something of a fuss of us, and of you. I thought everything was going to be all right, after all. She even financed Aaran to set himself up in business at the art gallery in Chelsea, although not with particularly good grace.'

Chrissie expressed surprise. 'I knew she was comfortably off, but didn't realise Grandmother was quite so wealthy.'

'Oh yes, she's very well placed indeed. The source of that wealth, however, is a bit of a mystery – questionable, you might say. Aaran certainly questioned it. Frequently. It was the main source of dispute between them, which was perhaps why she never really accepted him. She kept telling him he'd grown too much like his parents: his greedy mother and selfish father, who apparently had something of a reputation as a chancer, which didn't please Aaran one bit. I never met the man myself but I don't think Aaran and his father enjoyed a good relationship. Nevertheless, he remained steadfast in his loyalty towards him, as one does when you want a parent to love you and be proud of what you've achieved.'

'That must have been hard for you, when you knew Dad was really a good man.'

'He was indeed, although not good with money,' she admitted, with a sad smile. 'He'd always had plenty and never properly understood its value, then when Georgia funded the gallery he gave away far too much to that useless family of his. Later, when everything fell apart for us, he tried to win it all back through gambling, which naturally led to worse losses.' She gave a half shrug. 'Not that it matters. It's only money. It's people that count.'

Chrissie brought her gently back to the matter under discussion. 'I remember you said you visited Aaron's mother, and that in her dying days she told you the true extent of Georgia's lies and deceit?'

'Yes, and that's what it was.'

'Sorry? I don't understand.'

'What Peter told you was that lie, or rather the terrible secret. With her dying breath my mother-in-law carefully explained to me that Aaran, my husband, was my own mother's son. For some reason not fully explained, Georgia gave him away when he was still a baby, and because of some unfulfilled promise he had come back into her life.'

Chrissie felt as if her head was about to explode, as if she were somehow separated from reality or this was all happening to someone else. She must still be in shock, she told herself, for try as she might she couldn't get her usually quick mind to function properly. Nor her hearing either, for that matter. 'You surely aren't saying that it's true?'

'Yes, that's what I'm saying.'

'Heaven help us.'

'Indeed.'

'So that was the cause of the rows and arguments between you and Dad?'

Vanessa nodded. 'And the reason Aaran left me, although I confess we were so in love that we continued to see each other from time to time, at least until the war.'

Chrissie was staring at her hands as they lay clenched tightly in her lap. Her mind was racing now, thinking how this knowledge had so cruelly ruined her parents' lives. Then it came to her in a blinding moment of reality that it had likewise ruined her own life. Peter was right. Who would wish to be associated with the product of an incestuous relationship? The image of Ben's shocked face again floated into her mind. He'd seemed to dismiss Peter's comments as pure malice, as had she, but how would he react once he knew the accusation was true? It didn't bear thinking about. At this point Chrissie pushed back her chair and fled to the bathroom to vomit.

Chapter Twenty-Four

Chrissie spent a sleepless night tossing and turning and drinking endless cups of tea. By the early hours of the morning she was sitting on the end of the jetty, shivering despite the thick sweater and coveralls she was wearing. She kept going over everything in her mind, her sadness at losing Tom, castigating herself for grieving too deeply. It wasn't as if she was the only one to have suffered during the war. Then she'd foolishly latched on to the first man who was kind to her, allowing a dependence upon Peter to grow to such a dangerous level he'd got entirely the wrong idea, reading far more into the friendship than she'd intended.

As if that weren't bad enough, she'd made the greatest mistake of all by deciding to pry into her mother's past and resolve the family feud. Not only had she failed in her efforts to reunite Georgia and Vanessa, but she had destroyed her own chance of building any sort of relationship with her grandmother. Now she'd lost any hope of a future with Ben.

A lone fisherman found her in a weeping huddle of misery at five in the morning, and troubled by the sight of her forlorn figure at that hour, tied up his boat and came over. 'You all right, love? Weren't thinking of taking a dip, were you? Bit chilly this time of the morning.'

'I'm fine.' Chrissie struggled to smile up at him through her tears, liking the look of his concerned bearded face. But he insisted on escorting her safely back to her rented room, and the kindness from this complete stranger made her weep all the more.

The next few days were a jumble of confused emotions as Chrissie made some attempt to deal with the fallout. Vanessa had insisted that it was far too soon to approach Georgia for any further explanation. They'd just have to be patient. Even then she might decline to help, or Chrissie might be too afraid to ask, fearful of a yet worse relapse.

Having admitted that he'd deliberately befuddled her mother with sufficient gin sling to wheedle these secret horrors out of her, and perhaps realising that he'd got more than he bargained for, Peter meekly returned to London.

'But I want you to know that you may come home to me at any time, Chrissie dear. I'm willing for us to try again, and won't hold this moral slur against you.'

Moral slur! Chrissie almost choked on the words. It was as if she were soiled in some way. Did she feel unclean? she asked herself. A question her befuddled brain refused to answer. It preferred to keep hiding behind the invisible pane of frosted glass it had constructed for itself, protecting her from such matters as public censure.

But she still had to face Ben.

With some trepidation she arranged to meet him in their favourite spot by the lake, where they'd be private. Until this moment she hadn't realised how very much he mattered to her. Now she bluntly told him she would have to break off their budding romance.

'Why?'

'You know why.'

Ben's response was to put his arms about her and draw her to him, holding her even closer when she tried to push him away, thumbing the tears from her cheeks. 'No, you and I have something good going between us; I'm not going to call it off because some ex-fiancé or boyfriend, whatever he was, starts spreading nasty gossip. How can you be certain the words of a greedy woman, even if she was dying, weren't some perverted sort of revenge because Georgia refused to cough up any more money? It's a good time to lie, on your death bed, particularly if you're holding a grudge against someone. Your mother has probably got it all wrong.'

'Oh, Ben!' Tears stood proud in her eyes, and he kissed them away, one by one. She leant into his warmth, wanting to melt into him, body and soul, to become a part of him and banish these horrors from her mind. 'This ruined my parents' lives. I can't let it do the same to you – to us.'

'We won't let it. You've no other evidence that your father was Georgia's son.'

'Nor any that says he isn't.'

'Then there's only one thing to be done.'

'What's that?' She had never loved him more than in this moment.

'You must ask her.'

'But she won't see me.'

'She will if the request comes from my mam.'

The bedroom was sunk in gloom, the swathe of maroon curtains blocking out all natural daylight, the big bed itself barely visible, let alone the fragile figure that lay unmoving within the ghostly sheets. Chrissie dared hardly breathe as she sat beside it, steeped in nervous tension, anxiously waiting for her grandmother to wake, and yet dreading the moment when she did. It was desperately sad to see this normally vibrant woman lying here so ill, her still-lovely features in pale repose as if a waxen image, frighteningly like a death mask.

As she sat, watching and waiting for each breath, Chrissie studied the features more closely, seeking a family likeness between mother and daughter, as both were such strong, obstinate, passionate women, and both beautiful in their day. Still were, despite their advancing years. They each had full lips and a classically oval face, yet there were also differences. Their colouring, for one thing, Georgia being much darker. But then, if Grandfather had been fair that might account for a softer mix. And where Vanessa possessed dramatic winged brows, Georgia's grew stubbornly straight above her closed eyes.

Chrissie stifled a sigh. How tragic that their relationship had been fractured so long ago. And how would it ever be put right now that she had made things a thousand times worse?

'I know you're there.'

The eyes hadn't opened but the soft voice from the bed startled Chrissie. 'Goodness, I didn't even realise you were awake.'

'I have been for a while. I was wondering what you were thinking – if you'd devised yet more excuses for your treachery.'

Chrissie winced at her choice of language. 'That's a bit strong, although I do agree it was wrong of me not to come clean. I should have told you right from the start who I was.' The question she so longed to ask burned in her head, but she found herself quite unable to speak, too fearful of causing her grandmother further distress.

'Yes, you should.'

Choking with unshed tears and disappointment, Chrissie got slowly to her feet, realising it was too late now to make amends. Too much damage had been done to this old woman who was more frail than she might appear. How she longed to hug her grandmother, to feel some warmth emanate from her, some small sign of forgiveness. But the figure on the bed remained cold and unmoving, and she dare not risk hurting her further. At the door she paused to look back, a pleading in her voice that she made no attempt to disguise. 'May I come and see you again tomorrow?'

'You may do as you think fit. I doubt I'll be going anywhere.'

The sharp response cut to the heart of her. Had she ruined any chance of befriending this grandmother she'd never known? She'd made a promise to her mother that was impossible to keep without losing her own integrity. Now perhaps she'd lost everything by agreeing to the deception. It was a disturbing thought. She was about to close the door and quietly leave the old lady in peace, when the stentorian voice came again.

'Aren't you going to ask if what this so-called boyfriend of yours said was true? Don't you want to know if Aaran, your father, was my son?'

Chrissie stared at her, her first thought being that Peter must have spoken to her grandmother about this too. No wonder she was taking so long to recover from the shock. Almost too frightened to speak, she asked, 'Is he?'

'Sit down. I think it's time you heard the rest of the story.'

Chapter Twenty-Five

San Francisco

The bed may have been lumpy and flea-ridden, the sheets threadbare and the blankets stinking of cheap beer, but I felt a wild exultation that I had at last escaped what had become very like a prison on Nob Hill. It was astonishing how easily I had achieved it. Just walked away as if for an afternoon stroll in the park, although I had insisted the cab take a circuitous route so that I could check we weren't being followed. Now here I was, with my lover, the man with whom I intended to spend the rest of my life.

'I'm sorry this place is such a dive,' Ellis was saying. 'The only consolation I can offer is that there are plenty worse.'

'I can well believe it.'

'You have to be very careful which hotel you choose. I was warned never to be lured by someone who promises they know of a better place. More often than not it will be the complete opposite, and they'll charge you for the privilege of having taken you there.'

I put my arms about his neck and pulled him close. 'I don't care where we are, so long as we're together.'

Our reunion on this occasion was particularly ecstatic. Ellis was delighted and thrilled at the prospect of becoming a father, as I'd known he would be. Within minutes of his learning my news we were happily making plans, dreaming of a new beginning. But he became instantly alert when he learnt of my husband's reaction to the discovery of my little secret.

'He expected you to move back into his bedroom, even though he *knew* it wasn't his child? Or does he think it's his? Have you slept with him again?'

I rather loved this show of jealousy in him, even as I hastened to reassure him. 'No, my darling, I have not slept with him again.'

'How can I be sure of that?'

I smiled as I kissed him. 'Because I love *you*. To be fair, he has not touched me in months, rarely even speaks to me. He's far too busy in Maura's bed, or else exhausted by the hours of debauchery he indulges in at the houses of ill repute. Now, can we stop talking about Kemp and tell me all about your latest trip?'

But he wasn't in the mood for such talk today, only apologising for the delay of his return, due to necessary repairs which had held the ship in dock for a while in Singapore, then bad weather around the Cape. 'I swear that was my last voyage. I am done with adventuring now. All I want is to go home to England, and settle down to happy domestic bliss with you, my darling, and our child.'

'Oh, yes, please,' I cried, scattering kisses all over his beloved face – his mouth, his strong jaw, his eyes and ears, making him laugh out loud. Then he had to return my kisses, only with a much greater passion, the sheets tugged over our heads in an attempt to keep warm.

Yet my fears still niggled at the back of my mind, and later, when we at last paused for breath, I tried to explain that walking out of the house was one thing, but gaining my freedom completely quite another. 'Kemp will have his spies out looking for me the minute he realises I've gone. He will not let me go easily.'

'But why does he care when he clearly doesn't love you?'

'He sees me as a possession, an asset which proves his standing in society. He chose me for my skills in house management, for the way I can host his dinner parties for his political cronies. Because he considers me sensible, and careful with money. An ideal wife, apparently.'

'Nevertheless he has treated you badly, and you're entitled to apply for a divorce.'

'Once we're safely away, I most certainly will. But even if I had the money, that's not something I would dare to attempt while I remain in a city in which he wields such power. Nor can I run home to Mama. She would drive me back herself, push me in a handcart if necessary, ably assisted by my adoring sister. To them Kemp is so charming he seems an entirely different person from the greedy self-serving bully I know. When we are alone, he is so contemptible I could spit in his eye.'

'I could do a great deal worse than that.'

I flung my arms around him, terrified he might march up to Nob Hill that minute. 'No, you mustn't go near him. Kemp is so underhand, so devious, he would never fight fair. You'd only put both our lives at risk if you took him on. We really should get away from Frisco, as soon as we can. Remember, he threatened *your* life too, and that of our child. I'll be constantly looking over my shoulder if we stay here.'

Ellis gave a growl of frustrated fury even as he visibly struggled to control himself. Stroking my hair, that he'd tousled with his own eager hands a moment ago, he quietly conceded my point. 'You're right, but it's damned hard. I want to take him apart for what he's done to you. I'd feed him to the sharks if we were on board ship.'

'Ellis, please,' I begged, fearful of this great desire of his to protect me.

'Don't worry, I'll start making discreet enquiries about booking us a passage to Liverpool first thing tomorrow.'

While Ellis worked at the waterfront loading and securing freight, keeping his ears open for a cheap berth to Liverpool, which weren't easy to come by and at least thirty dollars each, I settled as best I could into life on the wharves.

'Conditions will not be comfortable. No privacy, no bunk to sleep in or even a seat to sit on, and fetid and unsavoury sanitary arrangements,' Ellis warned me. 'You have to book well in advance, and pay far more than we can afford, to get a decent berth.'

'I don't care what we have to endure,' I told him. 'So long as we get away safely.'

He cradled me in his arms, smoothing a hand over my swollen belly. 'And what about the baby? Wouldn't it be better to wait a few weeks more, till he or she is born? Giving birth on board ship is not something I'd recommend.'

I must have looked at him with such bleakness in my eyes that his heart swelled with love. He kissed me softly before holding me in a warm embrace. 'Don't worry, my love, I'll fetch the doctor when your time comes.'

And so we agreed to wait a while longer.

I bought some lye soap and scrubbed our room from top to bottom. I took the sheets and blankets to the Chinese laundry, which made some improvement, at least banishing the stink and hopefully the fleas that caused us to scratch all night.

Temperatures vary little in San Francisco but this winter seemed particularly grey, cold and damp. Despite this, I had never felt more gloriously happy. It was so wonderful to be with Ellis that I didn't care about the weather, about the fact we lived largely on soup for lunch and fish for dinner, squirrelling away as much of Ellis's earnings as we possibly could. We hid it in a sock under the floorboards beneath the bed. All that mattered was that we were in love, and we kept our hopes and dreams pinned on our planned escape. We ate rabbit stew for our dinner one day and thought ourselves kings.

I became a regular customer at the corner grocery store where potatoes were heaped in wooden crates beside onions, soap, candles and other ordinary goods. An old hag kept watch behind a makeshift counter, watching my every move with her bead-black eyes. Behind her, in the dim shadows, a tatty curtain served as a door to an inner room where I occasionally caught a glimpse of a group of rascally-looking coves playing poker. The place reeked of tobacco smoke and mice, possibly dead rats, but I was always studiously polite to her, and washed everything I bought there twice over.

The old hag rewarded my good manners by being surprisingly helpful. She told me where to buy the freshest fish, which we largely lived on as it was the cheapest food available. And there were times in those first weeks when I wish I'd paid more attention to Cook's attempts to teach Prue and I how to cook. I valiantly tried to emulate her crab cakes but failed miserably. Nonetheless, Ellis ate them without complaint.

The woman also taught me how to distinguish the loafers and thieves, gamblers, pimps and crimps – as well as how to take care of myself in this labyrinth of streets which even the local police refrained from visiting. Never turning your back or speaking to anyone you didn't know seemed to feature loudly in her little homilies.

'This is the place where you'll find all the dirty, degraded, hopeless bummers and two-bit greenhorns who are drawn to this town by the promise of riches in the mines, and end up in a dive like this with the rest of us poor fools.' Then she would laugh out loud, mouth open wide, revealing only a few blackened teeth. 'Handsome gal like you should watch out someone doesn't offer you the sort of employment your mother wouldn't approve of.'

Now I was the one to laugh. Poor dear Mama would faint clean away if she even *saw* me in this filthy little grocery store, let alone being involved in anything immoral. Such as sleeping with my lover, for instance. I shuddered, glancing instinctively over my shoulder.

Every day I begged Ellis to find us a berth, but he would shake his head, insisting my health and safety, and that of our baby, was paramount. 'You're quite safe here, I promise you. Kemp would never venture into these parts.'

I couldn't argue with that. Also, money was seriously tight, and we needed to save every dime and cent we could for the journey. 'Don't worry,' I told the old woman. 'We have plans. This is just a temporary stop-off for us.'

This comment caused her to laugh so much she had to hold her aching sides, the rolls of fat at her waist falling over her plump fingers. 'Wish I'd a dollar for every time I've heard that one.'

In the second week she asked about the baby, and I agreed it was my first, that we hadn't been married very long. It seemed safest to keep up the lie. Then one day I felt I'd gained her friendship sufficiently to ask a favour. I was carefully counting out the carrots, turnips and potatoes I needed to make soup, which I'd boil up later on the old stove out in the yard, fuelled largely from driftwood, that was shared by all the tenants. 'Were anyone to ask after me, I'd be obliged if you didn't mention that I was living round here.'

She regarded me out of slitted eyes. 'Now, who'd be likely to ask, I wonder?'

'I don't know. Could be anyone.'

'And how would I know if it was you, in particular, who they were looking for. Do you have a name, girl?'

'Yes, it's G—' I almost told her, but stopped myself in time. 'My name isn't important. If anyone describes me to you, you haven't seen me around, right?'

She pursed her lips, carefully considering my request. 'And how would you make it worth my while not to see you around when you come into my store every day of the week? My, that's a mighty pretty shawl you're wearing. Keep me plenty warm in winter, that would.'

I handed over the shawl, together with my thanks, then bought the vegetables and left.

It took the best part of a month but by mid-February, after much wheedling, I won Ellis over, reminding him there would be a doctor on board, so we'd be as safe on the ship as in this den of iniquity, constantly looking over our shoulder. At last he told me the news I'd most longed to hear.

'I've managed to get us two cheap tickets in steerage,' he said, excitement deepening his voice to an even greater richness. 'We have two choices. There's a ship leaving on Friday next, but since we don't quite have enough money yet we'll have to settle for Thursday the nineteenth of April.'

'I wish we could leave right now, this minute.'

He chuckled softly as he kissed me. 'Me too, but hopefully you'll have had the baby by then.'

'I doubt it.' It was madness contemplating sailing so near to my time, and it seemed such a long time to wait, but nothing would stop me now. I had no intention of allowing Drew Kemp to so much as touch this child. 'How much does it cost? Will we have enough money? Oh, I feel so guilty not being able to contribute.' The few dollars I'd managed to bring with me in my purse had long since been used up.

Ellis enfolded me in his arms, pressing his lips to my forehead. 'It doesn't matter. All I care about is that we only have to endure this place for a few more days, then we will be free. I love you, sweet Georgia.'

'And I love you.'

We carefully counted out the money in the sock, almost enough for our tickets, confident we could save the rest in time, including a sweetener to the colleague who'd found the berths for us. Then we went to bed and held each other close in warm contentment.

It was still raining the following morning when I hurried to the corner grocery store to buy some bread to go with the latest batch of soup – cabbage this time. Head down against the blustering rain I ran full-tilt into a bulky figure. 'Oh, sorry,' I cried, but as I made to step back, arms closed about me and lifted me from my feet.

'Gotcha, little lady, at last. Now hold still and mind your manners. Your husband will pay me a nice little bonus if I take you back without any bruises showing, and I really wouldn't like to spoil the merchandise.'

I didn't need to look into his face to recognise that voice. It was Big Billy. Only this time there was no sign of my little friend, Eddie the Weasel.

I should have realised that my husband would have someone watching me all the time, following my every move. Had Maura betrayed me yet again? I was transported to the house in the back of a fish wagon, smuggled in through a back door, then carried up the back stairs wrapped in a sheet and tossed on to the bed. I felt filthy and stank of stale fish, but before Kemp allowed me to make use of the bathroom he curled one hand tight about my throat and laid down the new house rules.

'You will never, I repeat, *never* do that again. Understand? There is nothing that makes me more angry than being made a fool of. You will remain here, in this room, until I say different.'

'You can't keep me as a prisoner,' I squealed, furiously defiant.

'Oh yes I can. Fortunately, the servants, your family, our various friends and business colleagues are unaware of your little adventure. They believe you were unwell, that you took to your bed because you feared you were losing the baby, that you asked for there to be no visitors, not even your maid, as you wished to be quiet and alone. That is the story I told them, and you will stick by it. Is that clear?'

I nodded, quite unable to find the strength to resist. I

could feel my child moving and kicking within me, as if eager to be born and get on with life. But what kind of a life would it be, with this man as a father?

I could kick myself for confiding my fears to the old hag at the corner grocery. No doubt she'd put the word about that someone was looking for me, and good old Billy Goat Gruff had heard the tale and put two and two together.

Lecture over, I was permitted to bathe, then sent to bed, like some recalcitrant child. I did not ask for a maid, nor was one offered to me. Because of the lie Kemp had told, no one had even missed me, and the few notes on my dressing table from Mama and Prue were nothing more than little lectures against my feeling sorry for myself, rather than expressions of concern.

Prue's attitude when she called to take tea a day or two later reinforced that view. 'You don't seem to appreciate your own good fortune,' she scolded me, with all the wisdom of her eighteen years. 'I envy you your fine husband, beautiful home and wonderful life.'

What could I say? My sister had never been able to see through the gloss to the reality of life, rather like Mama. I refilled her cup and said nothing, all too aware of my husband's condemning gaze.

'You should be forever at dear Drew's side, demonstrating your loyalty and affection as a good wife should, not wallowing in self-pity. He has protected your foolish desire for solitude these last few weeks, while I have protected your husband from the ladies of Frisco who circle like sharks at the first sign of a lonesome male.'

'I cannot imagine how I would have coped without your regular visits,' Kemp assured her with simpering insincerity.

'Any woman would be a fool to neglect such a handsome man,' Prudence cooed, casting him a sidelong look of adoration which caught me quite by surprise.

Goodness, was the silly girl flirting with my husband before my very eyes? But then my sister would flaunt her charms at anything in trousers.

'A man would not feel so neglected had he a wife as pretty and accommodating as yourself, Prudence.'

I turned my face away, determined not to react to this foolish game they were playing, nevertheless the words slipped out of their own volition. 'By accommodating I assume you mean obedient.'

'Not something you could be accused of, dear wife.'

'Georgia has ever nurtured a strong independent streak beneath that quiet exterior, while I have never been one for rebellion.'

I stared at my young sister in disbelief, remembering the fuss over the rouged cheeks, the low neckline of her gown, her refusal of countless offers of marriage. But I bit my tongue, anxious not to irritate my husband further, or appear affected by this silliness. And as Prudence continued to flirt and cast coy glances at Kemp I made a private vow to speak to my foolish sister later about the dangers she ran by such hoydenish behaviour.

I mentioned it the moment Kemp withdrew to leave us to our sisterly chatter, as he termed it. 'What do you think you're doing?' I challenged her. 'Fluttering your eyelashes at him in that immodest way. What if he were to take your silly flirting seriously? Where might that lead? Into dangerous territory, I tell you. He's not a man to tease like your foolish young beaus.'

Prudence tossed her head, and laughed. 'Goodness, what an old fuddy-duddy you are turning into, Georgia. I do declare you're jealous.'

'I am not jealous, I'm concerned – for you.'

She came briskly to her feet. 'Then pay better attention to your husband, and less to your own selfish needs. If Drew seeks feminine attention elsewhere you have only yourself to blame. Why, you haven't even called or written to us, not since we came for dinner in January. Mama was vexed.'

'So you choose to punish me with this sort of petty nonsense?'

She folded her hands primly at her waist, looking more like our mother than ever. 'Having a baby is a perfectly natural event, and Mama and I think you are making far too much fuss over this pregnancy.' So saying, she flounced off, leaving me in tears. It was not our first sisterly quarrel, but right now I rather wished she'd offered her support to me, instead of to my husband.

The house felt oddly lonely without Maura's bustling presence. She wasn't there to soothe me with a cold compress when my head throbbed with pain, or to bring a stool for my feet when pains shot up and down my legs, and I desperately needed her to rub my aching back. Not for a moment did I imagine my husband had banished her from his life, quite convinced he'd set her up in a house of her own somewhere, where he could visit her at will. He did not volunteer the information and I was too concerned with my own situation to enquire.

March was crawling by in a blur of misery, but if I was not to miss the April sailing that Ellis had taken such pains to acquire, and worked so hard to pay for, I realised I must do exactly as my husband told me. I must be the most obedient wife in the entire city. My fear was so great that each day, each hour, stretched endlessly before me.

Would I ever be free?

First, I reclaimed the freedom of the house by pleading to be allowed out of my room and sit in the parlour for a few hours each morning. A few days after that I was permitted to take a short walk out in the afternoons, accompanied by a maid, as I had used to do with Maura. I was never allowed out alone, nor out of my husband's sight unless someone was with me at all times.

Yet my mind was obsessed with escape. I would leave taking no bag this time, no cab, and hopefully with no Big Billy following me.

Could I appeal to his vanity? I wondered. I took a chance. With this plan in mind, I offered him my most humble apology, even to calling him by his first name. 'I'm so sorry, Drew, for being so foolish.' He looked at me in pleased surprise. Encouraged that my ploy was working, I continued, 'I really can't imagine what came over me. I must have been overcome with some crazed madness. I stayed in a dreadful little hotel close to the wharves. You wouldn't believe the squalor or the stink of the place. I hated it and was absolutely miserable there.' I sent up a silent apology to Ellis for this betrayal. 'It was all a terrible mistake. I swear I will never be so stupid again. I have been a poor wife to you, and, since you have sent Maura away, I promise I will mend my ways, I swear it.' I began to weep.

I could see him struggling to believe me. 'I'm glad to hear you say so.'

'Can you ever forgive me?' I looked up at him with tear-filled eyes, but there was still a strong hint of cynicism in his next words.

'You will have to hope that I do, otherwise life could become remarkably difficult for you. But I do need my wife by my side. In fact, I've organised an impromptu cocktail party tomorrow night.'

I was dismayed. 'Oh, but I could not possibly attend, not looking like this,' I said, indicating the unseemly size of my belly.

'Why should I not be proud of your condition?' He gave that twisted, private smile of amusement, as if he knew something I didn't. 'You well know how much I would welcome a son.'

I stared at him, not for the first time marvelling at the strange way his mind worked. Most men would abhor the idea of taking on another man's child, yet Kemp seemed to welcome it, or else enjoyed giving that impression to prove he was still very much in control.

He leant forward and whispered in my ear. 'This one will do for now. We'll call him the stand-in, shall we, until the right one comes along? And we'll make sure the next one is all mine.'

I shuddered at the thought, but the next evening, as befitted a dutiful wife, I dressed in my finest and handed round canapés and smiles with equal measure, as instructed.

April was upon us and Kemp seemed to be everywhere, scarcely taking his eyes off me for a second. Only my certain faith in Ellis and his love for me kept me sane. It was well-nigh impossible for him to contact me, yet I knew in my heart that he would be waiting for me on the pier, no doubt for some hours before the ship was due to sail on the early morning tide of Thursday the nineteenth of April.

On Tuesday the seventeenth, Kemp arranged for us to visit the opera. Caruso was playing Don José in Bizet's *Carmen*, and Mama, Papa and Prudence were to accompany us. A grand family occasion, no less.

I was a bag of nerves, which fortunately everyone put down to the fact that I had been unwell, and it was but two weeks to my confinement. I knew different, however.

As I prepared for the opera I felt my heart thudding in my breast. Might there be some opportunity during the show for me to slip away to the powder room, and then call a cab? The prospect of arriving at Pete's Place in the grubby little alley off Battery Street in my blue velvet gown gave me justified cause for concern. And would Ellis be there, waiting for me? What if he was out working on the docks somewhere, unloading cargo? Would the old codger let me in looking like a grand lady, or leave me out in the street to fend for myself and risk being robbed blind, or worse?

'How charming you look, wife,' Kemp said, interrupting my thoughts. 'You may not be quite so pretty as your sister, but you most certainly possess elegance and style, even in your present condition. I feel almost proud to be your husband.'

I glowered at him, distrustful of this sudden rash of compliments.

'Now, do not overtax yourself this evening, my dear. I shall be keeping a very close watch on you. We can call for a carriage at any time should you experience a twinge of distress, or feel the slightest bit unwell.'

I glanced up, wary of this veiled warning. 'I'm fine, thank you,' I coolly informed him, then strode away to check on Mama and Prue. They would be returning with us after the performance, staying overnight for convenience of transport, as it would be late when the opera finished.

We drove to the Grand Opera House in Kemp's newest acquisition, an expensive Buick motor car. I dread to think how he raised the funds for that, but it was not the only automobile gracing the front entrance of the opera house, which was almost invisible behind a trail of similar vehicles, carriages and broughams of every description. The less fortunate, or more prudent, travelled by cable car.

The evening passed in a blur of glorious music and singing, gentlemen in stiffly starched collars and tailcoats, and beautifully gowned ladies glittering with diamonds.

Mama was looking particularly fine in a gown of black lace set off by her emeralds.

Sadly, Kemp kept his word over keeping a close eye on me, even to insisting that my dear sister accompany me to the powder room. I knew better than to try any sort of escape with Prue around. She was my sweetest, dearest friend as well as my beloved sister, but her attitude towards my husband was still that of a capricious young miss. Attempting to explain everything that had happened in my marriage to her simple mind was quite beyond my skills. I accepted defeat, and hoped for better luck on the morrow.

When the curtain finally fell on the closing notes I almost sighed with relief, but, true to San Francisco's reputation as the town that never sleeps, the evening was far from over. The ladies donned their gold lamé and fur-trimmed cloaks, and we went off to dine at Tait's, where champagne corks popped and oysters were served.

I could barely eat a thing and the scent of dawn was in the air by the time I fell exhausted into bed, far too highly strung for sleep. I was counting the hours to the following afternoon when I would don my Easter bonnet and somehow or other escape the house and take a stroll in the park, no matter what. It would be my last chance to escape, and hopefully Ellis would be waiting for me in our usual spot by the Japanese Gardens. He would take me in his arms and kiss me, and with not a penny to my name, carry me off to England, where at last I would be safe from this callous, immoral brute I had married. Then I would set legal matters in hand, and we could marry and settle to a happy life together for ever and ever.

These delicious thoughts were still playing and replaying in my mind when, at twelve minutes past five on the morning of the eighteenth of April, 1906, the earthquake struck.

It felt as if some giant hand had taken hold of the entire house and was shaking it in fury, venting their wrath for alleged misdeeds. I woke with a start to find the huge mahogany wardrobe advancing towards me. There was a great rumbling, crashing, sliding, wrenching and grinding, then the bed seemed to rise into the air and I was flung sideways, landing in the corner of the room where I banged my head on the wall, but not before I saw the floor open and the bed, still with Kemp inside it, slip sideways and disappear into the vortex that opened beneath it. I thought I would never forget the look of dazed shock on his face.

Chapter Twenty-Six

I must have been knocked senseless for a while, as when I woke I stared in numb disbelief at the sight before me. The mahogany wardrobe had come to rest at an angle against the far wall. Chairs and other pieces of furniture lay scattered about like broken matchsticks. And where our bed had once stood, where I had reluctantly suffered Kemp's presence beside me these last few weeks, yawned a great black hole. I closed my eyes, not wishing to recapture the moment when Kemp had slipped into that abyss, his mouth and eyes wide open in a silent cry of shocked appeal. I could barely believe that I had survived. I lay huddled in a corner of the room not daring to move an inch in case the entire edifice tumbled about my ears.

With any quake comes the fear of fire. It was imperative that I get out with all speed, find Mama and Papa and Prue. Check on the servants. Yet for some reason I could not move, couldn't instil any sense of urgency into my shocked brain. Everything seemed to have happened in slow motion, even the dust settling floated slowly down with casual disdain.

I couldn't hear a sound: no screams or cries for help, no rumbles or vibration in the broken building. Nothing but an eerie silence. It was as if the entire city were too shocked to move or even breathe.

I struggled to gather my thoughts. Everyone knew that San Francisco was prone to earthquakes. Due to the San Andreas fault, and the Hayward and San Jacinto faults, we suffered countless tremors every year as the plates constantly shifted against each other and stress built up. But I had never experienced anything of this magnitude before. The last quake of any size had been almost half a century ago.

Strict codes about construction had been put into place since then, and I felt grateful that the house was at least still standing. But I had to get out. I couldn't stay here another second.

Flexing my limbs, I checked that my fingers and toes, legs and arms were all working properly. Then very gingerly I pushed away some rubble and dragged myself into an upright position. I was alive, and apparently in one piece. All I had to do was cross the floor and walk away. The door was mere feet away, yet to my confused brain it looked like miles. Somehow I reached it, the door hanging by one hinge as I stepped through it, and within seconds I was out on the landing. My success must have put new life into my legs because

I managed a stumbling run to Mama's room.

I found her calmly dressing. There was no sign of my father. 'Ah, there you are, dear. Can you find my emeralds? I'm afraid I left them carelessly lying about last night when I retired, as it was so very late, and now I can't find them anywhere.'

'What do emeralds matter? Are *you* all right, Mama? Where's Papa?'

She looked at me then with tear-starred eyes. 'I don't know, darling, not for certain, and I daren't look. But I do recall his cry, and a window smashing.'

As one we turned to stare in horror at the window, which was ominously empty of glass. I ran to look out and there Papa was, half buried under a pile of rubble in the street below. I could just make out his bare feet and the hem of his nightshirt. The urge to scream and cry out was almost unbearable, but this wasn't the moment. There was no time for grief right now.

'Now where did I put my dratted gloves?' Mama was saying, eerily calm.

I turned back into the room. 'Forget about your gloves, forget your emeralds. Mama, we must find Prue and get out of here. Now! A fire could start at any moment.'

'Nonsense, we have an excellent fire department which has ensured that all buildings are fire-proofed and the city properly equipped.'

I was pushing her towards the door. 'I'd rather discuss the merits of the fire department outside, if you don't mind.'

At that moment Prue burst in, well-nigh hysterical.

Enveloping us both in a warm hug of relief, she cried, 'Where is Papa? And Drew?'

'Not now, Prue. Let's get you and Mama out first.'

'Ah, there they are.' Breaking free of my grasp Mama stepped across a broken floorboard and pounced upon a glittering pool of green. She clutched them in her hand with joy. 'Now where are your clothes, Georgia, Prue? You cannot go out in your nightgowns. What will people think?'

Even in the midst of chaos, proper etiquette must be adhered to. I managed to find a few clothes for Prue and myself, and we quickly pulled on as many layers as we could, since that was the easiest way to carry them. Only then did I persuade my mother to evacuate the building.

Once out on the street I ran to check on Papa, but could see at once it was hopeless. A huge pile of rubble from the upper floor of an adjacent building lay on top of him. Rather poignantly, I covered his bare feet and said a small prayer.

Prue began to weep as I held her close. 'Come now, dearest, chin up. He would want us to concentrate on helping Mama, and to think of our own survival.'

I gathered together those of the servants I could find, some of the men already clearing rubble in case there were other survivors. It would not be a pleasant task. We must have made a sorry sight, no one knowing what to do next, yet already Mama was complaining about having nowhere to sit.

'I'll find you a chair,' I began, but my heart was racing

with fear at the thought of venturing back into the house. Fortunately, one was found lying in the road and she settled upon it as if she were the Queen of Sheba awaiting her minions to restore order to her universe.

'My jewels,' she suddenly cried. 'I stowed the box away in its usual place before we left for the opera. Where is Maura? You must get her to run along and fetch it for me.'

'Maura isn't here anymore, Mama, and your jewels are at home on Geary Boulevard.'

'Then *you* must go and fetch them, dear.'

I stared at her in horror, instinctively recoiling from the prospect of walking anywhere amidst this turmoil. Then I thought of Ellis. Might collecting my mother's jewels also allow me the opportunity to look for him, in the park perhaps, where we used to meet? Besides, there were our own servants to think of: Mrs Sharpe, our cook-housekeeper, and John, our driver, the maids, and Ruby the skivvy. How were they faring? 'Maybe we should check that the house is at least standing, and that the servants are safe and well, not to mention our neighbours.'

Mama grasped my hand in a grip tight enough to express the urgency of her demand. 'My jewels are of *paramount* importance. They may be all I have left.'

More important than the woman who has cooked and ordered your household for the last thirty years? I wondered. But I didn't speak the thought out loud.

'All right, but you'll both have to come too. I'm not leaving you alone. Who knows what would happen if we split up? We must stick together at all costs.'

Oh, Ellis, where are you when I need you? my heart cried.

The maids and servants had all disappeared by this time, no doubt gone in search of their own families. And some of our equally shocked neighbours had set off to walk downtown in search of breakfast, almost as if they imagined their favourite restaurants would be open as normal to cater to their demands, not dealing with their own catastrophe.

Mama expressed a desire to go with them. 'I could kill for a cup of hot coffee,' she mourned.

'Coffee?' I stared at her in bewilderment. We seemed to be facing Armageddon but all my mother could think about was food.

To my amazement, coffee and hot rolls were indeed being served just two blocks away at the new Fairmont Hotel. From here we had a good view of the city and could see columns of smoke springing up here and there, indicating that fires had already broken out.

All about us were the mansions of the millionaire pioneers of '49, those who had struck it rich. I caught glimpses of them through the windows, scavenging through their priceless treasures, desperate to save their fine collection of oil paintings, their Persian rugs, glass and china. But they were running out of time. Advancing upon them was an unstoppable wall of fire.

San Francisco had developed originally on the back of the Yukon gold rush, both as an embarkation point for prospectors on their way to the Klondike, and where the lucky ones had come to invest their new riches. As a result, the downtown skyline had grown with many eight-, nine, and even ten-storey buildings. Now, as we walked through the familiar streets we saw that taller buildings had toppled on to smaller ones, floors had concertinaed down, one upon the other. We experienced a deep sense of unreality, feeling like strangers in our own city. The streets themselves had lifted and split, water mains broken open with water gushing up through the cracks, leaving none to fight the fire. Telegraph poles lay where they had tumbled, crackling wires long since gone dead. Communication in this fine modern city was now lost. The oddest thing was that often on one side of the street damage could be trifling, while on the other would be complete devastation.

I'd hoped to hire a carriage for Mama from Conlan's on California, or at Kelly's livery stables on Pine Street near Van Ness Avenue, but by the time we found the stables there were no horses left at Kelly's, and we could as easily reach Geary Boulevard as Conlan's. We kept on walking, my mother leaning heavily on me, bitterly complaining about the state of the world.

'You just cannot get the service these days,' she mourned.

A woman passer-by stopped to tell us that the City Hall was in ruins. 'All the bricks were just shaken from the dome, like a child's toy rattle, leaving only the steel frame. Market Street is piled high with the wreckage, so don't try going down there.'

'We won't,' I assured her, and she hurried on to some unknown destination.

Mattresses, pianos, books and pictures, hats and shoes and other treasured possessions littered the sidewalk. Streams of people were heading for the Golden Gate Park, hoping for sanctuary. Many were carrying their few precious belongings, women looking fat with all their clothes piled on, just as Prue and I had done.

I longed to go with them, in case Ellis was there waiting for me. I felt so weary I longed to lay my head on his strong shoulder and weep. But there was no time for such weakness, or to search for my beloved. I could only trust in God and keep faith that he was safe and well. My own future must wait until I had seen to Mama, found her precious jewels and some form of transport for her and Prue out of the city. For my part, I had no intention of leaving until I had found him.

It was pitiful to see such anguish all around us. An old woman, wrapped in a blanket, weeping over her dead son. A young boy struggling to carry his terrified dog. A young mother pushing a pram loaded with her personal treasures, a baby screaming in her arms. At least her child was alive. And a middle-aged man in a tattered tailcoat staggering by as if he were in a dream, or more likely a living nightmare. I stopped him to ask if he was all right.

He stared at me with those same dull unseeing eyes. 'Last night I was worth three hundred thousand dollars, now I have nothing. Even my family is gone.'

What was there to say? I put my arms around him for a moment and held him close. Then he wandered off like some bemused down-and-out drunk.

By the time we reached the house on Geary Boulevard

we were all exhausted, both emotionally and physically. Even my strong no-nonsense mother was openly weeping. And she hadn't demanded more coffee for three whole blocks.

'It's still standing!' Prue cried, and to my joy I saw that she was right. Yet surely not for long.

Looking back over my shoulder I saw the flames coming ever closer. Showers of hot cinders rained down everywhere. A blustering offshore breeze, reeking of the scorched remains of hundreds of ruined homes, fanned giant billows of smoke, inciting the fire to a raging furnace that devoured block after block at astonishing speed. My eyes were streaming, and poor Prue was suffering from a coughing fit.

'We must hurry,' I cried. And then almost sobbed with joy as I saw a familiar round plain face, and a grubby figure running towards us.

Maura fell into my arms, as delighted to see us as we were to see her. I couldn't believe how ridiculously pleased I felt as I hugged her tight. 'Where have you been all these months, you silly girl? I've missed you. Are you all right?' My feelings for my erstwhile maid remained ambiguous. Was she my friend, or my enemy? I still couldn't decide. Had she spared me from worse attentions by sleeping with my husband, or ruined the chance of creating any sort of relationship between us? Not that this was the moment to examine that conundrum, as there were far more important concerns on our minds. Besides, Kemp must surely have died as the bed slid into that dark pit of hell, and to my shame I felt little grief.

'What are you doing here, and where is Drew?'

This, not unnaturally, was her first question. I gave a little shake of my head, and squeezed her hand, seeing how tears at once filled her eyes. So she really did love him? 'Papa too is gone. I'm intending to take Mama and Prue to the ferry, then they can catch a train to Washington. They're to stay with Aunt Candice for a while.'

'Just until the house is presentable again,' Mama put in.

Glancing back at the encroaching flames I doubted it ever would be. 'But first we've come to rescue Mama's jewels,' I explained, and Maura gave me one of her enigmatic smiles.

'That's why I'm here too. I had the same thought, but don't worry, I've buried them in the back garden, Mrs Briscoe. Your jewels will be quite safe there, safer than with us, or in the line of that fire,' she added.

'I want them in my own hands,' Mama protested, but I disagreed.

'No, Maura is quite right. Anyone could steal a box of jewels off any one of us. How could we, mere females, protect ourselves? There'll be looting soon, and heaven knows what crime. And the flames are just two blocks away. There's no time to save any more possessions.'

It was afternoon by this time and I feared my mother couldn't take much more. Nor could Prue, as we were all exhausted. 'We'll retrace our steps, find somewhere safe to spend the night, then I'm taking you to the ferry, Mama, first thing in the morning. Come on, we must go. Now!'

All night the city burnt. By dawn the sky was blood-red, marred by a thick pall of smoke in shades of ochre, rose and lavender. There seemed little hope of ever seeing the sun again. Whole buildings were broken, tilting at impossible angles; twisted columns and pillars stood as if petrified by the flames.

And over all lay a brooding air of silence.

I'd never witnessed anything like it. With not enough water to fight it, and the dynamite blasts to create firebreaks often making matters worse as surrounding buildings couldn't be damped down, the fire had swept the entire district below Sansome. We heard that it had jumped Kearny then devoured Chinatown, gobbling up shops and houses with their pretty balconies with as much ease as it did the paper lanterns and carved wooden dragons which gave the district its unique character.

Hand in hand, we stumbled on. As did hundreds of others, many dragging their trunks and luggage, their children and themselves, up and down San Francisco's unforgiving hills, only to meet a wall of flame at the top and have to run for their lives in the opposite direction, often leaving everything behind.

The fire scorched down the corridors of Frisco's long streets, destroying all in its path and leaving gutted ruin in its wake. The very heat of the flames cracked solid stone, crumbled great pillars, and bent iron and steel into a newly sculpted art form.

Finally we reached Union Square where we managed to grab a few hours' sleep huddled together on the grass, along with our fellow refugees. The lucky ones slept in government tents, cooking supper on stoves they'd salvaged from their homes.

'No point in trying for the ferry yet,' they told us. 'The roads are blocked all around with hundreds of refugees desperate to get a boat for Oakland.'

'And the authorities are being hampered by crowds of sightseers pouring off the ferry,' someone else put in. 'Coming to gawp at the scenes of horror and cluttering up the roads and sidewalks. "Earthquake tourists", they're calling them. And tempers are growing ugly.'

I had no wish to have Mama caught up in an affray, and my fragile sister was suffering yet another fit of weeping that might never stop. I thought her close to a breakdown and certainly too exhausted to walk another yard. It seemed that for now we must stay put.

Ten days later we had set up camp in Golden Gate Park. The fires had died at last, leaving our city a smoking ruin, in parts little more than heaps of ash. Some streets were already being cleared of rubble and trailing wires, burst pipes mended, but few buildings were safe to enter, so here we were, sleeping in makeshift shelters or government-issued tents, our throats parched with the acrid taint of smoke, our clothes blackened. Every morning I would stand patiently in the bread queue while Prue did the same in the soup line, and Maura would go off to find a grocery store that might be open and bargain for a scrap of meat or fish. Even if she was successful the task always took her hours, but she was so restless she persisted in her daily search, quite unable to sit still.

Mama sat beneath a piece of corrugated iron atop a pile of boxes and broken chairs, demanding that Prudence, Maura and myself wait on her hand, foot and finger, in lieu of the servants she'd lost.

'I am bored with fish soup,' she would complain, as if we might conjure up a little caviar for her instead.

'And do find me a proper bed, dear. I really cannot tolerate lying on this heap of old coats for much longer.'

'There are no beds, Mama. The fire burnt them all, remember?'

'Then something must be done. There are plenty of troops around – ask one of them.'

'I believe they have more important things to do with their time,' I patiently explained. 'Are you cold, Mama, would you like to borrow my shawl?' I was worried as her skin was flushed and she had a persistent cough. Maura had managed to buy her some linctus, yet it persisted, growing steadily worse, and I wasn't sure if I was the only one to notice that the scraps of fabric I'd torn from my petticoat for her to use as handkerchiefs, were stained with blood. She winced occasionally when she moved, and was having problems breathing. I suspected she'd been injured in some way during the quake, and was dealing with the pain in her usual stalwart fashion, by not complaining but becoming increasingly crotchety.

'I cannot get a moment's sleep with these noisy neighbours. Do ask them to be quiet, dear. I have one of my heads coming on.'

Our 'noisy neighbours' were a jolly Jewish family who had managed to salvage their piano from the wreckage of their home and were now entertaining everyone on this cool April evening with a rendition of 'John Brown's Body' and 'Row, Row, Row Your Boat'. The quality of the playing would not have impressed Papa one bit, but was keeping everyone's spirits high. I was certainly not going to ask them to be quiet. But I was beginning to think we needed to take my mother to a doctor.

'No, Mama, I can't do that. They generously allow us to use their stove, whether heating water in a tin can for your coffee, or cooking any food we manage to buy with our rapidly diminishing funds. Let me stroke your head for you.'

'And that's another thing,' she complained. 'Prices are quite outrageous. I believe some grocery stores are shamelessly profiteering, putting up prices to ridiculous levels. We should complain.'

I had to agree with her there, but again had to soothe her as the outburst brought on a fit of coughing.

'They say the government is taking measures to stop that,' Prudence tried to reassure her, but to no avail. Once Mama was in one of her moods, nothing we said would improve it, and for once she might have good reason.

What she failed to see in her despair was the spirit of good neighbourliness that was evident all around us, the courage and ingenuity of our fellow refugees as they instinctively built themselves shelter out of whatever they could find: broken window shutters and fire-blackened doors, tables covered with blankets, beds made out of torn sofa cushions and old coats. San Francisco had turned into a shanty town. People had nothing, and we seemed to have less than most, apart from Mama's emerald necklace which she wore constantly, hidden beneath her dirty clothing.

Yet children still played on the grass thinking it all some jolly picnic, women furnished their nests, and men fetched and carried without complaint, rigorously making plans for a new future. The old and sick were tended and cared for, and food and water shared equally with all and sundry. It was heart-warming to see how goodness and humanity prevailed.

Somehow or other, we had all learnt to cope in our own way.

'Look at me,' Prue said, her voice filled with pride. 'I'm cooking crab.'

'Indeed, Mrs Sharpe would be proud of you. Well done, dearest.' I said nothing of my own first efforts at cooking crab cake at Pete's Place on the Barbary Coast. I hardly dared to think of that time, or my longing now for Ellis.

All day and every day I looked for him. I'd been convinced that he would be here, in the park, waiting for me. But as there were thousands of people in this ramshackle oasis, I could not find him. It was an impossible task, but I stoutly refused to believe that he might be dead. How could he be when I loved him so?

Much as I might try to be the practical sensible one, I could feel my child kicking and moving within me, and dared not consider what was going to happen when the time came for it to be born, which could be any day now. I certainly no longer felt able to trek to the ferry.

'How will we ever get Mama out of here?' I asked,

when, after criticising the overcooked crab, she'd fallen into an uneasy slumber, her once lovely face creased with anxiety and pain.

We three girls were sitting listening to the music, savouring the peaceful stillness of the night as I told them my fears. 'She is seriously ill. We need to get her to the ferry, to a hospital.'

'Are you planning on leaving yourself?' Maura asked.

I shook my head. 'Not yet. There's something – someone – I need to find first.'

She nodded, glancing briefly at Prue but not betraying my secret, although I could see she understood exactly to whom I referred. 'I'll take Mrs Briscoe to the ferry, if you like,' she offered. 'I have one or two errands of my own to make.'

I looked at her, half in surprise and half in gratitude. My one-time Irish maid was still a mystery to me. She had not revealed where she had been staying these last months, nor why she should suddenly take it into her head to rush to protect Mama's jewels. Could I trust her? I had little choice in the circumstances. 'That's most generous of you, Maura, but I'm curious to know what sort of errands you could possibly have.'

That shuttered look came over her face again. 'You think I have no life of my own, just that of your maid?'

'You aren't my maid anymore, but my companion and very dear friend. At least I hope you are. And of course I think you have a life of your own.'

I just wondered what it was.

There was a small silence while I waited for her to explain, then her lips curled into a private little smile. 'I have things to do, people to check on. It won't take long. There's talk of navy hospital ships arriving alongside the Embarcadero, with surgeons and nurses on board, tending the sick before transporting them to safety. I'll see Mrs Briscoe safely on to one of those. We can go first thing in the morning, if you like.'

'Bless you, I'd be most grateful.' I turned to my sister. 'What about you, Prue? Will you go with her?'

'No, I shall stay with you. You'll need someone with you when the baby is born.'

I rather thought I'd prefer Maura as a practical assistant in such circumstances, but could hardly fling my sister's kindness back in her face. In any case, I welcomed her company and had no wish to be left alone to face the ordeal. 'You are a sweet girl, the best sister anyone could have,' I said, hugging her.

They left shortly after dawn, a lavender-pink light struggling to break through the grey mist that still hung like a pall over the city.

Mama protested a little about the fact I refused to accompany her, but not too much once I promised her that I would go, that very day, to the first-aid centre set up in the Pavilion. Even so, Prudence and I wept a little as she hurried away with Maura, not knowing when, or if, we might see our mother again. But at least she would be in safe hands with the navy.

We did as we'd promised, and saying farewell to our good neighbours set out to seek medical help at the makeshift hospital. But we never did reach the Pavilion. Instead, I found Ellis.

Chapter Twenty-Seven

So excited were we at finding each other again that we both started talking at once, then unable to help ourselves we hugged and kissed, oblivious of Prue watching wide-eyed. Ellis said how he'd looked for me everywhere, and having failed to find me, had been working with the authorities: damping down fires, delivering food and blankets, whatever he could do to help. When he ran out of breath, I explained that my father had not survived the quake, how we four women had found shelter in the park, and how Maura had taken my sick mother to the hospital ships that very morning. Then I calmly announced that Kemp was dead.

He stared at me in disbelief, as well he might. This was the last thing we'd expected when we'd contemplated the difficulties of my procuring a divorce. But then the world had changed overnight.

He said not a word, but I shall never forget the look of complete disapproval on Prue's face as he kissed me, holding me in his arms with such loving relief I believed he might never let me go. 'I thought *you* were dead,' he said at last, squeezing the very breath of life out of me that he'd just rejoiced in finding, making me giggle with joy.

'Oh, ye of little faith,' I teased. 'I knew in my heart I would find you again, my love.'

He smiled. 'Didn't I say our time was yet to come? We were destined to be together, you and I.'

And keeping hold of his arm, I turned to my sister with a smile. 'Don't look so cross, dearest. Not all marriages are happy ones, and mine most certainly wasn't.'

Twin spots of colour glowed in her cheeks. 'You betrayed Drew?'

'Not before he had committed what can only be described as the worst of sins, and all hope was lost of there ever being happiness between us.'

'What could he possibly have done that is worse than adultery?'

I winced at the word, accurate as it might be. 'He slept with prostitutes,' I told her bluntly, seeing no other answer would serve.

She blenched, every vestige of colour leaving her lovely face. 'It's not true. How can you say such a thing?'

I put my arms about her, giving her a warm hug. 'I'm afraid it is true. You are such a romantic, sweetheart, and I do not intend to fill your lovely head with gruesome descriptions of all my husband's sins, which were legion.

You must simply trust me that the marriage was doomed from the start, and you know that I have always loved Ellis.' I gazed lovingly into his face. 'I did my duty to Kemp. Now, nothing and no one will keep us apart.'

As if to reinforce this point, Ellis smoothed a hand gently over my swollen belly. 'There are plenty of hasty marriages going on right now, for a whole variety of reasons – sometimes because people have nowhere to live and are obliged to share a house, lovemaking in the face of death; or they've lost all their family and loved ones. People are clinging together and celebrating their survival by starting a new life. So must we. If this child is to have a father, and a name when it is born, then we should find a priest quickly and do the same.'

And in the middle of the sidewalk, in amongst the rubble, with passers-by stopping and smiling, he went down on one knee and proposed. 'I have loved you since first I set eyes on you, darling Georgia, and would be honoured if you would agree to become my wife.'

'Oh, yes, please,' I cried, kissing him, and our unexpected audience burst into an impromptu applause.

We were married within the hour, standing on the steps of St Mary's Cathedral on Van Ness Avenue, as it still wasn't safe to enter the church. Fortunately, the building had miraculously been saved from total destruction through the valiant determination of a team of helpers wielding endless buckets of water. But our hasty marriage wasn't a moment too soon. The familiar words of 'I do' had hardly left my lips when I felt the first nagging shaft of pain in my back.

Smiling up into my new husband's face I asked him how long he thought it would take us to get to the Pavilion.

'Why?'

'Because I believe I'm about to go into labour.'

I gave birth on a mattress on a straw-strewn floor, while doctors and nurses bustled about using their skill and patience to help those who still hadn't been shipped out, despite being close to collapse from exhaustion themselves. Operating tables stood empty now, but dressings and medication were still laid out with clinical precision, together with enamel pans and basins, and all manner of instruments. I couldn't have had better care, and I thought no woman in the world was more fortunate than I. I had escaped death, and, despite the difficulties, the birth had gone smoothly.

My mother, however, had been less fortunate. She'd died within moments of reaching the waterfront. Maura had been with her to offer what comfort she could in Mama's final hour. Prue and I wept at our loss, preferring to remember our mother in her heyday, when she'd ruled the roost at Geary Boulevard with style and panache. And dearest Papa too. They had always been stern parents, but not unloving.

Now, almost a week later, we were about to embark on our new life in England.

It had been agreed that Prue and Maura would come with us. The house on Geary Boulevard was nothing more than a burnt-out shell, so there seemed little reason for any of us to remain in Frisco. Tickets had been bought, plans put in place, and here we now were, standing at the ship's rail, waiting for the tide. And for Maura still to arrive. Prudence was carrying the baby. I had a bag of food and clothing for it, and Ellis was loaded down with whatever else we'd managed to salvage to make the journey more comfortable. We made a bedraggled but contented little party.

My eyes kept scanning the crowded quay, worrying Maura might be too late and miss the boat. Where was it she went on these mysterious errands of hers? The ship's hooter sounded, ropes were being untied; any moment now they would raise the anchor and we'd set sail.

'Oh, here she is,' I cried, suddenly seeing her hurrying up the gangplank. 'Thank goodness for that. Where have you been, you silly girl? I thought you might miss the boat.'

She came running along the deck, a large bundle strung across her back. All her worldly possessions, no doubt. She stopped before us, quite out of breath, but her next words took my own breath away. 'I've come to say goodbye.'

I stared at her in disbelief. 'Goodbye?'

'I've decided to stay. You were right, I do have a soft spot for John, our driver. We've been secretly walking out for some time. What's more he's asked me to marry him. So I intend to stay on in Frisco.'

'Oh, Maura, I'm so pleased for you.' I hugged her warmly, delighted that my erstwhile companion had found happiness at last. I wanted everyone to be as happy as me. I was free, about to begin the new life with Ellis we had so long desired. Let everyone be as joyous. 'But will you be all right? What will you do?'

'We've decided the city will resurrect itself better than ever, and we'll find other employment.'

'Oh, but I shall miss you. We haven't always seen eye to eye, you and I, but we muddled through, eh? You must promise to come and visit us one day in the English Lake District.'

'I would love to, but there's a problem. A couple, actually.'

I frowned. 'What sort of problem?'

'There's something you need to know, but first let me give you this.' And she handed over my mother's jewel box. 'I dug it up for you. You'll need them in this new life of yours.'

'Oh, Maura, how kind of you. I'd thought them lost forever, my mother's heritage.' Tears filled my eyes, and I hugged her in warm gratitude. 'But you must have something too, a memento of us all.'

'No, no,' she demurred. 'I don't deserve anything, really.'

'Of course you do.' I was rummaging through my mother's diamonds and sapphires, rubies and pearls. Prudence was already wearing Mama's emerald necklace, hidden beneath several layers of clothing. 'Here, take this turquoise brooch, it's so pretty and will suit your colouring.'

She kept shaking her head, even as I pinned it to the collar of her coat. 'You need to see this,' she said, and opening the bundle, to my complete astonishment she brought out a baby, sound asleep, and put it into my arms. I gazed upon the small face, bemused. 'This is my baby,' she said. 'Drew's and mine, cared for by a friend.'

I stared at her, uncomprehending, the shouts of the crew making ready to sail fading to nothing in my shock. 'Yours? Yours and . . .'

She nodded, giving a little self-deprecating shrug. 'Drew Kemp wasn't an easy man to refuse, and I think it all went to my head a bit: playing mistress of the house. And there is a charisma about him.'

If that was true, I confess I'd never discovered it. I couldn't even understand why my own sister bothered to waste her charms on him. 'So that's why you went away, to have the baby?'

She half smiled. 'You never guessed?'

'Not for a minute, though it seems obvious now.'

'And what does John think of all this?' The question came from Ellis who was regarding Maura with some sympathy.

'Well, that's the problem, to be sure. If I'm to marry John, I can't keep it. He loves me, but I haven't told him about the baby. He'd never accept it, do you see? Not another man's child. I want you to take it.'

'*Me*?' I couldn't believe what I was hearing, what she was asking of me. This girl, my Irish maid, had slept with my husband, given birth to his child, and now wanted me to relieve her of the burden of it so that she could marry her sweetheart. Ellis had started to say something about the ship making ready to sail, that if she was to stay in

Frisco she should disembark now, but he too was struck silent, standing paralysed with shock. He looked at the child in my arms, so soft and vulnerable, a fragile new life, then at me, a question in his eyes. And the kind of warm understanding for Maura's situation that I'd come to expect from this man. I was less forgiving.

'You cannot be serious, Maura. This is your child, your own flesh and blood. How can you give it away? You must love it?'

She was shaking her head. 'I made sure I didn't. I left all the caring to my friend so I wouldn't get to feel anything for it. I want to marry John, d'you see? It's my best chance. I love him and don't want to lose him. It'll be hard enough starting again, without explaining to him all that went on. Let this child be part of a proper family in England, with you. You'll do right by it, I know you will. I've done a lot for you, Georgia, over the years. Do this one thing for me.'

She'd used my given name, as if we were equals now in the face of disaster, which I suppose we were. The world, *my* world, seemed to have flipped upside down, and I was helpless to stop whatever was happening as everything I'd once known tumbled about me. I was struck speechless and again turned to Ellis, seeking his opinion, his help. But before we had time to even discuss the matter we both realised that Maura had still more shocking news for us.

'There's something more. Kemp is alive.'

I swayed on my feet, and it was not caused by the lurch of the ship. Ellis's arms came about me, as if fearful I might fall. There was a pounding in my head now, a drumming of sound that blocked out all sensible thought. But my voice, when I found it, was little more than a whisper. 'What did you say?'

'Kemp is *alive*?' This squeal of delight came from my sister, of all people.

Ellis's face was chalk white. 'Are you absolutely certain?'

'The iron bedstead saved him. He was rescued suffering only superficial wounds and a sprained ankle, which has now been strapped up, and he's fine. He apparently spent hours attempting to salvage his prized belongings before being forced back by the flames. I've seen him. That's who I've been visiting these last weeks.'

'Oh, my God! Did you tell him about me, that I too had survived?' I asked, the familiar fear exploding in my chest.

'No,' Maura shook her head. 'I lied for you, Georgia. But then I've done that before, haven't I?'

I was struggling to take this all in, the full implications only just starting to penetrate my befuddled brain. I was married to Ellis now. But how could I be if Kemp wasn't dead? I turned to him, leaned into his strength. 'I can't lose you now. We have to stick to our plans. I can't stay here. I won't go back to him.'

He held me close, the babe tucked between us, but his eyes were on Maura. 'We have no objection to caring for your child, Maura, if it will help you find happiness with John, and you're sure that's what you want.'

'I'm sure.' Her gaze was steady, and as unreadable as ever.

'But I ask you, for Georgia's sake, not to tell Kemp that you have seen us. You owe her that much at least.'

I felt as if I were burning up inside, my gaze scorching hers as I begged for my own happiness, my life. 'All I ask is that you don't ever tell him I'm alive.'

'I won't tell, I promise.'

'Thank you.'

A sailor approached Maura. 'If you're leaving, ma'am, you'd best go now.'

Then my Irish maid put her arms about me and hugged me. 'Thank you, Georgia. I'll never forget what you've done for me, for my child. Keep her safe.' There were tears in her eyes, and in ours, as we bid goodbye, watched her walk away down the gangplank. Only when she'd gone did I turn around, seeking my sister's support. But I couldn't see her anywhere. 'Where's Prue?' Feeling a sudden prick of panic, I cried out. 'Where is she? Where's my sister, and my child?'

'There she is,' Ellis suddenly cried out, his voice filled with alarm. Prudence was hurrying down the gangplank, our son in her arms.

'I'm staying too,' she shouted. 'I'm going to Drew. I love him, always have. You betrayed him, and he deserves better.'

'My *child*!' I screamed. I started forward but I was hampered by the baby in my arms. Ellis ran the length of the deck, shouting to the sailors to stop the ship, to let out the gang plank again, but it was too late. Prudence was already standing on the quay, the gap of water between ship and shore gradually widening, yawning before us like a chasm.

'He's *my* child now,' she shouted up to me. 'You've always had everything: husband, child, lover. Now it's *my* turn. You know how much Drew wants a son, and I know he wouldn't want me unless I can give him one. I'll let him think this child is his, yours and his. And I promise I'll not tell him where you are, or ask anything more of you, ever!' Then she turned and ran.

My knees would no longer support me and I sank to the deck screaming with grief and despair. The ship was drawing further from the shore with every beat of my aching heart, and there was nothing we could do. Ellis looked as desolate as I felt, holding me tight as both of us sobbed for our lost son while I cradled Maura's baby in my arms.

'So my father, Aaran, is actually the son of you and Ellis?' Chrissie said, wanting to be sure she had it all sorted in her mind. The entire family was by now gathered together in the library, where Georgia sat by the fire in her cosy dressing gown telling the end of her remarkable tale.

'That's correct. And Vanessa is really the daughter of my one-time maid, Maura, and Drew Kemp. I confess, though, that I have always thought of you as mine, and loved you as if you were my own,' the old lady said, her eyes soft as they rested on her adopted daughter.

'Which means that Aaran and I are not related?' Vanessa asked, in breathless tones.

'Not at all. I desperately regret not explaining that to you properly when you challenged me with it all those years ago. But I was afraid that my children would all be shamefully branded as illegitimate, and I would face the ignominy of jail for bigamy. I thought I could convince you without revealing quite everything, but you were young and headstrong and flounced off. Try as I might, I could not find you.'

'Oh, Ma, I don't care about being illegitimate, and I would have kept your secret, never let them take you.'

'I doubt any of us would have had the power to stop the legal machine from grinding us all to dust. For that reason I was terrified of your going to America.'

'I can see that now,' Vanessa said. 'If only I'd properly understood.'

'I wanted to return myself once, to retrieve my son, but Prue threatened to expose me as a bigamist if I so much as set foot on American soil. I loved my sister dearly, still do, but she stole my son. I could never forgive her for that. She wasn't a bad person, just rather selfish and foolish, considered no one's feelings and needs but her own. Sadly, Prue's life did not turn out as well as she'd hoped. She remained the spoilt greedy child she always had been, and became filled with a bitterness which ultimately destroyed her. Kemp did not change his ways, you see. He became embroiled in many more charges of fraud and graft, which is why she broke her promise never to ask anything more of me, and constantly begged for money to dig them out of yet another hole. She even resented not being given more of Mama's jewels. I had to cash those in long since, to pay her off year after year.

'He did at least marry her, for the sake of Aaran, even though he knew the boy was not his son. And Prue stuck with him, through thick and thin, but Kemp was never faithful, as you might imagine. There were always other women. It was not a happy marriage, and his financial successes gradually turned into failures, much of his profits paid out in fines and bribes, and to lawyers.

'When I refused to finance their profligacy any further she had the gall to send Aaran, my own son, to plead her case. Maura was dead by that time but Prue had continued to keep the promise Maura made, and told no one of my existence. Now she threatened to reveal all, to destroy my family, and me. I might have given in to her pleas, as I generally did, but I wanted an end to her demands, her blackmail. I had to stop her ruining your life as well as mine, so I put my foot down once and for all. Kemp died soon after that, no doubt one scandal too many taking its toll. Consequently, she took her final revenge on her deathbed by telling Vanessa that Aaran was my son, without explaining that Ellis was his father, or that Vanessa was in fact Maura's daughter, fathered by Kemp. It was a selfish, wicked thing to do.'

'And with dreadful consequences,' Chrissie softly added, giving her mother's hand a comforting squeeze.

Vanessa said, 'It destroyed us. Aaran and I loved each other so much we couldn't bear to be apart. I started to drink, he got involved in gambling, all to offset the misery and loss we felt. We did meet secretly from time to time, right up to the war, and always firmly believed what my mother-in-law had told me. Aaran was so determined to protect Chrissie, he actually fabricated his own death by pretending he'd been killed at Dunkirk.'

'What did you say?' Chrissie was staring at her mother now in disbelief. 'Are you saying that Dad isn't really dead?'

Vanessa smiled. 'He's very much alive and well, still living in London, if in straitened circumstances, working hard to pay off the debt he foolishly ran up. He rings me often to ask how you are, darling, and misses us both dreadfully.'

'Oh, Mum, I can't quite take this in.'

She laughed, looking young and beautiful again, quite her old self. 'You must, because this means he can come home, and we can be a family again.' Then mother and daughter were both crying, hugging each other with joy and relief.

A beaming Georgia said, 'It would seem, Chrissie dear, that your interference has paid off. Digging up family secrets and dusting off the past has been a good thing, after all.'

A few days later, when Aaran himself arrived, the family reunion was complete. It was a most joyous occasion. Georgia welcomed her son with open arms. And for Chrissie to see her father alive and well, to have him hug her and tease her was more happiness than she'd ever dreamt of. The rest of the family had to be sent for, of course: Ryall and his snobby wife, the twins and their children. A huge celebration dinner was arranged at which old wounds would at last be healed, the family feud finally brought to an end.

Ben and Chrissie managed to escape the melee as he

took her hand and pulled her out into the garden. 'So does this mean that you aren't going to break up with me, after all?' he asked, his eyes bright with love as he dropped a kiss on to her soft mouth.

'I might just consider keeping you on for a while longer,' she admitted, slipping her arms about his neck. 'I mean, there's still work to be finished on the bookshop, isn't there?'

'How much longer do you reckon you'll need me? Another week maybe? A month?'

'It's hard to say. What do you think? Is it a long job?'

'I'm afraid so, it could take at least a lifetime.'

Chrissie sighed with pleasure. 'That would suit me perfectly, so long as Karen has no objections.'

'No problem. I'll get her approval in writing, then there's no comeback,' Ben agreed, kissing her some more. 'All legal and above board, on the grounds that in our family there will be no secrets. And all promises will be kept.'

'Have you any particular promise in mind?' Chrissie asked, eyes closed as their kisses grew ever more passionate, and desire kicked in.

'Only to love me for ever. Could you manage that, do you think?'

'Now that's a promise I can easily keep.'

Author's Note

The characters and story are entirely fictional, but all the locations featured in the book are as real as I can make them, including the historical details of San Francisco. Some liberties have been taken with the timing of the Bowness-on-Windermere Water Festival for the purposes of the story.